Praise for L. R. Braden

A Drop of Magic
—First Horizon Award for a debut author title

A Drop of Magic
—Eric Hoffer Award for Science Fiction and Fantasy

A Drop of Magic
—Hoffer Grand Prize short list

"Questions and secrets come out of the shadows, and I still love this series!"
—Matthew Shank, Librarian and NetGalley Reviewer on *Courting Darkness*

"Readers can't tear their eyes away as they become one hundred percent immersed in all the excitement of Alex's life."
—Eva Millien, BookBub reviews on *Courting Darkness*

"Action packed from start to finish."
—Lovabull Books Blog on *A Drop of Magic*

"The world building is great . . . a definite read for lovers of Urban paranormal with a strong female main character."
—Evan Garron, consumer reviewer Goodreads and Amazon on *Faerie Forged*

"Great world building and characters, a gripping plot, and a surprising and excellent ending."
—Anna Maria Giacomasso, NetGalley reviewer on *Faerie Forged*

Other Titles
by L. R. Braden

The Magicsmith Series

A Drop of Magic, Book 1
Courting Darkness, Book 2
Faerie Forged, Book 3
Casting Shadows, Book 4
Of Mettle and Magic, Book 5
Chaos Song, Book 6
Lies and Illusion, Book 7

The Rifter Series
(set in the Magicsmith Universe)

Demon Riding Shotgun, Book 1
Personal Demons, Book 2
A Demon Faerie Tale, Book 3
Dancing with a Demon, Book 4

Casting Shadows

The Magicsmith Book 4

by

L. R. Braden

Magical Realms Press

This is a work of fiction. Names, characters, places and incidents are either the products of the author's imagination or are used fictitiously. Any resemblance to actual persons (living or dead), events or locations is entirely coincidental.

Magical Realms Press
PO BOX 24
Broomfield, CO 80038

Print ISBN: 978-1-968414-07-8

Published in the United States of America.

Previously published by BelleBooks

We love to hear from readers!
Contact us at:
MagicalRealmsPress.com
LRBraden.com

Cover design: Debra Dixon
Interior design: Hank Smith
Photo/Art credits:
Woman (manipulated) © Jetrel | Dreamstime.com

For Alice, who grew up way too fast.
I'll love you forever.

Chapter 1

THE BRAKES ON my old Jeep groaned as I slowed, then followed the green turn arrow through an intersection. Above the surrounding buildings, clouds glowed with ribbons of sunset like someone had spray-painted streaks of fuchsia and sapphire across the sky, and long shadows cloaked the street down which I drove. At the far end of the block, orange lights flashed by the side of the road. I eased off the gas and swore.

Maggie's gaze swung from the gently swollen belly she'd been rubbing happily to the front windshield and locked on the mobile checkpoint on the approaching corner. Her thick black curls bounced with the sudden motion. She cut her eyes to me. "Can you—"

"I'll be fine."

"I didn't think the ultrasound would take so long. I wouldn't have—"

"It's fine, Mags." I set my hand on her wrist and smiled. "This isn't my first test."

Despite my words, my heart was racing. The new governor of Colorado had pretty much turned the local branch of the Paranatural Task Force into his own private army. PTF mobile checkpoints had gone up the day after Anderson's State of the State Address in conjunction with his newly implemented curfew. Any paranatural caught out after dark, registered or no, was taken to one of the detention camps resurrected from the Faerie Wars. Luckily, the basic test they performed on street corners wasn't enough to identify me as the fae halfer I was, thanks to my immunity to iron.

That didn't make the process any less nerve-wracking.

The brakes groaned again as I pulled up beside the checkpoint, knuckles white on the wheel. A woman in a PTF uniform and an orange safety vest stepped around the Jeep's front end and tapped my window with a flashlight. Swallowing, I lowered the glass.

The warmth pumping through my vents escaped into the bitter

night, and cold air rushed in to take its place.

"License and registration." The woman sounded bored. Her cheeks and nose were red compared to the rest of her pale skin.

Reaching past Maggie's knees, I pulled the registration from my glove box and handed it over with my license.

The woman squinted at my ID, then swung her light up to study my face.

I blinked and cringed away from the light as spots flared in my vision.

Lowering her flashlight, the agent passed my credentials back through the window and stepped back. "Stick out your arm."

I pushed my arm out the open window, my elbow resting on the frame. The cuff of my new winter coat rode up a bit, exposing a strip of silky, black fabric wrapped around my wrist like a bracelet. The black band wasn't exactly my style, but I wasn't wearing it for its aesthetic value. The ribbon was basically an emergency phone call to a fae who owed me a favor. I'd been foolish enough to take it off a few weeks back. Maybe if I hadn't, my friend Oz would still be alive. I wouldn't make that mistake again, no matter how much it itched or how badly it clashed with my wardrobe.

An older man stepped up beside the woman. He was also dressed in a PTF uniform and safety vest, but he wore a bright-blue knit cap with a fluffy pompom and a pair of purple rubber gloves. He carried a small box, and from it he pulled a thin black cylinder that would be used to prick my finger.

I wrinkled my nose, but held my arm steady so they could do what they needed. There was a pinch of pain as the needle broke the surface on my index finger, and a shiny red dot swelled on my fingertip.

The man squeezed my finger and tipped my hand so three bright-red drops fell into his little box, which was filled with iron shavings. A crude test, but iron was still the fastest, most effective indicator of fae heritage. In everyone except me anyway. Maggie, the female agent, and I all stared at the man, who stared into the box. Then he snapped the lid closed and jerked his head in a nod.

I exhaled and forced myself to smile at the agents. *No faeries here. Thanks for keeping the streets safe from all those dangerous magic users. And while you're at it, why don't you go jump off a cliff.*

They circled the car, the man stopping off at the back of their van to swap out my test box for a new one, and repeated the process with Maggie. Once she passed, they waved us on and the next car in line took our place.

We drove for two blocks before Maggie broke the silence. "Sorry again, Alex. I shouldn't have called you."

"I'm glad you did." I pictured the image the nurse had put on the monitor of the squirmy little baby in Maggie's tummy. I'd almost cost that little guy his life by hiding my true identity from Maggie. I was going to do all I could to make it up to them. "What are faerie godmothers for?"

ICE CRUNCHED UNDER the Jeep's tires as I pulled into the clearing in front of my house and cut the engine. Two mounds of snow sat to one side. One pile of white hid the car I'd driven back from the fae reservation after abandoning its owner, Kai, to a fifty-year prison sentence. The other covered a yellow VW bug that belonged to my ex-coworker/new roommate, Emma, who'd taken up residence in Kai's old room. Since neither vehicle could reliably traverse the mile of steep, slick, mountain road that was my driveway, the two cars had become ice sculptures while Emma and I shared my Jeep.

Pulling my jacket tight around my neck, I stepped into the night.

The last light of the dying day had faded from the sky before I headed up the winding road of Boulder Canyon after dropping Maggie off at home. With the city lights far behind me, stars filled the spaces between the clouds, shining down like pinholes punched in the ceiling of the world. On my porch, a bright circle of yellow light illuminated a man in jeans and a t-shirt. He sat atop the narrow rail with his back against a supporting post, one leg bent while his other dangled over the side. His chin was tipped up as though he'd been enjoying the star show, but his eyes were closed. A long fall of silver hair draped his shoulder and trailed over his crossed arms.

"A little cold to be out with no coat, isn't it, Chase?" I dropped my gaze to his bare feet. "Or shoes?"

"It's worth a little frostbite for some peace and quiet. Besides, shifters run hot."

Shaking my head, I tromped through the snow to my front door. "What are the girls up to tonight that has you running for the hills?"

"Oh no." He finally opened his eyes, pinning me with his bright-green gaze. "I promised not to 'spoil the surprise.'" He made quotation marks in the air and rolled his eyes. Then he hopped off the rail, his bare feet slapping the snow-dusted concrete. "Should be safe enough now they've got you to focus on."

I snorted. "Happy to help."

Bracing myself for whatever "surprise" was awaiting me, I pushed the door open to bright lights and excited voices. Chase's little sister, Jynx, was bouncing like popcorn in a hot pan in the middle of my living room. With each rise and descent, her short, white hair flattened to her scalp then stood straight up. She did a spin at the top of each arc, causing the light fabric of her totally out-of-season sundress to flare indecently high. ". . . the flowers, of course."

"And I'll take care of the cake." Emma was smiling so wide I could have counted all her teeth. Nine metal rings jingled in her right ear as she did her own popcorn impression, the piercings exposed by the most recent of Emma's ever-changing hairstyles. One side of her head had been shaved down to her seldom seen, natural brown hair, while the other boasted medium-length waves dyed teal. Along with a blindingly bright-pink t-shirt, she was wearing a pair of black suspenders covered with tiny white skulls that clipped onto a pair of baggy, black cargo pants.

I paused in the doorway, watching the scene. Not long ago my house had been empty save for me. I'd gone days at a time without hearing another person's voice. Now it seemed like there was always activity, always chatter. Though Jynx's and Emma's current excitement level seemed high, even for them.

"What's got you two so wired?" I asked as I dropped my purse on a hook and kicked off my boots.

Jynx let out a *squee* of delight and bounced over to grab my hand. Emma darted over to grab the other. They both continued to jump, pulling me jerkily along between them in the worst-ever game of ring-around-the-Alex.

I yanked my arms down to my sides, tearing free of their grasp. "What's going on?"

Jynx threw her arms around me and squeezed until I couldn't inhale. "I'm getting married!"

I sputtered, looking down at the snowy hair of the petite fourteen-year-old wrapped around my waist. *No, not fourteen*, I reminded myself. *Forty-seven*. It was still hard to reconcile the energetic girl who'd become like a baby sister to me with the fact that, despite appearances, she was actually older than I was.

I patted the top of her head. "That's . . . uh . . ."

"Priceless." Chase perched at the edge of the couch, grinning at my discomfort.

Jynx stepped back, an earnest look on her face. "Will you stand with me?"

"Stand with. . . . You mean like a bridesmaid?"

She cocked her head to one side. "Um . . ."

"Yes," said Chase. "Something like that."

Jynx's smile sprang back into place. "So, will you?"

"I thought . . ." I glanced between the siblings, settling on Jynx. "I thought your parents didn't approve of Ava because she's not purely fae."

Jynx stopped bouncing.

I'd been surprised to learn Ava was a halfer, like me, thanks to a smidge of human blood on her mother's side. She was more fae than mortal, but even a single human ancestor meant she was only as old as she looked, which placed her at about twenty. It also meant she'd die one day, which I gathered was the reason Jynx's parents disapproved of their union.

"They don't approve." Chase slid off the armrest and moved to stand beside his sister, one hand resting on her shoulder. "But I do."

Jynx smiled up at her brother.

Chase looked down at her, but the smile he returned was strained. "When you find someone who makes you happy, you should hold them tight and never let go."

Jynx shifted her focus back to me. "Ava's coming over in the morning so we can start planning." She scuffed her toe in the rug. "Will you help us?"

Pushing aside my doubts about the speed with which Jynx and Ava had gotten engaged and the wedge it was sure to drive between her and her parents, I gave the bride-to-be a hug. "Of course I'll help."

Jynx and Emma started bouncing again, jabbering back and forth about possibilities for catering, and flowers, and dresses, and a million other variables on which I was unqualified to give opinions. Chase gave me a sympathetic smile, then pulled off his t-shirt and shifted, shimmering and melting into a medium-sized gray tabby with bright-green eyes. Stepping out of his jeans, he hopped up on the couch, curled into a little ball with his back to the room, and pretended to fall asleep. At least, I assumed he was pretending. I couldn't imagine anyone actually sleeping through the racket of the girls' chatter.

Sighing, I gathered up the shirt and jeans Chase had abandoned—a habit that was becoming increasingly regular—and tossed them in the room at the end of the hall.

Jynx's enthusiasm, and three pots of coffee, carried us well into the night.

Emma was first to call it quits, citing her opening shift at the bookstore café.

"How's business?" I asked. "I heard the shop got tagged again."

She nodded. "It's getting crazy. And Mom says she's gonna have to stop supplying the café. She'd rather break her contract with the bookstore than risk becoming a target. Besides . . ." She looked away. "I think she might be a Purist after all."

I grimaced and gave Emma's arm a commiserating squeeze. Her mom, Loni Yamada, ran the bakery where the bookstore's café got its fresh-baked pastries each morning. She'd lost her husband during the Faerie Wars, which left her to raise two daughters alone, so her hatred of magic wasn't entirely baseless. She'd flipped her lid when Emma took and passed the practitioner test—practically disowned her. And that had been *before* the anti-magic movement shifted into high gear. Witches might not be fae, but they were looked on with similar suspicion, watched and regulated by the PTF.

"She'll come around."

Emma smiled. We both knew my words were empty. There was no way to know if the rift between Emma and her mother could be repaired, but we could hope.

As Emma shuffled off to get ready for bed, Jynx stretched and yawned. "I'm turning in, too. Thanks for helping narrow down my options. It should make tomorrow's discussion with Ava much easier."

I chuckled. We'd managed to "narrow" Jynx's options from infinite to merely mind-boggling. She still had hundreds of dresses she liked, and thousands of meal options. If we whittled her choices in half every night, it would still take a year to plan this wedding.

Chase stretched, yawning wide enough to expose his fangs, and followed his sister to the room at the end of the hall that I used to use for storage. I'd moved out most of the shelves and built a wood-framed bed so the cats could have somewhere to sleep besides the floor. Especially now that *my* bed was no longer an option.

In all honesty, I sometimes missed snuggling up to a purring ball of fur as I fell asleep, but waking up next to the man I loved was worth the sacrifice.

A small twinge tugged at my heart, as it did every time the word "love" popped into my mind. I still hadn't been able to say it out loud.

Every time I opened my mouth, a nagging voice inside my head reminded me that there were still too many variables in our relationship, too many dead ends to avoid, too many reasons for one or both of us to run.

I shook my head and poured another cup of coffee. I had time. I needed to enjoy the now and not worry so much about the future. At least not until that uncertain future arrived.

I FORCED MY eyes open as they threatened to close and jerked straight up in my seat. Interlacing my fingers, I stretched toward the ceiling, twisting to pop my back. I'd been hoping the discomfort of my kitchen chair would keep my drowsiness at bay, but it seemed even the straight-backed wood wasn't enough to counter the call to sleep.

My coffee mug was empty . . . again. I glanced over my shoulder. So was the pot.

The ambient light brightened, then dimmed abruptly, and I glanced toward the front window. A car door closed.

I smiled.

James didn't knock, just let himself in with the key I'd made for him—a symbol of commitment I'd never extended to any boyfriend before. Sure, I had fae crashing at my pad right and left . . . but I wasn't in love with any of *them*.

My smile faltered. There was that unsettling word again.

I pushed back from the table and glanced at the clock on the wall. Nearly three a.m. "Busy night?"

James closed the door with his foot as he shrugged a thick, wool coat off his lean frame, exposing a perfectly fitted suit and a scarf the color of glacial ice.

My smile sprang back into place. I'd knitted that scarf myself, weaving magic into every stitch. Not only did the accessory match his eyes perfectly, I'd imbued it with every complex emotion I felt for James but couldn't seem to voice. He'd barely taken it off since I gave it to him.

"We had another transfer," he said, pulling off a shiny, black shoe. How he kept them so clean after tromping through the snow was a mystery.

"To or from?"

He met my gaze, shook his head. "A new member coming in."

I swallowed my disappointment. Every time James mentioned transfers, I hoped he meant Bryce was leaving to join some other vampire nest. What I wouldn't give to never see that psychopath again. Not that I'd had any reason to visit the vampire nest since assassinating the old master. From what I'd seen, and what James told me, the new master, Victoria, was keeping everyone in line. Even Bryce, the ex-master's sadistic lieutenant.

Dropping his second shoe on the rug, James straightened, and I stepped into his open embrace. His arms closed around me, strong and solid. His shoulder was just the right height for me to rest my head against. I trailed my fingers through the silky strands of his long, black hair and inhaled the spicy sweet smell of him. A contented sigh slipped past my lips as I relaxed against him.

Closing my eyes, I reached out with my mind, finding the place where James and I were connected.

Weeks ago, he'd saved my life by sharing a part of his demon-tainted soul. The transfer had resulted in a telepathic link that was overwhelming at first. Then I'd traveled to a fae realm—through a portal designed to kill vampires should they attempt to pass—and been forced to use my imbuing magic to change the demon infection inside me to . . . something else. Since then, the bond had been muted, but the connection remained—a steady pulse calling *I am here,* like the beat of a shared heart.

Following the threads of that connection, I crossed beyond the limits of flesh.

I missed you. James's thought rang inside my head.

Then you shouldn't stay away so long. I'd gotten better at framing complete sentences in my mind rather than shoving chaotic heaps of emotion at him like I did at first. *I thought you were going to cut back on your involvement with the nest once Victoria got established. She's had a month.*

Frustration leaked through the connection—some his, mostly mine.

I pulled back enough to look up at him. "She's been pressuring you to take a more permanent place in the hierarchy again, hasn't she?"

He smiled, but there was too much tension around his eyes. "I've had my fill of vampire politics. The only permanent place I'm interested in is right here, with you."

His words momentarily silenced the part of me that was always waiting to jump in with an "I told you so" when he abandoned me, as everyone eventually did. I twisted the ends of his scarf around my hands and tugged his head lower, pulling his mouth within reach. My insecurities evaporated when his lips brushed mine. He tasted like raspberries and alcohol.

"Mmmm," I murmured. "What have you been drinking?"

An image flashed through my mind—there and gone in an

instant—of a raven-haired woman in a red sequined dress.

I started to pull away, but James's arms tightened around me.

Only food.

Another wave of frustration surged between us as I was reminded again of all the reasons a relationship with a vampire was a terrible idea. Hard to feel special when your boyfriend was out sucking the necks of random women in a club or calling escorts in the wee hours of the morning.

You said yourself you didn't want to be a food source, and that's all those girls are. Food. Nothing more.

"I know." I *did* know . . . in my head. My heart was having a little more trouble coming to terms with the situation. "But couldn't they occasionally weigh three hundred pounds and have buck teeth?"

James chuckled. "Not a lot of call girls matching that description."

Sighing, I clamped a lid on my frustration and reminded myself that I wanted James, relationship warts and all. Despite his secrets, dietary requirements, and centuries of baggage, I was happier with James than I could ever remember being. I wouldn't sabotage that for my pride.

The image of Chase standing beside his sister suddenly popped into my head. *When you find someone who makes you happy, you should hold them tight and never let go.*

James's surprise was palpable. *I never pegged that cat for wise words, but he's got a point.* He pulled me tighter and whispered, "I'm not letting go."

I hugged him back, then stepped away. This time he released me, perhaps because he could read my intentions. I slid my hand down his arm until our fingers connected, and pulled him toward the bedroom.

Once a closed door separated us from the rest of the house, I found the bottom of his shirt and tugged it free so I could slip my fingers beneath. My hands slid along his sides, then traced up his spine to the ridges of his shoulder blades.

He inhaled sharply, shuddered, then tugged his shirt over his head and threw it to the floor. He pressed hard against me, filling the momentary gap. His lips tasted my skin, over and over, one kiss leading into the next.

Heat swelled through me. More clothes dropped to the floor as we stumbled toward the bed.

He threw back the covers and eased me down, making a cage with his body.

We moved in unison, clinging to the edge of control until our bodies tensed.

A ragged gasp escaped my throat.

He sank down beside me, breathing heavily.

Snuggled against him, my head cradled on his shoulder, I trailed my fingers over his sweat-slicked chest, half afraid, as I always was, that I would wake up from this wonderful dream and find myself alone.

His arm tightened around me. *You will never be alone.*

Smiling, I lifted the yellow crystal pendant resting against his sternum and rolled it between my fingers. The necklace had been made by my many-generations-removed grandfather, Bael, who also happened to be the fae Lord of Enchantment. It was imbued with the ability to absorb sunlight, which let James enjoy a close to normal life . . . for a vampire.

I had the same magic, the same ability to imbue, to change the nature of an object. If I could change the demon within him as I'd changed the portion he'd placed inside me . . . he wouldn't need the gem to protect him from sunlight anymore. He wouldn't have to drain the lives of mortals to keep his body from ripping itself apart. He could be, if not human, at least something close.

As James's breathing evened out and grew deeper, I opened myself up to my magic. I let my awareness drift over him, inside him—studying his connection to the demon as I did any time I got a chance to observe him with his guard down. The demon was like a disease, breaking apart the bonds of James's body on a cellular level. It was that damage that required the constant influx of new energy to repair. Of course, the demon was also what allowed James to heal at such an incredible speed. Somehow, the demon was killing him and keeping him alive at the same time.

"If you could be mortal again, would you?" I hadn't meant to ask the question out loud. It just slipped out as my groggy brain played with what ifs. But having asked it, I held my breath for his answer.

"An interesting question. One without an easy answer. What brought this on?"

"I've been thinking about how I changed that bit of vampire you put in me so the faerie portal didn't kill me trying to burn it out, and . . . What if I could do the same for you?"

He smiled, but his eyes were sad. "I have more than a 'bit of vampire' in me, Alex. Take away the demon magic holding me together, and there might not be anything left."

"Not take away. Change. The magic you put inside me is still there; our link is evidence of that. But what if I could use my imbuing powers to . . . tweak your magic. Shift it so it's not quite so"—I scrunched my nose—"demony."

Laughter rumbled through his chest. He traced a fingertip down the bridge of my nose, smoothing out the wrinkles. "An intriguing notion," he said. "One I'll consider." He kissed the top of my head and pulled me closer. "But not tonight."

I snuggled in against his warm side and let my breathing match the slow rhythm of his.

Chapter 2

PINK LIGHT FILTERED through my eyelids. Winter birds chirped outside. I slid my fingers over cold sheets, expecting to find skin, but the space beside me was empty. My heartbeat stuttered. I lifted my head a fraction, opened my eyes, and peered through the tangled curtain of my auburn hair.

"Looking for me?"

I swiveled to see James step out of my attached bathroom. Clouds of steam billowed behind him. His hair hung loose and wet around his shoulders. A teal towel wrapped his waist.

My gaze roamed over the hard planes of his abdomen. "If I knew you were in the shower I would have joined you."

"I didn't want to wake you." He sat down on the edge of the bed and leaned over to plant a kiss on top of my head.

I *harrumphed* and shoved him lightly away, falling back on my pillow. "Why are you up so early anyway?"

"I have to open the gallery this morning."

I crinkled my nose. "Isn't that what Joe is for?"

As James's right-hand-man, Joe handled most of the day-to-day running of the gallery.

James laughed. "Despite his super-human talent for organizing, he's only one man. He can't work every shift."

I tucked my hands behind my head and considered volunteering to help. My sculptures *were* displayed in James's gallery after all. It could be like a co-op thing.

I stared at the ceiling for a moment, then chuckled at my own optimism. I'd been sacked from my last job because I couldn't be counted on to show up for shifts. I wasn't exactly a poster child for dependability. Not an ideal candidate for, well, anything really.

James traced a finger along the underside of my arm and down my side. "I can think of something you're ideal for."

Sitting up, I planted a kiss on his lips.

"I really do need to go," he whispered, his mouth still brushing mine.

"No one's stopping you." I stared into the icy depths of his eyes, so close I couldn't focus properly.

Footsteps sounded in the hall outside my door. A moment later, TV voices filtered into the room.

I sighed and tipped my forehead so it rested against his. "I'll go make some coffee."

James graced my lips with one last kiss, then stood. "Saved by the roommate," he said, and wandered back to the bathroom.

Rolling out of bed, I tucked my toes into the fuzzy slippers on the floor, pulled on a long, loose t-shirt, and shrugged into my bathrobe.

I checked my cell phone out of habit. One missed call from David. My stomach clenched. There was a time, not long ago, when I would have called him right back. I deleted his voicemail without listening to it. He'd called every day since I stormed out of his apartment.

Maybe someday I'd forgive him for betraying me; for conspiring with my adoptive guardian Sol to spy on me; for pretending to be my friend. Maybe. But not today.

Leaving James to his meticulous grooming routine, I shuffled out to the living room.

"Morning, Jy—" I stopped at the end of the couch and squinted at its occupant. "Shouldn't you be at work?"

Emma pointed a remote at the television, cutting Governor Anderson off in the middle of a speech about making the streets safe.

"Maggie called, told me not to come in. Apparently someone chucked a brick through the bookstore window last night. There was glass everywhere. She's put a piece of wood in the window, but she's having trouble getting anyone to come fix it."

I sank onto the end of the couch. "Is she all right? Should we go help?"

Emma shook her head. "I offered. She says she can handle it, but the store's closed until further notice."

"Did she call the police?"

"Yeah." Emma's face screwed up like she smelled something foul. "They said they'd look into it. Just like they did when the place was tagged last week."

I bunched my fists until my knuckles hurt. The police were supposed to be impartial. They were supposed to protect *everyone*. But more and more these days it seemed like they were becoming a subset of the

PTF, which in turn was shifting more toward the hard line discrimination practices of Purity. Since Anderson took office, businesses accused of supporting fae had been boycotted, vandalized, and in one case burned to the ground. Everyone knew Purity fanatics were behind the crimes, but no one was doing a damned thing to stop them.

"Well," I said, looking for a silver lining, "at least you don't have to face your daily dose of awkward silence with your mom."

"Yeah." She crossed her arms. "Just the regular, 'I never want to see you again,' kind of silence."

All the words that came to mind sounded empty, so I just squeezed her shoulder and headed for the kitchen. "You want some—"

The sounds of a laboring engine broke through the morning quiet. Ice crunched. Through the large front window, a silver Range Rover pulled into view and came to a stop beside my Jeep. Light glinted off the tinted windows, making it impossible to see the driver.

I frowned and glanced at Emma. "You expecting anyone?"

She shook her head and turned to look out the window. Her eyes grew wide. The color drained from her suntanned cheeks. "That's my . . ."

Loni Yamada stomped through the snow, the sides of her dark-green parka flapping open to reveal jeans and a cream-colored sweater. Her steel-gray bun was hidden under a blue, red, and yellow winter cap. She marched straight to my front door and started pounding on the wood. "Emma! Are you in there? Open up!"

Emma seemed too stunned to move, so I trotted across the room and pulled the door open myself, hugging my bathrobe tight against the chill wind that snuck through the gap. "Mrs. Yamada, what are—"

She shoved past me, tracking snow across my rug. "Is Emma here? The bookstore was closed."

I shut the door, cutting off the outside cold, but Loni seemed to have brought a storm in with her.

"Mom, what are you doing here?" Emma stood. She'd found her voice, but her coppery skin was still washed out, her eyes too wide.

Loni closed the distance between them till they were less than an arm's length apart. She had to look up at her daughter, who was several inches taller. "Tell me she's here."

Emma frowned, a wrinkle creasing her brow. "Who?"

Loni shook her head in disgust. "May. Is she here? Have you seen her?"

Emma's frown deepened, but her confusion was answer enough for

Loni, whose hand whipped out to land an open slap across Emma's cheek.

"This is all your fault!"

Emma staggered back, fingers pressed to the red welt spreading across her skin. Her eyes were wide and bright with tears.

"Hey!" I pushed between them. "What the hell do you think you're doing?"

There were tears in Loni's eyes, too. As she looked up to meet my gaze, her expression crumpled. She lifted her hands to cover her face and began to sob into a bright-blue shirt, too small to be hers, that she'd been clutching in her left hand.

Emma and I shared a look. She seemed as much at a loss as I was. I set a hand on Loni's shoulder and steered her toward one of the faded fabric chairs of my mismatched living room set.

I sat on the couch and made my voice as gentle as I could. "Do you want some water?"

She shook her head.

Emma took the remaining chair so we were each isolated on our own piece of furniture. "Mom, what happened?"

Loni dropped her hands to her lap, revealing puffy red eyes and a wet upper lip. She stared at the blue fabric bunched in her fingers. "May's gone."

I looked at Emma, who'd gone so still she didn't seem to be breathing.

Emma's little sister, May, was eleven years old. She was a straight-A student, a musical prodigy, and a great help at the family bakery. She was sweet, considerate, and even-tempered. She was the kind of daughter every parent wished for but didn't believe actually existed. She was *not* the kind of kid to disappear.

"When I went to pick her up from orchestra practice," Loni continued, "all I found was this." She twitched her hands to indicate the blue shirt. "Her favorite hoodie. No violin . . . no May."

I swallowed. "Could she have gone to a friend's house and forgotten to tell you?"

Loni scowled. "You think I'd be here if it was that simple?"

I dropped my gaze.

"I've called around to everyone she knows." She cut her eyes to Emma. "Not that she has many friends since getting transferred."

Part of Anderson's reforms had been to pass a bill segregating public schools. Paranatural students—meaning anyone with magic—and those related to known paranaturals, were now being sent to private institutions.

Emma sank lower in her seat. Taking the practitioner test had done more than just confirm that she could work magic. It had marked everyone in her bloodline as possible practitioners, including May. "You think it has something to do with—"

"Of course," Loni snapped. "What else could it be? She's probably locked in a PTF cell right now."

"Did you call the—"

Loni killed that question with a flat look. "I can't get a straight answer out of the PTF call center." Her hands bunched into fists, straining the fabric of May's hoodie. "Apparently discussing their detainees breaks some sort of company policy. But what else could it be? Ever since you—"

I raised a hand to get their attention and stop Loni's tirade. Emma looked to be on the verge of collapse.

"May's a minor. If the PTF took her in for testing, you should have been notified."

"She's related to a para." She shot Emma another scathing look. "Who knows if human laws still apply?"

We were all silent for a moment.

Then Emma glanced at me. She bit her lower lip, worrying it between her teeth. Her lip ring wiggled and danced, scraping enamel. Finally, she said, "Do you think you could . . . um . . ." Emma took a deep breath. "I know you and your uncle aren't exactly on speaking terms these days."

It was my turn to go still.

"Don't call him that." The words hissed through my teeth like helium from a leaky balloon.

"Uncle" Sol was a big muckety-muck with the PTF. He'd be able to find out if May was being held. But he wasn't my biological uncle; that's just what I'd called him since he started coming around when I was a kid. He worked with my father during the war. He brought us the news of Dad's death. He checked in on Mom and me once a year no matter where we moved. He became my legal guardian after Mom's accident. He bought me the house I was currently sitting in. . . . He'd also hired David to befriend me in college for the sole purpose of having him spy on me. He'd exploited my vulnerability at a time when I had no one else to turn to and betrayed my trust. Until recently, I wouldn't have hesitated to call on Sol for help, but I already owed him one favor for getting my werewolf friends out of a jam with the PTF. Did I really want to owe him another?

Bile burned at the back of my throat.

But Emma was staring at me, her eyes full of desperation.

I took a deep breath and let it out slow. "I'll call."

Loni looked between Emma and me. She didn't know I had a direct line to a high-ranking member of the PTF. For once, she kept her mouth shut, probably sensing that something in the situation had changed. Maybe she was picking up on the hope in Emma's expression. Hope was dangerously infectious like that.

Sighing, I crossed to the bar that separated the kitchen from the living room and pulled my cell phone out of my bathrobe pocket. I found Sol's contact entry, took a deep breath, and pressed the call button before I could talk myself out of it.

Maybe he wouldn't pick up. Sol went out of the country on business a lot, and he was often too busy to—

The line connected on the second ring—a first in our long history.

"Alex?" His voice rang with surprise and concern.

Sol hadn't been as relentless about trying to reach me as David, but I'd erased a good dozen messages from him, unopened. I hadn't returned any of his calls, and here I was asking for another favor. I shifted my feet and took another steadying breath.

"Hey, Sol." It felt weird to leave the "uncle" off his name.

"What's happened? Are you all right?"

"I'm fine, but . . ." I gritted my teeth and looked back at Loni and Emma. "Could you check something for me?"

A beat of silence. Then, "What do you need?"

I almost smiled. Sol may not have been as altruistic as I'd always believed, but he'd never let me down when I needed something. "A friend's daughter is missing. She's related to a para, so we thought the PTF might have scooped her up for testing."

"Name?"

"May Yamada."

Key clicks filtered through the line. Sol was typing.

"I'm glad you called."

I bit my tongue.

"I've been trying to reach you."

I rolled my eyes. "Anything on May?"

"Give me a second. I'm looking."

A second passed. Five. Ten.

I drummed my fingers.

"Have you had any trouble since O'Connell?"

I hadn't told Sol what happened between me and O'Connell—the PTF agent who'd been bent on bringing me down—but there'd been a series of news reports about the suspicious fire at a Purity compound at the edge of the northeast Colorado waste—a lifeless area created by a large-scale magical clash during the Faerie Wars. Sol wasn't stupid. O'Connell's body had been recovered from the smoldering ashes. He'd been too badly burned to be identified by anything but dental records. Luckily, that damage had also covered the evidence of how he actually died. Namely, the magic knife with which I'd impaled him.

I still couldn't believe I'd managed to create a weapon out of smoke and magic. I could still hear the demon's parting remark as I cut off that unexpected flow of power. *Welcome.*

"Alex?" Sol's voice pulled me back to the moment.

"Did you find her?"

"I said she's not in the system. . . . You sure you're all right?"

"Yeah." I glanced over my shoulder at Emma and her mother, both waiting at the edges of their seats. "Thanks for looking."

I began to lower the phone, but Sol yelled, "Wait!"

Sol never yelled.

I sighed. He *had* just done me a favor. I lifted the phone back to my ear. "What?"

A heavy exhale. Was he surprised I listened, or just relieved?

"Something's going on in the PTF. I'm not sure what. I've been locked out of some files I had access to a few weeks ago. I've been left out of meetings, given bad information. . . . Someone is trying to cut me out of the loop. I don't know what's about to happen, but you need to be prepared. Do you have an exit strategy?"

"I'm sorry about your loss of clearance, but—"

"It started right around the time I did your last little favor."

My teeth snapped closed.

Sol had helped me spring three werewolves from PTF custody before they could be tested—one of whom had been Oz. I blinked away sudden tears at the thought of what came after, when we'd been rounded up by Purity and taken to the compound that was now nothing but ash. Sol's intervention hadn't been enough to save Oz, but that was on me, not him. I still owed Sol for his help. A debt he was sure to collect one day.

"I don't know exactly what's going on," Sol continued. "But I doubt it's good. Please, Alex. Pack a bag. Make a plan. Just in case."

I looked to the ceiling. "Fine."

"Thank you. And Alex?"

"What?"

"Forgive David."

I hung up the phone.

When I turned around, Emma and Loni were staring, statues of grief with tears running down their cheeks. They must have heard the disappointment in my voice when I'd thanked Sol.

"If the PTF doesn't have her . . ." Loni began, but her sentence was lost in a sob.

Emma stood and placed a hand on her mother's back. Loni didn't pull away, didn't yell. That worried me more than anything. Loni Yamada was a strong, outspoken woman. She yelled. Sometimes she hit. She didn't curl up and cry. The woman huddled on my chair was broken beyond recognition.

"We'll find her, Mom." Emma's voice shook, but at least she was still talking. "We'll find her."

I bit my lip, staring at Loni's raw pain. Then my gaze shifted to May's hoodie. I pointed at the fabric. "Could I see that for a second?"

Emma gave me an inquiring look. She knew I was part fae, despite my ability to handle iron, but I'd had no reason to explain exactly what my magic could do, until now. I tipped my head toward Loni, silently expressing that explanations would need to wait.

Loni glanced at me, then down at the shirt in her lap. She gave it an extra-tight squeeze, then let her hands fall open, freeing the fabric.

I took the hoodie and stepped to the side, out of Loni's direct line of sight. Taking a deep breath, I cleared my mind and reached for the fae magic deep within me. As an imbuer, I could sometimes read memories and emotions imprinted on objects, but only if they were strong. While I wanted to help find May, part of me was hoping I wouldn't glean anything from the hoodie. If I did, it would probably mean something terrible had happened.

But before I could find any clue May might have left behind, I had to wade through my own emotions, exposed by my magic like open wounds. I identified worry for May, sympathy for Emma, and discomfort at seeing Mrs. Yamada—usually so stalwart and stern—reduced to a quivering shell. As I sank past those emotions, the lighting around me seemed to shift, become brighter, more intense. I looked at the hoodie in my hands . . . but they weren't my hands. They were smaller, thinner, and the same rich tan color as Emma's.

I tried to finish the motion of pulling the hoodie on, but my arms wouldn't move. Nothing moved. It was as if my muscles had suddenly been fused in place. Panic welled inside me as I struggled to control my unresponsive body.

"You've been requested for a private performance," said a man's voice behind me.

I would have jumped, had I not been frozen in place. I didn't recognize the voice.

I tried to turn my head, to see who was speaking, and another wave of panic swept through me when my neck refused to respond. Some of the fear I was feeling was May's, but mixed with it was my own terror at the feeling of helplessness. I'd been a prisoner in my own body once before, unable to control my actions. It was not an experience I ever wanted to repeat.

There was a soft, scraping noise. My violin case, which had been resting by my foot, bumped my leg as the person behind me lifted it. Then a strong hand gripped my shoulder.

"Time to go."

There was a tug, and the blue fabric fell from my useless fingers.

I gasped and stumbled into one of the bar stools at the kitchen counter.

Emma and Loni both looked up. Loni frowned as though she'd caught me drunk in the middle of the day. Emma just quirked an eyebrow.

I swallowed the cold dread blocking my throat. May hadn't run off. She'd been taken, and there'd been magic involved. That wasn't information I wanted to share with Loni in her current state . . . or ever, really, considering her already militant stance on magic.

Straightening, I thrust the hoodie back into Loni's hands.

Emma wrapped her arm around her mother's shoulders. "Come on, Mom. I'll drive you home."

Loni stiffened for a moment, like she was going to argue, but instead she just nodded. She slid out of her chair, but remained hunched, making her a good three inches shorter than usual. With Emma's help, she shuffled heavily to the door, the blue shirt once more clutched in her hands. She didn't look around. She didn't say goodbye.

Emma grabbed her purse and coat from the hooks by the door on her way out. The Range Rover's engine turned over. Ice crunched again. Then silence.

I stood at the window and watched their taillights disappear into the trees, thinking about the pull of magic holding me in place—holding May. I still had no idea who had taken her . . . or why. Had Emma's abilities made her a target, as Loni assumed? The use of magic in her capture made PTF involvement less likely, though not impossible if they brought in one of the Church's sorcerers—the few practitioners capable of wielding offensive magic, trained to be humanity's strongest defense against the fae. Could May's abduction have anything to do with the "something big" Sol feared? Or was there another threat on the horizon?

I rubbed my temples. The PTF, the vampires, the fae in all their variety. There were any number of people who could have targeted May, though none had a clear motive. And if I didn't know *why* she was taken, there was no telling who could be next.

Do you have an exit strategy?

I crossed back to the counter where I'd set my phone, Sol's words ringing in my head. Whether or not May's abduction had anything to do with Sol's concerns about stirrings in the PTF, it wouldn't hurt to pack a bag in case I needed to run. But I wasn't the only one in danger.

Pulling up the number for the local werewolf alpha, who also happened to be my friend and neighbor, I tapped the call button again.

It took four rings before the line connected, and when it did the person who answered wasn't who I expected.

"Hey, Alex."

My heart skipped a beat, then came back double-time. "Sophie? Why are you answering Marc's phone? Did something happen?"

"No, nothing like that. I just . . . he's in the shower."

Silence rang across the line as I let that sink in. Seemed Sophie had gotten an upgrade from the dungeon where she'd spent her first stay at Marc's house.

"How are you doing?" It wasn't the conversation I'd intended to have, but I hadn't spoken to Sophie, Oz's ex and one of the paranaturals who survived the fire with me, since Marc carried her unmoving body away from the burning building where O'Connell died.

"I'm . . . alive." Left unspoken was the hanging, *but Oz isn't.* "I hear I've got you to thank for that."

Once upon a time, Sophie and I were friends. A lot had happened since then.

I'd accidentally led her into the attack that made her a werewolf. She'd inadvertently set me up to be kidnapped and tortured by a sadistic vampire. The two of us had been locked in a cage and forced to watch as O'Connell put a gun to Oz's head. I'd spilled my secrets, including some lies I made up about an iron vaccine for halfers, to try to save him. It hadn't been enough, and when the gun went off Sophie went into werewolf rage mode, shifting in full view of the rolling camera. Between the two of us, we'd hunted that bastard O'Connell down and killed him, but the damage was done. Oz was dead, and the footage of my confession and Sophie's transformation had disappeared. We could only hope it was destroyed in the fire.

"I—"

"Did you need something?" she cut me off.

I smiled. Same old Sophie. She never was one for teary displays of emotion. "Yeah, I wanted to give Marc a heads-up about a tip I got."

"The water just shut off. Let me grab him."

Muffled noises came over the line. A door opening. A soft conversation. Then Marc's voice. "Alex? What's up?"

"Sorry to interrupt your morning," I said dryly, "but I just had a chat with Sol. He thinks something's going down with the PTF. Something big."

"I thought you said we couldn't trust him."

I bit my lip. Sol had lied about having me watched, but I didn't believe he'd put me in danger. "The PTF cut him out of the loop shortly after he . . . assisted in your release. He told me to get an exit strategy in place. Seems like you might want to do the same. Just in case."

Marc sighed. "We've been ready to run since that memory card went missing in the fire."

I drummed my fingers against the marble countertop. "If anyone found that footage, it would have been released by now. The PTF would have been all over the evidence of werewolves. Not to mention my lies about an iron vaccination for halfers. Hell, that by itself would be enough to void the peace treaty . . . if they could prove it."

"Good thing it's not true," he said. "In any case, I've got a little off-the-grid place we can hunker down. Maybe we'll head there sooner rather than later."

"Good idea."

A moment of hesitation, then, "You're welcome to join us."

"At your safe house?"

"I wouldn't call it a house, but yeah. The PTF wouldn't find you there. Neither would Sol, if that's what you want."

Was that what I wanted? To disappear? To start over somewhere new?

That had been my mother's solution after Dad left. When life got hard, just pack a bag and go. Keep running so the memories of what you left behind could never catch up. I didn't have one continuous year of schooling from middle school till college. That was the first time I had a choice. The first time I stayed long enough to make a friend. Three even. Now Aiden was dead, David was a liar, and Maggie was in danger just for knowing me.

I sighed. Maybe Mom had been right.

Still. . . . "Thanks for the offer, Marc. Really, I appreciate it. But—"

"You're not coming."

"I spent my whole life running after my dad died. I finally have a home. I'm not giving that up unless I have no other choice." Besides, Emma wouldn't leave while May was missing, and I wasn't about to abandon her.

"All right, Alex. But promise me you'll pack a bag. If shit really does hit the fan with the PTF, you're gonna have to get out of there fast."

"I will."

I bit my lip, wanting to ask more about how he and Sophie were doing, how all the werewolves were doing, coping with the loss of Oz. He'd been my friend, but he was part of their pack, part of their family. And for Sophie. . . . Well, I'd gotten the impression he might have been something more.

But I couldn't find the words, and the moment passed.

"Take care, Marc," I said. "Take care of everyone."

"I will." It was the promise of an alpha, strong and sure. He would die before he'd let anything happen to his pack.

I disconnected the call and set the phone back on the counter with a sigh. If the werewolves went into hiding . . . I might never see them again.

Something twisted deep inside—the old, familiar pain of being abandoned.

But, no. Marc had invited me to join them. This time, it was my choice to stay behind.

Chapter 3

JYNX POKED HER head into the hall as I tucked my phone away. "Is the coast clear?"

I waved for her to come out. "I assume you heard all that."

She nodded. "Poor Emma. First her mom disowns her, now her sister's gone missing?" She took up her favorite perch on the armrest of the couch.

Chase came out of the back room wearing a pair of tight jeans and nothing else at the same time James opened the door to my bedroom. The two men pulled back from each other, then James gestured for Chase to precede him.

"There was a report on the news the other day about how many kids have gone missing lately," Jynx said. "The reporter thought they were probably halfer teens skipping town because of all the new anti-fae policies."

I shook my head. "May didn't just 'skip town.'"

I poured two cups of coffee and handed one to James, hating the question I was about to ask. But if the PTF hadn't taken May—and sorcerer involvement seemed like a stretch—that left a lot of less savory options. Not the least of which was being drained by a vampire and dumped where no one would find her body.

"Could a vampire control a person the way Merak controlled me without drinking their blood first?"

James frowned, then shook his head. "While I don't claim to know every talent of every vampire, our abilities stem from illusions. A vampire could fool a person into thinking they were doing certain things when they were not, but couldn't physically control that person without having established a blood bond." James blew a curl of steam off his mug. Then, perhaps sensing my uncertainty, continued, "Victoria has banned indiscriminate feeding for the time being, and Emma's sister would be too young to visit any of the nest's approved hunting grounds. I don't believe a vampire is involved."

I nodded, both relieved and disappointed. "That means May's kidnapper is most likely a fae."

Chase, who'd seemed absorbed in his own thoughts since emerging, looked up sharply. "What makes you say that?"

"Loni had a hoodie May dropped at the studio." I wrapped my arms around myself, remembering the fabric slipping from my fingers. "Whoever took her used magic."

Everyone present knew what I could do with my magic, so my words were proof enough.

Chase leaned against the back of the couch and crossed his arms. He seemed tense, as though preparing to face something he'd been dreading. "Does Emma's sister have any . . ."—he wobbled his head back and forth—"special talents?"

I frowned. "She's a really good musician, especially for her age. She plays violin, piano, and guitar, and she's composed a bunch of music for the orchestra she plays with." I shrugged. "Other than that, she seems like a pretty normal kid."

Chase nodded. "That could be enough."

"Enough for what?"

"Several fae children have vanished in the past few months, all with unique aptitudes."

"Full fae?" I asked. "Or halfers?"

Chase frowned. "As pure as we come."

"Were they here in the mortal realm?"

"Most vanished from their respective realms. Whoever is snatching these kids has access to fae portals."

That ruled out most humans, magic or no. "What else can you tell me about the missing kids?"

His lips pressed to a thin line. "Not much. The Shifter Lord has been investigating, but I'm not involved. I just overheard a few snippets when I went home last month."

"Then we should go talk to him."

"Her," Chase said. "The Shifter Lord is female."

A little whimper brought our attention to Jynx, whose frown was so deep it was almost comical. "Now? You're leaving now? But you promised to help plan my wedding, and Emma's already gone. Ava will be here any minute."

"It's just a quick chat." I glanced at Chase. "Right?"

He nodded. "A day, two at the most."

I winced, remembering that even a few minutes in a fae realm could equal hours here thanks to the time discrepancies between realms. Of course, it could work the other way too, depending on which realm you were visiting. "We'll be back before you know it. In the meantime, make sure Emma gets back from Loni's safely and let her know where I'm headed."

"She'll be mad you didn't take her," Jynx said.

I nodded. "But the fae realms are no place for a mortal." With any luck, when I got back I'd have some real answers for her about what happened to May.

There was a knock at the door.

Jynx jumped up. "There's Ava now."

Chase sniffed . . . and frowned. He tipped his nose up and inhaled deeper. He stiffened. His upper lip peeled back to expose his teeth.

"Jynx, wait," I called. Too late. She was already opening the door.

I moved to back her. There was a blur of motion, and James was at my side. I breathed a little easier.

The door swung wide, revealing a man in tan pants and a green sweater. He had wide-set Mediterranean blue eyes, white hair with crimson tips, and shimmered with a glamour that disguised his true features. When I focused past that glamour, I saw he also had furry fox ears and seven red-tipped tails.

I set a hand on Jynx's shoulder and pushed her gently to the side so I could face my guest directly. "Hello, Haru."

"Mica sends his regards." He nudged an oiled leather traveling bag by his foot that looked like a prop from *Lord of the Rings*. "He's calling in your debt."

I glanced over my shoulder. Chase looked like he was suffering from rigor mortis. I'd warned him about my deal with Mica, the not-quite-prince of Enchantment—room and board for a friend in exchange for helping me break Kai out of prison. The prison break had been a bust, but that wasn't Mica's fault. I was still on the line for my side of the bargain. Of course, I hadn't learned till later that Haru was Mica's intended house guest, or that Haru and Chase had a tumultuous history. In fact, I still wasn't sure what that history was.

I rolled my shoulders, trying to shake the feeling of Chase glaring daggers at my back. "Now's not really the best time for a visit to the mortal realm, Haru. Colorado just elected a new governor, and he's aligned with Purity. The PTF is really cracking down on unregistered fae. . . . I'm assuming you didn't pick up a visa on the way here?"

He rose onto the balls of his feet, peeking past me. "Yet I see two here right now. How can I not take that as a personal slight? Or are you going back on your word? You are mortal after all."

I balled my fists. "Of course not. If you want to stay here badly enough to risk execution—"

He sniffed. "I don't *want* to stay here anymore than you seem to want me here."

I frowned. "Then go home."

"I can't."

"Why not?"

He crossed his arms. His gaze slid to the side. "Mica tricked me into agreeing to this little"—he waved a hand at my house—"arrangement." His next words were quieter, intended only for me. "He holds my oath."

Laughter erupted behind me. Chase was holding his sides when I turned to look at him.

"The great trickster got tricked? Oh, that's just precious."

Haru lifted his chin, but didn't respond.

I stepped back from the door, pulling James with me, and waved Haru in.

Haru lifted his bag and stepped over the threshold.

Chase stopped laughing.

I closed the door, cutting off the flow of winter air that had already dropped the temperature in the room by at least three degrees, and muttered, "Won't this be fun."

"Shall I stay?" James asked. "I can call Joe and—"

"No. You said it yourself, he can't work every shift. Besides,"—I clasped his hands with both of mine—"I've got another favor I need from you."

"Oh?"

"Since it seems Chase and I are going to the reservation, I want to drop off Kai's car." My chest tightened at the thought of surrendering the last evidence of Kai's presence. "We'll need a ride when we get back."

James looked down at our joined hands. His thumb slid over my knuckles. "I don't like the idea of you going beyond my reach."

"All the more reason to consider my proposal from last night," I whispered.

"What's this?" Haru said, dropping his bag at the end of the couch. "You're leaving?"

I nodded. "Chase is taking me to see the Shifter Lord. I should be back in a day or two."

Haru had gone terribly still except for a muscle that jumped along the side of his neck. He took a deep breath and let it out slowly. "I'll send Mica my condolences. If you're working with the Shifter Lord, I doubt I'll see you again."

I frowned. "What do you—"

"Ignore him," Chase said. "He's just bitter."

"Bitter? Is that what you think I am?"

"I said it, didn't I?"

"As opposed to you, who—" He snapped his mouth closed. His nostrils flared. I could almost hear Haru's teeth grinding as his jaw worked.

I cleared my throat and turned back to James. "You should go. I'll call you when I get back so you can come and get me."

He pulled me farther from the others, staring over my shoulder at Haru. *Are you sure it's wise to let him stay?*

I gave my word. I might not be bound by the same rigid rules as the fae, but a promise is a promise. It should be fine as long as Chase isn't under the same roof, and he'll be with me. Emma and Jynx can handle Haru. I hoped.

He pursed his lips, perhaps sensing my doubt.

I set my hand against his cheek. *Everything will be fine.* I rose onto tiptoes to kiss him. Then I shoved him toward the door. "Now get going."

James looked reluctant, but grabbed his coat and followed my instructions.

"So," Haru said, hefting his pack onto his shoulder, "which room is mine?"

I shook my head. "I've got a full house right now. If you insist on staying—"

"I do."

"—all I can offer is the couch."

He snorted.

"Mica said even the floor would be fine when we made our deal. If you don't like the terms, take it up with him."

"If you're leaving," he pointed out, "your bed will be empty."

"Not an option."

He *tsked*. "Your hospitality is lacking."

"So I've been told. Again, if you don't like it, you don't have to stay."

His lips peeled back, exposing clenched teeth. "Yes, I do."

I shrugged. "Whatever trick Mica played to get you here has nothing to do with me."

Sighing, he tossed his bag back onto the end of the couch. Then he seemed to remember something and pulled an envelope from the front pocket.

"I don't appreciate being used as a messenger," he said. "But I've got a letter from your boy-toy in the dungeon."

His words jolted my system like a fork in an electrical outlet. I reached for the envelope, but he jerked it out of reach.

"What's the magic word?" he chanted in a sing-song voice.

I grinned, showing all my teeth, and responded in the same nursery-rhyme tone. "Hand it over or I'll smash your face in."

He raised an eyebrow, but lowered his arm.

I snatched the letter, shooting him a glare, and retreated to one of the armchairs where I turned the envelope over and over in my hands. There were no markings on the outside save a small water stain in one corner.

"What, no gratitude?" Haru asked.

"Be happy," Jynx called to him from the edge of the room where she'd been silently watching her brother, a deep furrow on her brow. "I heard it's traditional in the mortal realm to shoot messengers if the recipient doesn't like the news."

Chase rolled his eyes.

Haru just stared at her, as though trying to decide whether or not to laugh. Then he glanced at Chase and the mirth faded from his expression like a slate wiped clean.

Hands shaking, I gently tore open the sealed flap and slipped out a heavy piece of yellow paper that had been folded three times. I spread the letter on my lap, smoothed its creases, and began to read.

Dear Alex,

I heard about the deal Bael offered you for my freedom. I imagine you're probably beating yourself up about the fact that I'm still in prison, but you made the right decision. While I serve my lord with my life, I do not wish to be used against you. Despite your bloodline, you are not yet sworn to Bael's court, which means you're free to make your own choices. Don't give that up for my sake. And don't drown yourself in guilt. I've no doubt I will see you again someday. In the meantime, though I know it goes against your nature, try to stay out of trouble.

Your friend,
Kai
PS-Thanks for the candy. Please send more if you get a chance.

A drop of water splashed the paper, smearing the ink, and I quickly wiped my cheek to avoid blurring any more words. Closing the letter, I looked up at Haru. "How did he seem?"

Haru glanced over his shoulder. He'd moved to examine the photos and trinkets displayed on my mantel—mostly souvenirs of the places I'd lived with my mom. He shrugged. "Resigned. Bored. How does anyone feel facing fifty years of the same four walls?"

A crinkling sound reached my ears and I glanced down to find Kai's letter crumpled in my fists.

There was a muted popping sound in one corner of the living room as Ava, Jynx's soon-to-be-wife, stepped through a shimmering oval of distorted air. She stomped her feet, shook her head so her long red pigtails flopped across her face, and rubbed her arms vigorously. "Sorry for portalling directly inside, but it's *freezing* out there."

She looked up for the first time, and froze.

"Um . . . am I interrupting something?"

Taking a deep breath, I pushed to my feet. "Congratulations on getting engaged."

Ava smiled so wide it looked like it should hurt. "Thanks."

"I know we were supposed to do some wedding planning today, but Emma's sister has been kidnapped and Chase is taking me to the Shifter Realm to follow up a lead." I gestured to Haru. "This is Haru. He'll be crashing on my couch for a while. Jynx can fill you in on the details later."

"That's . . . um . . ." She cast Jynx a confused look.

I stuffed Kai's letter into the pocket of my bathrobe and tugged the gaping collar a little tighter. "Now, I'm going to take a shower and put on some real clothes for my meeting with the Shifter Lord." I looked between Haru and Chase. "Try not to kill each other."

CHASE AND I rolled down the main street of Crestone, Colorado in Kai's tan Toyota—Chase curled on the passenger seat as an unassuming gray tabby. Crestone marked the last human habitation before the PTF checkpoint—supposedly the only access through the towering iron wall that marked the boundary of the fae reservation. The town was a mecca for religious advocates—a jumbled congregation of every faith imaginable. Churches, mosques, synagogues, temples, and shrines lined the streets.

Just shy of the edge of town, a line of protesters waved signs on the steps of a building sporting a One Earth banner. One Earth was a political group directly opposed to Purity—a group who believed our world could, and should, be shared equally with all comers.

I slowed as we passed the scene. Men, women, and children shook signs and fists. One man was snapping pictures of everyone who entered or exited the building.

A hail of tiny pebbles pattered against my windshield. No, not pebbles. I squinted at the debris. They were curls of thin gray metal.

I cut my eyes to the sidewalk. A tiny boy was tossing handfuls of iron shavings into the air like confetti.

Knuckles white on the steering wheel, I fought back a shiver and held my pace until I passed the crowd. Then I stepped on the gas to put Crestone in my rear view.

I turned the car up a slushy, gravel path leading off to the left of the main road. Over a hill and past a little copse of trees, a run-down farmhouse came into view. A towering willow dominated the front yard. To the side of the house were the first few cars of the collection that spread around the back of the property. Kai's car was part of that fleet— vehicles modified specifically for fae use, made with a minimum of iron. Soon Kai's car would be back in the lot, waiting for the next needy fae to claim it.

I rubbed my chest, trying to ease a sudden tightness in my lungs. It was stupid to get upset about losing a car that wasn't mine to begin with, but Kai's car was the last physical connection I had to him. Once it was gone, all visible evidence of him would be cut from my life.

Swallowing the lump in my throat, I eased the car past the rotting split-rail fence that marked the protective barrier around the house. I waited for the twinge of magic I'd felt the first time I passed, but there was nothing. Last time, I'd had a tiny piece of vampire soul inside me that the barrier reacted to. This time, I didn't register as a threat.

I cut the engine and opened my door. Chase yawned, stretched, and climbed into my lap.

"Any day now." I gestured out the open door.

He followed my hand with his whole head, stared at the slushy ground for a moment, then swung his green gaze back to me. "Meow."

Snorting, I scooped Chase onto my shoulder and swung my legs out of the car. "Too prissy to get your paws wet?"

Needle-sharp claws pricked my shoulder.

"Scratch me and I'll bury you in snow."

Chase made a little chuffing sound, but his claws retracted.

I paused on the welcome mat in front of the door to the way station and kicked off as much mud and slush as I could. Then I took a deep breath and let myself in.

The house was just as I remembered from my last visit, full of the warm, rich smells of cooking coming from the kitchen to one side of the main area. The other side of the room was taken up by a trestle table and picnic benches, while the center held mismatched furniture, a small coffee table, and a reception desk. Three closed doors lined the back wall.

The little old woman who managed the place was up to her elbows in soapy water beside a teetering stack of dishes—also mismatched—at the kitchen sink. She glanced over her shoulder and smiled. "Go ahead and sign in at the desk. I'll be with you in just a moment."

I glanced at the reception desk that sat just past the living room furniture, but shook my head. "We're not staying. Just dropping off one ride"—I lifted the key to Kai's car—"and looking for another."

Chase pushed out of my grip and jumped away from me. He blurred into a shimmering streak and landed in the form of a naked man crouched on the hardwood floor.

"Is Otis here?" he asked.

I shifted my gaze back to the woman and did my best to ignore the scene in my peripheral vision as Chase straightened.

"He's taking a nap. I'll run and get him as soon as I'm done here. In the meantime, you can put that key up on the wall." She nodded to a pegboard of dangling keys behind the front desk. "Just match the colors."

I gripped Kai's key so tight it bit into my palm as I stepped around the desk with its guest book and display of postcards. The key in my hand had a bright-blue rubber cap covering its end, so I found the peg with a matching blue square painted below it. I slid the key onto the peg, where it dangled by its plastic ring. Kai's car was home. Nothing of my friend remained in the mortal realm save my memories.

"Why so solemn?"

I glanced back at Chase, then quickly shifted my gaze to the ceiling. "Aren't you going to put something on?" I gestured to the box of clothing near the front door, left out for just such occasions.

"Why?" He stepped closer, just shy of brushing up against me. "Do I make you uncomfortable?"

Gritting my teeth, I lowered my gaze to stare straight into his eyes. "You wish."

He smiled and shrugged. "Best get used to this. Where we're going, your prudishness will be the oddity."

I stepped around Chase and dropped into one of the threadbare chairs arranged in a loose circle in the middle of the room. In the kitchen, the old woman was drying her hands on a checkered towel. She hummed happily to herself, seemingly oblivious to Chase and me.

Chase dropped onto a couch across from me.

I frowned. "Are you serious . . . about me being the oddity?"

He stretched out, draping his arms over one end of the couch while his feet rested on the armrest at the other. "Absolutely. If you stare at every naked person you see in the Shifter Realm, you're bound to piss someone off."

"You don't wear clothes there?"

"Most of us don't even wear human bodies there." He shrugged. "You'll see."

The old woman's pinkish curls bounced as she waddled to the far-right door on the back wall. She opened it enough to reveal a carpeted area and the edge of a dresser. Then she slipped inside and pulled the door closed behind her.

I tipped my chin toward the door. "Do they live here?"

"The caretakers? Of course." Chase pointed to the doors one by one, starting with the one the woman had vanished behind. "Caretaker apartment. Bathroom. Dorm."

"Have you ever stayed here?"

He shook his head. "Most people passing through here have somewhere they need to be. But every now and then there's a delay, or the timing of a visit doesn't work out quite right. When that happens, it's nice to have somewhere to crash."

"I imagine coordinating is tricky when the realms move at such different speeds."

He shrugged. "It can be. That's one of the reasons we like using the mortal realm as a crossroads, neutral ground as it were. No one wants to stay in enemy territory longer than they have to."

"Is that why the fae realms don't connect directly to one another?"

"It's one reason." He closed his eyes.

Taking the hint, I turned to stare out the small window to the side of the front door. A light flurry of snowflakes had started to fall, spinning on the breeze so it looked more like they were dancing than falling.

I pulled out my cell phone. There was hardly any signal here. Once I crossed into the reservation, there'd be no reception at all.

I typed a quick text to James, letting him know we were about to drop off the map.

The far door opened once more and Otis, the stick-thin old man who acted as the official taxi for fae who didn't want to pass through the reservation checkpoint, stepped out. A loose sweatsuit draped his frame. His eyes were bloodshot, his skin was pale and drawn, and gray hair stood off his head in crazy, sleep-matted tufts.

"Heard you need a ride." He shuffled, barefoot, to the middle of the room.

"That's right." Pushing to my feet, I slid my phone back into my pocket. "Can you take us?"

He glanced at a clock on the wall. "Not my regular shift."

"But he's got nothing better to do." His counterpart smiled as she stepped into the room. "Isn't that right?"

Otis grumbled and shrugged. He lifted his arms, palms up. "Let's go."

Chase rolled to his feet and gripped one of Otis's hands. I took the other and scrunched my eyes shut.

My ears popped. There was a moment of silence, then birdsong filled the air. The scents of baking bread and soapy dishes were replaced by those of pine needles and rotting leaves. I cracked open one eye, remembering the disorientation that made me puke the last time I did this, but the world wasn't spinning. My feet were planted firmly on a field of trampled snow.

Otis cleared his throat.

I glanced at his frown, then down at his bare feet resting in slush, then to our clasped hands. I released him and took a step back.

"Next time," he said, "keep to the schedule." Then he popped out of existence like a collapsing star.

Out of habit, I pulled my phone out and glanced at the bars. No service, as expected. I was officially incommunicado until I got back on human land. I powered down the now useless phone and tucked it away.

"This way." Chase crossed to the edge of the clearing and stepped into the woods.

I hustled to keep up, glancing around as I walked. The trees quickly grew denser, snagging my clothes and hair as I passed. A bitter wind tickled the back of my neck and pinched the tips of my ears with aching cold. The birds stopped singing. Was their silence in response to us tromping through the forest, or was something else out there?

I inched closer to Chase, nearly stepping on his heels. I was suddenly grateful for his escort through the forbidding forest.

Wiping my palms on my jeans, I pulled my jacket tighter around my neck and shifted my gaze to Chase's smooth back to avoid freaking myself out with every snapping branch and shifting leaf. Chase was still completely naked, his bare feet stepping on snow and frozen pine needles. How could he not be freezing? Come to think of it—

"You don't have a car," I blurted.

He shot an incredulous look over his shoulder, then turned back to navigating the woods. "An astute, if bizarre, observation."

I shook my head, rattling my thoughts into focus. "How do you get back and forth from my house to here when I'm not there to drive you?"

Chase pushed past a prickly bush and let the branch go to slap me in the chest.

"Ow." I growled. I shoved the branch aside, then closed the distance between us again.

"Jump lines," he said.

"Hmm?" I rubbed my palm where the bush had scraped my skin.

"That's how we get around."

"What's a jump line?"

"A group of travel-talent fae who've agreed to serve as conveyors, like Otis. He's one of the busiest since he's right next to the reservation, but there are others spread all over the world." He stopped in front of another prickly bush and turned to raise an eyebrow at me. "Or did you think fae flew on planes like humans when we travel?"

"Honestly, I hadn't really thought about it before now."

He shrugged. "We don't advertise the jump lines. If the PTF found them, we'd be in trouble."

He lifted one drooping branch of a bush as though opening the door of a mansion and gestured with a flourish to a moss-covered hole at the base of a large granite boulder. "In you go."

I looked from the hole, to Chase's grin, back to the hole. "Excuse me?"

"This is the portal to the Shifter Realm."

I pointed to the dank, dark crack in the ground. "This hole? Seriously?" I shook my head. "You're messing with me."

His smile widened. "Suit yourself."

Melting into his cat form, he darted beneath the falling branch and disappeared into the hole.

Nothing moved in the forest.

"Chase?" I called.

There was no answer.

I looked around at the towering trees that all seemed to be leaning toward me. Something crunched behind me. I spun toward the sound, but found nothing.

Chiding my overactive imagination, I turned back to the hole where Chase had abandoned me and glared into the darkness.

"I hate you."

I dropped to my stomach and crawled inside.

Chapter 4

COLD, ROUGH ROCK scraped my palms as I slid into the darkness. Damp, musty air filled my lungs. There was barely enough space for me to squeeze through, and my body blocked out the light of the surface world. Even my enhanced fae eyesight couldn't pierce the gloom. I reached out blindly, fingers groping, but found only empty space bounded on the sides and ceiling by solid rock. The ground was covered in wet, sandy soil.

I continued to inch forward, cursing Chase with every name I could think of. Going was slow as I shifted one knee, braced my hands, and slid my body forward, then repeated the maneuver with the opposite leg. I bumped my head twice. My knees were bruised, and I was pretty sure my palms were bleeding.

Bracing my hands once more, I shifted forward, pushing with my left leg, and flopped onto my belly like a beached whale. Except this time, I didn't come down on level ground. My stomach lurched as I pitched forward, bending at the waist. I caught for a moment with my hips and legs on the shelf, but my momentum, coupled with the steep angle, began to pull me over the lip. There was nothing to grab, nowhere to brace. It was like the walls of the cave had suddenly fallen away. The gravel beneath me shifted as I scrambled for purchase, building to a tiny avalanche that carried me, screaming and flailing, down the earthen slide.

I curled my arms around my head, trying to protect myself from whatever landing was coming.

The chute was smooth, and I quickly gained speed. The slide curved several times, once banking so steeply that I rolled onto my back. I stopped screaming after exhausting my second breath and instead just cringed, waiting. . . .

Warm light lit my eyelids—which I hadn't realized I'd closed—and the air suddenly went from cold and damp to desert dry. The ground fell away. For a moment I was weightless. Then gravity took hold again, and I dropped like an express elevator.

My shoulders hit first, but the ground gave way in a puff of dust as my momentum carried me another few feet along its surface. A moment later, I came to a stop. My heart was pounding, my breath fast and ragged. I was still in one piece.

It hurt to unclench my arms. My strained muscles cried out in protest as I spread out on the surprisingly comfortable ground. I opened my eyes and blinked up at a lavender sky.

I hadn't asked Chase what the Shifter Realm looked like, but it hadn't occurred to me that the sky might be a different color.

I scraped up a handful of earth and lifted my arm. Fine, white sand sifted between my fingers to be carried away on the breeze before ever reaching the ground.

"How long are you going to lie there?"

I rolled to my knees and spun toward Chase's voice in one fluid move. Then I launched myself at him, for once not caring that he wasn't wearing clothes. "I'm going to kill you."

He skipped out of reach, hopping up onto a nearby rock. "That's gratitude for you. Show a girl the secret entrance to a magic land and she tries to strangle you."

Baring my teeth, I tried to shake the sand out of my clothes. It was everywhere. My hair, my bra, my socks. One of my boots felt like it had a whole dune nestled under the arch of my foot. "You should have warned me about the hole. At least I could have gone in feet first."

He shrugged. "Come on. We've got a bit of a walk ahead of us."

Grumbling, I stomped after my guide, white sand falling in my wake.

The shifting dunes of fine powder I'd landed in were cradled in an alcove of towering white rock that opened onto a wide plain. The sand became coarser near the mouth of the alcove and took on a reddish tint. Short trees with sparse, sprawling canopies dotted the cracked red ground.

Far to my right was another outcropping of rocks, and resting on a high shelf was a lion with a shaggy mane, and paws the size of my head. Its tail swished. A long pink tongue flicked out to lick its nose. Its yellow gaze was fixed on Chase and me. Perhaps it hunted creatures foolish enough to tumble through the hole from the mortal realm. Or perhaps it was a guard. After all, I couldn't tell a shifter lion from a real one. Either way, Chase didn't seem concerned by its presence, and it made no move to attack.

Beyond the trees and rocks, mountains of red sand dominated the horizon. Waves of shimmering heat rose off the dunes. The sun was a ball of blazing white, much lower in the sky than it had been when I'd entered the portal hole in the mortal realm.

I shaded my eyes.

Above the desert sands, something circled. It was much too big to be a hawk, but all I could make out was a span of long white wings.

"What's that?" I asked, pointing to the unfamiliar shape.

Chase glanced up. "Griffin."

I tripped. "As in part bird, part lion?"

"Don't worry, they stick to the dunes."

We paused at the top of the last hill before the sand spread into the wider desert. I put my hands on my hips and took a deep breath of dry air. "Do we have to cross that?"

Chase matched my pose. "Do I look like a desert creature?" He pointed off to my left. "We're going that way."

I followed his finger. The line of sun-bleached rocks that sheltered our landing pad tapered off nearby, revealing a steep incline of land covered with forest that brushed up against the edge of the sand in a long, dark line. The scrub brush and sparse trees of the desert grew abruptly thicker and more diverse. Leaves broadened. Trees grew taller.

Taking advantage of our momentary pause, I pulled off my boot and dumped what seemed like an impossible amount of sand onto the ground. "How far is it to the Shifter Lord's house . . . palace . . ." I waffled a hand in the air. "Whatever?"

"About six miles."

I slipped my boot back on. "Are we walking the whole way?"

"Something wrong with your feet?"

I snorted and stepped around him, heading for the end of the rocks that marked the beginning of the forest. Hiking happened to be one of my favorite pastimes.

WIPING A TRICKLE of sweat out of my eyes, I pushed aside a leaf twice the length of my arm with my free hand and received another shower of dew. I'd been a fool to call this vegetation a forest—it was a jungle. Steam rose off the ground, filling the air with humid mist that became trapped under the dense canopy. I'd stripped off my coat and tied it around my waist. My shirt was soaked through, the sleeves pushed up above my elbows. I felt like a dumpling in a pressure cooker.

A wide array of birds swooped and darted among the branches above, filling the air with song and streaks of color. Tiny, black, squirrel-like creatures no bigger than my palm darted through the undergrowth, and a group of golden-haired primates that must have outweighed me by at least a hundred pounds swung from branch to branch above, watching as I struggled up yet another nearly vertical slope. We'd crested the first ridge, plunged into a deep ravine, then crossed a dozen more, each taller than the last.

My foot slipped in the loose, rich soil coating the hillside, and I lost a good three feet of progress before grabbing a stiff vine to arrest my slide.

"How much farther?" I called to Chase's sweat-slicked back. From what I could see through the canopy, the sun was sitting just above the horizon. I did *not* want to be stumbling through the jungle when it set.

He just shook his head and pushed through yet another barrier of vegetation.

I was crawling on my hands and knees by the time I reached the flat shelf at the top of the hill where Chase waited. Straightening halfway, I propped my hands on my knees and panted like an Arizona dog in August.

Chase's smile was wide as ever.

I wanted to smack him, or at least say something biting, but I didn't have the breath.

"Congratulations," he said. Then he stepped to the side and pulled back one of the enormous fronds blocking my view beyond the ridge. "This is Matua'aiga."

I stepped to the edge of the cliff. Despite the steep drop near my feet, the valley below was wider than the slot-canyons we'd been traversing. A broad river flashed between trees that, while still dense, didn't completely obscure the ground. On the far side of the river, a gentle mountain slope rose in a series of hills dotted with pines and broad-leafed trees I might expect to find in New England rather than a rain forest. Interspersed among the trees were buildings that blended so perfectly with their surroundings I almost missed them.

A cool breeze blew up the valley, drying the sweat on my skin. I closed my eyes and spread my arms wide to welcome it. Then I opened my eyes and took another look at the little village in the trees with its camouflaged buildings. "I expected the lord's estate to be more . . ." I hesitated, picturing Bael's keep—towering walls of white marble surrounded by the bustling city of Abonaille Malmür. "Different."

"More different?" Chase laughed and pointed downstream. "The court proper is another two miles that way." He patted me on the shoulder and started down the slope. "We'll stash you at my house while

I run ahead to make arrangements."

I pulled up short. "Wouldn't it be faster if I just came with you?"

He paused, balancing easily on the steep incline, and looked back at me. "This isn't Enchantment. You're not a member of this court. And oath or no, you're Bael's kin." He gestured to the intricate tattoo spiraling up my exposed forearm—the charm Bael had imprinted me with to strengthen my fae blood and claim me as family. "Best not to parade you around the court if we can help it." He shook his head and resumed his descent. "A nice, private meeting. That's what we want."

Frowning, I rolled my sleeves back down to cover my arms. It was uncomfortably warm, but the temperature was dropping along with the sun, so I wasn't likely to collapse from heat stroke. Using a nearby vine for support, I started after him. "If it's not safe for me here, how is leaving me alone in this village going to—" My foot slipped and I landed hard on my butt. Luckily, I still had a grip on the vine.

One of the golden-furred monkeys who'd been keeping pace with us dangled from a nearby tree. He hung sideways by one arm and one leg, and *chuffed* as though laughing at my stumble.

"You'll be safe enough," Chase called back without stopping to check if I was all right. "Now focus on what you're doing. It'd be a shame to come all this way just to break your neck on the last descent."

Pursing my lips, I concentrated on my footing until we reached the edge of the river. The monkeys continued to watch, but didn't follow us down.

On this side, the river was lined by large boulders at the base of the mountain, while the far side lapped quietly at a sandy bank. Beyond that bank, a group of deer-like creatures munched the blooms off flowers in a wide meadow.

A bridge spanned the river a little way upstream, though it seemed to have been grown rather than built. Thick vines snaked together to create a wide tube cradled on either side by a fine mesh of thinner vines.

"You sure this will hold me?" I'd seen fae walk on snow without making a dent. Sometimes they forgot humans had to obey the laws of mass and gravity.

"I've seen an elephant cross this bridge," Chase said as he hopped lightly onto the central vine. He didn't bother touching the guide lines, just trotted across the swinging bridge and jumped to the sand at the far end.

I held the guides on both sides, and carefully placed one foot in front of the other. The collection of vines that made up the base was a good six inches wide, but it was slick with spray from the river and the whole bridge swayed with each step.

"I thought your charm was supposed to make you more fae." Chase crouched, trailing a stick through the damp sand to carve a pattern while he waited. "Shouldn't you be more . . . nimble?"

I stepped off the end of the bridge. "I'm still mostly mortal."

He glanced up. "How do you know?"

"What do you mean?"

He used his stick to point at my right arm and the now covered tattoo. "How do you know how much it's changed you? Maybe you're ninety percent fae now and only ten percent human."

I shook my head, not liking the way the thought rattled around, knocking other worries loose. I spread my fingers and inspected my dirty but scratch-free palms. I thought of the knife I'd forged from smoke and magic, and the speed with which my burns had healed after my confrontation with O'Connell. Not vampire fast. Not even fully fae fast. But way beyond human.

"Would it be so bad?" he asked. "What does mortality give you that's worth hanging on to?"

I opened my mouth, but closed it when nothing came out. What were the benefits of mortality?

He shoved his stick point down in the sand and brushed off his hands. "Just a little farther."

My legs were cramped from the steep jungle hills, so even the relatively gentle climb up the slope on the far side of the river made them ache. The first building came into view about a hundred yards from the river, but I almost missed it. Each corner of the house was supported by a thick cedar tree. Thin branches stretched between the trunks, connecting the trees together, and between the branches pale, stucco-like mud formed the walls. The building wasn't just sitting between the trees . . . it was built into them.

"How?" I pointed to the wall, noting how the branches had grown in a circle to allow the placement of a window.

Chase shrugged. "Shifters tend to live pretty closely with nature fae. Most of the houses around here were grown by dryads."

"The houses were *grown?*" I shook my head, smiling. Talk about living in harmony with nature.

A branch snapped to my left, and I caught sight of a bushy red tail darting into the underbrush. Starlings and jays chittered in the branches overhead.

More buildings appeared, each stretching far into the towering trees. Balconies sprouted from the sides like shelf fungus with rope bridges drooping between them. As the buildings increased in number, so did the animals. Creatures I would expect to find in the woods like the deer and fox were joined by other, more exotic beasts. A bone-white python draped the branch of a nearby tree. Two wolf pups and a kitten tumbled together through the tall grass. A raccoon waddled across the path, striped tail swishing. It paused for a moment, assessed me, then continued on.

I raised an eyebrow. "Are all these animals . . .?"

"Not all of them. Some are just animals." He grinned. "Can you tell the difference?"

I rolled my eyes.

Here and there, human-shaped fae mingled with their animal brethren. They meandered along the paths and crossed the bridges overhead, stepping over cats, lizards, children, and other obstacles. There was a wide range of skin, hair color, and body types, all on full display.

Chase had been right. I definitely stood out. I was the only person wearing clothes.

"Welcome to my humble abode." Chase pulled back a curtain of what looked like Spanish moss over the entrance to one of the houses just off the central clearing.

I ducked under his arm and stepped into a large, round room. A layer of soft, springy moss covered the ground like a carpet, and arcs of bramble frames created windows that filled the room with natural light. Stairs grew out of the wall to my left, circling to the floor above. At the back of the chamber two arches led into adjoining rooms. A set of wooden chairs sat to one side of the room beside a table with a polished stone top.

"Sorry I can't offer you any refreshments," Chase said as he stepped in beside me and let the curtain drop, "but I haven't had cause to stock the pantry in, well . . . a long time."

"Weren't you here just last month?" I asked. "While I was in Enchantment?"

"Here in this realm, not in this house." He pointed to the stairs. "Bedroom's up there. There's a basin where you can get cleaned up." He lowered his arm and turned to face me. "Make yourself comfortable, but *don't* leave the house."

I crossed my arms. "I hate doing nothing."

"Then don't do nothing," he said. "Just don't leave the house." He lifted the mossy curtain once more.

"When will you be back?" I asked.

"When I've convinced the lord to speak with you." He stepped outside and let the curtain fall.

I moved to the entrance and lifted the edge of the moss. A gray tabby streaked across the clearing and disappeared into the bushes on the far side. My muscles strained to follow. I hated the idea of sitting idle. But this was his realm, not mine. If he believed a private meeting was safest, I'd follow his lead. I let the curtain drop back in place.

I looked down. My boots were muddy. My pants and coat were streaked with green and brown stains from my many falls. I lifted an arm, sniffed, and recoiled. With a sigh, I headed upstairs. At least I could use this time to get clean so I didn't look and smell like roadkill when I met the Shifter Lord.

Chapter 5

CHASE'S BEDROOM was huge—the full size of the lower level. As I stepped inside, my boots made trails in the pale dust that coated the floor. A four-poster bed wide enough that I could have lain spread-eagle in the center and not touched either side sat against one wall. The frame and corner posts were carved from smooth black stone with flecks of gold that sparkled just beneath the surface. I ran my fingers over the stone, then pressed down on an edge of the bed, dislodging more dust. Silk sheets covered a mat of something soft and yielding. Probably wool shaved from shifter sheep or feathers shed by the many birds that sang in the branches just past the room's balcony.

I pictured Chase curled up as a cat on the back of my worn fabric couch. Not exactly the luxury he was used to if this was how he usually lived. But the dust indicated a longer period of neglect than the handful of months Chase had been spying on me.

There was a dresser beside the bed, and on it was a large stone basin full of surprisingly clean water. I'd seen similar bowls in Enchantment. No faucet, no drain, and the water was always clear and warm no matter how much grime you dumped in it.

Shaking the dust off a cloth that showed how long it had been since the basin was last used, I wiped the sweat and grime off my face, neck, and arms. Then I ran the cloth over a silver mirror on the wall, clearing the dust enough to see myself. I reached up and tugged my ponytail tight, tucking away a few loose strands, brushed at the stains on my jeans, wiped the mud off my boots, and dropped the cloth next to the still perfectly clear water. Then I turned to explore the room. Chase had done no end of snooping into my life. Turnaround was fair play.

Several shelves grew from the wall near the bed, each holding a collection of books. I blew a plume of dust off them and ran my fingers over worn leather covers, reading the spines. Most were in a language I couldn't understand. I picked one up and flipped through it. The script was unintelligible, but there were pictures. It seemed to be a storybook about a mouse who defeated a horrible monster with three heads and bat wings. A child's fairy tale, or a historical account. In the Shifter Realm, it could be either.

I placed the book back on the shelf and continued around the room.

A desk carved from the same shimmery black stone as the bed was positioned beneath one of the windows. I looked out at a darkening sky. The lavender of the afternoon had deepened to violet, and streaks of red marked the sunset.

The top drawer of the desk held a dry inkwell, three stained quills, and several sticks of charcoal. The next contained a stack of papers. Curious, I flipped through them. They were sketches. Plants, people, animals, landscapes. Some of the drawings had notes scribbled in the margins, labels about texture or color. Some were the barest outlines of shapes; others were detailed ink drawings that seemed about to walk off the page.

When Sol crashed my Christmas party he'd asked how Chase and I knew each other, and Chase had said he was a fellow artist. So much happened right after that, I'd all but forgotten the conversation. I'd have to compare notes with him once life settled down enough to get back to my art.

Closing the drawer, I stepped away from the desk and continued my inspection. In the farthest corner of the room, tucked behind a steamer trunk, was something covered with an oilskin cloth.

I lifted one corner, then pulled the whole sheet away. Canvases were stacked in the corner, each bearing an evolution of the sketches I'd found in the desk. Portraits of exotic animals, unbelievable landscapes, all depicted in vibrant colors and strong strokes. Chase wasn't just a hobby artist. These were masterful paintings.

I flipped past canvas after canvas, appreciating his technique, his compositions, the way he captured light and motion. About halfway through the pile, I stopped at a painting of a white tiger with sapphire eyes lying in a field of wild flowers. Behind her sat a two-tailed kitsune with one paw resting on her side, and sitting on her rump was a gray tabby. I pulled the painting out for a closer look, squinting in the dying light.

Haru said he and Chase had grown up together. And there'd been another, a girl. I dredged my brain for the name Jynx had given me.

Nia.

Whatever happened between the three of them was the source of animosity between Chase and Haru. A love triangle perhaps? Or something more tragic?

"I see you found a way to entertain yourself."

I spun to find Chase standing in the room's entryway. He remained just outside, as though prevented from entering by some invisible barrier.

"I . . . I just . . ."

"Please put that back."

I tried to remember any other instance of Chase saying "please" and couldn't find one.

Carefully, I placed the painting back where I'd found it and tucked the oilcloth around the stack. "Were you able to arrange a meeting with the Shifter Lord?"

"I'm here, aren't I?" He gestured to the window, where the last streaks of sunset were fading from the indigo sky, and the pale glimmer of the first stars were coming out. "She's waiting outside."

I tensed. I'd never met *this* lord, but Bael hated to be kept waiting.

Chase turned and disappeared back down the stairs, and I hastened to follow. The main chamber was darker now that the sun had set, but a layer of tiny glowing flowers shone down from the ceiling like domesticated stars. The light they cast was pale blue. Their glow might not have been enough for human eyes, but even a halfer like me could see pretty well in anything but pitch black. The dim glow was probably bright as daylight for Chase.

The clearing in the center of the village was aglow with the same bluish light as Chase's house. Tiny, bright flowers sprouted from the grass along the sides of the paths and trailed down moss from the bridges above. Dark shapes swooped through the night, and shadows moved in the forest. A few human-shaped fae still ambled through the town, but most of the inhabitants watched the nighttime world through shining animal eyes.

Chase led me back along the path toward the river. When we reached the wide grass field, he dropped to one knee and lowered his chin.

I glanced around. There was no one in the field. Not even a mouse could be seen scampering through the grass.

"Um . . ."

A sudden gust of wind knocked me onto my butt.

There was a soft *whomp* as . . . something . . . landed on the ground.

I stared at the creature in the middle of the field as it drew up to its full height. The glowing flowers were sparser here, casting dim light and deep shadows, but I picked out enough details to make me shudder.

Leathery bat wings as long as I was tall folded down to lay along golden-furred sides. A black, scaled tail dotted with foot-long quills lashed the grass. The creature was settled on its haunches, with four clawed paws each as big as my head. Muscular front legs tapered up to a human-shaped torso, though soft gold fur covered her breasts. Thick, reddish-brown hair cascaded over a purely human neck and framed a wide face divided by a long, sharp nose. Pools of ink stared from below golden eyebrows. There was nothing human about those eyes. Long, pointed ears protruded from either side of her face, and twists of curling black horns crowned her head. She was beautiful . . . and terrible. She took my breath away.

"My lord." Chase hadn't moved from his bow. "May I present Alex Blackwood, of the mortal realm."

I shifted my gaze to the smooth curve of Chase's back, wondering at the significance of his aligning me with the mortal realm rather than Enchantment, which I would have thought more normal from a fae perspective. Surely the Shifter Lord was aware of my relation to Bael. That's why she'd sent Chase to spy on me in the first place.

The dark eyes lowered as the lord bobbed her mostly human-looking head, but her gaze never left me.

I wasn't sure what the proper bowing angle was for this particular encounter, so I bent slightly at the waist but kept my back straight and my chin high.

Her lips curved up—not quite enough for me to see the shape of her teeth, for which I was grateful.

The Shifter Lord moved forward, four pawed feet padding across the field.

I straightened, willing my knees not to shake as the monstrous form loomed closer.

Five steps away, the lord began to shimmer, and it was a slender woman who crossed the remaining distance between us. Passing Chase without a downward glance, she scooped up both my hands in a loose embrace. "Lady Blackwood. Such a pleasure to meet you."

I blinked. The woman's body and face bore a complexion similar to mine, but her limbs faded to purplish-black just below her knees and elbows. Her wings had disappeared but her horns and tail remained. She fixed me with a gaze that was black from edge to edge. When she spoke, the tips of tiny, pointed teeth flashed between pink lips.

I swallowed, and the sound seemed to echo through the eerily still field. "Shifter Lord."

"You may call me Anika. I understand you are looking for missing children."

"A missing child," I corrected. "A girl, not quite twelve years old. She's the sister of a friend."

Anika nodded and released my hands. I hadn't realized until then how long and sharp her nails were. No, not nails. Claws.

"A number of children have gone missing in recent months." She tipped her chin up, looking toward the stars.

I followed her gaze, but looked away when I couldn't find any familiar constellations.

"I also have a friend who has asked for help. Her daughter was taken."

"I'm sorry."

Her gaze dropped back to my face and she frowned. "What have you to be sorry for?"

I shook my head. "It's an expression . . . a show of empathy, commiseration."

She made a little *hmm* sound in her throat. "I would like to help my friend, but I cannot go where the child has been taken."

"You know where the missing girl is?"

She nodded. "And who has been abducting these young ones."

"But?" I prompted.

"But they are beyond my reach."

She leveled her full scrutiny on me like a physical burden. My knees began to shake. My palms grew sweaty.

"I believe you and I may be able to help each other, for both our friends' sakes. I will share what information I've been able to gather, if you will be the savior these children require."

"Savior?" I took half a step back.

"Make no mistake. If the children are not rescued, they *will* die. And not by any natural means."

I waved a hand to indicate both her present form and the place where she'd landed. "If a fae lord can't save them, what hope would there be for someone like me? I'm nobody."

"Hardly nobody. But you're right, if this were a matter of raw power, be it strength or ability, you would be entirely outclassed." She gestured to Chase, still crouched in the grass. "Even he would be a better choice."

"Then why ask me?"

"Because of where they are. Now, do we have a deal?"

Clearly she wasn't going to give the details away until she had my cooperation. I took a deep breath through flared nostrils and tried to unclench my jaw. "You're sure the girl I'm looking for will be there?"

"I can't promise you will find the child you seek. I can only tell you she fits the profile of the other stolen children."

"Okay." I gave one curt nod. "Deal."

"Excellent." She clapped her palms together like a child who'd just been told they could have a second dessert. "The missing children have been taken to a place only accessible through the Realm of Enchantment."

No wonder then that she wanted my help. Despite Chase's introduction, Anika clearly intended to take advantage of my connection to the Lord of Enchantment.

She set a delicately clawed hand on my shoulder. "Tell me, have you ever heard the name Shedraziel?"

A memory tickled the edge of my mind, but the thought flitted away before I could grasp it. "It sounds familiar, but . . ."

"She is a powerful fae who made quite a name for herself during the war with the mortals. So much so that she was accused of war crimes and imprisoned at the end of the conflict as one of the stipulations of the Peace Treaty. Her prison lies in a shallowling—a small space split off from its parent realm."

"And that parent realm is Enchantment."

She smiled like a proud parent whose slightly dim child had nonetheless managed to come up with the right answer. "I cannot enter Enchantment nor safely send my servants without leave from the lord. Leave he will not grant."

I shook my head. "If this person is in a prison, how could she be stealing kids? Or aren't fae prisons guarded?"

"Oh she has guards, and wards, and worse . . . but she is a wily one, and she has had time to find ways around her situation."

"The war only ended a generation ago. That's barely a blip for most fae."

"When you are here," she indicated the field around us, "does the same amount of time pass for your friend in the mortal realm?"

"No. Each realm has a different speed."

"The rules of a shallowling are set when it is made. In the case of

Shedraziel's prison, Lord Bael wished her to have time to . . . reflect . . . on her choices."

"So more time passes there?"

"Yes."

"How much more?"

Anika lifted one shoulder in a surprisingly human gesture. "Shedraziel has had several mortal lifetimes to reflect."

The hairs on my arms and the back of my neck shivered as though stirred by a cold breeze. If May was in a place like that . . . how much time might have passed in the day she'd been missing? "Where do the kidnapped children fit in?"

"I don't know why Shedraziel started collecting children, but I cannot imagine the purpose is anything but nefarious. For one, she is only abducting those with unique or extraordinary abilities." She gestured to Chase again, who may as well have been a statue for all he'd moved. "Chase has told me your friend's sister is a musician."

"She's talented, but hardly the best in the world."

"But the best for her age perhaps? Talent in the young is always more desirable than talent in the old due to its inherent potential."

"If this Shedraziel person *is* the one abducting kids, that means she's broken out of her prison. Wouldn't Bael have noticed?"

"She has not escaped her prison, merely found a way around it. My information says she is still locked away."

"Then Bael can just pull the children out."

Anika nodded. "He could." She pinned me with that unsettling gaze again. "But *will* he?"

I frowned. "Why wouldn't he?"

Another shrug. "I find it hard to believe Lord Bael is ignorant of his general's activities."

"General?"

"Did I not mention she earned a name for herself in the war? She was a force to be reckoned with among mortals and fae alike. As such, she was named Bael's general and led the largest military force during the conflict."

"But he still imprisoned her."

"He had no choice. Shedraziel would not abide by the terms of the treaty, and both sides knew it. She continued to kill even as the leaders negotiated for peace. Even Bael could not control her. I believe *that*, more than anything, is what convinced him to imprison her, and it was his wounded pride that caused him to compound her punishment. It is that same pride that now stands in our way. I doubt Lord Bael will accept his failure to contain Shedraziel a second time. But if you believe you can get through to him . . ." She lifted a clawed hand. "By all means, try."

I wasn't at all sure Bael would listen to me. Despite being related, we barely knew each other, and the last time we'd tried to strike a deal we'd both walked away empty-handed.

I never retreat.

I rubbed my upper arms, recalling Bael's words. Anika was right about his pride being a problem, but that didn't mean he couldn't see reason.

"Should that fail," Anika continued, "the entrance to Shedraziel's prison lies far to the east of Bael's stronghold."

That familiar tickle of a half-remembered thought came back, pulling my attention like the buzz of a persistent fly. When I attended the Winter Festival in Enchantment, Bael had asked one of his underlings about wards in the east. He'd mentioned disappearances, and an old problem that gave him trouble from time to time.

"I must warn you, Shedraziel is a masterful enchantress. The power of her voice alone is enough to bend the will of many fae, to say nothing of mortals. If you face her directly, you will not succeed. Not as you are. Should your plea to Lord Bael go unheeded, your best chance will lie in stealth. To that end . . ." She moved to stand directly in front of Chase.

He rose smoothly to his feet, meeting and holding the gaze of his lord.

"You understand I cannot send an agent into Enchantment without grave political repercussions?"

Chase nodded.

"If you are detained, you will receive no aid."

Another nod.

"Then I declare you a free agent, your oath revoked."

A shudder rippled down Chase's body.

She turned to me. "Chase will accompany you, but not as a vassal of the Shifter Realm. From this point on, I can offer you no assistance. The shifters' position among the courts is too precarious to risk open confrontation with another realm. Especially one as powerful as Enchantment."

A lump the size of a boulder lodged in my throat when I tried to swallow. "I'll do what I can, but I can't promise much."

"I require no promises."

"What's your friend's daughter's name?"
She smiled. "Zeraldi."
I nodded. "I'll try to bring her home."

Chapter 6

SQUINTING INTO the darkness, I watched Anika's retreating form as she skimmed through the star-studded sky above the white sand alcove by which I'd arrived in the Shifter Realm. Given the time-sensitive nature of my mission, she'd offered to carry us back to the edge of the desert. It had definitely been faster than bushwhacking through the jungle, but I was pretty sure the sensation of dangling over open space in the grip of scaled fingers with razor-sharp claws was going to make for a few sleepless nights in my future.

I gestured at the barely visible Shifter Lord. "Can you do that?"

Chase raised an eyebrow. "Fly?" He lifted his arms as though judging their potential as wings.

I snorted and traced a finger along a small tear in my sleeve where one of Anika's nails had snagged the fabric. "Be multiple things. I've only ever seen you as a cat and—" I gestured to indicate his current form.

He lifted one shoulder. "Depends on the species. Most young shifters have a human-esque form and one animal form. As we grow older, we may adopt new forms. My mother, for example, has three animal forms."

"And you?"

A muscle in the side of his neck tensed, clamping his jaw shut. He turned away, moving toward the hole we'd tumbled out of. Well, I'd tumbled. Knowing Chase, he'd probably landed on his feet.

"What about the halfway thing? Is it normal to be multiple things at the same time, or is that because she's a lord?"

"Other way around," he said. "Part of why she's a lord is because she can do that. And no, I can't. It's a rare ability, not unlike your own."

"Imbuing?"

He nodded, pausing just outside the small, dark opening. "She's able to add components to the core of her being, changing her base struc-ture." He glanced over his shoulder, emerald eyes flashing in the dim light of the stars. "She's a chimera."

Then he shifted to the small gray tabby who slept on my couch, and darted into the hole.

Chimera. I pursed my lips. A legendary creature who possessed the attributes of a number of distinct animals. Another myth humans didn't know was real.

I looked at the palm of my hand, turning it this way and that to catch the light.

I was part human, part fae, a blend of two races. But there were lots of halfers.

I thought back to the first time I passed through a fae portal, when the barrier magic had tried to burn the vampire contamination out of my body. I'd twisted it, made it a part of me to protect the gift James had given to save my life. And that piece of him was still there, linking us. That part of him had become a part of me, inextricable. I'd changed my core, my base structure. Did that make me a chimera too?

I shook my head. Then I crawled in the hole after Chase, leaving the soft light of the stars behind. Dry sand slid between my fingers and under my knees, then gave way to cold, solid stone. I moved slowly, reaching each hand as far as my fingers could stretch, searching for the incline I'd slid down on my arrival. But the tunnel remained flat.

Eventually, my fingers crunched dry leaves. A pine needle jabbed my palm. I slithered forward on my knees and elbows and emerged in speckled moonlight beneath the camouflaging branches of a prickly bush. Chase pushed the brambles to one side and offered me his hand.

I eyed it, half-expecting the fae equivalent of an electric buzzer hidden in his palm, then slipped my fingers into his and scrambled to my feet.

I blinked up at the sky. What I'd mistaken for moonlight was actually the first blush of dawn. Stars still dotted a bruised sky in the west, but the clouds peeking over the eastern horizon were aflame with the first light of day.

Chase followed my gaze skyward. "What do you want to do?"

I sighed, weighing options. "I need to talk to Bael as soon as possible, try to convince him to check on Shedraziel's prison. At least we can verify if she has the kids."

Chase continued to watch the sky, notably not offering his opinion of my plan.

"Anika didn't seem to think Bael would be inclined to help." I chewed the end of my thumbnail, which had developed a sharp burr during our trip, and considered ways to strengthen my position. Then a thought struck me. "What if Emma asked?"

He shifted his gaze to me, the dawn light illuminating his frown. "What do you mean?"

"From what I understand, the fae justice system is centered around wronged parties seeking their own justice or requesting the intervention of a lord. If *I* go to Bael, I'll be asking for a favor. One he might refuse, or accept at a cost I'm unwilling to pay. But if *Emma* asks, she'd be working within the fae justice system as May's relative."

He pursed his lips and turned his face up once more. "Her presence would lend weight to your argument. If he's willing to listen."

"So I get her the audience, and she makes the request."

I patted my pocket, feeling the shape of my cell phone. "Let's hop back to the way station so I can get some reception. Emma can get here in just over three hours, then we'll jump to Enchantment."

I glanced down at the tiny cave that led to the shifter realm. It was nearly invisible beneath the bush. Even knowing it was there, I wouldn't be able to distinguish it from any other rocky hole. Could I identify the trees that marked the portal to Enchantment without a guide?

"Come on," Chase said. "If we run, we can be in the field before Otis arrives for his next scheduled jump."

"No rest for the weary," I grumbled.

OTIS POPPED INTO existence three feet to my left while I was doubled over my knees, trying to catch my breath. Chase hadn't been kidding about having to hurry, but we'd made it.

The teleporter lifted his arms, palms up. Chase gripped one hand without hesitation. I dragged my feet, filling my lungs more slowly. As soon as my fingers were twined with his, Otis jumped. A flash of light whitewashed my vision.

When I blinked, the forest had been replaced by rustic cabin walls. The scent of pine needles and rotting leaves became soap suds and yeast. Four loaves of bread sat rising on the kitchen counter, and two muffin trays were soaking in the sink.

Releasing Otis's clammy hand, I reached for my pocket. My phone came to life before I had the chance to touch it. *Ding. Ding. Ding.* Each sound marked a notification. Apparently I'd missed some calls while I was gone.

Maybe May had been found. Then my excitement went flat. If May wasn't missing any more, what would I do about Zeraldi? I'd promised

Anika I'd try to bring her back.

Tugging the phone from my pocket, I decided I'd speak with Bael no matter what. Even if May was safe, Bael should know Shedraziel's prison was no longer secure.

The phone continued to *ding* as I lit the screen. Just how many calls had I missed?

I pulled up the notification bar. There was Emma's name, as I'd hoped, but also James and Sol. Then there was David. I counted the messages. Four, five, six. . . . I frowned. This was way beyond his daily attempt to beg forgiveness.

Chase peeked at my screen. "Popular today, aren't you?" He tapped David's name. "Have you forgiven him yet?"

I pulled the phone out of reach. "None of your business."

Clasping his hands behind his head, Chase stretched. "I'm not sure why you made such a fuss in the first place. What he did was not so different from the circumstances under which I came to know you, and you don't hold that against me." He narrowed his eyes. "Or do you? Is that why you offered Jynx a bed and not me?"

I opened my mouth, closed it. It was true Chase had come into my life to spy on me. He hadn't made any attempt to hide that fact when he asked to stay with me as thanks for saving my life. So why did learning David was spying on me hurt so much more? Was it because he'd lied about it? Because his deceit involved not one, but two people I'd thought I could trust? Or was it because David had been my first real friend, the first person I'd opened up to after losing my mother, and now I couldn't shake the feeling that our connection was a lie?

I glanced at Chase, then back down to the phone in my hand. David swore he'd reported to Sol strictly for my own good, that our friendship was real. Was I being too hard on him? Maybe I should forgive him.

The front door of the way station banged open and the female caretaker strolled through, a tray of dishes in hand. Her pale curls were tucked under a blue silk scarf, a gray shawl draped her shoulders, and white knit gloves protected her fingers from the morning chill.

"Oh good," she said when she saw us. "I was hoping you'd be back today."

I frowned. "Why?" It had been my impression the woman's routine was pretty much the same no matter the comings or goings of her guests.

Setting her tray on a counter, she hooked a thumb toward the door. "Because now I can stop delivering meals to that bloodsucker camped out in the driveway."

Otis shook his head. "I told you to leave him be. He can't cross the barrier. He's not our responsibility."

"Maybe not," she said. "But I won't let anyone go hungry. Not even one of them."

Otis threw his hands up with a, "Bah," and marched through the far right door in the back wall.

"Wait." I held up one palm as though stopping traffic. "There's a vampire here?" I glanced out the window. The pale streaks of dawn had reached the treetops, turning them golden in the morning sun. "In the day?"

The woman nodded. "I assume the tinting on his windows protects him. He doesn't come out during the day. Just leaves the trays I put out in the evening outside his car so I can collect them in the morning."

"He doesn't leave his car during the day?"

"As far as I can tell, he's never left his car, day or night." She shrugged. "But the trays come back empty, so . . ."

Stuffing my phone back in my pocket, I jogged out the front door of the way station, down the rickety wooden steps, and along the dirt path that led to the main road. Chase trotted beside me on four gray paws. As I moved along the path, I turned my attention inward. Finding the thread that connected me to James, I plucked it like the string of a harp. The feeling rippled out, found its other end, and echoed back to me.

James was close. Closer than he should have been.

At the top of the first hill I could see the split rail fence that marked the edge of the way station's property, and the barrier that prevented hostile forces from coming any closer. Just beyond that barrier, parked on the shoulder of the dirt road, was an unfamiliar black car with darkly tinted windows.

James was out of the car before I reached the bottom of the hill, and I ran straight into his open arms. The thread between us, stretched thin when we were apart, thickened to a cable when we touched, anchoring us together. I tipped my chin to plant a quick kiss on his lips, then stepped back. Happy as I was to see him, James's being there was all wrong.

"I told you I'd call when I got back. What are you doing here?"

A dark look clouded his expression. "You can't go home."

I narrowed my eyes, fighting back a surge of panic.

You can't go home.

How many houses, trailers, apartments had I been forced to abandon over the years as Mom dragged me around the country. But my house in Nederland was different. It wasn't a stepping stone. It was a Home, capital H. It was the one place I could always go back to.

"What are you talking about?"

James pulled a phone from his pocket and made a few gestures on the screen. Then he turned it toward me.

Chase grew to human height and peeked over my shoulder.

Together, we waited for the YouTube ad to finish so we could see what had caused James to declare my house out of bounds.

At first, I didn't understand what I was seeing. The video was bad, grainy and pixelated. Then a face came into focus. My face, grimy and streaked with tears. Dried blood and swollen skin marked a gash on my forehead. I was looking at the camera through a set of steel bars.

My abdomen clenched, making me thankful I hadn't yet eaten breakfast. Sweat sprang out along my spine while my mouth went suddenly dry.

The missing memory card from O'Connell's camera . . . the video of my confession . . . proof of the existence of werewolves . . .

I closed my eyes, hiding from the evidence in front of me. It couldn't be. All the secrets. All the lies. For nothing.

Then my own voice crackled through the phone's speaker. "My name is Alex Blackwood, and I'm a halfer."

My eyes snapped open, focused on the video as the same scene played out from a different angle in my memory.

The me in the video looked to the side. In my mind, I pictured Maggie, hurt and scared, on a soiled mattress in the corner of our shared cage. "I found out months ago, and kept it secret from the PTF."

"How can you handle iron?" O'Connell's voice came from off screen, but it made me shiver in the here-and-now as though he was standing right in front of me and not burnt to a crisp in the building where he'd imprisoned us.

"A genetic anom . . . luke." Static crackled through the speaker and the video fuzzed out for a moment. Apparently the memory card hadn't survived entirely intact.

The next clear image showed me gripping the bars of my cage, shaking my head. "—rum. It doesn't work on full fae, but it can reduce—"

Another break in the video. Then five *pops* that made my blood run cold. The image was still fuzzy, colored snow dancing across the screen, but in my mind Oz was falling to the floor, five red stains spreading across his chest.

My breath came in short, fast bursts, making me dizzy, and bile rose to the back of my throat despite an empty stomach.

The video came back into focus showing Sophie, my human friend turned werewolf, mid-change. Fur coated her body where the tatters of her clothes fell away. Her face stretched, bones popping. Her teeth grew to fill a long, narrow jaw. Then she tipped back her head and howled.

Chapter 7

I SHOVED THE phone away as disjointed images of Sophie sinking two-inch fangs into my calf and worrying it like a dog with a bone flashed across the screen to a soundtrack of growls and screams. I didn't need, or want, the reminder. My back and leg had healed surprisingly well thanks to an infusion of magic that I still wasn't sure I understood the source of. The healing properties of my fae blood had definite limits. Limits I'd brushed up against before. The near-miraculous healing I'd somehow initiated was something else altogether. Something I didn't want to look at too closely.

Welcome. A demon's smile faded into the swirling smoke of my memories.

Stiffening my shaking legs, I rubbed my hands over the goosebumps on my upper arms. "When did the PTF release the footage?"

"Never," James said. "The footage was leaked and spread by an independent journalist. It hit the internet yesterday and it's already been picked up by every news agency in the country, maybe even the world. People haven't been face to face with proof of paranatural violence like this since—"

"Since the war." I shook my head. With footage of a rampaging werewolf compounded by my confession about being able to handle iron, garbled though it was, the Purity movement would have more supporters than ever.

Taking a deep breath, I braced for more bad news. "What was the PTF's response?"

He shook his head. "They're under almost as much fire as the fae." He swiped his phone screen a few times, then handed it back to me.

There was no ad this time, just streaming video of what looked like a press release. A woman with dark skin and dozens of long, thin braids that faded from black at the roots to light brown near the tips stood at a podium in front of the cameras in a form-fitting business suit. A bar of text scrolled across the bottom of the screen. *Everly Harris, Paranatural*

Task Force Regional Director for the Western United States, addresses allegations of corruption and negligence within the PTF.

"I assure you, we at the PTF are taking these allegations seriously. We have not yet been able to verify the source or authenticity of the video that went viral yesterday, but we have been in communication with various paranatural representatives as well as the heads of numerous government agencies to determine the validity of these disturbing images. I will personally be heading up this investigation with the full support of the PTF, and backing from the Church's sorcerers. I ask that if you have any information on the people featured in this video to please contact your local PTF office. Whether this was a hoax intended to stir up fear among the human public or a genuine documentation of a new threat, I will get to the bottom of it."

Cameras flashed and reporters in the foreground raised their hands. James took the phone back and cleared the screen. "That woman, Harris, took over the Denver office last night. Apparently she's making it her base of operations during the investigation."

"Not surprising," said Chase. "Alex's name was clear on the video. I doubt it would take a government agency long to track her down."

You can't go home.

My house. My studio. The knickknacks I'd collected with my mother. The picture on my mantle of David, Aiden, and me in Mexico that was a reminder of happier times. I'd never see them again.

My eyes burned. The road blurred. I balled my fists. Even dead, O'Connell was screwing with me, getting the revenge he'd sworn to have what seemed like a lifetime ago.

James squeezed my shoulder. "It's all right, Alex. We can—"

I brushed his hand off and shook my head. "No, it isn't. Nothing about this is all right."

James frowned. A ribbon of pain filtered through our connection—hurt feelings at the way I'd brushed him off.

He didn't reach out again, not with his hand, but a comforting warmth settled inside me. A steadying presence. I may have lost my home, but I was not alone. Things might not be okay at the moment, but they *could* be made right.

I took a deep breath, met James's gaze, and nodded.

"I think we should go back to the reservation," Chase said.

"What?" I spun to face him. "I can't just—"

"You were planning to go back anyway. May and Zeraldi, and who knows how many other children, are still missing. Still in danger. You can't go home with the PTF hunting for you. At least in Enchantment, you'd be safe."

"I agree." James stepped around me so he was standing next to Chase, his dark hair and tailored clothes a sharp contrast to the shifter's silver tresses and bare skin.

I pursed my lips. They weren't wrong, but I hadn't intended to head to Enchantment until Emma joined me. I needed the authority her presence would provide if I wanted to get Bael to agree to my request. Besides, if my house was no longer safe, Emma couldn't stay there any more than I could. I focused on James. "Where are Emma and Jynx?"

He shook his head. "I've been unable to contact them since the video's release. I can only hope they were wise enough to leave your home when they realized the threat."

Marc and the werewolves would have bolted as soon as the whispers started. Had Emma done the same?

"If Jynx thought she was in danger, she would've headed to Crossroads. It's an evacuation point for the fae." Chase met my gaze. "Remember the jump lines I told you about?"

James frowned. "Crossroads?"

Despite the dire circumstances, I couldn't help but smile. It wasn't often I knew more about the paranatural community than James, but Crossroads was a strictly fae establishment, complete with charms and enchantments to keep out humans and the like. If James didn't know about it, those spells must have been tuned to trick vampires as well.

My sense of one-upmanship was short lived, though, as the word "evacuation" sank in.

I pulled out my cell phone.

James lifted a hand, pointing at my phone. "You should get rid of that. Pull the battery out at the very least."

I tipped my chin toward the slim phone still in James's hand. "What about yours?"

"Burner," he said. "Can't be traced."

I considered the device in my hand—a homing beacon waiting for some government desk jockey to ping the GPS. But I needed all the information I could get. "In a second."

I clicked my voicemail icon and held the phone to my ear. Sol's message was first. Another warning. He was going off the grid, but hoped he'd be able to speak with me again soon. "Keep yourself safe, Alex."

The second message was from David, as was the third, and fourth.

Where was I? Was I safe? Had I seen the video? His voice crackled with an edge of hysteria in the later recordings, and my heart twisted.

The next message was the one I'd been looking for, the one from Emma.

"Don't come home, Alex. It's all over the news. Jynx and I are packing what we can, but—" She cut off abruptly. In the silence, I could just make out the distant whine of sirens. "Shit. Jynx, we gotta go." Emma's voice cut off as the message ended.

David's voice drifted into my ear again as the next queued recording began to play, but I didn't register his words. The police had gone to my house. Or maybe it had been the PTF. Did they have sirens? It didn't matter. I was a fugitive. I couldn't go home.

". . . how things ended up between us." David's words chipped their way into my brain, forcing me to focus. "Maybe, someday, I'll see you again. I hope so. Goodbye, Alex."

My brain played back the words I'd heard but hadn't understood the first time around. David wasn't taking any chances. He was going into hiding, dropping off the grid. Had he made this plan with Sol? Would the two of them join up somewhere?

I shook my head. It didn't matter, so long as they were safe. I pinned my lower lip between my teeth. I hadn't forgiven them. Now I might never get the chance.

The last message began to play. A woman's voice I'd heard only once before, rich and firm. "Ms. Blackwood, my name is Everly Harris. I work for the PTF. It's my job to find the truth behind the video that was released this morning. I've been informed that the police went to your house this afternoon but were unable to locate you." A brief pause, as though she was deciding which path to take. "I'm flying to Denver tonight. I urge you to turn yourself in. I promise that if you do, no harm will come to you."

As silence rang through the line, I lowered the phone from my ear.

"That Harris lady wants me to turn myself in."

Chase snorted. "Of course she does. You'd be doing her job for her."

"If I explained what really happened . . . that I was abducted and coerced . . . that O'Connell . . ." I shook my head, unable to complete the sentence. Even if Harris believed me about what O'Connell had done, she'd still have verification of a halfer immune to iron. Maybe I could pass the basic tests that filtered fae from humans, but if the PTF went poking through my blood I was pretty sure they'd find *something* paranatural.

"Are you going to turn yourself in?" Concern buzzed through my connection to James as he spoke. He did *not* like that plan.

"If I thought it would actually help. But . . ." I shook my head.

James relaxed, his shoulders dropping half an inch.

"I need to find out what happened to Emma and Jynx when the cops showed up. And Maggie. She might not have been clearly visible in the video, but if they found out she was there . . ."

"There was nothing on the news about any of them being arrested," James said.

"You think the capture would have been advertised if they were?" Chase asked.

James shrugged.

"Let's find out." I pointed to James's burner phone. "Can I borrow that?"

He handed it over.

I tapped Maggie's number in from memory, pressed the call button, and held my breath.

The call connected on the second ring, but it wasn't Maggie who answered. The knot in my stomach grew tighter.

"Hello?" Maggie's husband, Charlie, sounded nervous. His voice was tight and a little too high.

"Charlie, where's Maggie? Are you guys all right?"

"Alex?" His voice jumped another octave. "They've taken her for questioning. They're—"

"Ms. Blackwood?" A woman's voice cut in, smooth and sure. "My name is Everly Harris. I'm currently leading the PTF investigation into your rather controversial video."

I struggled to swallow. "What happened to Charlie?"

"Mr. Rohne is fine. Your call has simply been redirected to my office."

"That video was a lie," I said. "O'Connell was threatening the lives of my friends. I only told him what he wanted to hear."

"And the wolf?"

I bit my lip. I could maybe convince her my confession was false . . . but Sophie's transformation?

"The quickest way to clear this all up is for you to turn yourself in. Tell us your side of the story."

I thought of Maggie, Emma, Jynx, and everyone who was in danger because of their connection to me. Then I thought of May, trapped in Enchantment, losing who knew how much time—how much of her innocence—every moment I dithered in the mortal realm. I was the only one who could reach her.

I disconnected the call and stared down at the phone. Maggie was in PTF custody. There was nothing I could do for her. But she was a purely human citizen. I had to believe they wouldn't hurt her.

I looked at Chase. "Do you know the number for Crossroads?"

He raised an eyebrow and gestured with both hands to his naked body. "You think I make a lot of calls? And a fae bar's not exactly gonna be listed in the phone book."

I glanced over his shoulder. "Do you think the way station—"

"I'll ask." Chase shifted before I could get another word in and darted back to the building in a streak of gray.

Sighing, I handed the phone back to James, who pulled the battery from the back. I did the same with mine, then put battery and phone in opposite pockets as though mere proximity might bring the device back to life.

I took the moment of privacy to take hold of James's hand, reassuring myself with the warm thrum of our connection.

He smiled, and pulled me into a full embrace. "We'll figure this out."

I nodded, my cheek against his shoulder. I hadn't mentioned the second reason for my reluctance to turn right around and go back to the reservation. My relationship with James was no secret. If the PTF was looking for me, he was in danger too. And unlike Chase and me, he couldn't find sanctuary in another realm. Not so long as the demon in his soul was present.

He stroked a hand over my hair and whispered, "I'll be fine."

Sometimes I hated that he could see so much of what I was thinking and feeling, especially when we were pressed together like this. But right now, it was nice not to have to voice my worries. Not to struggle for words.

Chase was back a moment later, shifting smoothly to human as he reached us. "They had the number, but I couldn't get through. Got one of those robot voices saying the line was out of service."

I stepped back from James, but didn't release his hand. Did a disconnected line mean Crossroads had been compromised? If so, Jynx and Emma would have no safe haven.

"Don't panic yet," Chase said. "Targe may simply be locking the place down."

I nodded, hoping he was right.

"So." James swung our joined hands to draw my attention. "Where to?"

I flicked my gaze between the two men. Neither blinked. Neither offered an opinion. I was the fugitive. It was up to me to decide.

"We'll head to Crossroads," I said. "I know time is a factor for May and the others, but we've got a better chance of getting her out if Emma's with us. Besides, I can't leave without knowing she and Jynx are safe."

"And if they're not at Crossroads?" Chase asked.

I circled to the passenger side of James's car. "We'll cross that bridge when we get there."

Chase shrank back to his cat form. I opened my door, and he slipped into the back seat where he curled into a furry gray ball on the black leather.

James settled behind the wheel and started the engine.

As he turned the car back down the dirt road, I tapped my knuckle against the window. "Whose car is this anyway?"

"It's on loan from the nest. One of many they keep on hand for . . . discreet operations."

It took less than ten minutes to get back to human habitation. I squirmed in my seat as we passed the city limit sign for Crestone, recalling the anti-magic protest we'd passed in front of the One Earth building on our last trip through.

James turned off the main street at the first opportunity, headed for a narrow country road that led out the west side of town. The meandering path would eat precious time, but we'd be less likely to draw unwanted attention.

Three turns later, we found a wooden blockade stretched across the road with the words "road closed" painted across the boards in big black letters. A uniformed PTF agent stood behind it. He waved us to the right, pointing to a small "detour" sign. It seemed someone wanted all traffic to and from the reservation to pass straight through the center of Crestone.

James eased the car back toward Alder Street, the town's main thoroughfare.

In the day I'd been gone, the scene in front of the One Earth building had spread to engulf the whole town. Buildings were shuttered. Closed signs dangled from nearly every window along Alder Street. Men and women with steel batons patrolled the sidewalks, many in PTF uniforms.

Just before the road curved toward Birch Street and the way out of town, a heavy-set man in aviator lenses and a PTF windbreaker stepped into the road, waving us to a stop.

I stiffened in my seat. I could pass a fae blood check, but my face was all over the internet. There was no way an agent wouldn't recognize me. My heartbeat ratcheted up. Leather creaked as I gripped my seat.

James eased the car to the shoulder. "Stay calm."

"But—"

"Trust me."

A flush of cool calm washed through me, carried through our connection. James had a plan. He wasn't worried, and his confidence lent me confidence.

I relaxed my fingers and tried to slow my breathing. I glanced in the rearview mirror, but Chase was no longer on the back seat.

The PTF agent rapped against James's window. He hadn't removed his sunglasses, so all I could see when I looked at his eyes was silver. Close-cropped brown hair stood stiff on his scalp, barely shifting in the wind. The skin around his mouth and neck was tan, rough, and wrinkled. Gray and brown whiskers peppered his chin.

"Security check," the man said when James's window was down. "What's your business in Crestone?"

"We were attending a meditation seminar at the Dharma Sangha Mountain Center."

The man grunted. "Are either of you registered paranaturals?"

"No."

"I'll need to check." He pulled a blood test kit out of his pocket. "Put out your arm please."

James did as he was told, extending his arm out the window so the man could prick his finger. Three drops of blood were squeezed into a small, clear container with a layer of iron shavings at the bottom, which the agent held up in front of his aviators.

He shook the vial, then tucked it back in his pocket and circled around the car.

I had my window down before he reached me, arm extended. I didn't want to give him any reason to study my face.

A fresh needle came out of the man's pocket. He popped off the cap and jabbed my index finger. My blood splattered the iron shavings in the bottom of a jar identical to James's. Again the man lifted the jar as though the quality of light might make a difference to the test results. Then he nodded and stuffed the jar back in his pocket.

"Might want to avoid Crestone for a while. Not the most . . . meditative . . . place at the moment." He slapped his hand twice on the roof of our car and made a twisting motion with his index finger. Farther along the road another agent lifted a hand in acknowledgement. We'd passed our test. We were free to go.

When we passed a sign that said "Leaving Crestone, come back soon!" I sank back against my seat. My muscles felt wrung out. I hadn't even realized I'd been so tense until that tension was gone.

Chase slunk out from under my seat and shook himself in the space between my feet.

"At least you didn't have to get jabbed with a needle."

Giving me a flat look, he twitched his ears and hopped over the center console to curl once more on the back seat.

"I thought for sure he'd recognize me."

The corner of James's mouth lifted. "He wasn't looking for a blond with brown eyes."

I glanced over, studying the profile of his satisfied smirk. "You changed my appearance."

"I changed his perception," he corrected. "Vampires are illusionists, not enchanters."

"And what did you look like?"

His smile grew. "A portly, balding businessman with a bulbous nose."

The car was silent for a moment, then I burst out laughing. James joined me and the car echoed with our mirth.

It felt good to laugh, and I carried on slightly longer than I might have under normal circumstances, burning off residual adrenaline. When the laughter subsided, I wiped my eyes and turned my attention to the rolling hills beyond the windshield. I had a feeling there wouldn't be many occasions to laugh in the coming days.

Chapter 8

CRESTING A HILL on US Highway 36, I squinted at Boulder spread out in the valley below. Light glinted off windows and the backs of cars as they raced along the road ahead of us. The sun shone from a pale-blue sky that stretched horizon to horizon. The traffic leading into Boulder moved steadily until we passed Foothills Parkway. Then it slowed and stopped. The lanes leaving the city were dotted with evenly spaced cars where there should have been bumper-to-bumper traffic.

I frowned, a knot of worry twisting my gut.

As we rounded the bend that would merge us onto Twenty-eighth Street, I spotted the cause of the slowdown. Checkpoints had been set up across all the lanes entering and leaving the city. The exit for Baseline, the last escape route before the checkpoint, was blocked off by a police cruiser. We were being funneled into a choke point where people in uniforms checked each vehicle before sending it on its way.

Two cars ahead of us, a cop lifted a printed image to compare with a female passenger whose red hair was a few shades closer to orange than my own.

A lump lodged in my throat. "Can your illusions get us past this?"

The steering wheel creaked in James's grip. "I don't know."

The orange-haired woman was waved on. We inched forward.

I gripped the door as our turn came. We rolled into place, even with a stand of harsh floodlights that shone despite the adequate morning light. A cop with a pot belly and receding hairline tapped on James's window while a tall, blond man approached my side of the car.

"Evening, officer," James said with an easy smile.

I forced my face to relax and rolled down my window.

The blond cop looked at the picture on his clipboard. He studied my face. Then he glanced over his shoulder.

I looked up. There was a traffic camera pointed directly at me.

The blond man pressed a hand to his ear and nodded.

Cold seeped through my limbs. I spun to James. "They've seen us."

My back slammed against my seat as the car rocketed forward, engine whining. Guns were pulled from holsters by the officers on the side of the road. They leveled their weapons. Bursts of noise were followed by a rapid series of metallic *pings* as bullets bit into the doors and trunk of the speeding car.

There was a loud *crack*, and an opaque spiderweb appeared on my window. Wind whistled through the dark hole at its center. The windshield bore a second, smaller web, like a cataract blocking my view. A deformed wad of lead rolled off the dashboard and fell to the floor.

The gunshots faded behind us as James swerved around the SUV and the car with the orange-haired woman that had been waved through ahead of us. He jerked the wheel hard to the left at the first intersection. Rubber screeched. Our back wheel jumped the curb, then dropped back to the street with a bone-jarring thud.

Sirens wailed behind us. Lights flashed in the rear view.

"Hold on!" James swerved around a blue pickup and took a hard right on Folsom. He was leaning forward, eyes narrowed, deep lines of concentration etched on his face.

I was hanging onto the "oh shit" bar above my door for dear life, my other hand braced against the dash.

The outline of our car seemed to haze, creating a double image as though I'd crossed my eyes.

I blinked and shook my head.

"One more," James said.

This time, when he careened around the corner, the car seemed to split in two. While James and I moved west, a copy of our car, complete with duplicate passengers, continued to the north.

James pulled into the Folsom parking garage and cut the engine. A second later, a stream of cruisers zipped north, lights flashing, sirens blaring, chasing an illusion.

"That won't keep them distracted for long."

"This car's too conspicuous." I unsnapped my seatbelt with shaking fingers. "Crossroads is about two miles away, northwest of Chautauqua."

He nodded. "Let's head for the creek. There's an underpass on Folsom."

"But that's the wrong direction. And it's where all those cops are headed."

"We need somewhere without cameras," he said. "Trust me."

Sighing, I climbed out of the car. My legs wobbled, and I held the door for a moment to catch my balance. Gray pock marks decorated the side of the shiny black car.

Chase hopped down to the pavement. If the turbulent ride had unsettled him, he didn't show it.

Together, we slunk out of the parking garage and along the path to Boulder Creek. The sirens, which had grown quieter with distance, were getting loud again. James's illusion must have worn out. Or maybe someone watching the traffic cams had noticed our detour and called it in. Either way, we didn't have much time.

We ducked into the underpass. Fast food wrappers and pieces of cardboard littered the ground, blown into corners and against the concrete pillars. There weren't any other people.

"Now what?" I asked.

James stepped close and wrapped one arm around my waist. With the other, he scooped my knees. "Hold tight."

I wrapped my arms around him, burrowing against his neck. The scent of raspberries and nutmeg wafted off his skin.

He glanced down at Chase, who tipped his head sideways, twitched his whiskers, and meowed.

"We'll meet you at Chautauqua Park," James said. He bent his knees and gripped me tighter. Then he ran.

The world blurred by in streaks of color. Even if a camera did catch us, we would have looked like a shadow passing in front of the lens. Wind roared in my ears. My hair whipped around my face, stinging my cheeks. I clung to James, feeling the rhythm of his muscles and the steady beat of his heart as he carried me across town.

All at once, the wind cut off. The world came back into focus.

James was standing on a shoveled path along the northern edge of Chautauqua Park. Beside us was a wide, grassy field covered in a thin layer of snow. He leaned down until my feet rested firmly on the sidewalk, then straightened. He wasn't even breathing hard.

Reluctantly, I unclasped my hands and stood on my own. My heart was racing like I was the one who'd just sprinted across town. "That was amazing."

"Glad you enjoyed it." He brushed a wisp of hair back from his forehead and sighed.

I frowned. While he didn't seem tired, he did look a little pale. Well, paler than usual. "When's the last time you fed?"

He waved the question away. "Don't worry about it."

I pursed my lips.

A car passed on the nearby street. The frosted branches of winter trees blocked us from casual view, but I still felt exposed. I rubbed my hands over my upper arms. "How long do you think it will take Chase to catch up?"

James smiled. "Not *too* long. Cats are pretty fast."

Especially cats who also happened to be fae. But even a fae couldn't keep up with a vampire moving at full speed.

A moment later, a gray tabby came bounding up the street.

Chase leveled his green glare at James. His furry sides were heaving. His paws were wet.

I thought about teasing him, but decided against it. It's not like *I'd* done any work to get there. Instead I said, "Let's get moving, shall we? The sooner we're off the street the better."

Chase took the lead, and I laced my fingers with James's so our joined arms swung like a pendulum between us as we walked. We didn't have far to go, just a couple blocks. Strolling along the sidewalk hand-in-hand with James, I almost felt like the normal person I was pretending to be—just a woman out for a stroll with her boyfriend. Nothing to see here.

Talk about looks being deceiving.

Chase stopped at the mouth of the alley leading to Crossroads.

As James and I approached, he pulled up short. "Perhaps I should wait here."

I turned. "Why would you say that?"

"The fae are not fans of my kind. Your associates thus far have been more tolerant than most, but shifters have a certain . . . blasé attitude toward other paranaturals, and Malakai knew me personally. That will not be the case in a fae sanctuary."

He wasn't wrong about the fae's feelings toward vampires. Even Kai had his reservations about James—and James was a saint compared to most of his species. But leaving James alone and exposed on the street was not an option.

I tightened my grip. "You go where I go. If anyone has a problem with that, they can take it up with me."

He squeezed my hand, a brief pulse of appreciation.

When we reached the mouth of the alley, Chase trotted to a door midway down its length and scratched at the weathered wood.

James stopped two steps into the alley and swayed on his feet. His eyes grew glazed and distant. Then he turned as though he planned to leave.

"Hey." I tugged our joined hands, bringing his attention back to me.

He frowned. "I . . ." He glanced around the alley, then took a step back straining my grip. "I'm not sure I can proceed, despite your desire to remain together."

I looked around the alley too, but there wasn't much to see. Just some soggy newspapers and a rusty trash bin. Of course, what was stopping James wasn't visible. On my first visit to Crossroads, Kai had told me there were powerful spells on the place. Spells that kept it hidden from those they didn't want poking around.

The door to the club opened and a nine-foot troll who looked like he was carved from solid rock faced off with the tiny gray cat who'd called him out.

Chase meowed once, then looked back at me as though asking, "What's the holdup?"

The troll, who I'd learned on a previous visit was named Arthur, turned to look at me as well. If rock could show emotion, I'd say he looked concerned.

"James is . . . having a problem. I think the spells around this place are affecting him."

Chase continued to stare. His tail flicked once.

Arthur frowned, the corners of the craggy fissure that was his mouth turning down. I half-expected flakes of rock to chip off his face.

James stiffened, squeezing my fingers. He was looking up the street to his left.

A woman in a tattered coat was pushing a shopping cart loaded with random odds and ends down the sidewalk toward us. There was nowhere to hide in the mouth of the alley, not with James stuck as he was.

The wheels of the shopping cart squeaked as she approached. She was looking right at me.

"You're still disguising us, right?" I asked under my breath.

"I was, but . . ." James frowned. "I lost the illusion when I got disoriented. It's back in place."

"How long were we exposed?"

His lips pressed into a grim line and his words traveled silently through our link. *I don't know.*

The woman continued her steady progress, trundling along, hunched over her cart, until she was standing right in front of us. Then she paused.

I tensed, ready to run.

"Spare some change?" She held out one hand. Her ring finger

peeked through a hole in the tip of her grime-coated glove.

"Sorry." I patted down my pockets. "I don't have any."

James reached inside his coat and pulled out a wallet. He withdrew two crisp twenty dollar bills and set them on the woman's palm.

Her fingers snapped closed on the money and disappeared into her coat pocket.

"Thank you," she said with a smile, and pushed her cart past us.

We watched her until she turned the next corner. She never glanced back.

"We need to get inside." I turned back to James and grabbed both his hands with mine. "I have an idea. Close your eyes."

He shook his head. "It's not something I'm seeing that's the problem."

"Kai said the spells around this place were designed to make people ignore it. I don't think you'll have any problem if you can just make it through the door."

"Except I get disoriented before I can get anywhere near it."

"That's why you have me." I tightened my grip on his hands and poured as much confidence as I could through our link. "Close your eyes and trust me. Forget about where you are and what you're trying to do. You don't need to get to Crossroads. You just need to keep holding my hands."

When James's eyes were closed, I called to him through our connection. *Stay with me.* Then I took a step back.

James's grip grew crushingly tight on my fingers. He shuffled forward.

I took another step, pulling with the invisible cord that connected us.

Stay with me.

This time he moved faster, shifting before my weight had settled. The next step we took almost in unison.

I moved toward the door, glancing over my shoulder as I went, keeping up the silent litany of encouragement. When I was in danger of stepping on Chase if I went any farther, I paused. Arthur was filling the doorway.

"Please," I said. "Let us in."

Arthur's stony frown was still in place. His flint black eyes flicked between me and James.

"Meow."

Arthur looked down at Chase, who sat tall and straight in the damp alley.

"Meow," he said again.

I looked between them, unsure if trolls could understand cats. James's hands shook in mine. A glance showed beads of sweat on his pale skin. I focused on the bouncer. "Please."

The mountainous shoulders slumped. The frown deepened and the rocky protrusion of his brow sank lower, hiding his deep-set eyes. Then he stepped back, clearing the doorway.

Sighing with relief, I pulled James over the threshold.

Chapter 9

JAMES LURCHED forward when he crossed into the dim entryway as though a force that had been pressing against him suddenly fell away. He dropped to one knee, one hand still gripping mine while the other pressed to the floor. His eyes remained firmly closed. He was pulling in deep breaths, as though he'd just come up for air after a particularly deep dive.

I rubbed my free hand over his back. "You made it."

His eyes opened slowly, but when his gaze locked with mine it was bright and alert. Whatever fogging effect the spells in the alley caused had vanished, leaving cold, clear blue.

He pulled our joined hands to his lips and kissed my knuckles. "Thank you."

Chase stepped between us, furred tail lashing our shins. Then he stepped lightly down the hall.

"Come on." I pulled James to his feet and led him toward the bar.

Noises filtered down the corridor, but they weren't the sounds I usually associated with the place. There was no music, no stomp of dancing feet, no drunken merry-making or raucous laughter. All I could make out as I walked was the subdued murmur of voices and the scuff and shift of bodies unable to hold still.

When I rounded the corner leading to the main room, I froze. Dozens of fae stood around the bar. There were sidhe, pixies, a kelpie, a harpy, even a backoo. There were also some species I would need my encyclopedia to identify. Chase slipped between the ankles of the nearest fae, quickly disappearing in the crowd. Every face in the room was turned away from me . . . toward a large screen on the back wall behind the stage where a band should have been playing.

On the screen, the local news showed a line of people marching into the PTF testing facility in Denver. I'd been there once before, passed through those glass doors to the vaulted atrium where a too-cheerful desk attendant handed out ID bracelets and visitor badges.

Armed PTF agents in full riot gear held the doors open as the line of people shuffled past. Men and women in business suits stood between those in t-shirts and jeans. Some people looked like they'd just rolled out of bed or been pulled out of the gym while others wore high heels and fur coats. Children were scattered throughout the group, clinging to the arms of parents.

The shot zoomed out, and a pouty-lipped woman with thick, black hair and a microphone stepped into the frame. "As you can see from the line behind me, the Denver PTF facility is full to capacity with registered halfers who've come in for retesting in response to Director Harris's call to action earlier today."

A fast fade changed the view on the screen to the inside of a conference room. Everly Harris stood in a pale-gray suit with her shoulders back and her chin high. She was framed by a pair of potted plants with wide, waxy leaves.

"We at the PTF are requesting all registered halfers come in for retesting. Once it has been confirmed there is no change to your status, you will be free to go. Those who do not come in voluntarily will be brought in for questioning at a later date." The threat in Harris's tone was unmistakable. Come in . . . or else.

Harris's face froze mid-speech, locking it in a ridiculous expression with her eyes half closed and her mouth making a pursed "O" shape. Then the scene shrank to hover in an upper corner of the screen so we could once more see the reporter.

"So far, no discrepancies have been found, leading many to believe the claim of iron-resistant halfers was a hoax."

"Alex!" A high-pitched voice called from somewhere in the middle of the crowd.

Chase emerged from between a pair of eloko legs. Behind him, a ripple ran through the gathered fae until Jynx pushed past the last line of bodies and burst into the open. She raced the last few steps and slammed into me, arms wrapping my ribs like a vise.

"I'm so glad you're okay." Before I could return her hug, she jumped back, glaring. "Why did you come back? It's not safe here. The PTF is looking for you."

"I had to make sure you and Emma were all right. Speaking of which . . ." I scanned the crowd. More and more faces were turning in my direction, their attention pulled from the drama on the television screen to the one happening behind them.

"I'm here." Emma waved a hand as she emerged from the gap Jynx had made. She came to stand beside me, but didn't offer a hug. "Did you learn anything about May?"

I nodded, my mouth suddenly dry.

Hope lit Emma's face. "What did—"

"Let's find a quiet corner to talk," I said. Almost every face in the room was turned in our direction now, and most of them did not look friendly.

I glanced at James. He was holding very, very still.

"Alex Blackwood." The crowd split like metal shavings pushed back by the force of a magnet to reveal a large man with a barrel chest, tree trunk arms, and a shock of flame-red hair. Behind him trailed a smaller, slimmer figure whose hair was the same shade of red.

Ava smiled at me from behind her uncle's back, but the smile was strained, more a tightening of her face than an expression of pleasure.

"What trouble have you brought into my bar today?" Targe, the owner of Crossroads, folded his arms across his wide chest and glared down at me.

I tightened my grip on James's hand, both in a show of solidarity and to give myself a much-needed boost of confidence. The last time I'd been in Targe's bar I'd gotten drunk on a faerie drink called ambrosia and caused a scene. He'd kicked me out, and so far as I knew, hadn't yet lifted the ban on my return.

"We came looking for Jynx and Emma," my gaze flicked past Targe, "and Ava. I wanted to make sure they'd gotten out of my house all right."

"Well, as you can see, they're fine." He didn't move, a wall of unhappy man blocking further entry. Honestly, I found the troll less intimidating.

"Right . . . well . . ."

"We request sanctuary," Chase said as he stepped up beside me, once more in human form. And once more totally naked. Apparently a room full of strangers seeing his junk didn't bother him in the slightest.

Targe's gaze shifted to Chase, then back to me, then continued to my other side where James stood statue still. "A vampire can't claim sanctuary."

"He won't cause any trouble," I said. "I promise."

"Throw them both out," someone shouted from the crowd.

A murmur of agreement rippled through the fae.

Targe cut one hand to the side like he was chopping wood, and the murmurs stopped.

"Your face is all over the news, along with claims about a treatment to fool the PTF iron tests."

"I was lying when I said that, stalling for time, trying to save the life of a friend." My throat constricted on the last word.

"Now you show up with one of *them*"—he jerked his chin toward James—"begging for sanctuary."

"We just need a safe place to talk for a few minutes. Then we'll be out of your hair."

"You've upset a lot of people, Ms. Blackwood. The PTF aren't the only ones with a bone to pick."

The crowd behind him was starting to stir again, and it finally struck me that James being a vampire wasn't the only reason I wasn't welcome here. These fae were hiding from the PTF and the angry humans calling for war . . . and they blamed me.

My face began to tingle. I took a deep breath.

"I'll take them to the back office." Ava set her hand against Targe's arm. "Keep them out of the way."

Targe's orange-stubbled jaw shifted side to side, as though he were swishing the idea around to see how it tasted. Judging by his expression, it left a sour flavor.

"Stick to the back room," he said. Then he turned and marched back to his station behind the bar at the center of the room, fae once more parting around him.

"Come on." Ava tugged my sleeve. She, Chase, and Jynx walked closest to the fae, providing a moving barrier for Emma, James, and me as we made our way around the perimeter of the room and through a door at the back.

Ava pressed the door closed when the last of our little group cleared the threshold.

I waited a beat, then moved to the plastic blinds that covered the one window in the room, which looked back into the bar rather than offering any view outside. A few fae still faced the office, but most had turned back to the TV where scenes of unrest continued to scroll past.

"They blame me for having to hide," I whispered.

"They're scared." Ava hopped onto the large oak desk that dominated one side of the room.

I turned away from the window. "I'm glad you guys are safe."

Jynx smiled at Ava, pride lighting her face. "Ava portalled to the house as soon as she saw the news. She got us out just before the police broke down the front door."

"We barely had time to grab a few necessities, but we packed a bag for you too." Emma gestured to my suitcase, propped in a corner beside her backpack.

"That's great, thanks." I should have made packing a go-bag a higher priority, but who would have thought shit would go to hell so fast? I crouched in front of my bag and unzipped the main section, finding my knife, gun, and a collection of random clothes. On top of it all was the carving of a gaala—a six-legged deer-like creature—I'd gotten from Bael. I'd kept the keepsake on my dresser beside my silver sword—which was notably absent. I lifted the tiny sculpture. "Why'd you bring this?"

Emma frowned. "I didn't. Maybe it fell in when I was grabbing your clothes."

I stared at the carved gaala. While the creature was made of wood, I'd seen it walk, and even fly, thanks to Bael's enchantment. It was entirely possible the little guy had packed itself to avoid being collected by the PTF.

Emma settled onto a faded orange couch with sagging cushions and folded her arms across her abdomen. "So . . . what did you find out about May?"

I tucked the gaala back inside the bag and took a seat beside her.

Chase and James remained standing, each with their arms crossed, while Jynx snuggled up next to Ava on the desk.

"We've got a good idea who's been taking kids," I said. "Not just mortals, but fae too. She's in a pri . . . in a place attached to the Realm of Enchantment, so I'm going to go talk to Bael and see if he can get them out."

I'd almost said she was in a prison, but Emma didn't need to know May was in the hands of a war criminal, not when she already looked like death warmed over.

"Did you—"

The office door opened, and we all jerked to attention.

"Are you always this popular?" Haru said as he slipped through the opening. "I seem to recall you receiving a similar welcome in Enchantment."

My surprise was followed quickly by a twinge of guilt. I'd forgotten about Haru. He would have been at my house as well when the police arrived.

He was still in his human form, though his ears and tail were clearly visible. I was reminded of Anika with her mix-and-match body. Did

Haru's ability to hold a partially changed state mean he was stronger than Chase?

"I see you survived your encounter with the Shifter Lord," he continued. "So what did you think of the old bird?"

"What do you want?" Chase asked.

Haru smiled, his Mediterranean eyes twinkling. "To lodge a complaint." He swung his attention to me. "Your hostess skills are sorely lacking."

"Noted. But you're free to go now. Whatever deal you had with Mica, I doubt he'd insist you stay in a house under PTF control."

"I promised to stay with *you*, so stay with you I shall. Besides"—again his eyes twinkled like sunlight on water—"your escapades could prove quite entertaining."

Chase snorted and turned his back on the kitsune. "Ignore him. His sense of humor is undeniably warped."

Haru pulled out the tall leather chair behind Targe's desk and dropped into it, tucking his hands behind his head. "You would know."

I shook my head. Curious as I was about the animosity between Chase and Haru, and the part Nia had played in their falling out, we had more pressing concerns. "We need to head back to the reservation immediately. The place where May is likely being held moves through time faster than here."

Emma frowned. "You mean like how you went away for over a week but said you only felt a couple days had passed?"

"But the other way. Every moment that passes here could be . . . well, a lot longer for May."

What little color remained in Emma's cheeks drained. Even her lips seemed pale.

"How long?"

I shook my head. "I'm not sure."

"Roughly two thirds of a year passes there for every day here on Earth," Haru piped, his feet now propped on the corner of Targe's desk.

The world seemed to slow. My vision drew in, focusing on the soft leather soles of Haru's shoes. May had been missing nearly two days already. She'd been eleven, almost twelve when she was taken. How old would she be when we got her back?

I inhaled, forcing air into my tight lungs. The tunnel vision faded, revealing the rest of the room's inhabitants slightly out of place from where they'd been when my brain took momentary leave. Emma was doubled over with her head between her knees. James's hand rested on her back. Jynx and Ava were huddled tight together, mirrored frowns on their faces. Chase was glaring at Haru like he wanted to vault the desk and strangle him. Chase had probably known the time ratio but kept it vague for the benefit of the mortals involved.

I forced a swallow past the lump in my throat and croaked, "We need to get back to the reservation." I shifted my gaze to the girls on the desk. "Ava, can you reach that far with your portals?"

She shook her head, red hair tumbling over her shoulders. "Not even Targe can do that, but he's a member of a jump line. That's why so many fae are here. They're planning to run a jump soon for fae who don't want to hang around to see how things sort out with the PTF."

Chase uncrossed his arms. "When's the jump scheduled?"

"Tomorrow morning."

Emma shook her head, pushing to her feet. "That's too long."

I rose as well and set what I hoped was a calming hand on her shoulder. "I agree. Four and a half hours by car beats spending the night here, even if it only saves a few hours. We need to leave now."

Chapter 10

"WHAT ABOUT THE security checks at the edge of town?" James asked.

"I could jump you outside the city," Ava said, then frowned. "But then you wouldn't have a car."

I looked at James. "Where's Joe? Could you call him to meet us somewhere?"

He shook his head. "Joe's the one who told me what was happening. When he called, the PTF was already at the gallery looking for us. Even if he wasn't detained, he'll be under surveillance."

"Do you think—"

A knock at the door interrupted my train of thought. Targe's fiery hair appeared in the gap. Deep lines created shadows around his eyes and mouth. "Y'all had best come see this."

He pulled back before anyone in the office could ask a question.

I glanced at Ava, who shrugged, then around the room, finding the same confused, wary expression on every face.

Giving Emma's shoulder a pat, I slipped out the still open door, the others close on my heels.

The main room of the bar was just as we'd left it. Every face was turned toward the big TV above the stage. No one even glanced in our direction.

Then I saw what had captured their attention.

A wolf snarled inside a cage, but the animal was far too large to be mistaken for something you might see in a zoo. Tattered strips of fabric littered the ground around it. Denim. Cotton. The padding and snapped elastic strap of a bra. Sophie was no longer the only werewolf whose shift had been caught on film.

Everly Harris's face replaced that of the snarling werewolf.

"As you can see from this footage sent in by our Dallas office, we have now been able to confirm the existence of a paranatural species that can change its shape from human to that of a large wolf."

Lights flashed in Harris's face, reporters snapping photos to run with their front page stories. From offscreen, a voice asked, "Is it true the creature is immune to iron?"

Harris's many braids bobbed with her nod. "The fae delegations claim to have no connection to this species. They insist it is a native of Earth, like the practitioners."

"And there's no chance they're lying?" the same voice cut in.

"Fae cannot lie. Not even to save their own lives. As I'm sure you're aware, we tested that theory exhaustively during the war. Whatever this creature is, I think it's safe to say it did not come from one of the fae realms."

Another bout of camera flashes.

"Do you agree with the Church's statement that these creatures are humans possessed by demons?"

I shuddered at the word *demons*. An image of smiling fangs filled my vision.

"We've not been able to confirm, nor deny, any such claim. What is abundantly clear is that these creatures, whatever they may be, are dangerous. To that end, all available sorcerers have been called up to deal with the threat. Every PTF and law enforcement agency in the country and around the world has been given a directive to bring in anyone suspected of being a"—she twitched the first two fingers of each hand in the air—"'werewolf,' or of being connected to them. Here in Colorado, we've already apprehended several humans suspected of harboring these beings."

The TV cut to footage of a tall, thin man being shoved into the back of a police car, hands cuffed behind his back. The man had dark skin and close-cropped hair. Just before ducking into the seat, he glanced at the camera. A pair of thick-framed glasses perched on his nose.

My pulse stuttered. My knees felt like rubber.

Luke was a local practitioner. One of only three known to operate in Colorado. He was also Emma's teacher and the man who kept Marc's pack healthy when they needed more than a super-fast metabolism. He'd saved Sophie. He'd saved me. He'd been keeping the werewolves' secret for years.

Had the PTF known, or were they just rounding up anyone with a suspicious background? Would all the registered practitioners be brought in for questioning, along with anyone who'd taken a sick day that happened to correspond with a full moon?

A white ribbon appeared at the bottom of the screen, overlaying the image of Luke being shut in the cruiser. Text scrolled along the banner. *Reward offered for information on the following people.* My name and description marched across the television, followed by those of Marc, Emma, and James.

I looked away as the names of my friends were replaced with people I didn't know.

James pulled his gaze away from the TV to meet mine. A flash of silver swirled through his eyes, there and gone in an instant, and a shock wave rippled through our connection. James's demon was stirring, rising with his anger.

Murmurs broke out around the room.

Targe stood nearby with his arms crossed, his eyes fixed on the screen as more images of people being marched out of buildings and loaded into government cars rolled past. Names continued to slide across the news ticker. Most of the other fae were still watching as well, but a few glanced in my direction.

I bit my lip. I didn't like the way some of those fae were looking at me. "We should leave."

"The police and PTF are out in force right now," James said. "We'd be exposed on the street. And we still don't have a sure way past the checkpoints."

"They can't have every road out of town covered. We'll just avoid the main streets. Do you know how to hot-wire a car?"

He raised an eyebrow. "You want to steal one?"

I shrugged. "We're already fugitives."

Targe turned toward us, frowning. "I can't let you leave the bar right now."

My jaw dropped. "Just a second ago you didn't want us here."

"The enchantments protecting this place are weakest when some-one is entering or leaving. We can't risk it. Not with this"—he gestured to the screen—"wolf hunt in progress."

"But—"

He held up a hand. "I'm putting this place on lockdown. We'll all leave tomorrow, at the scheduled jump time."

He moved away, weaving through the crowd, talking to the fae, soothing nerves. A plan was in place. The jump would happen tomor-row. The enchantments would keep us safe till then.

Some of the fae continued to grumble, but most subsided, moving to claim booths along the outer walls of the room. A few nasty glances were still being thrown my way, but most of the fae ignored my little group.

Emma gripped my arm. "We can't wait, Alex. You said time is passing faster for May. We need to leave *now*."

"You can't," Ava said. "You heard Uncle Targe. He locked the bar. That means no one in or out without his say so."

Emma glared at Ava. "Your uncle's not the boss of me."

"But he's the boss of this bar, and he controls all the enchantments around it. If he says no one leaves, no one leaves."

I fingered the ribbon around my wrist. "What if we didn't use the door?"

Ava shook her head. "I won't disobey Targe. And even if I wanted to, I couldn't. We'd have to leave the building for me to open a portal."

"What about a shadow walker?"

She shook her head. "Same problem. They could move around inside the bar, or outside, but they couldn't cross the threshold." She turned to Emma. "I know you're eager to leave, but waiting really is your best chance to help your sister. If you left now, you'd probably get grabbed by the PTF between here and the reservation. If you travel with us in the morning, we'll get you there without having to risk being out in the open."

"It's only a couple extra hours, Emma." I set my hand on her shoulder. "I know—"

She shook me off. "No, Alex, you don't! You have no idea how I'm feeling. May is trapped in some faerie prison, and it's *my fault*."

I frowned. "No it's not."

"Why else would they take her? It's because she might be a practitioner. And the only reason anyone knows that is because I took that stupid test."

I hugged myself. Anika said children with exceptional abilities were being taken. Being a practitioner was certainly exceptional, but there was no guarantee May would have the gift just because her sister did. Would Shedraziel have taken May on the chance she could do magic? I glanced around the room. Most of the fae had settled into groups. Only a few looked up at Emma's outburst. I tightened my fists until they shook. I couldn't be sure Emma was wrong, but I *did* understand how she felt.

"I told you Kai extended his trip."

Emma frowned. "What does that have to do with—"

"He didn't." I swallowed past the lump swelling in my throat. James moved closer and placed a hand on the small of my back. Our connection grew stronger through that contact, lending me support as I struggled with the next words. "He's serving a fifty-year sentence in Bael's dungeon . . . for a mistake *I* made."

Emma stared, her eyes round and wet. Her chin quivered. She looked to be on the verge of an emotional collapse. And who could blame her? Her sister was trapped in a time-sucking prison for which she blamed herself, her mother hated her, and her mentor had just been arrested.

"Then you know why I have to make this right," she said.

"And we will. But letting our emotions run wild isn't going to help May. We need to keep our heads." I felt like a hypocrite as the words left my lips, but it was good advice even if I didn't always take it myself.

Emma's lower lip trembled, but she straightened her shoulders and nodded.

"Come on." Jynx placed a hand on Emma's back and pushed her toward the office. "Let's find something to distract ourselves."

Emma shuffled along under Jynx's direction, her expression stony. Ava followed behind.

"You lot are depressing," Haru said. He glanced toward the bar, where Targe was serving drinks. "I need a pick-me-up."

Chase rubbed a hand over his jaw as he watched the girls walk away. His forehead was wrinkled in thought. Then he turned to follow Haru. "Excuse me."

Chase and Haru found places at opposite ends of the bar. The girls disappeared into Targe's office and the door shut behind them. I bit my lip.

James moved so he was standing directly behind me, his arms wrapped around my waist. "You are not responsible for your friends' hardships." He spoke into my ear, tickling my skin with his breath. "Nor is it on you alone to fix them."

Sighing, I leaned back into his solid presence. "I *feel* responsible. It was O'Connell's obsession with me that led to the wolves getting caught. My deal with Mica brought Haru to the mortal realm. And Emma . . ." I shook my head. "Everyone around me suffers. Sometimes I feel cursed—like I cast a shadow over everyone who knows me, tainting them. "

"People would suffer regardless. That is a fact of life. You do not bring the darkness." He pulled me tighter against his chest. "You are the light that exposes it. I, for one, am richer for knowing you, and I'm not the only one who feels that way."

"You're biased." I twisted to plant a kiss on the corner of his smile. "But thanks."

Chase strolled up to us.

I raised an eyebrow. "Done drinking already?"

"I haven't started yet," he said. "I have an idea to kill some time and lift everyone's spirits, but I need your help."

"What did you have in mind?" I asked.

He grinned. "A wedding."

I glanced at the office door where the girls had disappeared. "Now? Do you really think this is the time to—"

"Distract everyone from their anxiety and worry?" He shrugged. "We're all stuck here till morning. We can either spend the time glaring at each other, or throw a party and drink the night away." He hooked a thumb over his shoulder toward the bar. "Targe's on board. He's eager to keep the gathered masses distracted. Besides, the girls wanted to get married at Crossroads. With things the way they are, who knows if they'll get another chance?"

THERE WAS A knock at the door to Targe's office and James slipped inside, pulling the door closed behind him. "How's it going in here?"

James had been helping Chase and Targe decorate while Emma and I got the brides ready. Though, in truth, most of the work had been done by a small nisse woman who'd managed to turn a collection of spare cloth into the lavish blue gowns Jynx and Ava now wore. *Go, go magic.*

"We're just about done," I said, twisting a small purple flower into the garland that would sit atop Jynx's head. Emma was putting the finishing touches on a similar crown for Ava. It had been good for Emma to have the distraction, but she'd been quieter than usual and her eyes were puffy and red.

Jynx and Ava were tittering together under the nisse's needle in the corner as she tucked hems and adjusted seams.

James nodded. "I'll tell them five minutes." He leaned in and gave me a peck on the cheek. "See you out there."

The door clicked shut. My hands stopped moving. I stared at the garland of flowers, then looked up at the smiling girls. They'd both agreed to Chase's plan as soon as he mentioned it, plunging forward with the same reckless abandon they'd shown in the rest of their relationship.

I sighed, trying to quash the anxiety making my legs twitch and bounce. Jynx and Ava were clearly in love, but despite what stories would have us believe, love wasn't a cure-all. Quite often, it was the culprit behind the greatest hardships in life. Ava was mortal, like me. Jynx was not. No matter that Ava was mostly fae, or that my tattoo charm had shifted the balance of my blood, halfers didn't live forever. Someday, our faces would haunt the memories of the immortals we loved as they continued through the centuries without us.

I cleared my throat. "Are you two really sure about this?"

Jynx and Ava looked over. Their giggles faded.

"What do you mean?" Ava asked. "Of course we are."

"Until death do you part." I set the flower crown aside and looked at Jynx. "Then what?"

Her expression grew dark. "You sound like my mother."

"Maybe your mom just doesn't want to see you get hurt," I said.

"She doesn't want to see me happy either." She gripped Ava's hand. "Ava makes me happy. She won't hurt me."

"Not on purpose, but—" I shifted my gaze to Ava, feeling like a traitor. "You have mortal blood. Whether a few drops or a gallon makes no difference. Someday, you'll die, and Jynx will have centuries still."

"Or she could be executed by the PTF as an unregistered fae and I could spend the rest of my life mourning *her*. Fae aren't indestructible. And yeah, she might have to live with my memory longer than I would hers, but that wouldn't make my pain any less. We're only taking the chance everyone takes when they fall in love." She glanced at the closed office door. "Maybe that's a chance you're not ready to take yet, but we are."

I stiffened and felt my cheeks grow warm. Was I just projecting my own doubts and insecurities? Sighing, I rubbed the back of my neck. "I'm not saying you two shouldn't be together, I just . . . want to make sure you've thought this through. Marriage is a big commitment."

Jynx frowned. "I know what I'm getting into." She looked at Ava. "I know Ava won't live as long as I will, but I'll never love anyone else." Her words rang through the room like a promise, and I realized the ceremony was just for show. Jynx and Ava were already bound to walk this path. She turned back to me. "Will you stand with me, or not?"

I picked up the garland, carried it over, and placed it atop Jynx's head. Then I set a hand on each of the girls' shoulders and smiled. "Let's do this thing."

Emma placed her creation on Ava, who quickly wrapped several thin red braids around her crown to hold it in place. The remainder of her hair was twisted into an interconnected net of strands courtesy of

Emma's deft fingers.

"Everybody ready?" I asked.

They each nodded, and I pushed open the office door.

Glittering streamers and strings of flowers hung from the rafters in graceful drapes above the bar's dance floor. Colored lights cast a dim blue glow around the perimeter of the room while warm spotlights lit a path from the office door to Targe and Chase, who stood together on the far side of the room. Fae stood in two neat rows on either side of a path strewn with flower petals.

Despite most of the bystanders having no connection to Ava or Jynx, everybody in the room was part of the living hallway. Maybe they were just eager to have some way to pass the time and get their minds off the evacuation, but I think Targe's promise of an open bar for his niece's reception was a big motivating factor in getting one hundred percent participation.

Haru was standing near the middle of the fae on the right side. He'd been surprisingly quiet about Chase's idea, offering none of his usual humor. Perhaps even he recognized the seriousness of the promises Jynx and Ava were about to make.

Targe had changed into what looked like a gray tunic with a plaid sash. Chase was now wearing loose black slacks and a purple shirt with the top button popped. When we reached them, I smiled at Chase and I stepped to the side, filling the empty space between him and James. Emma stood beside Targe on the other side.

I slipped my hand into James's and whispered, "You guys did a great job."

"As did you."

Jynx and Ava came up the aisle together, walking slower than Emma and I had. When they reached us, I expected Targe to start the whole "Dearly beloved" speech I'd heard at pretty much every wedding I'd ever attended, but he didn't. Instead, he took one end of a long strip of red fabric. Chase held the other. Together they looped the cloth over and around the girls' joined hands. Then they stepped back.

"By all I hold dear," Jynx began, "by the truth in my blood, I swear myself to you, forever."

Ava repeated the same phrase, but while she spoke I noticed several of the gathered fae shake their heads or look away. As a halfer, the "truth" in Ava's blood wasn't binding. She could change her mind, back out of her promise at any time. For Jynx, forever meant forever.

I glanced up at James. He wasn't a fae; he could lie, but the level of commitment required in our relationship wasn't equal. I could promise him the rest of my life. He couldn't say the same. I closed my eyes, imagining the coil of silver demon that would keep him alive long after I was gone.

Releasing my hand, James wrapped his arm around my shoulders and hugged me tight to his side. *Stop worrying. You're missing the ceremony.*

I opened my eyes.

Jynx and Ava leaned over their joined hands and kissed. Targe cheered. The rest of the room followed suit. Then the neatly formed lines dispersed. Most of the fae headed straight for the bar. Music burst through the speakers. People began to dance.

I blinked. "That's it?"

Chase grinned. "Best to get the formal part over with quickly." He clapped his hands and rubbed them together. "Now we can move on to the reception."

He headed for the bar, where Targe had enlisted the help of two other fae to serve drinks. Emma followed him. Jynx and Ava were already on the dance floor. I looked up at James. "Shall we?"

Lifting my hand, he pressed a kiss to my knuckles.

We spun and laughed, weaving between other dancers, clinging to each other when our bodies came close, straining like magnets when we moved away. Smiling faces whirled all around us, lost to the music. Chase's distraction had been a success.

Then an earsplitting *boom* broke through the beat of the music, a section of wall collapsed, and I was blown off my feet.

Chapter 11

HIGH-PITCHED ringing filled my ears, and the world spun as I shook my head to clear it. Shadows danced in piercing beams of light that swept across billowing clouds of dust. I coughed and curled around an ache in my right side from where I'd slammed into a wall.

Fingers wrapped my upper arm. I jerked away. Then James's face came into focus. His lips moved but the ringing in my ears drowned out any words.

He pulled me to my feet.

I swayed as a wave of dizziness hit me, followed by more coughing. Even after my vision cleared, it was hard to see. The overhead lights had blown out in the blast. Flashlight beams swept through drifting clouds of dust. Bodies were scattered around the room. Some moved, others didn't. One wall had been reduced to splintered wood and plaster dust. Debris fell from the ragged edges of a gaping hole, and through that breach, men and women in tactical gear advanced with guns drawn.

The ringing faded. I could make out raised voices, though I couldn't tell if it was the fae or the advancing troops doing the yelling.

I spotted Emma clutching the edge of the bar, her disheveled teal hair drooping over one eye. She saw me and began making her way through the rubble in my direction. Behind her, Chase hopped on top of the bar and scanned the room. I waved to draw his attention, but his gaze passed over me and continued on.

Targe emerged from behind the bar and swung his arms in a wide arc. A patch of sifting dust began to shimmer. He cupped his hands to his mouth and bellowed. This time, the words broke through my dazed senses.

"Everybody through!"

Fae began pouring from every corner of the room toward Targe's portal. The floor vibrated with the force of the stampede.

"On the floor!" screamed a PTF agent, swinging his weapon toward the nearest fleeing fae.

A green-skinned woman with willowy limbs and pale-yellow hair dropped mid-stride, a feathered dart stuck in her arm. A bronze-skinned nixie collapsed to my right, crumpling like a cut marionette. A pixie with shimmering wings fell from her flight, landing on the crowd bunching up around the portal.

The PTF advance slowed as some of the fae turned to face their attackers head on.

Screams rent the night as mortals fell to teeth and claws.

A flashlight beam swept over a braided net of bright-red hair a few feet away. I clambered over the uneven floor toward Ava. More fae fell, mostly near the advancing troops who were still shouting for everyone to freeze. James stuck to my side as we struggled against the flow of the crowd.

I dropped to my knees beside Ava and grabbed her shoulder. She cringed and lifted her head. Blood ran from a gash near her temple. Cursing, I cupped the sides of her face. Her eyes rolled for a second before coming to rest on me.

"Can you stand?" I had to shout to be heard over the racket.

Ava blinked slowly, staring at my face.

A second later Emma dropped to one knee on Ava's other side.

"Targe's got a portal open," she hollered. "We need to go."

I squeezed James's arm and pointed to Ava. "Can you carry her?"

Nodding, he scooped up the disoriented girl.

Chase's face appeared in front of me, eyes wide and full of worry. He gripped my shoulders. "Have you seen Jynx?"

I shook my head.

He turned to face the chaos near the collapsed wall. "I can't leave without her."

"I'll help you look," I said, then turned to James. "Get Ava to the portal."

James frowned. "I'm not leaving you."

Ava was looking around now. She raised a hand to her wound, pulled it away, and stared at her red-tipped fingers.

Then James dropped, taking Ava with him. He barely managed to keep his hold so she didn't tumble from his arms. Chase reached for Ava and I reached for James. Together, we managed to slow their fall, but we couldn't arrest them completely. We all ended up on the floor.

I pulled a feathered dart out of James's calf and tossed it away. I cupped the side of his cheek and turned his face toward me. His eyes were glassy and unfocused. His lips parted as though his jaw had gone slack.

Emma, the only one of our little group still standing, gasped. When I looked up, she wasn't paying any attention to us. She was pointing over our heads.

I followed the direction of her finger.

It was hard to make much out through the crush of fae around the bar, but a second later, the fae scattered in panic. I spotted Targe's mop of bright-red hair. The burly leprechaun lay on his side, a feathered tuft sticking out of his chest. Our exit had been cut off.

The remaining fae made a run at the PTF agents, and the only remaining exit.

I gripped Ava's shoulder, pulling her attention. "Targe's down. Can you open a portal?"

Her eyes were scared saucers. Her lip quivered.

"Ava," I snapped. "Can you do it?"

She shook her head. "I can open a portal, but . . . I don't know the location of the next jump point."

A second wave of agents pressed forward, plugging the gap. These bore three-foot iron-coated riot shields. The agents with guns continued to pick off any moving fae from behind the mobile wall. A small orb was lobbed from somewhere behind that line. I tracked the arc through the sweeping lights as it sailed toward the back of the room.

"Don't look!" Chase's palm slammed into the side of my face. I turned away from the blow, my eyes closing involuntarily from the impact. A second later, bright light shown through my scrunched eyelids and a wave of dust and debris slammed into me. My ears were once again ringing.

Carefully, I opened my eyes and blinked. Many of the fae near the back of the room were down, hands pressed to their heads. The agents had used the fae's natural ability to see in darkness against them. After adjusting to the gloom of the room, the flash from that grenade had blinded them, at least temporarily.

The PTF troops pushed forward with renewed force.

"Get us out of here," I shouted at Ava. "We're sitting ducks."

Emma was on her butt beside James now, either to make herself less of a target or because she'd been knocked down by the blast. She was blinking and wiping watery eyes. Guess she hadn't gotten them closed in time.

With Chase's help, Ava struggled to her knees, swayed, and swung her arm in a large arc. The air began to shimmer.

"Hold her steady," Chase said to me.

I took Chase's place, bracing Ava's shoulders to keep her stable.

Chase set a hand on Ava's outstretched arm. "Keep it open as long as you can. I'll find Jynx."

Stripping out of his dirty purple shirt, Chase dropped to all fours as a gray tabby and darted into the chaos. As a cat, he could move faster and he was a much smaller target.

"Emma," I said.

She swung her face in my direction, but I could tell she was having trouble seeing.

"Ava opened a portal. It's about two feet to your right. You need to go through."

"What about the rest of you?"

"We'll follow. Now go."

Nodding, Emma crawled to her right, and with a few more directions managed to pass through Ava's portal.

The fae nearest us took notice. The tide of those rushing the exit shifted again as several fae broke off and darted through Ava's portal. As they went through, more began to turn. It wouldn't take long for the PTF to notice the new breach.

James, sitting beside me, gripped my leg.

There. The word resonated through me. He pointed, and I swung to follow the line of his finger.

Haru leapt over the fallen form of a rock troll who'd just punched a hole through the PTF line. He stumbled when he landed, thrown off balance by the body draped over his shoulder. His passenger's legs bumped his chest, draped in a long train of blue fabric.

Releasing Ava, I spun in the direction Chase had run, cupped my hands to my mouth, and shouted, "Chase!" Then I made an exaggerated gesture toward Haru, which served the added purpose of drawing Haru's attention.

A streak of gray darted between stomping feet to fall in line a step ahead of Haru, leading him back to us.

With the others on their way, I tucked myself under James's arm.

"Time to move," I said, pulling him to his feet.

Silver swirled groggily through the icy depths of his eyes, glinting unnaturally in the dim light. Was the fae tranquilizer loosening James's grip on his demon? The last thing we needed right now was an out-of-control vampire.

We shuffled to the portal, jostled by the fae swarming in on either side. There was a brief, twisting sensation as we passed through the shimmer, then we were standing on asphalt under a street lamp. Snow drifted through the air and my breath came out in a cloud.

I shivered. I'd left my coat in the office at Crossroads . . . along with the bag Emma had packed for me.

Fae continued to stream out of empty space behind me, darting off as soon as they cleared the portal. With the jump line compromised, it was every fae for themselves.

"Alex!" Emma struggled through the fae swarming around us. She gave me a quick hug, then ducked under James's other arm. His feet scraped the ground with each step, but his head didn't loll as it had a moment before. The silver in his eyes was becoming more pronounced. It seemed the demon in him was fighting off the tranquilizer.

"Take James." My shout was eerily loud in the suddenly quiet night.

"But—" Emma grunted as I shifted the remainder of James's weight to her.

Once free, I darted back toward the portal, swerving to avoid a collision with the evacuating fae. I could see the shimmer of air, like flecks of ice frozen in place. Taking a deep breath, I jumped through . . . and landed on the asphalt on the far side.

I stumbled and spun around. I could still make out the distortion of the portal. Fae were still erupting from the far side.

Frowning, I tried again.

This time I slammed into the back of an eloko who'd just appeared. He twisted to growl at me through bared teeth, then scampered away toward the nearest alley.

"I can't get through." I looked at Emma, panic sinking in.

She shook her head. "Maybe Ava's portal only works in one direction."

I opened my mouth, but at that moment Haru burst into existence in front of me. He charged half a dozen steps down the street, Jynx bouncing precariously on his shoulder. Chase—once more on two legs—soared through the portal a second later. He grunted when his shoulder hit the ground, rolled over twice, and flopped onto his back. When he opened his arms, Ava looked up from where she'd been clutched against his chest.

I blinked, and looked back at the space where the portal had been. The shimmer was gone. Two bloody stumps rested on the dark street.

One was an arm, severed just above the elbow. The other was half a foot.

Bile rose in the back of my throat. I clamped a hand over my mouth and turned away, taking deep breaths of the frigid air until my stomach settled.

Haru circled back to our little group and lowered Jynx's limp form down beside her brother.

Ava scrambled off Chase, making him grunt again. She knelt beside her new wife and cradled one pale hand.

"How is she?" I asked.

"Only sleeping," Ava said, relief thick in her voice. "She'll recover when the drugs wear off."

Chase sat up, looked down at Jynx, then up at Haru. An expression I couldn't identify passed across his face. A muscle in his jaw twitched as if he were clenching and unclenching his teeth. If I had to guess, he wasn't happy Haru had been the one to save his sister. His hands balled into fists.

"Why did you save her?" Chase's words were a whisper.

"You'd rather I left her?"

"You could have just run, saved yourself." He crossed his arms. "That's what you're good at, after all."

Haru looked away, but a flicker of emotion tightened his features before he hid his face. Frustration? Shame?

Chase pushed to his feet so he was no longer looking up at Haru. "This settles *nothing* between us."

I moved to James's side, resuming my position as a human crutch. "The important thing is that we all made it."

"Not all," Ava whispered. Blood still coated one side of her face, and the area beneath it looked swollen.

My chest tightened. I'd been so relieved to find all the people I cared about had made it to safety, I'd forgotten about Targe. Ava had lost her uncle. And who knew how many of the fae left behind had been her friends or acquaintances.

"I'm sorry," I mumbled. The words were inadequate.

She sniffed and nodded, never taking her gaze off Jynx.

I looked around, taking in the cold, dark street. Slush collected in the gutters. Snow drifted through cones of light cast by evenly spaced street lamps. The towering silhouette of an apartment building loomed on the far side of the street. Light shone through a few of the windows, but most were dark. On the near side, beyond a sidewalk coated in salt crystals, a wrought-iron fence guarded the snow-covered, rolling hills of a golf course. I didn't see any street signs.

"Where exactly are we?" I asked.

Ava finally looked up from Jynx. She glanced around the street, then wiped a wrist under her nose with another sniff. "Westminster."

Haru's eyes widened. "You sent us to England?"

I shook my head. "There's a Westminster in Colorado about a half hour east of Boulder." I looked to Ava for confirmation. She nodded.

"In any case," I continued. "We're too exposed here on the street."

Emma shifted her feet on the far side of James and hoisted his arm higher on her shoulders. "Any chance you can get us to the reservation, Ava?"

She shook her head, red braids wiggling along her back like snakes. "I've got one, maybe two jumps left in me. A trip like that is at the very edge of my ability even when I'm well rested."

"Then we need to find somewhere to hole up for a bit." I glanced at James, who still drooped between Emma and me. "Obviously our houses are all out."

"What about a hotel?" Emma asked.

I frowned. "My face was on every TV in the country, and James is in no condition to cast an illusion. Besides, hotels have security cameras."

"The nest," James said. His voice was airy and quiet, as though he were talking in his sleep.

"The what?" Emma asked.

I bit my lip. True, the vampire nest was secure from the PTF, at least for now, but there were plenty of other dangers there. Despite James's reassurance that the new master vampire was nothing like the previous sadistic bastard we'd put down, I wasn't eager to put myself at the mercy of an unknown predator.

Chase was pacing beside Jynx. "Bad idea. Vampires and fae . . ." He shook his head. "We don't mix well."

"Wait, *vampires*?" Emma's voice rose an octave.

"Victoria . . . will grant . . . asylum."

Chase stopped his pacing and pinned his green gaze on James, his eyes flashing like reflectors. "And if she doesn't?" He spread his hands wide. "We are hardly in a position to defend ourselves."

"As in suck our blood, vampires?" Emma asked.

"Do you have a better option?" I asked Chase, honestly hoping he did.

He pressed his lips tight and turned away, fists on his hips.

"I'm not eager to bunk down with the vampires either, but—"

"Ha!" Haru's outburst made us all jump. "Sorry," he said, waving a hand. "I just . . . the mortal capacity for lies is so . . ." He trailed off into laughter.

"If you don't have anything constructive to say, keep quiet," I said.

"But honestly," Haru continued, ignoring me. "To say you won't bunk down with them even as you're snuggled next to one?" He gestured to James.

Emma gasped and jerked away. The sudden loss of support on James's other side was more than I could make up for, and James went down to his knees.

"You're a . . ." Emma's eyes were wide and bright.

I glared at Haru, then turned my attention to Emma. "We don't have time for this right now, Em. I'll explain everything later."

She nodded, but she didn't take her eyes off James. She didn't even blink. I couldn't blame her; she was still pretty new to the paranatural world. Luke had told her about werewolves, and everyone knew about the fae . . . but vampires? They were the monsters that gave the monsters nightmares.

"If no one's got any better ideas, I say we head for the nest. If James says Victoria will grant us asylum . . ." I looked down at the top of James's head. His cheek was pressed to my hip. I had my fingers bunched into his shirt to prevent him sliding any farther. "I trust him."

"Can't say I've ever had occasion to visit the local bloodsuckers," Ava said, looking up at me. "Where exactly do you want me to send us?"

"Denver," I said. "To a club called Abandon."

Chapter 12

AVA STOOD AND waved a hand through the air, creating the telltale shimmer of a portal. "This is as close as I can get us."

Apparently fae like Ava could only open portals to places they'd been—something about having an anchor point. She'd never been to Abandon, but I'd given her the cross streets.

Chase lifted Jynx off the ground, cradling her to his naked chest. His breath puffed out in short, angry clouds. He stepped through the shimmer and disappeared.

I glanced at Haru. "You don't have to come with us."

He frowned. "I told you, I—"

"Made a promise to Mica. I know. But that was before the PTF was actively hunting me. I'm sure, given the choice, he'd rather have you back in Enchantment. Besides"—I shifted my gaze to the space where Chase had disappeared—"we don't need any added drama right now."

Haru crossed his arms. "So you're casting me out because Chase had a tantrum?"

I shook my head. "I'm giving you the option. I'm sure you've got plenty of ways to get back to the reservation on your own. And unlike the rest of us, you don't have a reason to crash with the vampires."

He was quiet for a moment. Then he said, "I appreciate the offer. You're right. Mica would not require me to stay in the current situation. But if it's all the same to you, I shall."

"Why?"

He shrugged. "I find this group amusing."

"If that's the only—"

"And"—he raised a hand to cut me off—"I've been running from this long enough."

I chewed the inside of my lip, wondering how much conflict his presence would add. "What exactly happened between you and Chase?"

"Really, Alex?" Ava said. "Do we have to do this *now?*"

I waved a hand at the portal. "When am I gonna get another chance?"

But Haru took the opportunity to follow Chase, turning to smile at me as he stepped through and disappeared.

I gritted my teeth.

Let them be. The words echoed through my muted connection to James. Even his thoughts seemed sluggish. He tipped his head so he could meet my gaze. "Chase and Haru are both raw from old wounds." He took a deep breath. "Despite the old adage about time . . . such wounds do not heal on their own. Sometimes they must be reopened."

I frowned, but nodded. Whatever had happened between Haru and Chase, they had the right to deal with it on their own. I'd do my best to butt out.

I knelt beside James so I could get his arm around my shoulder again. "Come on, let's get you through."

Emma took a step forward. "Should I . . .?" She gestured to James, but didn't take up her previous position.

I shook my head and straightened, pulling James up with me. "Stay and help Ava, make sure she gets through okay."

She bit her lower lip, scraping a metal ring against her teeth. "I didn't mean to . . . I mean . . ."

"It's all right," James said. "I can understand why you'd be afraid." He turned his head just enough to focus on Emma. "You were right to be. Sanctuary or no, keep your guard up in the nest."

Emma paled.

Stop scaring her. I shoved the words through the link I shared with James, unsure he'd hear them.

James frowned at me. *Anyone who does not fear a vampire is a fool.*

"Guess I'm a fool then," I grumbled and shuffled us toward the portal. James's feet scraped along the asphalt with each step, but he was holding more of his own weight. I cast one last look back at Ava, Emma now standing by her side, and passed through the portal.

My stomach twisted. My ears popped. I looked around at a street similar to the one I'd just left. This street, however, had apartments on both sides, and graffiti decorated the bricks. Soggy papers clogged the gutters, and one in three street lights was broken or burnt out, casting the area in deep gloom. The cloud cover that had been overhead was breaking up, letting pinpricks of light from the distant stars shine through. The moon was either still covered or already set.

"Took you long enough," Chase complained. He cut his eyes to Haru.

I pulled James forward to clear the area in front of the portal. A second later, Emma and Ava stepped through. Ava was clutching Emma's arm as if she was dizzy or exhausted, maybe both, but at least she was standing on her own two feet.

"This way," I said and started toward the intersection that would lead us to Abandon, sticking to the shadows as best I could.

James sagged against me. Chase, Haru, and Ava all donned glamours. Chase even created the semblance of clothes to cover his naked body. Jynx hung limp in his arms, her still fae features turned toward his chest. Ava's glamour covered the blood on her face, but she stumbled like a drunk against Emma's steadying grip. Only Haru, bringing up the rear, seemed inconspicuous.

I worried my lower lip between my teeth. With the exception of Jynx, we could probably pass for a group of bar-hoppers who couldn't hold our liquor. If we were lucky, the club patrons wouldn't look at us twice. But an unconscious fae—

The club is closed tonight. James's response broke into my thoughts. *Not enough weeknight traffic to warrant staying open.*

Well hallelujah for savvy business practices. Now all we have to do is get there without anyone calling the cops.

Six blocks separated Abandon from the place where Ava's portal had dumped us. They were the longest six blocks of my life.

Distant sirens made my heart race, but they remained a directionless threat echoing through the night, never materializing. PTF headquarters was far to the south, but their reach was wide. I pictured Everly Harris standing in front of a wide window on the upper floor of a skyscraper, surveying the city below. And there we were, scurrying like rats through a maze under her merciless gaze.

We rounded the final corner that brought us in sight of the renovated church that housed the vampire nightclub. The neon sign was off. The doors were closed. Three cars sat in the parking lot to one side of the club.

I looked at James. "Should we just knock on the front door?"

"That'll work," he said. "They'll see us on their cameras anyway."

I sighed. I really didn't like this plan.

Our group crossed the last hundred feet of cracked sidewalk to the double doors of the church. Shifting my grip on James, I lifted my hand to knock.

The door on the right swung inward before my knuckles hit the wood.

"Well, well," came a familiar voice. "If it isn't Alex Blackwood."

Goosebumps sprang up over my entire body. I lowered my hand slowly and stared into a face from my nightmares. I swallowed to steady my voice. "Bryce."

A pale scar marred his otherwise dark complexion, starting an inch above his right eyebrow and tracing a jagged line over his eyelid to tapered off just above his jaw. The eye itself was whole, though the lids puckered slightly at the edges where the wound crossed it. Vampires could heal from almost anything—except concentrated UV. Bryce would always bear the evidence of the light-infected wound I'd given him. Judging by the hatred burning in his eyes, he'd love to return the favor.

My fingers itched, wishing for the handle of my light-imbued blade. But the knife was gone, lost with my other possessions when we fled Crossroads.

"I need to speak with Victoria," James said.

Bryce held my gaze for another moment, then swung his attention toward James. He sneered. "You look like shit."

James pulled himself a little straighter. "Tell your master I am here."

Bryce wrinkled his nose at the command, but stepped aside. When the last of our little group cleared the threshold, he slammed the door behind us.

"I saw you on the news, Alex," he said as he brushed past us to move into the lead. "Not your best performance. I much preferred the way you screamed in Merak's throne room."

I bit my tongue, willing the memories of torture down. Rising to Bryce's bait would gain me nothing.

He led us through the open dance area. Racks of lights hung from the vaulted ceiling, but none were lit. Only a smattering of emergency lights along the outer walls cast any glow. In a far corner of the room, past the confessional-slash-make-out-closets and the abandoned bar, we entered a corridor that ran along the edge of the room and stopped in front of a nondescript door with a small white placard that read: *Employees Only*.

Bryce pulled the handle and gestured toward the looming darkness framed by the open door. He smiled at me, the scar across his eye made the expression lopsided. "I'm sure you remember the way."

A memory of bouncing over Bryce's shoulder as he carried me into the dark earth slammed into me. I tightened my grip on James to steady my shaking hands.

A wave of comfort poured from James, dulling the memory, soothing my nerves. *You are not alone this time. I will not let him harm you.*

I appreciated the sentiment, but it would have been more comforting if James could stand on his own.

"Perhaps we should wait here while you tell your master of our arrival," James said.

Bryce shook his head. "Standing orders are to bring you straight to her." He shifted his smile to James. "She had a feeling you'd be stopping by after Alex's time in the spotlight."

I glanced back at the others. The fae were huddled close, as though they didn't want to risk touching anything but each other. Chase and Haru didn't seem to realize they'd taken up stances back to back. Emma's eyes were huge. Her gaze skittered over the interior of the club, as if expecting to find a neon sign proclaiming, "Here be vampires."

"The others can wait here," I suggested. "I'll go with you to see Victoria."

Emma grabbed my sleeve, her gaze drifting past me to Bryce. "We should stick together."

"You'll be fine here." I glanced at Chase, who nodded. If things went sideways, he'd get the girls out. "I'll come get you once we've cleared things with Victoria."

I patted her hand, then pried her fingers off my arm. "Just stick with Chase and Ava."

Haru snorted and folded his arms.

Bryce tapped a shiny black shoe against the ground. "Are you coming, or not?"

Straightening my shoulders, I took a deep breath and walked with James through the tunnels that led to the heart of the vampire nest.

THE THRONE ROOM was much as I remembered it; and yet, not the same at all. Arches lined both sides of the room, creating aisles through which I could see branching hallways. But where those aisles had been cast in shadow by the flickering light of blue torches on my previous visits, the areas behind the arches were brightly lit with the warm glow of electric lights and lined with gathered curtains that reduced the echo of my steps. The open area where I'd fought for my life against Merak and his vampire hoard was dotted with sofas, love seats, and chaise lounge chairs. The high ceiling bore two crystal chandeliers, and Merak's dark-wood throne had been replaced with a wide, gilt-framed chair with white velvet cushions. A plush throw rug covered the dais itself, hiding the hard stones where Merak had met his violent end, and I almost met mine.

I stared at the clean steps—at the veneer of comfort and luxury draped over them. Last time I'd seen them, they were covered in blood. I'd been reborn on those steps.

Without meaning to, I sought that part of myself that had come from James, the piece of demon-tainted soul he'd split off to save me. I glanced at him. There had to be a way to change him the way I'd changed that sliver inside me. A way to rid him of the demon without losing the magic that kept him alive.

"This way," Bryce said. He'd been a perfect match to the dark depravity of Merak's lair, but he looked out of place in the opulence of the newly decorated throne room. Out of place and uncomfortable.

We followed him through one of the arches and up a connecting hall.

Bryce rapped his fingers lightly against a door, then pushed it open and gestured for us to enter. He didn't follow, but pulled the door closed behind us.

"I expected you hours ago." A set of heavy curtains parted at the far end of the room. My gaze snapped to a woman with silky black hair cascading to her thighs and eyes like emeralds. "Oh! And you've brought a friend."

She said "friend" in the same tone a parent might use when referring to a toddler's stuffed animal.

"Alex, this is Victoria, the new master vampire of Denver," James said, gesturing to the woman. "Victoria, this is Alex Blackwood."

She gave me a wide smile and slid through the curtains so she was standing in front of the bed. Heat crept up my limbs and seeped into my cheeks. She was bare-ass naked. Her smooth, tight skin was the color of thick cream . . . and was there ever a lot of it. My gaze slid down her lithe body. She was as beautiful and inviting as the old master was dark and scary—a perfect match to the redecorated throne room.

This was the ex-girlfriend James had invited to town?

"We can . . . um . . . wait outside . . . while you get dressed." There seemed to be a disconnect between my brain and my mouth as I continued to stare at all that perfect skin.

She waved my words away. "I've heard so much about you, Alex. I've wanted to meet you for a while now, but James seemed reluctant to bring you around." She shifted her gaze to James and quirked an eyebrow. "I'm glad he finally changed his mind."

"Circumstances have changed," he said.

Victoria took three graceful steps to a nearby chair, lifted a piece of translucent ivory fabric off the back, and slipped it over her shoulders. The robe was a mesh of intricately woven lace that did nothing to hide what it covered. Long, slim fingers tied the two ribbons in a bow over breasts that strained the fabric. Below that single point of contact, the robe draped like a waterfall over curves I couldn't tear my eyes away from.

"I apologize for not meeting you in the audience room, but I was just turning in for the day." Her voice was deep and rich, and carried the hint of an invitation.

Despite her words, I got the feeling her bedroom was exactly where she'd wanted to be when James came to visit, though she'd probably expected him to be alone. While the night was wearing on, there was plenty of time before dawn to put that bed to a different use than sleeping.

That realization was enough to rattle me out of my stupor. I grasped the invisible thread that connected me to James and thought as hard as I could. *Is this where you spent all those late nights discussing policy?*

James tightened his arm around my shoulders and cut his gaze sideways to meet my glare. He smiled. *Jealousy looks good on you, but don't get carried away. We need her help.*

I gritted my teeth in what I hoped would look like a smile and turned back to Victoria. "It's our fault for calling so late. We appreciate you seeing us."

She slid a pair of lace panties up her legs, wriggling slightly to pull them in place.

An uncomfortable warmth seeped through my abdomen. I absently scratched an itch on my right arm.

"Victoria . . ." James's voice held a note of warning.

She made a pouty face and said, "Sorry, force of habit."

The warmth that had been spreading through me abated, as did the itch that indicated I'd been the target of magic.

I frowned. "What did you—"

"Merak enjoyed the taste of fear," she said.

I shivered. I knew all too well what Merak liked.

She dropped onto a velvet chaise with the fluid grace of a panther. "I'm partial to lust."

I glanced at James. The unwelcome heat I'd experienced was replaced with a writhing mass of angry snakes, hissing and snapping.

He frowned. *Not now, Alex.*

"Please." Victoria gestured to a nearby couch. "You two look done in."

"That's actually why we're here," James said as I lowered him to the seat.

I dropped beside him and rolled my shoulder, happy to finally have his weight off it.

"I'm sure you're aware of the PTF's current search." James set a possessive hand on my thigh. "We, along with five others, require a safe place to rest . . . just for a few hours."

Victoria slid the tip of one crimson-nailed finger along her lower lip. "You know I'm always happy to offer you the protection of my nest . . . for a price."

I tensed, but James increased the pressure on my thigh in clear warning. This was *his* negotiation.

He fixed his gaze upon Victoria and shook his head.

She pursed her lips into a little pout. "A favor, then. One day of sanctuary."

James nodded. "Agreed."

"My offer stands," she smiled, "should you ever find yourself in need again."

She leaned forward to reach across the open space between couches, her breasts nearly spilling out of her robe, and lifted my calloused hand between her soft, smooth fingers. "It was lovely to meet you, Alex. Please come see me again when your schedule is less . . . hectic."

I nodded, pulling my hand back. Then I slipped my arm behind James and helped him to his feet, eager to be out of this room.

One mission accomplished. We'd managed to arrange a safe place to sleep, surrounded by bloodsucking murderers. Time to tell the others.

I CLOSED THE DOOR of my temporary bedroom and leaned back, resting my head against the hard wood. Chase and Haru were standing watch in the hall—Haru because he was the least exhausted of us, and Chase because he didn't trust Haru to do the job properly. Ava, Jynx, and Emma were next door. I sighed. This was hardly the wedding night anyone expected.

I pushed away from the door, kicked off my shoes, and slipped into bed still fully dressed. Promises or no, I wanted to be ready to run should Victoria's hospitality turn south. James was already in the bed, sans shirt, and lifted an arm in invitation. I snuggled close, tucking against his side and resting my hand over his heart beside the ever-present crystal pendant.

Picturing Victoria's perfect skin, I asked, "What's the standing offer Victoria mentioned?"

"The same one she's been pushing since she got here. She wants me to join her nest. Pledge myself." He murmured the words into my hair and followed them with a kiss on the top of my head. "But I'm pledged to another."

Smiling, I closed my eyes and relaxed against him. "Good answer."

I matched the smooth rise and fall of his chest, the rhythm soothing some of my anxiety as the laundry list of impossible tasks ahead of me ran through my mind.

Once Ava was rested and Jynx was awake, we'd be headed for the fae reservation so I could talk to Bael and rescue May, but the portal to Enchantment was warded against vampires. Victoria had offered one day of sanctuary. One. I was happy James showed no interest in swearing himself to Victoria and her nest, but without her continued protection, James would be alone in the mortal realm once the rest of us crossed over. And while he might not share my spotlight as public enemy number one, he was still a wanted fugitive, thanks to our relationship. He'd be vulnerable . . . unless I found a way to circumvent the portal wards by the time we arrived.

I tilted my head so I was looking up at his chin. "Have you given any more thought to my idea about changing your demon?"

His chest stilled for a moment, then resumed its rise and fall.

"I have," he said. "But I haven't reached a decision."

I rolled slightly so I was propped on my elbow and could look at him properly. "What's holding you back?"

"Uncertainty, for one thing. What you're suggesting has, as far as I know, never been attempted. What makes you think you can even affect the demon within me?"

I shrugged. "It's the same demon that was inside me. On a different scale, I admit, but still."

"And what if you *can?*" He traced his knuckles down the side of my face. "As a vampire, I'm strong and fast. I'm useful to you. What if changing me . . . changes that?"

I frowned, then I glared as his words took root. "You think I'm with you because you're *useful?*"

I pushed away, intending to sit up, but he wrapped his arms around me to hold me in place.

"I would never think you so shallow," he said. "But maybe I am. From my perspective, a man who cannot keep the woman he loves safe is . . . well, no man at all. And you are by no means an easy woman to keep safe."

I stilled and studied the lines in James's face, the shadows in his eyes. I didn't know how old he was, not exactly, but he definitely came from a very different time. When he'd been human, before he was turned, what had chivalry looked like? How hard was it for him to watch me face danger time and again?

I settled back against his chest, hands folded under my chin. "If you want to keep me safe, the best place to do that is by my side."

"And if I become mortal?"

I stretched to place a gentle kiss against his frown. "Then we'll be mortal together."

His gaze slid to the side and became unfocused.

"At least let me see if I can even affect your demon," I suggested. "If not, this is all moot."

He pursed his lips, clearly reluctant, but he nodded.

Shifting my gaze, I traced the ribbons of silver through James's veins, following them out from the shadow at the center of him. The demon was a part of James . . . but also separate, part of an ancient creature who spread through hosts like a parasite.

I tugged at a single silver thread, separating it from the knot of energy at James's core, finding the barbs that anchored it. Then I wrapped my magic around it. I needed to dissolve the demon into James, make it an indistinguishable part of the whole rather than a separate entity to keep in check. That's what I'd done with the piece inside me. I'd absorbed it, redefined it. I could do it again.

I twisted the thread the way I'd twisted other materials with my magic, the way I'd twisted the piece of demon within me, shifting it closer to what I wanted—healthy human tissue fused with magic. Not the chaotic, self-destructive magic of a demon, but ordered, controllable magic.

I pushed and pulled the silvery substance, smoothing it into James's natural energy, blending the two together. The silver started to bleed out, fading to match its surroundings.

James gasped and grabbed my wrist, pulling my hand away from his chest and breaking my concentration. The section I'd been changing reverted to silver.

He was staring at me, wide-eyed. "You really can do it."

I was breathing heavily, as if I'd just run a race. "I can." I grinned. My experiment had been a success.

A single strand was a long way from complete conversion, but I could do it. I knew I could. Though, considering how much energy that small change had taken, I'd need to rest first. "Give me a good night's sleep and a decent meal, and I'll be ready to tackle your demon when we get to the way station tomorrow."

"Tomorrow," James said in an oddly flat voice, his eyes still wide. The fact that he could be free of his demon within a day seemed to have hit him like a cancer patient being told there was a cure to their terminal disease.

Exhausted but happy, I set my cheek on his shoulder and let the warmth of my success pull me toward sleep.

Chapter 13

I STEPPED THROUGH Ava's sixth, and final, portal. Chase waited a few steps away, wearing baggy shorts and a loose gray sweater. Jynx was tucked against his side. She was awake and walking on her own, but her buoyant energy was absent. Her half-lidded eyes were dull, her shoulders slumped. Haru stood a little ways off, hands in his pockets. Behind him, the tan Toyota I'd returned on my previous visit to the reservation sat at the end of a line of fae-friendly cars waiting to be loaned out.

Emma burst into existence beside me, took a quick look around, and went to stand next to Jynx. She bounced on the balls of her feet and wrung her hands. She'd been a ball of raw nerves since we left the nest, clearly anxious to get to May. Neither of us mentioned what we might find when we finally reached her.

Turning, I held my breath and studied the shimmering patch of cold, afternoon sunlight through which I'd come. Despite Ava's assurance that her portal bypassed the wards around the way station, I'd breathe easier once James was through.

A polished shoe settled on the matted leaves that coated the ground. Then another. James took a deep breath, and I let mine out. He stepped away from the portal, moving to stand beside me. I touched his arm, finding comfort in the spark of connection that jumped between us.

A moment later Ava stumbled through. She dropped to her hands and knees. The shimmer behind her vanished.

I rushed to kneel by her side and placed a hand on her back as she gasped and panted.

"You did it, Ava," I said. "You got us to the way station."

She nodded, unable to speak. She'd been skeptical that she could make all six jumps necessary to get us there without more substantial breaks in between. But Emma's impatience coupled with the threat of PTF discovery kept us moving since we left the nest.

"Come on," I said, pulling her arm across my shoulders and lifting her to her feet. "Let's get you inside."

The six of us made our way to the front of the way station, tromping through a track of slushy, brown snow and mud which left the ground looking as if there'd been a stampede around the little farmhouse. I pictured the crush of evacuating fae around Targe's portal before he collapsed. How many made it through?

Haru pushed through the front door. The rest of us followed, tracking muddy prints across the porch and into the common area that served as kitchen, living room, dining room, and check-in station. The ever-present little hob woman was in the kitchen. As usual, the smells of fresh-baked pastries, meat fat, and mingled spices hit me like a slap to the face.

My stomach clenched, a growl ripping out of it. Vampires didn't keep a lot of food on hand that those of us with mortal digestions could eat. So while James had gotten a much-needed chance to feed thanks to a pretty redhead Victoria sent his way, breakfast for the rest of us had been a sparse affair. I licked my lips.

"Come on in. Make yourselves at—" The woman who manned the way station gasped and the tray of iced cinnamon rolls she'd been holding hit the floor with a clatter, pastries scattering. She clutched the counter behind her with one hand. With the other, she pointed one knobby-jointed finger at James and spluttered, "The wards."

Ava slipped out of my grip and planted herself at the head of our little group, hands outstretched in a placating gesture. "It's okay, Nell. The wards are intact."

"But . . . but . . ." The woman's eyes narrowed, still focused on James. "How'd you get through?"

"I brought him," Ava said. "We portalled in."

The old woman finally swung her gaze to Ava. Pale curls bounced against the woman's skull as she shook her head. "You should know better. The wards are in place for a reason."

"I mean you no harm," James said.

"We're on our way to the reservation," I added. "Then we'll be out of your hair."

Piercing eyes stared at me out of an avalanche of wrinkled skin. "Otis is resting. He's been ferrying fae to the reservation all morning."

"How many have come through?" Ava asked.

The woman sighed and, kneeling, began picking up the spilled rolls. She kept one eye on James while she worked. "Six evacuation shelters ran their lines after hearing what happened at Crossroads."

Ava wrung her hands, probably thinking about Targe. "How many others did the PTF raid?"

Nell shook her head. "None. But people are scared. They're jumping ship while they can."

"Any word what happened to those captured at Crossroads?" I asked.

Nell glanced at Ava, then back to me. "Sent to the detention centers, I'm afraid."

I nodded. That made sense. I looked at Ava's pale profile. At least the captured fae should still be alive.

Ava hugged herself. "How did they even find us?"

I thought of the homeless woman with her shopping cart begging for change, and the gap in James's illusion. Had there been time for her to identify us? A call to the tip line might have gotten the PTF close enough to notice the aversion spells on Crossroads.

My face tingled as I went suddenly lightheaded. Was it my fault the bar was compromised?

"I hate to interrupt," Emma said, stepping forward. "But we're kinda in a rush."

The woman's pale curls bobbed in agreement. "You and everyone else. I'll go roust Otis."

With one last glare at James, she shuffled to the bedroom door, slipped through, and closed it behind her.

Chase led an ill-looking Jynx over to a floral patterned couch. Ava followed, and the two girls slumped together on the sagging cushions. Chase set his hands on his hips and looked up at the ceiling. "You two should head for our parents' house."

Jynx's eyes became round as saucers, and she blurted, "I'm going with you!" at the same time as Ava, stiff beside her, said, "But they hate me!"

Chase shook his head. "Neither of you is in any condition for a trip to Enchantment. You can wait here if you want"—he gestured to the room around us—"but there's no guarantee the PTF won't find this place."

I sat down next to Ava. "I don't think Jynx's parents hate you. They only opposed the marriage because of your mortality." I met James's gaze. "No one wants someone they love to suffer that kind of loss."

Chase had gone very still when I started talking, but when I mentioned loss he shuddered and looked at Haru, who'd been keeping to himself on the far side of the room.

"But you've made your vows," I continued. "There's nothing they can do or say to change that. You can afford to be the bigger person here. Mend your bridges while you still can."

"Alex is right," Chase said. "There's no reason for you to hide from our parents any longer. The union is struck. They'll have to accept it."

"But—"

"Go home, Jynx." Chase rested a hand on his sister's shoulder. "It's time."

She shook her head, jaw set. "Emma's my friend. I want to help."

I pushed to my feet, antsy to move. "With any luck, a quick chat with Bael is all it'll take."

The siblings exchanged a glance that made it clear how unlikely they thought that outcome was.

"Regardless," I continued. "We've got this covered. You two should rest, recover . . . and celebrate. You're married now, after all."

Jynx stuck out her lower lip. "Our reception *did* get ruined . . ."

Ava stroked Jynx's arm. "We could have another."

Jynx took a deep breath and nodded. "When you guys get back, and everyone's safe, we'll have another party. The biggest, best party ever."

Everyone being safe seemed like a deal-breaker, considering what was going on in the mortal realm, but I plastered a grin on my face. "Sounds great."

Emma was shifting her weight nervously from foot to foot. "If that's settled, can we get going? May's already been gone two days."

"Almost." I crossed back to James and took his hand in mine. "There's one more thing we need to do."

Deep lines framed James's frown. "I'm not sure."

"I can do it." I lifted his second hand as well, clutching his fingers against my chest. "You saw that last night."

He nodded, but remained silent.

I felt along our link and found turmoil. Hope and fear swirled together and around each other like oil and water, making me dizzy.

"If you're worried about your usefulness—"

The door behind the check-in desk opened and Otis shuffled out, his thin frame more hunched than usual. Dark circles drooped below his eyes.

Nell pushed past him and started pulling platters of raw meat out of the fridge. "Just let me get some food in him."

Otis glared at each member of our group. His lip curled when he got to James. "Nell said you were here." He shook his head. "But I ain't taking you through. Your kind ain't welcome beyond the wall."

"If my plan works," I said, "James's *kind* won't be an issue by the time you're done with your lunch."

Otis grunted and shuffled to the bathroom.

"Alex, we need to talk." James looked around at our gathered friends, then pulled me toward the front door.

I waited until we were alone on the porch with a closed door between us and everyone else before I spoke. "I know there are still . . . uncertainties, but we're leaving for the reservation in a few minutes. It's now or never."

James shook his head. "Not true." He set his hands on my shoulders as though holding me steady. "This is too fast. Much as I want to stay by your side, I can't commit to this."

I frowned. "You've said time and again that you don't like being separated from me when I cross realms."

"I don't."

"And that you hate having to feed off innocent people just to survive."

"I do."

"And that you—"

James placed a finger against my lips. "There are reasons, lots of reasons, why I do want to try this. That doesn't mean it's a good idea."

I crossed my arms. "I don't want to leave you here, alone, with the PTF hunting you while the rest of us are off in another realm."

"And I don't want to watch you leave . . . without me . . . again. But even knowing you can change the demon within me, we don't know those changes will allow me to cross the fae wards. Nor what side effects there might be. And even if everything works exactly as you hope it will"—he looked away, studying the mud beside the porch—"I'm not sure I want to change."

"You . . ." I stepped back, breaking his hold, as all my old insecurities came flooding back. *You're just a passing fancy. He'll use you and leave you. You can't rely on anyone but yourself.*

I shook my head. "So despite what you've said, it doesn't really bother you to suck the necks of other women and spend your nights with a succubus, or that we'll never walk under the sun together if your magic charm breaks, or that I'll grow old alone while you stay the same age forever." The words rushed out in a torrent as the strain of the past few days tore down the dam around my emotions. I looked away, ashamed, but also relieved. All the ugly, petty worries I'd been brooding over had been thrown into the light for him to see.

James watched me for a moment, maybe gauging if I was done. Then he closed the distance I'd put between us. He didn't touch me, but he bent so he was looking into my eyes. His consciousness caressed my raging thoughts.

"Your concerns are not petty, nor were they a secret. I don't hold them against you. But I have been as I am for centuries, and I've struggled to find this equilibrium with my inner demon. To risk that so suddenly . . ." James took my hand, rubbing my knuckles with his thumb. He dropped his guard enough to let me see his indecision. "One thing immortality grants is patience. As you once so eloquently told me, 'I'm not saying never. I'm saying not right now.'"

I pictured Jynx and Ava at their wedding, and the way I'd grilled them about their decision to commit despite the many obstacles in their path. I'd definitely been projecting. I sighed. "I have no right to ask you to change. It's just, when I started thinking it was possible . . ."

He nodded. "You wanted a partner without so many complications."

I grimaced, hating that he was right. Here I was, part fae, part human, wanted by the PTF, related to the Lord of Enchantment. Who was I to complain about complications after James had accepted all of mine?

"Promise me you'll be here when I get back from Enchantment," I said.

"Promise you'll come back in one piece."

"Deal," I said. "And while I'm there, maybe I can learn a little more about how imbuing people works, eliminate some of the uncertainties . . . just in case." I grabbed the handle on the front door. "Now let's see about getting you some accommodations."

When James and I stepped back inside, Jynx, Ava, and Emma were studying the coffee table with feigned concentration. Otis was squared off against a mountain of steak, biscuits, and gravy at the trestle table, and Nell was scrubbing a large ceramic pot at the kitchen sink.

Haru stared at us, unabashed. "Lover's quarrel?"

Chase glanced at James, then shifted his gaze to me. "Everything all right?"

Ignoring Haru, I nodded to Chase and headed for Nell in the kitchen, James in tow. "My friend needs a safe place to stay until we get back. Shouldn't be more than a couple of days." *Assuming Bael grants us an audience right away, agrees to inspect the prison, and finds the missing children without incident.*

Nell wiped her hands on her apron, looked from me to James, and shook her head. "We'll likely have more fae coming through here, fleeing PTF raids. A vampire would . . . complicate things."

"He's no threat," I said.

"And if another guest decides there should be one less abomination in the world?" She pinned James with a stern look, as though daring him to say he wouldn't defend himself if attacked.

"I thought the way station was supposed to be neutral territory," I said.

"For fae. Your friend should never have been here to begin with."

James stepped around me. "What if no one knew I was here?"

Nell wrinkled her nose. "Hard to miss a vampire in the common room."

"You have a storm cellar. I saw the doors around back."

She frowned, then raised an eyebrow. "You want to hide in our cellar?"

"Seriously?" I asked, turning him to face me.

He smiled. "A cellar would hardly be the worst place I've had to hide."

I crossed my arms, sick to death of the world's widespread bigotry. Mortals, practitioners, fae, werewolves, vampires. There wasn't a single group that wasn't despised by another. "This is bullshit."

"This is reality," he said. He turned back to Nell. "Please."

Nell pressed her lips to a thin white line and looked past my shoulder to Otis, who'd taken a break from eating to listen to our conversation.

Otis shook his head and grumbled, "You and your strays." Then he tucked back into his food.

"You're not to come out until your friends return to claim you," Nell said.

I breathed a sigh of relief.

James nodded. "You have my word."

"I'll be warding the cellar doors just the same."

THE CELLAR WAS cold, dark, and musty smelling, but vampires were used to that kind of thing, right? At least he would be safe.

I arranged the blanket and pillows Nell had given me and turned to James, who stood stoop-shouldered on the stairs, his head scraping the ceiling of the low entrance. His arms were full with a tray of food and two bottles of red wine. It seemed Nell's hostess sensibilities wouldn't allow her to let a guest go hungry. Even an unwelcome one.

"Not exactly the Marriott," he said, stepping in fully and straightening. "But it'll do."

"Wishing you'd taken me up on my offer now?"

"Maybe." He set his load on a barrel to one side and wrapped his arms around my waist, pulling me to him. "You always seem to get into trouble when I let you out of my sight."

"In fairness, I've gotten into plenty of trouble while you were watching." Smiling, I stretched onto my tiptoes and pressed my lips to his.

He hugged me tight, deepening the kiss and making my pulse quicken. Warmth spread through me, inviting. . . . But May was waiting.

"I have to go," I murmured against his mouth.

He breathed a deep sigh that warmed my cheeks and stared into my eyes from inches away, his forehead pressed to mine. "Be careful. And come back soon."

Chapter 14

DEEP SNOW crunched under my boots, and I pulled in a breath of cold, crisp air untouched by industry. I shivered and hugged myself, burrowing into the warmth of an oversized orange sweater I'd borrowed from the way station's collection of discarded clothing.

Chase, in the form of a small gray tabby, brushed against my ankle, arching his back. He looked up with big green eyes, meowed once, and darted into the trees. I bit my lip and watched him go. A shifter spy wouldn't be any use in my meeting with Bael, so he'd use the opportunity to scout out the entrance to Shedraziel's prison . . . just in case Bael wasn't in a cooperative mood. The plan was to meet back at the way station when we'd finished our respective tasks. If we didn't have May by then, we'd need to plan our next move.

Emma stood a few feet to my right. She blew a puff of steamy breath into her hands and looked around, wide-eyed. "So this is really another world?"

"In a manner of speaking," said Haru. He looked up at the blue sky.

"It looks a lot like the mountains we just left," Emma said.

"Looks can be deceiving." He whistled, an ear-splitting shrill, and pointed toward the trees.

An eloko—a three-foot tall fae with green skin covered in leaves—stepped to the edge of the clearing.

Haru held up a single finger. The eloko nodded, and faded back into the forest.

I took Emma's hand. "When we get to the keep, let me do the talking."

Haru laughed. "Because you did such a great job the last time you were here. Tell me, will you be paying Malakai a visit?"

I glared, but he just smiled, Mediterranean eyes twinkling.

The eloko came back. In one hand trailed a set of thin, leather reins attached to the head of a large gaala with chestnut-brown fur and broad antlers. The beast snorted steam from wide nostrils and pawed the ground with one of its six hooves, scraping the snow he otherwise walked on top of without leaving so much as a dent.

Emma stared at the beast. "It's just like your little sculpture," she said. "But huge."

"If you're done gawking"—Haru shoved his shirt into Emma's arms—"feel free to wear it. The wind can get rather cold."

Emma frowned. "What are you—" Her eyes widened as Haru dropped his pants, then pushed those into her arms as well. He was now standing buck naked in the snow.

"Shall we?" He gestured for us to mount the gaala.

Emma turned to me and whispered, "Why is he naked?"

"Haru's a kitsune," I said. "Just don't lose any of his clothes. He'll want them at the other end."

I jumped up and managed to get my chest onto the gaala's back. Then I swung my leg over, sat up, and scooted forward to make room for Emma. She scrambled up behind me and wrapped both arms around my waist, Haru's clothes pinned between us.

"Hold on tight," I cautioned, tucking my hair up under the knit cap I'd also borrowed. "It's a little startling when they take off."

Haru shimmered for a second, then dropped to all fours on white paws. He shook his head and all seven of his red-tipped tails.

Emma gasped.

Haru stepped in front of our gaala. He and the beast locked gazes for a moment, then the gaala snorted. Haru took off like a shot. His legs gobbled up the open space of the clearing and he launched into the air, paws continuing their motion as though pounding against an invisible track.

The gaala charged after, climbing just in time to miss the treetops at the far end of the clearing. Emma squeezed so hard I thought I might pop when we tilted up into the sky, but she eased up a little as we evened out.

The feeling of galloping across the sky was amazing, but the sick weight that had been growing inside me since Loni announced that May was missing soured the experience, making the half-hour ride feel like an eternity.

The last time I'd flown into the city of Abonaille Malmür, I'd ridden with an entourage. We'd come at night, homing in on the beacon of the glowing city. This time, the white marble buildings blended with the snowy cliffs of the mountain they clung to, making it impossible to spot save for the blue ribbon of the river that split the city in two before plummeting to the forest below. Like last time, we pranced through the sky high above the bustling streets. Unlike last time, we did not head directly for one of the many towers of Bael's keep.

Haru alighted on smooth stone in front of a massive set of wooden doors. They had to be at least twelve feet high, and nearly as wide.

By the time my gaala's hooves clacked against the marble street, Haru was striding toward the gate on two naked legs. A pair of green and leather liveried guards watched him warily. One was a pale, gold-haired sidhe, with thin, sharp features whose hand rested on the hilt of a curved blade at his waist. The other guard was a panotti, with long leathery ears dangling nearly to her knees. She clutched the shaft of a spear with both hands.

I tightened my grip on the gaala's reins, wondering if I was supposed to dismount or not. I was theoretically a member of the Court of Enchantment, and not a minor one, but having a title didn't mean I had any practical idea how to arrange a meeting with the Lord of Enchantment. What if he wasn't even home?

Straightening my shoulders, I slid off the side of the gaala and passed the reins to Emma. "Wait here."

She clutched the leather straps with white knuckles.

I trotted to Haru's side as he closed the remaining distance to the gate.

"Why didn't we fly straight to the keep?"

He snorted. "You think just anybody can cross these walls? Without an escort, we would have been shot down as intruders."

Haru and I stopped within striking distance of the guards.

"State your business," said the panotti.

I looked at Haru, but he just tipped his head toward the guards. Guess I was taking the lead.

"We—"

Haru cleared his throat.

I shot him a glare and started again. "*I've* come to see the Lord of—"

Hinges groaned. Behind the guards, one of the enormous doors shifted. When the gap was wide enough, someone stepped out. She was tall and slender, with severe features made even more severe by the tight braids that held her flame-red hair away from her face. She tossed the edge of a green cape behind her shoulder and pinned me with her indigo gaze.

I nodded to the Captain of the Court Guard. "Hello, Rhoana."

"Lady Alyssandra," she said. "We've been expecting you."

EMMA CLUNG TO my side, strangling the life from my arm with her viselike grip as we followed Rhoana into the keep. Her wide-eyed gaze swung from side to side as we crossed the living carpet of the entrance hall and climbed one of the spiraling staircases lining its walls. A variety of fae moved through the halls, each wearing the green and leather livery of Bael's court. Almost everyone we passed did a double take, some staring openly at the human in their midst, others averting their gaze and hastening away.

How long before the fae purists heard there was a mortal at court? Would they target Emma? Or did they only care about human-fae mongrels, like me?

I bunched my fists. The sooner we got out of here, the better.

Haru, who'd reclaimed his clothes from Emma and trailed at the back of our little procession, peeled off as we approached yet another set of stairs.

"This is where I take my leave." He gave one flippant wave and headed down a side hallway without a backward glance.

"Wait, what?" Emma said. "He's leaving?" She looked from me to Haru's retreating form, then back to me. "I thought he was gonna help."

Rhoana snorted. "As if that lordless consort could help anyone." She started up the stairs. "This way."

The plush carpet of the upper floors muffled our footsteps as we headed for a familiar door. I'd walked these halls on my last visit to Enchantment. Once for a dinner that turned out to be a blind date, and once after getting caught trying to break Kai out of the dungeon. Neither meeting had gone particularly well.

Rhoana stopped in front of the door to Bael's private garden and knocked twice, then stepped aside and gestured for me to enter.

Swallowing past the lump in my throat, I turned the knob and stepped through, towing Emma along.

The musical burble of tumbling water filled the unnaturally warm air. Bael's garden was housed on an open balcony twice the size of my house. By rights, we should have been standing on barren ice and snow, high on the mountain peak as we were, but magic broke all the rules. To my left was a bush with stiff silvery stalks and leaves that shone like thin-pressed metal. Beside it, mustard-colored poofs drooped from slender purple reeds. To my right was a lattice overgrown with vines sporting huge, teal leaves and bursts of orange where petals as fine as strands of hair erupted from rust-colored pods.

Emma leaned so close her mouth was practically touching my ear and said in a stage whisper, "This place is incredible."

I shook my head. Of course Emma wasn't afraid of an alien environment where everything could probably kill her. Emma's glass was always half full.

"Over here." Movement caught my eye from behind the teal leaves, and I stepped around the lattice to find Bael lounging on a stone bench.

He wasn't what you'd expect from someone with the title Lord of Enchantment. He certainly hadn't been what I'd imagined my estranged grandfather would look like. Bael had the outward appearance of a nineteen-year-old boy with pale skin and a lithe frame. His long, purple-black hair hung in braids decorated with tinkling golden beads, and the cut of his clothes was straight from a Renaissance Fair. He looked up at me with eyes the color of flowing lava swirled with sparks of black and gold, and smiled.

"Emma," I said, "this is the fae Lord of Enchantment." I bowed, dropping my gaze to the ground.

Emma practically fell to her knees beside me.

"I was hoping you'd come." Bael's voice was young-sounding, but carried a thread of steel. "I've been worried."

I glanced up. The little gaala carving I'd lost at Crossroads was standing on Bael's knee. He stroked one finger down its back.

"As I understand it, things have grown rather . . . tense in the mortal realm. It seems our treaty with the mortals may be coming to an end." He flicked his wrist and the gaala galloped through the air to land on the branch of a nearby tree. "Best you remain by my side until things settle down."

I straightened. "I appreciate the offer, but the current tension between the humans and fae isn't why I came."

He raised an eyebrow and interlaced his fingers. "Oh?"

I shifted my feet, then raised my chin and pulled Emma up beside me. "Emma's sister has gone missing. We have reason to believe she's been taken by a fae named Shedraziel."

Bael stiffened. "And what reason might that be?"

"May wasn't the only child taken, and not all the children are mortal."

He pursed his lips. "So a fae gave you Shedraziel's name and sent you here." Sighing, he pushed to his feet. "Did you learn nothing from your previous visit? My enemies are legion. They do all in their power to sow doubt in my court, to weaken my position." He crossed his arms. "What proof do you have that she took your friend? Vague hints from an enemy lord? This is likely a plot to sow discontent between us."

"If the person who sent me is wrong, if there is no breach in Shedraziel's prison, surely the simplest way to prove it is to check."

The gold and black specks in Bael's eyes spun faster, caught in a fiery torrent. "And give credence to the claim that I cannot maintain my own borders?" He lifted his chin. "I will not."

"Please, your lordship," Emma said. "She's just a child. If there's even a chance—"

Bael raised a hand and Emma's voice cut out mid-sentence. She set her fingers against her throat and turned to me, mouth gaping, the beginning of fear in her eyes.

I glared at Bael. "Did you just—"

"You have permission to address me," he said. "She does not."

"It's *her* sister that's missing. She has the right to seek justice."

"Within *her* abilities," he said coolly. He clasped his hands behind his back and paced along the marble path that wove between the plants.

Pursing my lips, I took Emma's hand and I pulled her to follow. Dangerous though it might be for her in Bael's presence, I wasn't about to leave her alone.

We walked to the outer edge of the balcony, where all of Abonaille Malmür spread beneath us. Bael stood at the railing. A sinking feeling made my steps leaden. The last time I stood there, Bael had offered Kai's freedom in exchange for a deplorable favor. I'd turned him down flat.

"If you're worried about appearances, just let me go alone." I set a hand against my chest. "A quick look to see if the kids are there with no one the wiser. We can say I'm touring your realm."

"You?" He scoffed. "A nameless child? Shedraziel would devour you." He shook his head, then crossed his arms and looked out over the city. "I might be willing to consider a prison inspection."

Emma bobbed to the balls of her feet, but the bowling ball in my gut settled lower. Nothing from a fae was free. If Bael wasn't interested in justice—which he'd already made clear—he was looking to bargain.

"Your price?" I asked.

"You know what I want."

I gripped the banister until my fingers ached.

He smiled. "I'll even pardon Malakai, per my original offer."

Emma glanced between us, frowning. When I didn't respond, she tugged at my sleeve and gestured to Bael as if to say, "Just give him what he wants."

"What he wants," I said through clenched teeth, "is a child."

Emma swung her focus back to Bael, mouth hanging silently open.

He lifted both palms skyward in a weighing gesture. "A child for a child. What do you say?"

Chapter 15

EMMA'S GAZE SWUNG between Bael and me as I struggled *not* to say all the things that sprang to mind. I'd made it clear during our last encounter that I had no interest in becoming Bael's brood mare. Clearly, he wasn't willing to take no for an answer.

In the end, the lord always gets what he wants. Kai's warning echoed through my memory.

Finally, through gritted teeth, I managed, "I will *consider* your offer."

The words burned like acid in my throat, but I couldn't deny him flat out . . . not with May's life hanging in the balance. If there was no other way, I'd have to consider his deal. But I wasn't out of options yet.

"Wonderful." Bael clapped his hands. "Then I look forward to your favorable response. But don't take too long. If the girl you're looking for *is* with Shedraziel, she won't last long."

I clenched my jaw.

"In the meantime, you and your guest are welcome to the accommodations of my keep."

He waved a hand at Emma, whose hand jumped back to her throat.

I gripped her elbow and whispered, "Is your voice back?"

She looked up with wide, wet eyes, glanced at Bael, and squeaked out a timid, "Yes."

"Good." I turned my attention back to Bael. "While I appreciate your offer of accommodations, Emma and I will be headed back to the mortal realm."

Bael's lips turned down. "With the mounting unrest?" He shook his head. "I'm afraid I can't allow that. You're far too vulnerable."

I stiffened, my fingers balling to fists at my sides. But the last time I'd let my temper get the better of me at court, I'd landed a friend in prison—and Kai had been a valued Knight of the Realm. Who knew what Bael might do to Emma, a lowly human? I took a deep breath.

"We have matters to attend to at home. I cannot accept your offer at this time."

"Eager to get back to the vampire you've been bedding?" He raised an eyebrow, then set one finger against the side of his chin. "Or was it the shifter spy? I was disappointed to discover how much Malakai and Hortense left out of their reports."

Heat flooded my cheeks. From its perch on my dresser, the little gaala would've had a perfect view of everything that happened in my bedroom. Was Bael able to see through the little creature? Or did he just get the highlights after the fact?

He waved a hand at Emma. "Send your associate to see to your mortal matters. You will remain here."

My blood boiled at the way he dismissed Emma like she was one of his servants, to be given orders and forgotten. I bit my tongue and counted to five to keep from blurting out something I'd regret. Kai would have been proud.

"I'd like to speak with Kai."

"Once you're settled," he said. "Tomorrow perhaps." He stroked his smooth chin in a way that would have seemed dignified on an older man but came across as comical on his impossibly young face. "Maybe I will move him above ground while you're here. Would you like that?"

I ground my teeth.

"And we can continue your training." He looked out over his domain, his expression growing distant. "I'm curious to see what progress you've made with the basics I taught you on your last visit."

Memories of a glowing dagger of pure energy popped into my mind. I *did* have a lot of questions about my magic. And as one of only three living imbuers, I didn't have a lot of options for mentors or answers. Answers like how to change James's demon without unraveling the magic that was holding him together.

I glanced sidelong at Emma. She was vulnerable here. The longer we stayed, the more danger she'd be in. I took hold of her hand. Her fingers were clammy in mine.

"Don't move," I whispered. I glanced at the goblin fruit hanging heavy and golden from a nearby plant. My mouth began to water. I shivered and pulled my eyes away. Even one bite of that magic fruit could turn a mortal into an addict, filling them with an insatiable need. "And don't touch anything."

She nodded, and I released my grip.

I joined Bael at the railing, setting my hands on the smooth marble and gazing out over the city. I could see more details in the daylight, but that somehow made it seem more ordinary than the ribbons of twinkling lights in the darkness that had marked the city streets the last time I enjoyed this view.

"How do you imbue a living being?" I asked.

He swiveled toward me, surprise written in bold strokes across his features. "You do think big, don't you?"

I kept my gaze on the city.

He chuckled and turned back to the view. "It's impossible."

I frowned. Fae couldn't lie, and there didn't seem like a lot of wiggle room in that statement . . . but I'd changed myself with magic. Why wouldn't it work on others?

"Are you certain?"

"I've been around a long time. You really think I haven't tried? If I could rewrite people as I saw fit, I wouldn't have to worry about traitors and dissidents in my court."

I shuddered at the thought of Bael overriding people's natures to make them more malleable. Much as I wanted to change James, it was a good thing Bael didn't have that kind of power or I'd be settled into a room at the keep looking forward to a lifetime of baby-making in the hopes of producing an imbuer to be Bael's heir.

Maybe what happened inside me was a fluke. Or maybe it hadn't been imbuing at all. Maybe something else had affected the demon inside me.

I stepped back from the rail and bowed to Bael. "I'll take my leave of you now."

He nodded. "Keep thinking big. Ambition is one thing humans and fae have in common."

Grabbing Emma's hand, I pulled her back through the garden and through the door to the hall. Then I tipped my head back and sighed. I'd managed not to agree to Bael's hospitality, but I had no way back to the portal on my own.

"Shall I escort you to your rooms?" Rhoana stood at attention a few feet away. Either she'd overheard our conversation, or Bael had made it clear I'd be staying before we even spoke.

There was no way I was going to convince Rhoana to let me go back to the mortal realm if Bael had given her orders to the contrary. And if Bael said the earliest I could see Kai was tomorrow, she wouldn't take me to see him either. My muscles tensed in frustration. Bael would drag everything out, burning precious time to try to force me into accepting his deal to save May. He might not be able to change a person's nature, but he wasn't above manipulating those he couldn't command directly.

I'd never been so happy not to be sworn into his service.

"Well?" Rhoana tipped her head slightly to one side.

"Actually," I said. "I'd like to visit Mica."

Her eyes widened slightly. "Why?"

Summoning every bit of etiquette training I could remember, I pushed back my shoulders and lifted my chin. I might not have sworn loyalty to Enchantment, but as Bael's recognized descendant, I was a Lady of the Court.

"My business is my own," I said. "Lead the way, or I shall find another servant who can."

Rhoana stared for what felt like an eternity, surprise and anger burning in her eyes. Not only had I pulled rank on her, I'd also called into question her competence. But I'd learned from my previous mistakes. I'd been careful with my words. Even the Captain of the Guard couldn't ignore a direct command from a court noble. And I never actually said she didn't know the way. I'd only implied it.

A cold smile spread across Rhoana's lips. She bowed—a perfect, stiff bow. "This way, *Lady* Alyssandra."

MICA SAT ON A chair opposite the velvet couch Emma and I were sharing. His long, blond hair was tousled, and he wore only a loose teal robe that matched the marbled blue and green color of his silver-flecked eyes. The collar gaped open, revealing smooth, pale skin from his chest all the way to his belly button. An equally rumpled-looking Haru lounged on a sofa near the edge of Mica's sitting room.

Emma's gaze oscillated between Mica and me. Her brows were pulled tight, wrinkling her forehead. "Lemme get this straight. Your grandpa wants you to make a baby"—she hooked a thumb toward Mica—"with this guy?"

I nodded. "That's the long and short of it."

"And that's his price for freeing the kidnapped kids?" She shook her head and sagged against the cushions. "What kind of person uses a baby as a bargaining chip?"

Mica and I shared a look. Trying to pry a baby out of unwilling participants was the least of what Bael had done in his lifetime. He was responsible for the death of a world, the decimation of an entire race. A little blackmail was hardly noteworthy.

I set my hand on Emma's knee and waited until she met my gaze.

"I'll do what I can for May," I said, "but—"

"Don't." She narrowed her eyes. "Don't you think for a second that I'd expect you to . . . to . . ."

"Whore herself out?" Haru supplied. "Abandon a baby to a psychopath?"

Mica shot him a reprimanding look.

Haru had been sulking since Emma and I showed up at Mica's door—interrupting their reunion.

"We've got another option," I said. Maybe. Hopefully. Assuming Chase had found a way into Shedraziel's prison while I was wasting time with Bael. "But not if we're stuck here under house arrest. Do you think . . . ?" I raised my eyebrows and glanced out the window. Mica had helped me sneak into the dungeon on my last visit. He'd spent decades wandering these halls. If anyone knew a secret route out of the keep, it would be him.

Mica stroked his jaw, much as Bael had done when thinking. The gesture looked much more suitable on his more mature face, despite the fact that Bael was several centuries older. "I think it's time I visited my aunt."

He glanced at Haru, who rolled his eyes, stood, and stalked to the bedroom door.

I watched Haru's journey, frowning, then turned back to Mica when the bedroom door closed. "I thought you weren't allowed to leave the keep."

"Lord Bael prefers to keep me close, but he can't prevent me seeing my aunt from time to time." He smiled—a wolfish smile. "I'm her favorite relative."

"Um, didn't you tell me your aunt was . . . well . . ."

"Crazy?" He nodded. "Without a doubt. She's also the one person in any world Bael doesn't dare cross if he can help it. If I say Marron wants to meet you—"

"You can't lie."

He raised an eyebrow. "Trust me. Marron *does* want to meet you."

Wherever Marron lived, it had to be less well guarded than the keep. That should make sneaking away easier. Getting to the portal unobserved would be another obstacle . . . but one problem at a time. Besides, I was eager to meet Marron. She was, after all, the only living imbuer besides Bael and me. If Bael couldn't help me change James, maybe Marron could.

I looked at Emma, hoping she saw the wisdom of getting away

from Bael's influence. "We're not going to accomplish anything here."

She nodded, then looked at Mica. "Do you think your aunt—"

Mica raised a hand to block her question. "We'll talk later." His gaze flicked around the room, as though he was searching for something.

I pushed to my feet. "Then let's go."

HARU WAS WAITING at the gaala stables, once more in the form of a large white fox with seven red-tipped tails. His ears perked up at our approach, and he trotted over to Mica, brushing up against him like Chase sometimes did to me when in his cat form.

Mica dropped a hand and petted Haru's smooth fur. "All set?"

Haru flattened his ears and looked behind him, a low growl in his throat. I followed his gaze.

Three gaala stood in the courtyard, bridled and ready to ride. Rhoana stood between us and them.

My jaw tensed. How had she known? Was Mica's room bugged? Was that why he'd seemed reluctant to speak candidly?

"I understand you're taking a trip," she said, her gaze steady on Mica.

He smiled. "And you've come to see us off?"

She crossed her arms.

Mica matched her pose. "I'm going to visit my aunt. As you know, that's one of the privileges I'm still afforded."

"You're free to go." She pointed at me. "She's not."

"My aunt told me she wishes to meet her."

Rhoana narrowed her eyes.

"Surely Lord Bael would not disappoint his niece over something so small as an introduction to his granddaughter." Mica lifted his chin. "Or do you doubt my words?"

I stiffened. Fae couldn't lie, so calling him a liar would be the same as calling him a halfer—an impure mongrel. I'd learned that lesson the hard way the last time I was in Enchantment, and Kai was rotting in prison because of my slip.

"Then I shall accompany you." Rhoana's words ground out as though they were causing physical pain.

Mica relaxed, his expression becoming blankly cheerful once more, and strode to the lead gaala. "You're welcome to come along for the ride, but you'll have to wait outside." He swung onto the gaala and looked down at Rhoana with a smile that was all teeth. "You know how selective Marron is about her visitors."

Rhoana's jaw was so tight it seemed like her teeth should shatter. She stalked to the second gaala and climbed onto its back.

Emma and I shared the final beast. Once we were all seated, Haru launched into the air with graceful ease. The gaala followed.

Dusk fell over the realm as we soared above Abonaille Malmür. Lamps lit the city streets beneath my dangling feet. Then we crossed the edge of the cliff and the ground dropped away to the snow-blanketed forest far below. I gazed up at the two moons overhead as the first stars made their appearance in the night sky. Precious time was passing.

How much time had I wasted on Bael, believing he would do the right thing when presented with the evidence? I wouldn't make that mistake again.

Haru led us far to the left of the path we would have taken to the portal. After about twenty minutes, he dropped lower, skimming the treetops. The gaala followed. First Mica's, then mine. Rhoana brought up the rear.

A structure stuck up out of the forest ahead. It was still a mile or so off, but reflected moonlight allowed us to discern the shape of a crooked tower.

A break appeared in the trees, a snowy field shining bluish-white beneath the moons. Haru led us to it.

My gaala's hooves touched down on glittering snow, not even denting the surface. Emma slid off and sank into six inches of powder.

I looked around. The clearing we'd landed in was ringed in dense forest just like the one near the portal, but it was less than half the size.

"Does your aunt live in that tower I saw up ahead?" I asked.

"That's the one." Mica swung his leg over the gaala's back and dropped to the ground. He sank about a quarter-inch into the surface before gravity gave up. He waved for me to dismount as well.

I dropped next to Emma and frowned. The snow reached over the tops of my boots; my socks and pant legs would be soaked in moments. "It looked a long way off still. Why'd we land so far away?"

"You can't reach Marron's home directly." He glanced at Rhoana. "She doesn't like uninvited guests."

The guard captain sniffed. "I'll be at the portal while you conduct your visit." She reached into a pocket and lifted a glass marble about the size of her fist. "Send word to me when you're ready to return to the keep, and I shall come collect you." She narrowed her eyes first at Mica then at me. "Do *not* leave Marron's property without alerting me."

Mica smiled and waved, then turned and headed for the nearest edge of the clearing. Haru trotted by his side.

"Come on, Emma." I jerked my head toward the men—well, the sidhe and the kitsune—and started after them. She stuck to me like a shadow.

I glanced back once, after crossing the first line of trees, to see Rhoana glaring after me. I didn't look back again.

Chapter 16

MICA AND HARU wove easily between the tightldy packed trees, Mica on two legs, Haru on four. They sauntered along on top of the snow while we mere mortals had to plow through the drifts. Despite the late hour and the shadows cast by the towering trees, the moonlight reflecting on the snow cast more than enough light for even Emma's eyes. But the night, coupled with leaving the protection of the magically warmed city, brought a drop in temperature.

I shivered, and snuggled deeper into the fur-lined cloak Mica had given me before we left his rooms. Emma wore a similar piece of clothing, though hers was bright-blue lined with white while the one I'd taken was a simple tan and gray. Mica now wore a heavy, navy-blue tunic and dark-brown trousers, but he hadn't bothered with a coat. Haru's clothes were tucked in the bag Mica carried over his shoulder. Fae didn't seem to mind the cold.

Shortly after leaving Rhoana, Mica pulled to a stop, placed his hands on his hips, and tipped his head back with a noisy sigh. "Stars above, that woman scares me."

As I waded over to him, he pulled a small silver case from inside his shirt and scooped a fingerful of glittering dust into his mouth. The lines of tension around his eyes relaxed.

I glanced back the way we'd come. If Mica felt we were beyond Rhoana's hearing, it was probably safe to talk.

"You told Rhoana your aunt said she wants to meet me."

Mica glanced at me, a second dose of dust on its way to his mouth.

"But I was with you when you decided to say that. Your aunt wasn't. So how can it be true?"

Mica shrugged. "Aunt Marron told me years ago she wished she could meet an imbuer other than Bael." He snapped the silver case shut and tucked it back into his shirt. "And here you are."

"What if Rhoana had asked for specifics?"

"After I accused her of doubting me? She had no choice but to drop it or insult my honor." He frowned. "You've seen firsthand how that can turn out."

I looked away, trying not to picture Kai in his stone cell.

Emma blew a puff of warm breath into her hands and shifted her feet in the snow. "How much farther to your aunt's house?"

Mica started walking again. "Not much."

After twenty minutes of trudging through snow, my toes were numb, along with the tips of my ears and nose.

"Here we are." Mica stopped and spread his arms, blocking our advance. "Stay back. You don't want to get within reach of those vines."

I squinted into the shadows beyond Mica's arm. The snow ended abruptly at a wall of bright-green vines that blocked our path. The barrier stood about eight feet high, stretching from tree trunk to tree trunk like fencing between posts. Each vine was as thick as my wrist and twined so tightly with its neighbors I couldn't see any way through. Unlike the trees around us, the living wall was oddly clear of snow.

In the distance, the lopsided tower I'd seen earlier rose above the vegetation. The tower itself was little more than a silhouette against the bruised sky, but orange light shone from tiny windows, illuminating rough-hewn stone and giving the structure shape. It still seemed a long way off.

"How do we get through?" I asked.

Mica extended his arms before him, palms out, and took a step forward.

The mass of vines began to writhe.

Emma gasped.

I took a step back.

Dozens of vines uncoiled from the wall, snapping back and forth like loose rigging in a storm.

Haru flattened his ears and whined. He stayed well back from the lashing whips.

Mica took another step forward.

"Are you crazy?" I reached out, thinking to pull him back, but he stepped out of reach.

Fast as a flash, a snaking green tendril whipped out and drew a thin red line across one of Mica's exposed palms.

He flinched and hissed, but held his ground. Blood welled from his broken skin.

The attacking vine curled back toward its base, its tip smeared with liquid like a pen dipped in ink. As it retreated, the other vines parted to reveal a bright-red bloom with triangular petals. The red-tipped vine slid over the flower, depositing Mica's blood on a tuft of purplish filaments at the center of the blossom.

As the tongue-like vine wiped itself clean, the entire mass seemed to shudder—a ripple that spread from the blood-stained blossom, through the wall, and beyond my field of vision. As the ripple passed, the vines settled down, coiling back into their brethren and falling dormant. Within moments, the forest was still and silent once more.

I took a tentative step forward. "Are you—"

Mica lifted a hand. Blood still streaked his palm. "Stay where you are."

There was a creak of wood and a scraping noise, as though someone was forcing a door open in a too-tight frame. Then a streak of warm, orange light spilled across the snow.

We all turned to the right.

A ragged section of trunk had swung open in a nearby oak tree, revealing a slice of another place. A fire burned merrily in a soot-streaked hearth. Books and scrolls lined shelves on the walls and stood in haphazard piles on the floor. The smell of cloves drifted out.

Then a shadow blocked the cozy scene, resolving into a person with wild, pink hair and thin arms and legs sticking out of what looked like a dozen tattered blankets sewn together.

"Kane!" A woman whose voice was at least an octave higher than mine rushed across the glowing snow and cupped Mica's face in her hands. She had to stand on tiptoes to reach. "The night is cool and dry. Shall we hide beneath the heather and keep each other warm?"

Mica gently pulled the woman's hands away. "I'm Kane's son, Aunt Marron. Mica. Remember?"

I stared wide-eyed at the new fae. The hope that had been growing in my chest twisted into bitter ropes around my lungs. Despite what Mica had said, I'd assumed Marron would be at least a little useful. But if she couldn't even recognize her nephew . . .

Marron settled back on her heels, tipped her head to one side, and frowned. Then a light sparked in her lavender eyes and her smile sprang back in place. "Mica! How good of you to visit." She looked around. "But what are you and your friends doing out here? Come in, come in." She made a "come" motion with both hands and backed into the tree she'd stepped out of.

Mica rubbed one hand over the back of his neck and glanced at me. Then gestured to the glowing tree. "After you."

Crossing the threshold was like passing from one world to another. Snow dripped off my boots onto a polished wood floor. Heat pressed against my cheeks and thawed my fingers back to tingling sensation as I left the frozen night behind. Emma pressed in behind me, and I stepped to the side and bumped into a thick couch with faded green fabric half-buried in papers. On the far side of the room, a colorful rug lay in front of the merrily crackling fire. To my left sat a long, irregularly shaped wooden table. Bark lined its edges. The surface was buried in books.

Behind me, glowing snow twinkled under the double moons, the image hanging in space like it had been cut from a different scene and inserted into Marron's living room. I peeked around the hole in space. The cluttered but cozy room continued as if unbroken by the doorway when seen from the other side.

I returned to an angle where I could see the forest we'd left. A gust of frosty air snuck through on Mica's heels as he joined the rest of us. Then the snowy scene winked out of existence and all I could see around me were the walls of Marron's tower. Dark windows dotted the stones, but I didn't see a single door.

"Guests, guests!" Marron clapped her hands. "It's been so long since I've had guests."

Now that she was fully illuminated by the fire, I could make out more details about our hostess. She wore a young body, similar in features to Bael, but lines creased the skin around her eyes and mouth. What I'd taken for stitched-together blankets at first glance was actually a dress made of layers of other garments all Frankensteined together. There were at least four different skirts, two shirts, and what looked like an evening gown. The outfit flared and fluttered as she spun around the room like a top.

She paused for a moment to squint at Haru, who'd shifted back to his two-legged form and was pulling a loose, white shirt over his head. "Such a fuzzy fellow." She frowned. "Why so cold?" Then she was off and dancing again.

I cleared my throat. "Can we talk freely here?"

Mica nodded and dropped to the fireside rug. "We left Bael's eyes and ears at the barrier."

"Good. We—"

Marron came to an abrupt stop with her nose less than an inch from my own.

Startled, I tried to back up, but my legs hit the couch and buckled. I fell onto the green cushions, scattering a pile of papers to the floor.

Marron looked down at me with lavender eyes. Ebony specks drifted in that sea of purple, moving more like snowflakes in a haphazard wind than the uniform spiral I'd grown accustomed to among the sidhe. She leaned in, bracing against the armrest, until she'd once more invaded my personal space.

"Nameless child," she said. "You have a question."

I frowned. "More than one, actually."

She shook her head. "It burns inside you like a light."

I blinked. "I did have a question about imbuing . . . but—"

"Ask it."

I glanced at Mica, who shrugged. I licked my lips. "Can you use imbuing to change a person's nature?"

"Not according to the king." She smiled. "But a king is not a god."

She did a back flip and landed lightly on her hands. Her pink hair stood on end, and her skirts bunched up around her chest. A striped stocking covered one spindly leg, while the other was bare.

"It's a matter of perspective." She resumed her dance around the room, walking on her hands with no more effort than she had her feet.

I sagged. She was bonkers after all.

She righted herself, pushing back the hair that curtained her face. "Objects don't care about the past or the future. They are what they are in the moment. But people . . ." She tapped the side of her head. "The king would make a soulless golem, and who wants to be that? People remember who they were and who they want to be. You can't change one without knowing both."

I sat up straighter. "So it *is* possible, if you know both who someone is and who they want to turn into?"

Marron started humming and skipped over to the large wooden table. She hopped on top and settled cross-legged among the books.

"Um . . . Marron?"

She continued to hum as she tore a page from one of the books and folded it into an origami butterfly. She seemed to have forgotten we were there.

I turned to Mica. "What is she—?"

He shook his head. "You're lucky to have gotten what you did. She's rarely so lucid."

Emma pulled a rickety-looking rocking chair closer to the fire and settled in it with a creak. She stared into the flames, wringing her hands. Was she thinking about May?

I watched Marron for another moment, then turned my attention back to the task at hand. "Can we reach the mortal realm from here?"

"Without a doubt," Mica said. "But you heard Rhoana. The portal you came through will be guarded. It might be wise to choose a different crossing point. There's one a little ways to the east of here that's not likely to be watched."

"Because it comes out in Ohio," Haru said, joining Mica on the rug.

Emma frowned. "How can that be right? Ohio is halfway across the country."

"This realm is smaller than ours," I said. I'd recently learned quite a lot about fae realms from history lessons with my tutors, Kai and Hortense. "Walk for an hour here and cross over; end up on the other side of the world back home." I turned back to Mica. "But we need to come out in Colorado to meet up with Chase."

Mica glanced at Haru, but the kitsune pretended to be absorbed by the patterns in the rug. "Is he the 'other option' you mentioned?"

I nodded. "Chase was scouting Shedraziel's prison while I spoke with Bael." I smiled bitterly. "He wasn't particularly hopeful about my chances of securing help."

"Because he's not an idiot," Haru muttered.

I ignored the gibe. "With any luck, he'll have found a way into Shedraziel's prison."

"Getting into her realm is the least of your worries." Mica said. "Have you considered what you'll face inside?"

I braced my hands on my knees and tried to quell the sea of dread sloshing around my insides. "Bael's general from the Faerie Wars, Shedraziel."

Haru crossed his arms and glared at me. "You say her name so lightly."

"She's no simple fae," Mica added. "Not only was she Bael's general during the war against humanity, she was strong enough to be a lord in her own right, and I don't imagine a few hundred years of imprisonment has dulled her much."

I slumped back against the couch. "What choice do I have?" I raised a hand. "And don't say I should give Bael a baby."

Mica shook his head. "I'm no more inclined to provide him an heir than you are, but if you're going to face Shedraziel, you'll need more than pluck and grit."

I sank deeper into the cushion. I'd lost my light-imbued knife during the raid on Crossroads. Of course, that didn't mean I was defenseless. As I'd learned in my fight with O'Connell, magic could form a blade as readily as steel. But I wasn't eager to repeat the forging process—calling that much magic seemed to draw the attention of every demon in the Rift.

I shivered, remembering the chorus of voices, the sensation of incorporeal beings prodding my defenses, slithering inside me on the trickle of magic I so desperately needed.

"I'll need a weapon."

Haru snorted. "A blade will do you little good against one of the finest swordsmen in any realm."

I rolled my eyes. "If you don't have anything useful to say—"

"Haru's right," Mica said. "You'd never get close enough to use a blade. Shedraziel could enthrall your heart with no more than the power of her voice."

The Shifter Lord had said something similar—that I wouldn't stand a chance against Shedraziel's enchantments as I was.

"Stealth is your best option," Mica said. "A direct confrontation would be the worst-case scenario."

"Hope for the best; prepare for the worst," I muttered. A tight ache twisted in my chest. That had been one of Uncle Sol's favorite sayings. Had he made it clear of the PTF before Harris closed in? I had to assume he had. Sol was the kind of guy who had contingency plans for his contingency plans. Either way, I had bigger concerns at the moment. "The Shifter Lord said Shedraziel could enthrall 'lesser' fae." I raised my chin. "Would having a name protect me from her enchantment?"

Mica and Haru both went stiff.

When I first learned about fae true names, Hortense told me those names made their bearers more powerful. They also made the fae uniquely vulnerable to anyone who learned their true name, and they were *not* easy to get. She refused to elaborate on what kind of trial fae went through to acquire their true names, but she'd made it clear not everyone survived the ordeal.

Marron stopped humming. Her hands where frozen partway through folding a piece of paper. The corners of her mouth twitched up. Then she said in a sing-song voice, "Dance the path of shadows and flame to find your heart and lose your name."

Mica looked at her. "Actually, she's trying to *find* a name. Any advice?"

Marron resumed her humming. The torn paper in her hands became a tiny fox.

Emma looked at each of us like she'd just missed the punchline of a joke. "Alex, you already have a name. A couple, in fact, if you consider that Alex is short for Alyssandra."

I stared down at my hands bunched in my lap. "I mean a fae name. A *true* name."

"The kind used in binding spells?" Her eyes grew wide. "Can halfers even get those?"

We both looked at Mica.

He shrugged. "Anyone with fae blood can take the test. Whether or not they can pass . . ." He shrugged again.

"*If* I managed to get a name, would that make me strong enough to withstand Shedraziel's enchantments?"

Mica frowned. "I've no way of knowing how much a true name would bolster the strength of a . . ."—he waved a hand at me—"less than pure fae. It *might* be enough."

"It might not," added Haru.

"Prepare for the worst," I said. "If we don't manage to sneak past her, questionable protection is better than no protection at all. If I get Jedi mind-wiped right away, none of this will do May any good." I glanced at Emma, then back to Mica. "How long does the test usually take?"

"The naming trial takes place outside of time," he said. "Pass or fail, *if* you return, it will be like you never left."

Finally, a piece of good news. "How do I reach the trial?"

"If the Shifter Lord sent you in Shedraziel's direction . . ." Mica looked at Haru. "Any chance she'd open the way?"

Haru shook his head. "I don't presume to know what the traitor lord is up to these days, but the shifters can't risk pissing off Enchantment. They'll play it safe and hope someone else solves their problem for them."

Traitor lord? I tucked that piece of information aside for a later time. "Don't either of you have true names?" I asked.

Mica frowned. "We both do."

"Then why can't you show me how to get one?"

"There are only a handful of fae in each realm capable of opening the path to the testing ground." Mica lifted his palms. "Alas, I'm not one of them."

No way Bael would back me taking the test. Not when it could mean losing his best shot at birthing a new imbuer. I glanced at Marron. She now had a dozen paper animals lined up in front of her. I wasn't sure I wanted to walk any path she opened for me. Who knew where I might end up?

"Could Hortense do it?" My tutor had been unbearably strict in her lectures, but she'd proven willing to help me beyond memorizing texts and practicing etiquette.

Haru propped his elbows on his knees. "Even if she could, the court tutor is loyal to her lord. No one sworn to the Lord of Enchantment will undermine his wishes for you."

I frowned. "Then why are you two helping me?"

Haru waved the question away. "I'm currently unaffiliated."

I looked at Mica.

"I'm bored."

Emma pinned him with an incredulous look. "Seriously?"

He shrugged. "I've been stuck in Abonaille Malmür since I was a kid, shuffled into a corner and forgotten when it became clear I was unfit to be Bael's heir." He spread his arms. "This is the most distracting development to come my way in decades. How could I pass up being a part of it?"

"And the fact that you get to stick it to Bael without acting directly against him?" I asked.

He smiled. "That would be reason number two."

I didn't think Mica's reasons were as straightforward as he made them out to be, but since he seemed to be my only ally in the Court of Enchantment at the moment, I wasn't going to push.

I fiddled with the frayed end of the black ribbon wrapped around my wrist. "Could the shadow walker Galen open a path to the naming test?"

Haru raised an eyebrow. "And how would a little thing like you know a name like that?"

"Could he?" I pressed.

Mica nodded. "Without a doubt. But not from here. The heir of the Shadow Realm coming to Enchantment would stir up all kinds of trouble."

I stood up. "Then it's time to head back to the mortal realm. I've got a test to take."

"How?" Emma asked. "You heard the scary lady. She's going to be guarding the portal."

"To keep me from sneaking out," I said, grinning as a new idea began to take root. I looked at Mica. "But what if she's the one sending me through?"

Chapter 17

"QUIT FIDGETING," Haru said.

"It itches." I scrunched my nose, hating the way my skin crinkled. It felt like I was wearing an inch-thick layer of makeup over my whole body.

Mica continued to mumble barely audible phrases in a language I didn't know. His hands skimmed over my clothes, tracing my body. A faint glow lit his teal eyes, and the silver sparkles there swirled like dust in a sandstorm.

"Done." He dropped his hands to his sides. A sheen of sweat stood out on his face.

Emma stepped up to me, her eyes wide. "This is so creepy," she said, stepping around to see me from the side.

Mica gestured to a mirror hanging nearby. "What do you think?"

I stepped up to the mirror. Emma stood at my side. Looking back at us were two identical copies of Emma Yamada. Hair, face, clothes, even the pattern of creases around her narrow, brown eyes.

"That's incredible." I raised a hand to my throat. Even my voice was different. I turned to Mica. "But will it fool Rhoana?"

My plan for getting back to the mortal realm was simple enough. Bael wanted me to stay in Enchantment, but he'd made it clear he didn't care about Emma. She was free to leave. Only *she* would be *me*. But my whole plan hinged on Mica's enchantment abilities. If Rhoana saw through my disguise, we'd be toast, and Mica and I would be sharing a cell with Kai for the foreseeable future.

"The enchantment covers every trace of your fae blood. An *imbuer* could still tell the difference,"—he glanced at Marron—"but that shouldn't be a problem. There aren't any enchanters among Rhoana's knights strong enough to match me."

"I don't like this plan," Haru said. He was still sitting on the rug.

I turned to him. "You don't think it will work?"

"I didn't say that. Mica's magic is stronger than most."

I frowned. "Then what's the problem?"

Mica crossed his arms. "Don't tell me you're still sulking."

"I'm not sulking. I just don't particularly like the idea of playing chaperone on a naive girl's suicidal quest."

"I can't leave," Mica said. "And she needs a guide."

Assuming I passed my test and got a name, the plan was to reenter Enchantment through the unguarded portal in the Ohio reservation. Chase could get me to Ohio via a short detour through the Shifter Realm, but we needed someone who knew where the Enchantment portal was on the other side or there was no point.

"Besides," Mica added. "You agreed to stay with Alex until I said otherwise."

Haru and Mica stared at each other for a long moment. Finally, Haru looked away. "And I will, but I never agreed to be happy about it."

Marron's high-pitched laugh jolted our attention to the table where she'd been making her paper creations. As I turned, the army of tiny paper creatures burst to life. Origami birds and butterflies swarmed around us. Animals and insects surged across the floor and along the walls. A paper wing sliced the back of my hand as I flailed to keep the animated paper away from my face. The others were shouting in the chaos, waving their arms like I was to protect themselves. Then Marron was suddenly at my side, her fingers like steel around my arm.

"You already suspect, but you don't know. Don't be afraid little girl. He's a hypocrite."

She was gone before I had time to blink.

The paper creations continued past us, and the flames in the fireplace crackled and danced as the first creatures threw themselves on the pyre. In less than a minute, the room was empty of all but the five of us. Every last animal Marron had imbued to life had burned.

"Like moths to the flame." Firelight flickered in Marron's eyes as she stared sadly at the drifting ashes of her paper army.

Haru clapped his hands. "And on that cheerful note, as the mortals say, 'Let's get this party started.'"

Mica pulled his gaze away from the fire. He reached for the pocket containing his little silver case, paused, and dropped his hand back to his side. Then he stepped in front of the mirror Emma and I had used to compare.

"Stay quiet," he said. Then he waved a hand over the glass. Hazy smoke curled beneath its surface. After a moment, the smoke resolved into Rhoana's face.

"That was fast," she said. "Are you ready to return?"

"Alex isn't headed back to the keep just yet, but her human companion is eager to move on. Haru will bring her to you and escort her back to the mortal realm." He swiped his hand in front of the mirror again and the smoke cleared, taking Rhoana's face with it.

He turned to me. "The enchantment will break as soon as you pass through the portal. *Don't* let Rhoana or any of her guards accompany you."

I nodded and turned to Emma. "I'll see you soon. We're going to get May back."

She gave me a hug so tight my vertebra popped, then stepped back, her face grim.

Mica closed his eyes and muttered something. The glowing outline of a door appeared in the middle of the room. "Good luck," he said, and swung the door open.

I glanced back at Marron, who'd resumed her seat atop the cluttered table. Loose leather bindings with the remains of torn pages were piled around her. Her lavender gaze locked onto me, but her expression was empty.

Disappointment settled heavily around my heart. It seemed Bael was the only viable option for magic training after all.

I followed Haru through the doorway, back into the snowy night. The warm glow of the fireplace cut off behind me. I turned to see the rough bark of a solid tree trunk.

"Come on." Haru shoved a wad of fabric against my chest when I turned to him. "Don't talk if you can help it." He lifted a finger threateningly. "And don't squeeze me too tight."

I frowned. "Why would I squeeze you?"

Haru shifted to his fox form, but rather than shrinking like he usually did, he grew larger. He grew and grew until his furry, white shoulder was even with my face. Then he swung a muzzle full of finger-length teeth in my direction and blew a puff of hot air into my face.

I took a step back.

Haru dropped onto his belly. His Mediterranean blue gaze bore into me as if to say, "I'm waiting. . . ."

I took a tentative step forward and set my hand against Haru's side. His fur was soft, but cold.

He snorted again, and nudged me in the side with his nose.

"Okay, okay, I'm moving." I straddled his back and lay flat against his spine with his clothes pinned between us. Then I wrapped my arms around his neck.

Once I was settled, Haru lifted off the snow. He wasn't as wide, or as comfortable, as the gaala had been. His ribs shifted against my knees with each breath. Haru's muscles bunched beneath me. I tightened my grip, careful to stop short of "squeezing." Then Haru launched into the air.

The rocking motion of his body was more pronounced than the smooth rhythm of the gaala, and I found myself jerking alternately against his shoulders and hips. His legs bunched and stretched, gobbling up the night as the forest passed below.

I glanced back once, but Marron's tower was already shrinking in the distance, distinguishable only by a single orange window near the top.

The trip from Marron's to the clearing with the portal took barely five minutes, but my face was completely frozen by the time Haru's feet touched down in front of Rhoana. Three guards stood behind her. Two were sidhe whose dark complexions made them nearly invisible in the night, and one was a short green creature I thought might be a goblin. He had spindly arms attached to a compact body, a wide mouth, and small, close-set eyes.

I slid off Haru's side, sinking ankle-deep in the snow once more.

Rhoana glanced at the trees around us, then strode forward. She slid her gaze down to my toes, then back up to my face.

I hugged Haru's clothes tighter and tried not to squirm under her inspection. Would Mica's enchantment be enough? Even if she believed I was Emma, would she let me go?

"I can spare one man to escort you through the reservation." Rhoana's green cape swished as she turned back toward the portal.

Haru nudged me with his nose.

"That won't be necessary," I said. "Haru has agreed to guide me."

Rhoana glanced back at us, shrugged, and continued toward the portal. "Suit yourself."

The other guards stepped away from the two trees that marked the crossover point to the mortal realm. They continued to scan the trees around us. I really hoped Chase had already gone back.

Haru met my gaze, then stepped through the portal first. It was a risk, but if I really was the full-blooded human I was pretending to be, it wouldn't be safe for me to step onto the reservation alone.

As Haru's tails disappeared in the empty space between the trees, I stepped forward, risked one last satisfied glance at Rhoana, and crossed the portal.

"THAT'S A TERRIBLE plan!" Chase paced wall to wall in the cramped storm cellar. While Nell had removed the ward on the cellar upon my return so James could exit, Otis had refused to let a vampire back in the house, so we were all crammed in his hidey-hole under the way station. At least Haru had shrunk back to human proportions. "Do you have any idea how hard it is to get a name? There's a reason most fae don't attempt it until their second century, if then."

"Do you have a better idea?"

Chase waved at James. "Would you please talk some sense into her?"

James stroked a thumb over my knuckles, tracing the ridges and valleys of my skin. We sat side by side on the blanket bed I'd made for him. We'd barely spared time for a quick kiss before I launched into my explanation of what happened in Enchantment, but he hadn't released my hand since I arrived, and the steady reassurance of his presence gave me strength.

"From what I understand of the fae naming test, it *is* dangerous and not everyone comes back." James met Chase's gaze. "But if Alex believes it's necessary, she has my support."

Chase rolled his eyes with a groan and turned his focus back to me. "And if you fail your trial? Who will save Emma's sister then?"

I stared evenly into his wide green eyes. "You will."

He crossed his arms and turned away.

I gave James's hand a quick kiss, then pushed to my feet. "If anything happens to me, either before or during the prison break, I'm counting on you and Haru to get the children out."

"You shouldn't count on Haru," Chase said. "Use him as a guide if you must, but don't put lives in his hands."

Haru growled, a deep sound that shouldn't have come from a human chest. "At least I don't throw lives away for worthless causes."

"You know the odds this time," Chase said, "the goals and the stakes. So what are you even still doing here?"

Haru looked away. "I made a promise."

"Since when did that stop you from leaving?"

Haru and Chase bared their teeth at each other, both snarling.

"Enough." I stepped between them. "You two can have a pissing contest once this is over, but Emma and Mica can't cross into Shedraziel's realm, and James is stuck here on Earth. You two are the only backup I've got, so get your shit together."

Haru blinked and looked at Chase, his expression more confused than angry. "It's like being told off by an infant."

Chase nodded. "But she's right."

"Now that that's settled . . ." I returned to my seat next to James, whose expression was strangely shuttered.

"Everything okay?" I whispered as I sat down.

He nodded. "Just . . . thinking."

I prodded at our link, but he'd erected a wall to guard his thoughts. Frowning, I unwound the black ribbon on my wrist.

James set his hand on my arm, stilling me. "What if I could offer an alternative? Or at the very least, better odds?"

I frowned. "What do you mean?"

"You're willing to risk your life for your friends. I'm willing to risk mine for you." His fingers tightened on my arm. "Let's attempt to change me, so that I can accompany you."

I gaped, my mouth hanging open. "I. . . . There are still a lot of uncertainties."

"There always are in life. But you're not just headed into Enchantment to speak with Bael this time. You're sneaking into the prison of a powerful, and arguably insane, fae general, and your only support is a pair of quarreling buffoons." He gestured to Chase and Haru, who both looked as though they wanted to argue, but were cut off as James continued. "There's no way I'm staying behind this time. Not if there's any chance I can go with you."

I stared down at the ribbon in my hands. "I'll still need a name if I'm to be of any use against Shedraziel."

"And I won't stop you. But if you can risk changing to protect those you love, so can I."

I chewed at my lower lip. Having James by my side would certainly make me feel better, and there was no doubt another able-bodied person would increase our chances of rescuing May and the other kids. Though I couldn't shake the feeling I'd somehow pressured James into making this decision. And of course, there was no guarantee it would work.

"Bael seems to think imbuing living beings is impossible," I said. "But Marron suggested it could be done, if I know both who a person is and who they want to become." I shifted so I was facing James directly. "Who do you want to be, James?"

His mouth pressed tight and turned down. His brow crinkled in thought. "If possible, I would like to change just enough to pass the fae wards against vampires. I do not wish to lose my speed, strength, or ability to heal, but I'd love not to have to drink blood or avoid exposure to the sun."

I smirked. "So you want all the good parts of being a vampire without any of the bad ones."

He shrugged. "You asked."

I wound and unwound the silky ribbon around my fingers, staring at the slick fabric. "If we're going to attempt this, we should do it before I go into my trial. . . . We might not get another chance." I re-wrapped the ribbon around my wrist and tucked up the ends. "At least if I don't make it back, I'll know May has both you and Chase to save her."

"Don't even joke about that." James pulled me into a hug. "Now I'm tempted to say we should wait till you get back."

"Nope." I planted a kiss on his cheek and pulled back. "It's now or never."

He frowned. "You really like that saying. It's almost never true."

"Think of it as an expression of mortal mentality."

Chase, who still seemed sullen about being called a buffoon, was pacing near the cellar entrance. "Messing with magic you don't understand is a bad idea."

"By that logic, I should never do *any* magic," I countered. I turned back to James. "You sure about this?"

"Not in the least," he said. "But in the spirit of mortal mentality, let's do it anyway."

Chapter 18

I MOVED SO I WAS kneeling in front of James, his legs extended to either side of me. "Just relax."

I licked my lips and tried to follow my own advice. I'd been the one to suggest attempting this in the first place, but now that I was faced with actually *doing* it. . . . I felt like a doctor in an operating room, about to perform open heart surgery with only a child's drawing of a heart for reference.

Cool fingers cupped my cheeks. James pressed his forehead to mine. "Whatever happens," he whispered, "I will not blame you. *I* am choosing to take this risk."

I pressed my lips to his, savoring the sensation, the taste and smell of him. Then I sat back on my ankles and linked my fingers with his, resting our joined hands on his thighs. "Here goes."

I unfocused my eyes, following our connection deep inside him.

"Do you have any idea what you're doing?" Haru's voice broke my concentration.

I ground my teeth. "Everyone, be quiet."

I took a deep breath and tried again.

When I found the tangled knot of pulsing threads at James's core, I reached for my magic. What came to me was a rush of fear and doubt. My emotions were the gatekeepers to my magic. I'd have to deal with them first.

Tightening my grip on James's hands, I opened myself to my worries. Fear drenched me, seeping through every pore.

An image of smoky features and grinning fangs filled my mind. I hadn't seen a demon since the night O'Connell died . . . the night I killed him. I shuddered. I'd avoided doing any serious magic since then, afraid of what might be waiting for me when I did. For small things, the smoke didn't roll in, the demons didn't come. But what I was attempting now was no small thing.

And even if the demons didn't come, what if I failed? What if I changed James in some unforeseen way? What if I couldn't control my magic?

We cannot know what will happen until we try. James's voice was a warm caress inside my skull. *I am with you . . . always.*

Squeezing his hands until I imagined I could feel bones grinding, I pressed my forehead to his knuckles, closed my eyes, and pulled at my magic once more.

This time, the response was immediate. Ribbons of warm, pulsing, magic coursed through me on waves of fear, doubt . . . and hope.

I began separating the silver strands of James's essence, the foundation of what made him a vampire, tracing them back to their source. Then I wrapped loops of rosy magic around the knot of shimmering shadow from which the silver tendrils anchored in James seemed to spread. To make the change, I had to get past that shadowy shell to the core.

The shadow stirred. Sweat prickled across my skin and my hairs stood on end. The thing inside James had no face, no eyes, yet I could swear it was watching me.

I prodded the shadow, and the shadow pushed back. Some of my loops snapped. The silver ribbons snaked further, digging deeper.

James's breath sped up, coming quick and shallow. His hands were cold and clammy. His nostrils flared. Thick tendons strained in his neck and jaw.

My mouth went dry. Did the demon know what I was doing? Would it try to stop me?

I had to hit it all at once, now. I needed more magic.

Gritting my teeth, I sucked in a deep breath and tried to remember how I'd called the magic outside my body when I'd been fighting O'Connell. I'd been running mostly on adrenaline and instinct then. This time, I had to think.

I latched onto the tingle on the surface of my skin that indicated magic, and invited it inside. A little trickle at first, then more and more. I struggled to control the flow, to take what I needed without drowning in the excess.

Color washed out of the world, save for the mix of red and blue streams inside me and the vibrant silver strands of the demon inside James. Then the fog rolled in, thin at first, just a hazing of my vision. But it grew darker, and thicker. It began to take form.

I poured the combined magic inside me through my connection with James, slamming it into the shadow over his heart.

James grunted and jerked. His breath hissed between clenched teeth. His blood was on fire. The echo of his pain came back along our bond, but muted. He was holding it back, trying to protect me.

Let it go. I funneled more magic into the writhing silver nest, trying to pry it open.

The first demon took shape to my right. A frightful mask of tusks and burning eyes. Smears of smoke streaked like an afterimage when it moved.

"She's back," it hissed.

"She couldn't stay away," another said, loping closer on apelike arms.

Dozens of faces appeared in the smoke. Some with bodies, some without. Every mouth echoed the same word. "Welcome."

I cringed away from the demons, holding tighter to James's hands. The magic faltered. Silver pushed back against purple, stretching and straining.

No. I pushed harder, squeezing the silvery mass with my magic, looking for a chink in its armor.

"You aren't strong enough," the demons said.

"You don't know what you're doing."

"You're going to kill him."

"Let us help."

No! I could feel the demons pressing close, prodding the spaces where the magic flowed into me. I slapped invisible hands over the breaches, plugging holes and opening new ones in a frantic game of whack-a-mole as I tried to keep the flow of magic steady while barring entrance to the demons who sought to possess me.

"We could make you like him," they said in a chorus of voices that came from everywhere and nowhere.

"You could live forever."

"Be together forever."

The silvery threads bucked and twisted under the onslaught of my magic. James spasmed, his body going rigid. Then my magic pierced the shell of darkness around James's demon and poured inside. I followed, diving deeper. This was where the demon lived. The secret part of James I'd never seen. This was where I needed to make the change.

James thrashed like he was in the throes of a seizure, and I clung to him, desperate to keep the connection. He grunted and growled—animal noises made by a cornered beast. I couldn't see the color of his eyes since they were scrunched shut, his whole face pinched with pain, but I guessed they were more silver than blue.

Images flashed through my mind as I plunged deeper into James's subconscious. Crying children, burning buildings, blood dripping from broken bodies, a series of accusing eyes as faces flashed past.

James opened his mouth and screamed, the sound tearing out of his throat.

I continued to push, nudging the darkness in James closer to the surface, twisting the pieces of him together like a braid, then smoothing them until the seams disappeared. Patches of silver faded into the background of James's core, not gone, but hidden, camouflaged. My plan was working.

Another series of images flashed past, and every silver barb anchored in James's soul twisted, shredding him.

James screamed again, a sustained note that scraped my nerves. He bucked and struggled beneath me as I pinned him with my body. His mind pushed against our bond, trying to force me out.

The demons bombarded my defenses, clawing at my skin, wriggling past my barricades. They were in my head now.

"You're killing him."

"You'll fail."

"He'll die."

"Murderer."

Hang on, I begged. *Just a little longer.*

I continued to twist the core of silver threads, watching the changes sweep out along the trailing tendrils. But I was fighting on two fronts, and losing both. Silver drops seeped from James's core where I'd buried them beneath the surface, oozing like blood from a shallow wound. Where they emerged, healthy tissue turned black and fell to ash.

James was breaking apart, rejecting the union body and soul. He was going to tear himself to pieces.

I'd failed.

With a shriek of guilt and frustration, I tore my hands free of James and pushed away from him. I scrambled across the cellar floor, panting and sobbing. I slammed doors over every place where the magic poured in and felt a snap of whiplash as the threads tore free.

James continued to spasm. His teeth clenched in a solid grimace through which only a guttural hiss escaped. His body was out of balance. The demon taint was reasserting itself, trying to take over while James struggled to contain it. If he couldn't . . .

My chest constricted. I pressed both fists over my heart. I couldn't breathe. Couldn't think.

I can't lose him. I can't . . . I. . . . I took everything I was feeling, packed it tight, and shot it like a blazing bullet along our connection, straight at James's heart.

Fight!

His eyes snapped open—twin pools of liquid silver. The demon was awake. But a flicker of blue flashed through those mercury eyes.

Help me. James's thought was weak, desperate.

How could I help? I'd caused this mess by mucking about inside James when I didn't know what I was doing. What if whatever I tried next just made things worse?

James's eyes flashed blue again, but the color was quickly drowned out.

Shifting my focus, I watched the battle rage between James and his demon. On the surface, he was a statue, locked in anguish. Inside, flesh burned and reknit, strings of silver writhed along veins and strangled organs. Pulsing blue light pushed back against a swarming mass of silver-lined darkness. James's two natures were fighting for dominance in a way they probably hadn't since his induction as a vampire. And James was losing.

He needed more energy to fight, energy I could give him. But feeding him would feed the demon, too. I bit my lip till it bruised. I had to do *something*.

Moving to kneel in front of James once more, I tore open the collar of his shirt and pressed my hands flat to his chest. His skin was cold and slick with sweat.

I sent energy through our link. Not the chaotic, borrowed magic of the demons, but the steady crimson glow that rested at my core. The energy passed out of me and into him, adding a rosy presence to the silver and blue battle waging within.

Sharpening my focus, I shaped that warm glow into a wall and used it to hold back the demon where it threatened to overtake the cool blue light.

I'm here. I sent my reassurance into James, as he'd done for me countless times. *I'm with you.*

The blue pulses near James's core surged. Together, we pushed back the silver-slick shadow until it was once more contained—a waiting ball of malice. The silver vines stopped writhing, settling in place where they were.

I blinked, and met the watery gaze of icy blue eyes.

James smiled. Then his eyes slid closed. His head fell back against the wall with a dull *thunk*.

I could still see the damage from what I'd done. James's body was burned and scarred on the inside, though his exterior was as smooth and beautiful as ever. "I'm sorry."

He rolled his head from side to side. "My fault." His voiced was cracked and hoarse. "I didn't realize . . . when you said you had to know me . . ."

I considered the way James had tried to push me out when his memories were exposed. Had he been hiding something from me? Was that why the change hadn't worked? Or had I simply lost control of my magic under the onslaught of the demons and my own split focus?

Whatever the case, James wouldn't be crossing a fae portal anytime soon.

"PTF raids, experimental magic, prison breaks. . . . Is this what all your exploits are like?" Haru asked. "If so, it's a miracle any of you are still alive."

I glared at the mouthy kitsune. Not that he was wrong. But, if I hadn't been willing to take risks, there'd still be a murderous PTF agent assassinating halfers. A sadistic vampire lord would still be calling the shots in Denver, and James would be locked in a light-lined coffin for eternity.

And maybe Oz would still be alive and Kai wouldn't be facing fifty years in a fae dungeon. . . .

I sighed and set a hand over my cramped, growling stomach. "Any chance one of you could convince Nell to give me some food? I need to recharge before I attempt my next miraculous exploit."

BETWEEN THE TWO of us, James and I managed to put down a whole pot of stew and two trays of cornbread in under twenty minutes. By the time I was wiping up the last dregs of stew from around the edges of my empty bowl, I felt a million times better. James, however, still seemed tired.

"This isn't refilling your energy like it is mine, is it?" I asked.

He shook his head. "I'll need to feed soon."

"Well, it's not like Otis was gonna let you stay here again anyway," Chase said. "Especially since we don't know when, or if, we'll be coming back. Might be a good time to make your way back to the nest."

"Actually," I piped up, "I've been thinking about that." I licked the last crumbs of cornbread off my fingers and set my bowl aside. "*When* we come back from Enchantment,"—I shot Chase a reprimanding look—"we'll have May and who knows how many other kidnapped kids with us, and we can't just let them walk off a fae reservation through the front gate. Unsanctioned or not, proof that the fae were kidnapping children would be like dropping a match in a powder keg. We'll need a safe place to stay, at least for a couple nights, to regroup and figure out how to get the kids back to their families without giving the PTF another reason to start a war with the fae."

"You want to use the nest again?" James asked.

I shook my head. "We're fugitives, and Colorado is crawling with PTF agents right now. No way could we transport that many kids to a club in Denver without drawing attention. And as Chase pointed out after the raid on Crossroads, the PTF could be knocking on the way station door any day now, so I don't think we should stay here even if Nell and Otis were okay with housing a vampire and a bunch of mixed-species kids—which seems unlikely.

"But the portal we're using to get into Enchantment is in Ohio." I crossed my arms. "I think we should stay there. James, you can drive there while the rest of us are in Enchantment. You should have a decent head start, thanks to the time difference between realms. Rent a little place off the beaten path, somewhere that won't ask too many questions, and we'll all meet there when everything is said and done. Then we can plan our next move without the PTF breathing down our necks."

James pursed his lips. "I certainly don't mind lying low in Ohio until things cool down. But it'll take me most of a day to get there. You may have to wait on the reservation for a few hours."

I turned to Chase. "Is there a way station like this one outside the Ohio rez? Somewhere we could wait without raising suspicion?"

He nodded. "Smaller than this one, but it should suffice for a little while."

"Then that's settled." I gripped James's hand. "You'll join us in Ohio and secure a safe haven for our return."

He sent a flicker of gratitude through our connection. Gratitude that he would have a part to play—that he wouldn't be left behind, even if he did have to take the long way round.

I smiled at him, but the smile faded as anticipation of my next task settled over me like a weighted blanket. "Time to call Galen and see if my change goes better than yours."

I once more unwound the black ribbon from my wrist.

A nervous flutter filled my chest. Would Galen really come when I called? If not, I'd have no choice but to enter Shedraziel's prison without the protection of a name.

I swallowed the dry lump in my throat, tied three knots in the ribbon, and took a deep breath. Holding the knotted black silk taut between my hands, I licked my chapped lips and called out in a shaky voice, "Galen."

Chapter 19

I COUNTED TO ten, twenty, thirty in my head. Chase and Haru stood on opposite sides of the cellar, each with eyes that darted side to side, searching. James was a statue beside me. I held my breath, straining to hear something that might herald Galen's approach, but the only sound was the whistle of wind across the heavy shutters that blocked the way to the outside world. Shadows cast by the single bare bulb overhead swayed as Chase shifted his feet.

He hadn't come.

I set my jaw. I was going to have to rescue May without the protection of a name. Smooth fabric slipped through my fingers. I let the useless ribbon drift down to the dust-covered floor.

"This is a grim party." Everyone's attention swung to the deepest shadow in the corner of the room. An ash-gray face emerged from the darkness like someone stepping out of a thick fog. Amber eyes scanned our group as Galen stepped fully into the room. His black trench coat gave the impression he pulled the darkness with him.

Relief washed through me. "You came."

He frowned. "You called."

There was a crackling sound and the hairs on my arms and neck stood on end. The light above flared. Then an arc of lightning struck the ground in the center of the room with an echoing *pop*. Enzo, Galen's raiju companion, straightened up. He looked like an Asian gangster, with tan skin, fashion magazine hair, and thick tattoos climbing up the side of his face. Lightning danced in his eyes.

Another shadow detached from the wall. This one coalesced into a girl with skin and eyes the same color as Galen's, but her black hair was pinned up in a braided crown while his hung loose around his shoulders. She wore an ankle-length black jacket that parted just enough to show the lacy collar of her high-necked, midnight-blue blouse and a pair of black leather pants tucked into calf-high boots with black ribbon laces and three-inch heels. She looked around at the people crowding the cellar and wrinkled her nose. "Bit tight in here."

I looked the newest arrival up and down. I'd only met Galen's twin sister once, but there could be no doubt who she was when they were standing side by side. "I wasn't expecting so many people to show up."

Galen lifted his hands in a "What can you do?" gesture. "Enzo and Morgan were with me when I sensed your call. They refused to be left behind."

"Can we take this outside?" Morgan asked. "Or is there some reason you're all crammed in this dusty hole?"

Pursing my lips, I got up and pushed open the cellar door. Pale moonlight spilled over me. The others filed out one by one behind me, until we all stood in a loose circle behind the way station.

Morgan looked up at the warmly glowing windows. "Why are you squatting in the cellar rather than staying in the house?"

"That's not important right now." I turned to Galen. "I need your help."

"So I assumed." He tipped his head infinitesimally to one side. "What did you have in mind?"

I took a deep breath. "I'm going to get a true name. I need you to open a path to the trial."

Galen, Morgan, and Enzo all stared at me. Then Morgan burst out laughing.

"I like her," she said, wiping a tear from her eye.

Galen crossed his arms. "Sending you to your death seems poor payment for you saving me from the vampires."

"But you owe me a favor, and this is what I want."

"Why the sudden desire for a true name? I can't imagine such a thing would be of much use in your mortal life."

"Can you open the path, or not?"

"If that's really what you want."

"It is."

"Then my debt is repaid." He turned and waved one arm like he was wiping a screen. A pair of stone pillars appeared, each four feet tall and topped with a basin of burning oil.

I reached for James's hand, twining my fingers with his.

Galen caught the gesture. "Know that you must walk this path alone, for it is a journey inside yourself. Once you set foot on the path, there is no turning back. If you lose your way, you will be lost forever."

I turned to James, meeting his pale gaze. His skin was practically transparent in the moonlight, save for the deep purple crescents below his worried eyes.

He tucked a loose strand of hair behind my ear. His fingers traced a path down my cheek and over my lips. "It seems you're always going places I cannot follow." His fingertips continued down my neck until his hand rested over my heart. *Remember, no matter what distance separates us, I am with you, always.*

Stretching up, I stole a last taste of James's lips. I lingered against his soft skin for a moment, then pulled away and released his hand. "I'll see you soon."

Galen gestured to his companions. "Come, I have no desire to watch a child commit suicide."

Enzo nodded, but Morgan stepped away from her brother. "I'm going to stick around, see how this turns out."

Galen frowned. "Suit yourself."

He strode toward the deeper darkness of the way station's shadow, where the moonlight couldn't reach, but paused at the edge. "Good luck, Alex. For what it's worth, I hope you find what you're looking for." Then he stepped into the shadow and was swallowed by the darkness.

Enzo tipped his head in the slightest bow, then snapped out of existence with a *pop* and a flash that arced down toward the bare bulb in the cellar.

Chase stood to one side of the lit path, his arms crossed. "Last chance to change your mind."

I shook my head as I passed him. "If I don't make it back—"

"Don't." He raised his hand.

"—get them out," I finished.

A muscle jumped along his jaw and he wouldn't meet my gaze, but he gave a small, stiff nod.

As I stepped between the burning markers on either side of the path, the world grew murky. Dark fog rolled in from nowhere, obscuring the field behind the way station. I looked back. James, Chase, Haru, and Morgan stood in a semi-circle around me, but the color had drained out of them along with the surrounding landscape. Not only that, but they were all frozen. Not a hair fluttered. Not a breath stirred.

I took two more steps along the path, deeper into the fog. A second set of pillars appeared as their basins flared to life, casting a flickering orange glow over the obscuring mist. I glanced back again. My audience was gone, swallowed by impenetrable fog that had flowed in behind me. There was no way back.

More flames ignited as I walked through the swirling gray world, while those behind snuffed as I moved away. The smoky swirls grew denser, until it seemed I was walking through a tunnel walled off at either end. The path beneath my feet was laid with tightly-fitted stones the same gray color as the mist. I could have been walking in circles.

My legs grew weary, my tension flagged. The adrenaline I'd felt upon entering the trial faded as the monotony of the path wore on. What if halfers couldn't take the test after all? How could I pass a challenge I couldn't find? What if I just stumbled through this haze until I collapsed from exhaustion?

My steps slowed, then stopped. The same three sets of burning markers stretched before me. The same three sets behind.

Had it been arrogance to think I could pass a test designed for beings who'd lived a hundred years or more? Perhaps this endless fog was the test's way of weeding out the unworthy. What chance did I have?

I lifted my chin. I'd made the decision to enter the trial, to gain a name, and with it the protection I needed to face Shedraziel, if that's what it took to save May.

I closed my eyes and imagined May, shy and quiet, covered in flour from her mother's bakery. She'd been hanging around the bookstore practically since it opened—doing homework, writing music, waiting for the end of Emma's shift. And according to the Shifter Lord, there were dozens of other kids, just like her, trapped. Waiting. I couldn't fail here.

I took a deep steadying breath. I didn't have time for self-doubt. I had to find a way through this test.

"Arrogant."

My eyes snapped open. I scanned the fog for the source of the voice. It had been low, quiet, and somehow familiar.

The farthest flames on either side of me snuffed out, then the next two, shrinking my island of light. The stone pillar behind me disappeared, vanishing into the mist when its fire went out. The hazy swirls of gray smoke curled and coiled around me, shifting closer.

I clung to the one remaining point of light and fought to slow my racing heart.

Then the light went out.

I stumbled, the solid rock of the stone pillar vanishing beneath my hand. There was nothing but darkness around me, and the mist that had loomed beyond the light was suddenly pressing against me, thick and cloying.

My breath sped up. I coughed. The air was turning acrid, burning my throat.

A flicker of light flashed to my left, dull orange reflecting in the swirling clouds, turning the black world to gray once more. I stumbled toward the light.

The air grew thicker. My eyes began to water, my nose to run. My lungs ached. The soft *thud* of my footsteps became a *crunch crunch* noise. I froze.

The orange glow I'd been moving toward flared into a wall of fire, and raced to either side until it connected behind me, trapping me in its ring. In the suddenly bright light, I could see what I'd been walking on. The ground writhed with the hard shells and questing legs of thousands of insects.

I gasped and tried to kick the creepy-crawly things away.

"She thinks she's worthy." The dry rasp sounded behind me.

"She's a fool," a different voice said on my right.

"She's a murderer." This last voice made me shudder.

"No," I said. "Not you."

PTF agent Benjamin O'Connell stepped through the flames. His suit was charred and bloody, as it had been the last time I saw him. A gaping wound was visible in his chest—the place where I'd thrust my magic-made dagger through his heart.

I shook my head and took a step back. "This isn't real. You're gone."

"He's your latest victim," came a voice behind me.

I whirled to face it.

"Your latest . . . but not your first." A water fae with translucent skin stood in front of the flames. His arms ended in blackened stumps below the elbows, and his face was a pulped mess of seared flesh and crushed bone. Jagged, needle-like teeth stretched in a misshapen grin. "Remember me?"

I gagged on the smell of burnt meat and shied away from the first man I'd ever killed. "Neil."

Another figure stepped out of the flames to my right. He clapped his hands, as though amused by my answer. He was short and balding, and wore reflective sunglasses that mirrored the flames around him.

"You've left quite the trail of bodies," he said. "Almost as many as I have."

Agent Johnson tipped his head to peer over the top of his glasses. He touched the bloody tear in the PTF armor that covered his chest.

"You were a serial killer," I said. "I'm nothing like you."

But as the shades of the men I'd killed closed in around me, I found myself backing away from the accusation in their stares. I'd had my reasons. They were all bad men. They had to be stopped. But that didn't change the fact that I'd killed them.

My hands itched.

I looked down. Blood coated my sleeves and dripped from my fingertips, dark and thick.

The insects under my feet skittered away, swarming toward a single point. They rose, wriggling and twisting into the shape of a man. A cloak of midnight formed from the smoke and settled over the figure. Merak, the ex-master vampire of Denver, slid back his hood, revealing dark, deep-set eyes and pale skin stretched tight over a skeletal frame. A dark gash circled his throat. He gestured to Johnson. "He at least was methodical. You kill indiscriminately." He waved a hand around the circle. "Human, vampire, fae. All that's missing is . . . oh, never mind."

A shadow formed in the flame beside him. This one was hunched over, hands resting on the ground.

I gripped the front of my shirt, smearing it with blood, as details formed on the new arrival.

Merak smiled. "I guess you got one of those, too."

Oz looked up at me with lost eyes. Five holes decorated his blood-stained shirt.

I shook my head. "That wasn't me." I pointed an accusing finger at O'Connell. "You killed Oz."

"But why was he there?" Sophie stepped out of the flame next to Oz. She placed one hand gently on top of Oz's head, and stared at me with sad eyes. "Why were any of us?"

O'Connell raised his arms. "Don't you see, Alex? It was always you. Everyone else was just—"

"—collateral damage." Maggie stepped up beside Sophie, taking her hand. "I should have listened to Sophie that night at the concert. She tried to warn me about the dangers of being your friend. I thought I knew, but how could I when you wouldn't talk to me? You lied to protect yourself. I nearly died because of you." She set her free hand against her swollen stomach. "I nearly lost my child."

Tears pricked in my eyes. Was this what Galen had meant by the test being a journey within myself? I'd expected a physical trial, but this was more like a trial in the traditional sense, with all my sins and fears laid bare. How could I defend myself? How could I fight the past?

You can't. James's voice in my head was like a physical slap. It was distant, quiet, but a solid anchor in this shifting place. *The past cannot be changed. Only accepted.*

I twisted and turned, expecting to see him walk out of the fire like the other apparitions, but he didn't appear. *How can I even hear you? I saw you when I stepped through. You're frozen in time.*

And yet a piece of me is here with you. Warmth swelled through my chest. *Always.*

I set a hand over that warmth. "Thank you."

"How sweet," O'Connell said. "Taking comfort from a demon spawn. But then, you're practically a demon yourself."

"Magic isn't evil," I said. "Despite what people like you and Johnson believe."

He sneered. "Where do you think magic comes from?"

"Fae draw magic from within themselves." I frowned. "Practitioners pull it from the world around them."

"Well, you're half right."

"Poor Alex," Merak crooned. "Always one step behind."

"Never quite sure what's going on," Johnson added.

Neil's twisted grin grew wider. "Doesn't even know who she is."

The apparitions drew closer, closing in around me.

"I think she does," O'Connell said. He reached out a hand, palm up, revealing the dagger I'd used to kill him. The blade was translucent, glowing with a faint purple light. It was a blade forged of magic and desperation.

My skin itched with the memory of magic pouring into my body. I folded my arms over my abdomen. "What, you want me to kill you again?"

O'Connell smiled. "I offer you the same peace you've given each of us."

He closed his fingers around the handle and slashed.

I jumped back, but not fast enough. A line of burning pain opened along my forearm.

Thin fingers closed over my shoulder. Merak whispered in my ear. His breath carried the metallic scent of blood. "Scream for us, Alex."

He shoved me back toward O'Connell.

Neil's foot stretched out to trip me and I sprawled on the hard stones.

I tried to scramble up but Johnson's knee came down on my spine.

A painful gasp escaped my throat as fingers twisted into my hair, yanking my head back.

O'Connell approached with the glowing dagger, gaze locked on my exposed throat.

I looked past him. Maggie, Sophie, and Oz watched my struggle with flat expressions.

"Please," I begged. "Help me."

They didn't move. They didn't even blink.

"You've burned every bridge you've ever built," O'Connell said. "You destroy everything you touch. In the end, you will always be alone."

Always.

"I'm not alone." I gritted my teeth. "And I don't destroy . . ."

O'Connell lifted the dagger for a downward strike.

Opening myself to the magic around me, I stretched out my hand, fingers reaching. ". . . I create."

Purple light splintered in his hand. The dagger dissolved into a million shimmering sparks of light that darted and skipped like fireflies. I pulled those lights to my palm like a magnet drawing iron shavings. The blade reformed, and I closed my fingers around the glowing purple hilt.

Chapter 20

I SLASHED BLINDLY behind me. The weight lifted off my back.

I rose.

My attackers surrounded me.

I lifted my chin and tightened my grip on the dagger. "I've fought like hell to form some meaningful connections in this world, and I'll continue to fight, and kill, to protect them—to create a future I want, where the people I love can be safe." I turned to Johnson. "Maybe that makes me no better than you, who killed because you believed magic was a blight on the world. But it's who I am. I don't regret it."

Neil *tsked*. "No regret, huh?" He raised the stumps of his arms and two water spouts emerged from the ends, twisting and swirling like miniature hurricanes above his head. "Let's see if we can't change that."

He brought the storm crashing down on top of me.

I raised my arms instinctively, shielding my face from the driving rain, but I was knocked off my feet by the force. I tumbled backward, through the space where the ground should have been, and plunged into ice-cold water.

Bubbles danced around my face as an involuntary yelp escaped before I clamped my lips closed over the precious air. Above me, the ring of fire was a distant light growing fainter by the second.

I kicked toward the surface.

Something brushed my side. I jerked, twisting away. Indigo faded to black around me.

The glowing dagger still clutched in my hand provided a tiny sphere of illumination. Enough to show me I wasn't alone in the depths.

Arms reached through the murky water, fingers grasping, snagging my clothes, my hair, pulling me down.

I slashed with the knife, but my movements were slow, my limbs heavy.

Monstrous faces with sharpened teeth and translucent skin flashed at the edges of my vision.

The pressure in my chest mounted. I looked up. The ring of fire was shrinking again.

I kicked and slashed and flailed, striking the shapes in the darkness as I struggled up. But there was too much weight dragging me down.

Scraping one ankle with the toe of the opposite boot, I kicked off one shoe, then the other. Then I grappled with the fabric encasing me, tearing free of Mica's borrowed coat and the orange sweater from the way station. Clawed fingers darted out, shredding my clothes as they drifted into the black below me.

With the last of my energy, I kicked for the surface.

A wall of warm air slapped my face, and I fell forward onto my stomach as though I'd somehow dropped from above. I coughed and gagged, spitting water onto black mud while my mind tumbled in a dizzy rush. This trial was like some bizarre nightmare where the rules of physics and common sense held no sway.

"You would destroy us for the sake of *your* future?" Johnson's polished boots squelched in the mud inches from my face. "What about *my* future?"

I strained my neck to look up at him. His arms were open wide. He was staring at the horizon behind me.

The ground began to shake. The inch or so of water sitting on top of the saturated mud thickened and turned red. The coppery scent of blood filled the air.

I twisted to peer over my shoulder.

Row upon row of PTF troops stretched across the horizon, shrinking into the distance behind the first, crystal-clear line. Every soldier wore full riot gear, including masks that covered their faces, making them look like identical prints from a single stamp. They marched in sync, adding to the illusion they were all a single person somehow copied into infinity.

Blood lapped against my legs and sloshed over my wrists in a rising tide ahead of the troops.

I struggled to my feet, feeling each pounding step of the oncoming army rattle through my bones.

They crossed the distance between us impossibly fast, each step seeming to gobble up the land. I held my hands up, the shining knife still clutched in my fingers. They were nearly on top of me.

"Stop," I shouted.

The troops continued to march.

I tried to turn, to run, but my feet had sunk down deep in the mud and become trapped.

An elbow knocked into my ribs as the front line stepped even with me, then pushed past. A boot brushed my knee. A shoulder cased in iron-laced fabric crashed into my back as I bent to pull my leg free. Something solid slammed into my hip and spun me, twisting my ankle hard.

I fell.

One heavy boot came down on my wrist. Another kicked my side.

I tried to stand, but the mud was slick and the blows kept coming.

I curled into the smallest ball I could manage and lashed out with my knife, hoping to divert the nearest soldiers. For a moment, my plan seemed to work, as first one black-clad leg, then another, passed to the side of me.

Then the sloshing mud around me came alive with insects. They writhed and died under the booted onslaught. Centipedes and spiders crawled up me, seeking higher ground, and where they clung, shimmering gossamer lines attached to my clothes and skin.

"You fight forces beyond your control." Merak's voice rasped in my ear. I swore I could feel his breath on my cheek, but when I jerked to face him there was no one there.

Growling, I smacked and swatted, but each bug I brushed off was replaced by another, until silken strands dangled all over my body. Then, all at once, the strings pulled tight.

My muscles went rigid. My limbs stretched out, exposing me, making me an easy target.

The boots continued to rise and fall like pistons in a war machine.

I screamed and struggled as they came down on my legs, my arms, my torso, each step driving me farther into the mud and blood until I was drowning once more. But I was railing only inside my head, looking out the window of my eyes, powerless to move as I had been while in Merak's care, as May had been when she was taken. Like the insects I shared the ground with, I was helpless to stop the assault.

Just let go, whispered a voice in my head. *You can't win.*

The weight of my knife was still pressed in my palm. But an ocean, an army, the treachery of my own body. . . . These weren't things I could fight with a knife, magic or no.

The spark of an idea jolted through my mind. The knife wasn't just a blade in my hand. It was magic. Pure magic.

Doing my best to ignore the many bruises I was receiving, I turned my focus inward and pulled at the threads of magic holding the knife together. If I failed, the knife would simply fall apart as it had when I'd dissipated it after my battle with O'Connell. But if I was careful. . . . The magic became liquid. It slid over my skin, directed by thought and feeling, and where it passed, the gossamer threads snapped. I spread the magic thin over my entire body, then focused on hardening it into a shell. I pictured annealed metal stiffening under my hammer, growing more rigid with each blow.

The pounding of the soldiers' feet dulled to a distant pressure as the magic took the brunt of the impact. I was still on my back in the mud, but I could breathe again. I could move. I might only be a single force against the tides of inevitability, but I wouldn't just roll over and die. As the specters of this nightmare proved, I *could* make a difference.

The world shifted again, and my breath escaped in a *whoosh* as my back slammed against solid stone. The PTF soldiers were gone, along with the mud, blood, and insects.

Gasping, I rolled onto my side. The ring of fire blazed around me once more. Maggie, Oz, and Sophie watched with detachment, as though I were one of the bugs whose perspective I'd shared. Merak, Johnson, and Neil were gone, banished along with their torments. O'Connell, however, remained. He stood just inside the flames, ribbons of yellow and orange snaking over his skin.

"You speak of creating a future," he said, "but you've already lost it. Your secret is out. The world knows what you are. The humans hunt you. The fae use you. You'll never have a future with either of them. There's no place left for you."

I climbed to my feet, wincing at the various aches that sang out all over my body. The stones were rough and cold against my bare soles. My coat and sweater were still gone, but the clothes that remained were remarkably dry and mud-free, as was my hair and skin.

Channeling the thin-spread magic back into the palm of my hand with an ease I'd never experienced in the real world, I closed my fingers once more on the shining blade and narrowed my eyes at O'Connell. My chest heaved. My heart pounded. "Maybe I'm naive," I gasped, "but I'll keep fighting for the future I hope for."

He pursed his lips. "Will your power be enough to build that future?"

The blade in my hand shattered into a million sparks of light and faded away. Smoke drifted in front of O'Connell's face, coalescing into a gaping jaw and glowing red eyes—the face of a demon. "Or will you call on us again?"

The flames died down, their orange tongues snapping at knee-height. The roiling mist beyond grew darker, thicker. Faces formed in the shadows. Taloned fingers, flapping wings—the smoke beyond the ring of fire became a mass of monstrous bodies.

O'Connell disappeared, fading entirely into the demon who'd grinned at me in the burning wreckage of Purity's church.

"Welcome." One mouth formed the word, but it was spoken by a dozen different voices. The demon spread its long, leathery arms. "This is where you belong. With us. *This* is your future."

My skin itched and tingled. I shook my head. "No." I took a step toward the three remaining figures of Maggie, Sophie, and Oz. "I belong with them."

"You think so?" This new voice rooted me to the spot. It wasn't the cacophony of the demon's voice. It was high and rich . . . and familiar. A voice I never expected to hear again.

Tears formed in the corners of my eyes.

I took a deep breath, and turned toward the source.

My mother stood in front of the flames, her long red hair fluttering in the heat. She looked back at me with the bright-blue eyes I'd always envied—so much prettier than the dull gray I inherited from my father.

"Mom?" My voice cracked.

She shook her head. "I warned you, Alex. Keep moving. Don't get attached. You ignored the lessons I tried to teach you, and look at the result." She gestured to my friends. "You really think this is where you belong?"

"Yes," I whispered. "Isolation isn't strength. It's cowardice. It took me a long time to realize that."

"You can't count on anyone but yourself."

I recoiled from the familiar phrase, thinking of the family I'd built for myself. The way Maggie still called me for a ride and laughed at my jokes despite my lies and selfishness. The way Oz tried to bridge the gap between Sophie and me even as he lay dying. The way Chase had moaned and groaned, but nodded all the same when I'd asked him to save May. The way James's presence thrummed in my chest like a second heartbeat. "After Dad, you never gave anyone a chance. All you ever did was run away. But not me. I'm done running. I'm building a place where I belong."

She shook her head again. "Leave or be left."

"I'm not going to run."

"Then they will. One way or another, you'll end up alone."

Oz's gaze focused on me, sad, accusing. "I tried to be your friend. I suffered for you. I died for you. And you left my body to burn." His brows drew together over watery eyes. "I wish I'd never met you, Alex. Then I might still be alive."

Flames licked up and over his body, turning it to ash. He watched me as the fire consumed him.

Sophie's hand dropped into the empty space where Oz had been. She stared at her fingers, as if wondering where their support had gone. "You remember how happy I was? We used to meet for lunch and gossip about guys, and art, and nothing in particular." She smiled, but her eyes were too tight, her brow puckered. "All I wanted was to dance, draw, and meet a nice guy." She pointed an accusing finger at me. "Until you led me into the woods that night."

I gripped my left arm, imagining I could feel the bumps and ridges of the scars beneath my sleeve. I'd tried to save her. Tried and failed. I frowned. Had I ever apologized for that night?

"Now I'll spend my life hiding, being hunted," she said. "Alone but for the company of monsters." She looked up at me. "I wish I'd never met you, Alex. Then I might still be human."

I crossed the distance between us, stopping just short of the flames as they burned away Sophie's sad smile.

The flames settled down, dropping to barely an inch above the ground.

Shaking, I turned toward the last person in the fire.

Pale tracks streaked Maggie's cheeks. She cradled her stomach with both hands, shielding it. "The PTF raided my home, they threatened my family, they locked me away in a windowless room . . . all because I knew you." Her piercing, green gaze bore into me. "But then, I never really knew you, did I?" She looked away. "I wish I'd never met you, Alex. Then I might still be free."

The fire flared once more, climbing her sides. I stepped forward, reaching into the flames, but my hands closed on smoke that leaked through my fingers. Specks of ash settled against my cold skin.

"If you care at all for the people around you, let them go." The shade of my mother set one hand on my shoulder and gave a gentle squeeze. "Let it all go."

I rested my cheek against her hand. Tears spilled from my eyes. Every fiber in my body wanted to reach out, to wrap my arms around the mother I'd lost and let her take my pain away. I didn't need to struggle. I didn't need to lose any more.

I closed my eyes and fought the urge to move, strained until my muscles vibrated.

"I've stumbled," I said in a raspy voice. "I've made more than a few mistakes." I opened my eyes and lifted my head, hating the chill on my damp cheek as my skin lifted away from hers. "Other people have paid the price for my blunders. But giving up now would make their sacrifices pointless." I shook off her hand and stepped back. "I owe them more than that."

"You'll continue to fight even if it causes those around you to suffer?"

"I'll continue to fight because giving up would make them suffer more." I gestured to the empty space where the specters of my friends had been. "These weren't my friends. They were my fears. But the people they pretended to be are made up of so much more. Compassion. Forgiveness. Hope. That's what you failed to see in all those years hiding from the world, what you failed to teach me. Living isn't just not being dead. It's affecting the people around you and letting them affect you. You gave up on life long before that car accident." I set my hand over my chest, picturing all the people who'd become integral to my life. "I won't make that mistake."

Mother *tsked* and crossed her arms. "I never should have had you, Alex. If it wasn't for you, I'd still be alive. If it wasn't for you,"—she looked to the side—"I might still have him." A shadow stood, tall and broad, just beyond the dim orange glow. I squinted into the gloom. Then a sudden, cold wind tore at my hair and clothes, and snuffed the last, lingering embers of the fire. As the light faded, my mother gusted away in a swirl of smoke.

The world was darker than a moonless night. I blinked, unable to tell the difference when my eyes were open or closed.

Slowly, light leached back into the space around me. Not the flickering orange light of the flames, but a soft gray that rippled and roiled through the eerie mist that had closed in around me, no longer held back by the circle of flames. The demons I'd glimpsed earlier were nowhere to be seen, yet the feel of the fog sliding over my skin was like grasping fingers and scraping claws. The breeze that stirred my hair was a warm breath on the back of my neck.

The shadow I'd seen before my mother disappeared remained darker than the space around it. It moved through the mist, growing larger, becoming more solid. Definitely the shape of a man. He walked with a sure swagger, long limbs swinging, a slight bounce to his step.

I tensed as the man came closer, widening my stance, ready to fight. He stopped a dozen paces away. The haze continued to lighten around us until I stood in a world of uniform gray. Across that limbo, I faced a set of blue-gray eyes, so like the ones I saw in the mirror each morning.

My father frowned. "She always did have a flair for the dramatic."

Chapter 21

I STARED, UNBLINKING, until my eyes began to itch. When I finally let my focus spread beyond those murky blue orbs framed by crow's feet, I received another shock. The eyes I knew so well were set in a patchwork face that made my stomach twist to look at. It was as if someone had cut up a dozen photographs of my father and glued mismatched features onto a single frame. Some elements, like his eyes, were distinct. Others lacked detail, bearing only a passing resemblance to the man they were supposed to represent. His hair grew to different lengths and varied in color from dirty blond to nearly black. His nose lacked definition. His mouth turned down on one side, traced by a deep line. On the other, his lips pulled up in a laughing smile.

The Frankenstein father looked down at his hands. They too were mismatched, one thin and pale, the other one tan and so large it must have belonged to a different body.

"You don't remember me at all, do you?"

I stiffened as understanding sank in. Of course. O'Connell, Maggie, even my mother. . . . All their images were pulled from my memory. But the decade I'd spent with my father had been overwritten by twice that time of memories made without him, and the potency of his memory had faded. A creeping tightness spread through my chest. I'd avoided thinking about my father for years, but I hadn't realized how little I actually remembered about him.

He closed and opened his fist, stretching his fingers. "Not surprising, I suppose." Even his voice shifted as he spoke, like the cracking speech of a teenage boy.

His hands fell to his sides. He looked at me across the flat gray expanse. Then he shook his head. "Such a disappointment."

I rocked back at the impact of those words.

This is my test, I reminded myself. *He's a manifestation of my fears and worries.* . . . That logic didn't make his statement hurt any less. Gritting my teeth, I lifted my chin. "If you wanted to be remembered, you should have stuck around."

"Still harping on about that?" He planted his fists on his hips and shook his head. "Woe is me," he said in a high-pitched voice. "I've suffered a loss." He pinned me with a pitiless glare. "Grow up."

"I have."

"Bullshit. You're still blaming your past for your shortcomings—your fear of commitment, your fear of rejection, your inability to forgive. Hell, you can't even say 'I love you' to the one guy dumb enough to want you to." He took a step toward me. "You're pathetic."

My limbs started to shake.

What was I supposed to do? Was the test just to see how much verbal abuse I could stand? Did I have to admit the things he said out loud? Or was I supposed to argue, defend myself? But how could I defend myself from what was, essentially, myself—my own darkest thoughts freed and thrown back in my face.

"And on top of all that—"

I stiffened, bracing for his next assault.

"—you're a monster."

There it was. The condemnation I knew was coming. The judgment I'd dreaded since the day I learned I was part fae. Knowing my dad had lost his life fighting the fae, trying to rid the world of magic, there'd always been that little voice inside my head screaming that I was a traitor to my blood.

"I can't help the way I was born," I whispered.

"But you could have rejected it," he said. "If you had, your human friends wouldn't have been pulled into your mess. Hell, even your freak friends would have been better off. The werewolves wouldn't be hunted right now. Your faerie knight wouldn't be rotting in a cage. All you had to do was send Kai away, and you could have lived the rest of your life in peace, as a human."

I hugged myself, feeling suddenly cold in the cloying mist.

"But no," Dad pressed. "You had to play the hero. You had to explore your powers. You found excuse after excuse, but the truth is . . . you wanted to be special."

Was that true? Had I been making excuses to grow my magic, all while claiming I wanted no part of it? Even if I had, what was so wrong with wanting to explore my abilities? Why limit myself?

"And special you are." Father reached behind him and gripped the hilt of a sword I hadn't noticed peeking over his shoulder. "A very special kind of monster."

I raised my chin. "Being fae doesn't make me a monster."

"But you didn't stop at being fae. You kept reaching."

The shadows in the roiling fog grew darker.

"Bad enough you're contaminated with fae blood, but practitioner as well? You're a mongrel through and through." He pulled his blade free.

My blood froze at his utterance of the word *practitioner*. I'd had my suspicions. . . . The way I pulled magic from outside my body, harnessing more than my fae blood should have allowed. . . . The way I could see demons. . . . But was this really confirmation, or just wild speculation manifested by my mind?

The clouds formed arms and legs, wings and horns. Hazy eyes stared out of the darkness—an eager audience watching gladiators clash, knowing one would fall.

"If I'm a practitioner," I called, "whose fault is that?" I pointed one shaking finger at him. "Powers or no, magic must be in your blood."

He laughed. The sound was cold and hollow. "You think such a weak claim will deter me? If a practitioner father is what you want, so be it. You're as much a bastard as you are a mongrel—some folly of your whore of a mother. Perhaps that's why she wouldn't give you my name when you were born. You're no daughter of mine." He raised his sword in both hands. "You're an abomination."

He charged forward, mist swirling in his wake.

My mouth went dry. My muscles refused to respond.

The patchwork memory of my father brought his sword down. He didn't flinch. Didn't waver. He was going to kill me.

I dove to the side. Steel sparked against stone in the space where I'd been standing.

My roll was sloppy, and I slammed my hip on the hard ground, but I was still in one piece when I came up into a crouch.

The demons pressed closer.

"Call us." They said with one voice.

"Use us." They crowded in around me.

"Join us."

"No." I flapped my arms at the specters, dispersing them like the smoke they appeared to be.

Wispy maws grinned back at me. "Then die."

My father turned, prepared for another attack.

"Please." I lifted my hands, entreating. "Stop this."

"For the sake of humanity, magic must be purged from this world." He moved forward again. "Humans belong with humans. Fae with fae."

He swung, a wide arc meant to take his sword through the center of my chest.

I ducked, rolling once more.

"But you," he said. "You don't belong anywhere." He followed up with an overhead attack.

The tip of his blade tore through my jeans and across my shin as I sprang clumsily away.

"You think the fae will welcome you? Accept you?" He raised the sword again. "They were barely willing to tolerate you when they thought you were just a halfer. Once they discover what you really are, they'll destroy you as they once tried to destroy the vampires."

A cold shudder ripped through me as I recalled Kai's words from the night I'd first learned of the existence of vampires.

Magics don't often mix. When they do, the results are unpredictable and dangerous. That's how we ended up with vampires and werewolves in the first place. . . . They are abominations. No fae would help them.

I'd learned the hard way how impossible it was to hide one aspect of my life from another. If I continued to interact with the fae, they would eventually discover the truth. Then what? Would I be hunted? Executed? Or simply abandoned?

Dad straightened, his patchwork expression shifting to one of grim satisfaction. "You will never be welcome among them."

Welcome.

I glanced at the twisting shadows around me. They were keeping their distance, watching, waiting.

No. I focused on my father, on the sword he held, its tip darkened by my blood. I could fight on my own.

I found the place inside me where my fae magic resided and reached for it, calling it to me.

Nothing happened.

Frowning, I strained harder, but it was as if I was blocked by an invisible barrier. I couldn't reach my magic.

Desperate, I groped through the twisting tangle of threads that made up my core. I stroked the single silver thread I found there, hoping for advice, or at the very least, comfort. But James's voice had gone silent. The resonant thrum of *I am here* was barely a twitch in my questing consciousness.

A cold dread settled through me as I realized why I couldn't reach him . . . why I couldn't reach my magic.

Facing my crimes, my fears, and my friends had nearly broken my heart. But the ghosts of my parents pushed me over the edge. I'd locked down my emotions to keep from being overwhelmed, shoved away enough of the pain that I could function.

But magic—my magic—required me to be more than merely functional. It required me to be raw. I couldn't access my powers without leaving myself open to the full impact of my emotions.

I glared at the specter before me, thinking of all the anger, all the grief I'd felt at his loss. I'd pushed those feelings down deep so I could move on with my life. Was I strong enough to face them now? Or would they overwhelm me?

My father's mismatched mouth pulled into the semblance of a smile. Could he sense my dilemma?

Of course he could. He was a projection from my mind.

"Poor Alex," he said. "Still running."

Taking a deep breath, I tried to settle myself the way I did before starting a new project. Then I approached the door I'd unconsciously slammed shut inside myself. Emotions leaked around the edges like wisps of smoke, warning of the blaze contained on the far side.

I opened the door. The barrier blocking me from my magic shattered. I reached for my power, but a wave of anger hit me first, hot and fierce.

You're as much a bastard as you are a mongrel . . . an abomination.

I stared at the apparition before me—at eyes so like my own.

It had never occurred to me that my father could be anyone except . . . my father. But wherever my powers came from, the result was the same. I was a freak. Neither human, nor fae, nor practitioner. I was, so far as I knew, unique. And the one thing I knew about uniqueness was that people either feared it or coveted it.

You will never be welcome among them.

Despair slammed into me, cold and deep. It dampened my anger like flipping a switch. Doubt, grief, fear . . . these were the emotions I'd shut down. Anger was like an old friend compared to the drowning sorrow waiting behind it.

The patchwork memory of my father took a step toward me, the bloodstained tip of his sword rising. "Let me end your suffering."

My breath rattled as I released the air from my lungs. Tears flowed over my cheeks. My body suddenly weighed a thousand tons. I didn't have the energy to move it. Was this place amplifying my emotions? Or was this the result of pushing them aside too long, letting them fester?

James's presence rushed back along our link, a deafening scream. *You can do this! Don't give up!*

I blinked, then smiled.

I didn't belong with the humans. I didn't belong with the fae. So what? I'd make a place for myself with the people who could accept me, be they vampire, practitioner, or halfer. I wasn't the only freak out there.

The bloody blade came down.

My emotions continued to swell and surge within me, but I found I could ride the currents like waves on the ocean—so long as I didn't focus on the individual drops, it was possible to float on the surface.

I rolled to the side once more and steel struck the place I'd been.

Dad's eyes—the one thing about him totally in focus—narrowed. Leather creaked beneath his two-handed grip as he lifted the sword once more.

I took a deep breath.

I can do this.

My magic stirred, finally answering my call. I cradled the rosy glow, gathering it to my center. It wasn't enough. Not by itself.

My father prepared for another attack. He would never stop.

I looked at the demons around me. They smiled.

They had the power I needed. Power I could make my own if I could keep from being overwhelmed. I opened myself up . . . and invited them in.

Glowing blue sparks emerged from the mist like a field of fireflies rising from riverbank reeds. The frosty embers formed strands that trickled toward me—first in streams, then rivers, and finally as a tidal wave that threatened to wash me away.

Dad took two steps toward me, sword raised, but he seemed to be slowing as he moved, like a mechanical toy winding down.

Magic poured through my skin, filling me to bursting. My veins burned. My muscle fibers were tearing apart. It was too much. I couldn't contain it. I was going to have a burnout—the catastrophic result of a magic backlash when a practitioner lost control. I'd end up a walking husk with my magic and soul seared away. If I survived.

Except . . . part of me wasn't burning.

The warm core of my fae magic pulsed and mingled with the raw energy coursing through me, and where the two met, the tide was contained.

I focused on the feel of my innate magic, my fae magic. This was the source of my ability to imbue, to create, but it lacked the raw material to be powerful on its own. It was the hammer and the anvil. I considered the chaotic energy pouring through me. This was the raw material, the metal waiting to take shape. One was useless without the other . . . but together . . .

Dad's sword fell in an arc toward my face, strong and sure, filled with murderous intent.

I channeled the raw energy ripping through me toward my right hand, filtering it through the rosy glow of my fae magic. Purplish light poured into my palm, stretching, forming a blade faster than when I'd made the dagger with which I'd killed O'Connell.

Cold steel slammed into the translucent purple blade gripped in my hand.

My arm tingled from the impact. My muscles strained. I stared into my own warped reflection in the surface of my father's blade as it struggled to drop the last few inches to reach me.

Father *tsked*, just as Mom had done. He stepped back, pulling his sword away.

We stared at each other in silence as seconds stretched into minutes.

Then he turned his back on me. "You're a lost cause, not even worth finishing off."

He strode away.

My mouth dropped open. He was leaving? Did that mean I passed? Or failed?

I took a step toward him. "What about my trial? Is it over?"

He continued to walk.

"Hey!" I couldn't tear my gaze from his retreating back. It was an image that had haunted far too many of my childhood dreams. I tightened my grip on the sword of light shining in my hand. "Don't you walk away from me."

I moved to follow him, walking at first, then running. I lifted the sword.

"Answer me!"

I swung the bright blade down toward the exposed back of my patchwork memory.

My hand jolted to a stop. Sparks momentarily blinded me. When my vision cleared, an ebony blade of compressed shadows was pressed against my sword edge. Above the crossed blades, I stared into my mirror image. Except for the eyes. The eyes were all wrong. Swirls of black smoke instead of pale-gray sky.

I jumped back.

My reflection did likewise.

"What are you?" I asked.

She lifted one hand. "Can't you tell?"

Behind her, my father faded farther into the mist. The ache in my chest grew tighter.

"Let me pass."

She shrugged. "If that's really what you want." She shifted her stance, settling lower. "Make me."

I ground my teeth. I was tired of fighting, but this too must be part of my test. Could I keep going? I attacked.

Our swords clashed again and again. I swung and thrust. She parried and returned. We were evenly matched . . . except I was breathing hard. She wasn't.

We came together. Our blades locked. My breath stirred the hair around her face.

She shook her head. "How long are you going to chase the past?"

We sprang apart.

Beyond her, clouds roiled. I glanced side to side. I'd gotten turned around in the fight. My chest tightened. My father was gone . . . again.

My other self lifted her blade, using it to point to her right. "He's over there."

I frowned.

She swung her sword across her body, pointing it in the other direction. The mist there was a warmer color, tinted by a distant orange glow. "The way out."

She moved again, this time pointing her blade straight at me. I looked down the length of it, into eyes of swirling darkness set in the face from the mirror.

"The choice is yours." Her dark sword disintegrated, splintering into particles that scattered into the mist. "It always was."

My own blade split apart, sparks of light darting away. I stared at my empty palm. I hadn't meant to dispel the magic. I looked up again. Had she done it?

She spread her arms to either side. "Choose."

I looked from side to side. My father, or the exit. I still didn't have a true name. Did I have to find and defeat my father to get it? To prove I'd overcome my past? Or had I already lost and I'd just end up wandering this smoky landscape forever if I didn't escape now?

Not all who seek a true name will find one. My tutor's words echoed in my mind. *And not all return from the search.*

I'd entered the trial determined to find some protection against Shedraziel, but if the choice was to go back empty-handed or not at all . . .

The apparition let her arms drop to her sides. "Why do you fight?"

I frowned, thinking back to when all this started. Why had I accepted Kai's invitation when he showed up on my doorstep months ago? Why had I taken it upon myself to hunt down a serial killer, despite my lack of qualifications, when the police and PTF had failed? Why had I stormed a vampire nest to save James even after the werewolves refused to back me? Or jumped into the middle of Merak's gathered forces, outnumbered and outmatched, to save Oz, futile though that effort ultimately was?

I pictured Emma waiting by the portal in Enchantment, ready to infiltrate an enemy stronghold with little more than a few weeks of practitioner training and the will to save her sister. She'd be facing a battle-hardened fae so powerful that even other fae were afraid of her, while those strong enough to stop her sat safely on their thrones.

Despite the odds, even without a name, I wouldn't leave Emma to fight alone.

"I fight for the people I care about, because no one else will." I turned toward the orange glow.

I took two steps, then paused and glanced at the other me. She stood relaxed, watching. I bit my lip, then asked, "Are you a demon?"

She smiled. "Does it matter?"

I stared at the woman who looked so much like me but for the impenetrable black of her eyes. I hadn't felt the demons attack when I called for more magic this time, but I remembered the feel of them crawling inside me the day I killed O'Connell, and again when I tried to change James. "Kai said fae and demon magic were antithetical. But if I can use practitioner magic . . . can I be possessed?"

"Fae and demons aren't as different as your knight would like you to believe." She lifted her hand, a gold coin pinched between her fingers. "Two sides of the same coin. Order." She turned the coin. The back was identical. "And chaos. But what happens when you flip it?"

She flicked the coin into the air. It spun end over end, a golden blur. "Can you tell them apart?" She snatched the coin as it fell and displayed it on her palm. "Which side is up?"

I shook my head. "I don't know."

"Magic bends to the will of the user." She closed her fingers over the coin.

She hadn't really answered my question. Was she a version of me possessed by demons? Was that the future before me if I continued to use practitioner magic without proper training? But she didn't *act* like a demon.

I looked at my own empty palm and closed my fist. *The will of the user.*

I'd continue to move forward, no matter the dangers. I would face what came.

I moved toward the distant glow, bare feet slapping the cold stones. The woman who might have been me faded into the mist.

The haze in front of me cleared, revealing two stone pillars with blazing tops. Beyond them stood James, Chase, Haru, and Morgan, just as I'd left them.

I paused between the markers and glanced back. Uniform fog billowed behind me. The path was gone. I'd survived my trial . . . but I hadn't gained a name. If I returned now, it would be as a failure. I'd risked my life for nothing.

With a shuddering breath, I stepped past the pillars.

Chapter 22

AS I CROSSED THE barrier between worlds, a gust of wind ripped past me. And carried on that wind . . . was a name.

I staggered and fell, as every cell in my body was ripped apart and remade within a single beat of my heart. My knees sank into muddy earth. My fingers dug into the cold ground. I gasped, and ice filled my lungs.

Warmth seeped into my back.

I looked up. James's face was blurred by my unshed tears. He was kneeling in the mud beside me. One arm was wrapped around my shoulders. The other braced my chest, saving me from a complete face-plant.

"I did it," I panted. "I have a name."

He pulled me closer until my cheek rested against his chest, his chin on the top of my head. "I knew you could."

"You were there." I gripped his arm. "I heard you."

He hugged me tighter. "I told you, I'm always with you."

"I must admit," Haru said, "I didn't think she'd make it."

I glanced up, peeking past James's shoulder. Morgan, Haru, and Chase were standing in a loose line, watching me. I grew suddenly self-conscious of the fact that I was curled up in James's arms like a child. I wanted desperately to stay there, in the comfort and warmth, but everyone was waiting on me. Emma . . . May. . . . I closed my eyes and forced my muscles to reengage.

James loosened his grip.

I straightened so I was, if not standing, at least sitting on my own. I narrowed my eyes at Haru. "Thanks for the vote of confidence."

Morgan crossed her arms and pursed her lips, looking me over. "I would have given her fifty-fifty odds. She's not all that powerful, but my brother says she's crazy. I figure that gives her an advantage."

Chase stepped away from the others and moved to a pile of clothes I hadn't noticed beside me. The fur lining of Mica's coat and the bright orange of my borrowed sweater were easily recognizable, as were the boots I'd kicked off during my underwater struggle. Chase lifted them as though it were perfectly normal to find my clothes and shoes in a pile on the ground. "We've still got a long night ahead of us," he said, holding out my lost clothing. "Do you want to rest before we head out?"

Of course I wanted to rest. I was running on fumes. With all the jumps between realms, I wasn't even sure how many hours I'd been awake. But if I slept now, I'd be worthless for at least half a day. May and Emma didn't have that kind of time to burn.

Bracing against James, I climbed laboriously to my feet. The cold air blew through my thin shirt, making me shiver. The fabric on my left arm gaped open. It was matted with blood from a shallow slice along my forearm. My jeans flapped open beneath my right knee, exposing the gash I'd received from my father. It seemed not everything in that other place had been an illusion.

I took my clothes and boots from Chase. "I've got my name. I'm ready to face Shedraziel."

Haru huffed and rubbed one hand on the back of his neck. "Maybe your will won't be instantly crushed when you see her. That's not the same as *ready*." But I caught a flicker of respect in his gaze before he looked away.

"That's why you needed a name? You're going up against Bael's general?" Morgan's voice carried a note of awe, though it might have been more the, *Galen was right, she really is crazy*, variety than, *Wow, she's so impressive*. She looked between us. A small smile curved her lips. "So what's next?"

Chase frowned. "You've seen the climax of this little show. Alex survived. She passed her trial."

Morgan scrunched her nose. "*I'll* decide when the show is over." She shifted her gaze to me. Her half-lidded, amber eyes glinted with reflected light from the way station windows. "I think there's still plenty to see."

"You're welcome to stick around if you want," I said. "But we won't be here long. Chase is taking me through the Shifter Realm to the Ohio reservation. Then we're going back to Enchantment. As I understand it, high-level fae don't cross into other realms without permission."

She tapped her chin. "True, I'd be in trouble if I entered Enchantment . . . but the shifters hardly care who passes through." She glanced sideways at Chase. "And I'd have a guide. But you needn't take such a roundabout way. The trip between reservations via the Shifter

Realm will take what, three hours?"

"Two," Haru said.

She crossed her arms. "I could have you there in twenty minutes."

I blinked. Twenty minutes to cover half of North America? I glanced at Chase. He was frowning, but not like he didn't believe her. More like he was annoyed by the offer.

"What's in this for you?" I asked.

She lifted one shoulder in a delicate shrug. "Entertainment."

I frowned. First Mica, now Morgan. "What is it with fae nobles and boredom?"

Morgan's smile faded. "Do you have any idea how long eternity can be when nothing interesting happens?"

I cast a sidelong glance at James. From snippets of his memories, I had some idea of eternity, but only as a concept. I was mortal. I would never experience time that stretched on forever.

"Mortals are mayflies," she said. "That adds a certain . . . intensity to your actions. And you"—she pointed to me—"are a catalyst. Good or bad, stuff happens around you." She shrugged again. "I just want to watch."

I tightened my grip on James's hand. Maybe he wouldn't have to endure a lonely cross-country road trip to join us after all. "James, too?"

She looked at James and wrinkled her nose. "Promise me a play-by-play of your encounter with Shedraziel when you get back, and I'll let the vampire tag along."

I looked at Chase and waited for him to meet my gaze. Then I raised an eyebrow.

He shrugged.

"All right, Morgan," I said. "We'll take you up on your offer."

"But first," James said, "Alex's wounds need attention." He looked at Chase. "Ask Nell for hot water and bandages."

I HISSED AS JAMES wiped a warm, damp rag over the cut on my shin. The hot, spicy drink I was cradling in my hands sloshed in its mug, intensifying the scent of pumpkin wafting off it.

"Sorry," he mumbled, but he continued to clean mud from the wound. The black muck from my trial may have been an illusion, but the soggy ground I'd collapsed on after passing the pillars had been real enough.

I took a sip of my drink, savoring the heat as it flowed down my throat and through my chest, loosening knotted muscles. Nell had said it would help the healing process. From the pleasant burn, I suspected alcohol.

Sighing, I lowered the mug back to my lap. I was sitting on the blanket in the cellar again, my back pressed to the wall while James knelt over my outstretched legs. My arm was already clean and bandaged.

I studied James's features as he worked, noting the lines around his eyes, the sharp angle of his nose, the curve of his lips. *You can't even say "I love you" to the one guy dumb enough to want you to.* I took another sip from the mug.

"Did you hear it?" I asked. "When I came out of the trial?"

He frowned, looking up from where he'd just started wrapping the bandage. "Your name?"

I nodded.

His frown deepened. "Almost. You were wide open when you stumbled out of the trial. I had to slam down the link to keep it from spilling over into my mind."

I looked up, staring at the bare bulb in the ceiling until spots formed in my vision. "You didn't want to know?"

"A true name is precious, and dangerous. You need to keep it hidden."

"Not from you," I whispered. I thought of the way he'd pulled away from me when I tried to imbue his demon. He'd hidden the memories he didn't want me to see, the parts of his past he was ashamed of. I'd never be able to help him if he didn't open up to me completely. But trust worked both ways. "I want you to have it."

I found the corner of my mind where my true name had settled and showed it to James, sharing it silently through our link. "This is all that I am . . . the good, the bad, the ugly." I forced myself to meet his gaze. My drink sloshed slightly as the mug shook in my hands. "I hope, someday, you'll let me see all of you, too."

I closed my eyes and took a deep breath. "I love you."

No sound or motion emanated from the space in front of me. It was as though a James-shaped hole had been cut out of the fabric of reality.

Bracing myself, I opened my eyes.

James took a breath, and the James-shaped hole became a person again. One long-fingered hand rose to cradle my cheek.

"I love you, too." He leaned in and kissed me with warm, wet lips.

He'd said it dozens of times since we started dating, but somehow those words sounded different now that I'd said them too.

I set my steaming mug on the floor so my hands were free to trace the curve of his back as he held himself above me, our lips still locked together.

"Ahem."

James pulled back, twisting to face the cellar entrance, where Chase was peeking down the stairs.

"If you're all patched up, Alex, we really should get going." He stepped away, leaving the door open.

My cheeks felt sunburned. The corners of my lips pulled up uncontrollably. I felt like a teenager whose parents had just found a boy in her room. Except I hadn't had a boy in my room as a teenager . . . or parents around to find one.

I glanced at James. His eyes were twinkling.

Could a centuries-old vampire feel like a guilty teenager?

Grinning like an idiot, I downed the rest of my spiced ale while James put the finishing touches on my bandage.

"WE'LL HAVE TO do this in skips," Morgan said.

"Skips?"

She nodded. "If I keep you in the shadows too long, you'll die."

I coughed, choking on my own spit when I swallowed. I pounded my chest. "You never said this path was life-threatening."

"All good shortcuts are," Chase grumbled.

"And make sure you stay connected," she continued, as if we hadn't spoken. "Lose your grip and you'll lose your way."

Haru smiled grimly. "Which will kill you."

I rubbed my hands together, trying to work the chill out of my stiff fingers. "How many of these 'skips' are we talking about?"

She looked up, as though searching the stars. "We can probably make it in four." She held out her hand. "Ready to go?"

I took Morgan's outstretched hand. The two of us turned toward the three men—a vampire and a pair of shifters with unresolved issues. They looked uncomfortably at each other, frowning and shuffling their feet.

"Seriously?" I asked. "Sort it out."

"I'll go at the end," James volunteered.

Chase shook his head. "You don't want to put your life in Haru's hands. He should go last."

Haru crossed his arms and glared. "So you can drop me?"

"*I'm* not the one who abandons my friends."

Haru's jaw twitched. I swore I could hear his teeth grinding. Then he sighed. "Whatever. I'll take the end." He pointed at James. "But he stays between us."

"Fine by me," Chase said.

James and I shared a look. I felt his unease. I tried to send some reassurance his way, but this whole shadow road idea was seeming more and more like a mistake.

"Let's get this train moving," Morgan said.

Chase grabbed my hand and James moved to his far side. Haru dragged his feet over to the end of our procession, gave James an appraising look, then clasped hands with him.

Morgan squeezed my fingers. "Remember, whatever you do, don't let go." Then she walked into the deepest patch of darkness cast by the way station, pulling us after.

Nothingness enveloped me.

There was no light. No sound. I could feel myself breathing—my chest swelled and collapsed—but there was no external response. I could feel the pressure of Chase's and Morgan's hands holding mine, but that was all—as though they existed only in the areas of intersection.

I tried to speak, to ask if it was the same for the others, but while my mouth moved, no sound came out. Not even the whisper of air passing my lips.

I shuddered.

I continued to place one foot in front of the other, though there was no sound or pressure to tell me what I was walking on, nor any breeze to prove I was moving. Morgan's hand was my only guide, and even that was beginning to feel surreal, as though I was only imagining the pressure there. I held on tighter, afraid my sweaty fingers might slip free of the phantom grip.

My senses stayed at high alert, but the endless emptiness frayed my nerves. The back of my neck itched. My skin tingled as the hairs on my arms stood on end. My ears and eyes strained against the muffling darkness. Anything could be out there . . . watching . . . waiting.

The muscles in my legs continued to contract and relax. That meant I was walking, right? My eyelids drooped, giving in to the futility of trying to see. I searched for the beat of my own heart. I heard nothing. I felt nothing. In this place, I *was* nothing.

How long since we entered the shadows? How long until I unraveled completely and just disappeared into the black?

My toe connected with something solid and I pitched forward. I reached out instinctively to catch myself, realizing too late that I'd opened my hand.

My eyes snapped open. Pale strands of dry grass loomed in my vision for a split second before my face plowed into them.

Morgan snickered. "That's what you get for walking around with your eyes closed."

Spitting dirt, I twisted to glare up at Morgan. I looked to my right. Chase, James, and Haru stood in a line, all present and accounted for. None of them were holding hands.

I exhaled, relishing the sound and the feel. Then I pushed to my knees. "I can see why you can't stay in there very long." I set my palm against my chest, tracking the steady—if slightly too fast—rhythm of my heart. "I'm not sure how much more of that I could take. I felt like I was drifting away."

"That was only about three minutes," Morgan said. "Well within the safety margin for most fae."

I glanced at the guys. None of them looked particularly frazzled. Guess it was just me.

"Mortals don't do so well with sensory deprivation," I said.

Morgan nodded. "Good to know."

I looked around. The five of us were standing, or in my case sitting, in the shadow of a large barn with peeling white paint. Beyond the shadow's edge, dry grass glowed under starlight as far as I could see.

"Where are we?"

Morgan scanned the horizon, then shrugged. "Somewhere in Kansas."

I shook my head, astounded. "You really can get anywhere in the world like this."

"Anywhere there are shadows." She extended her hand. "Ready to go again?"

Chapter 23

MY EYES WERE open when I stumbled, gasping, out of the shadows a second time. Bright, overhead lights pierced my vision. My boots came down on concrete covered in chunky salt crystals.

Morgan released my hand and wiggled her gray fingers as if they'd gone numb.

I placed my palm against the brick wall beside me, taking comfort in the solid surface.

I peeked around the corner. We were standing next to a gas station convenience store. Four pumps stood empty under glowing fluorescent lights. A freezer hummed in front of the store, stocked full of ice no one wanted at this time of year. A pyramid display of wiper fluid filled one window. A poster advertising Pepsi products covered another.

"Where are we now?" I asked.

"Does it matter?" Haru countered. "We're somewhere between where we started and where we need to get."

"Missouri," Morgan said. "I stopped here so you could get a snack." She pointed at my hand—the one not pressed to the wall. It was shaking. "Sugar should help."

James set his hand on my shoulder. "I'll go. Your face made national news, after all. No telling who might recognize you."

I snorted. "Like they're not looking for you, too." But his comment had given me an idea. I smiled. "We'll both go."

"But—"

I held up my hand. "You get the snacks. I'm going to make a phone call."

"Shall I cast an illusion?" he asked.

I shook my head. "Let them see me."

A bell chimed when we walked through the front door. James glanced at me, uneasy, then split off toward the junk food. I headed for the register.

A young man with shaggy, blond bangs and a stained green smock stood behind the counter. His chin rested in his hand. He absently flipped pages in a magazine. He yawned and looked up when I stopped in front of him.

I plastered on a smile. "Could I use your phone?"

"There's a pay phone at the Denny's up the road."

"I don't have any change." I pouted out my lower lip and blinked a few times, trying to remember the way Sophie used to act when she wanted something from a man.

The clerk gave me a flat stare. "Not my problem."

So much for feminine wiles.

I took a breath, exhaled slowly, and focused on maximizing the speed and strength my fae blood granted me. Darting around the counter, I grabbed the front of the clerk's bright-green smock and shoved him out of the employees-only zone before he could trigger any kind of alarm. His butt hit the linoleum. His eyes and mouth were matching "O" shapes.

"Let me rephrase. *I am going to use your phone.*"

"Everything okay?" James stood at the entrance to the snack aisle, several candy bars and bags of potato chips cradled in his arms. I also spotted a Monster energy drink in each hand, bless him.

"All good," I said. "Just watch this guy a minute, will you?"

James stood over the clerk. He didn't touch him, just stared down the bridge of his nose with a stony expression.

The clerk's eyes somehow managed to get even wider. I was pretty sure he pissed himself.

The gas station phone was a simple wireless tucked under the counter. I lifted it out of the cradle and called Maggie's house.

"Hello?"

I gritted my teeth at the hollow quality in Charlie's voice, remembering his easy smiles and sympathetic eyes.

"Is the PTF still monitoring this line?"

"Alex? I—"

"We're here," came an unfamiliar voice.

"Patch me through to Director Harris," I said. "This is Alex Blackwood."

Something clicked in the line.

I stared up at the security camera on the wall behind the counter and counted the seconds.

The line clicked again.

"Finally ready to turn yourself in?"

"Are you still in Boulder?"

"I can be."

"I left town."

There was a moment of hesitation. Then, "That mess at the bar could have been avoided."

"You mean the *attack*? Where you *blew up* a wall and *shot* unarmed people?"

"With tranquilizers," she said. "And we didn't know how many fae would be in there. We were only looking for you."

The fingers of my free hand closed on the counter top. "I assume you can trace this phone."

"You're a long way from home. Why tell me? Just to gloat that you got away?"

"To let you know I'm gone. And hopefully, to avoid any more collateral damage."

"If you want to keep your friends—if you want to keep *the world* safe, let me bring you in. I promise no harm will come to you."

"Don't make promises you can't keep," I said. I pressed the off button and set the phone back in its cradle. With any luck, knowing I was out of the state would ease the pressure on my friends back home, if only a little. And if I was very, very lucky, I'd just shifted the center of the PTF's manhunt to a place I'd be gone from in a matter of minutes. "Let's go."

I rounded the counter and pulled the door open. The bell jingled. James gave the guy on the floor one last glare for good measure, then strode through the open doorway. He didn't pay for the food. I glanced again at the surveillance camera. Yeah, I was a criminal.

I turned to follow James, but paused on the threshold.

"Next time someone asks to use the phone," I called over my shoulder, "don't be a dick about it." I let the door swing shut behind me.

WE MADE ONE more stop on our way to Ohio—a snowy field near the border between Illinois and Indiana—where I scarfed the last candy bar James had tucked in his pocket and finished off the chips I'd stuffed in my sweater. When we stepped out of the shadows the final time, we were greeted by a blazing orange sunrise that filtered through the bare branches of a deciduous forest.

"Welcome to the Ohio reservation," Morgan said, slipping her hand out of mine.

I braced against my knees and took three deep breaths, enjoying the strain in my lungs, the noisy exhales, the sensation of being alive and grounded in the world. Ice-crusted leaves crackled under my feet. To my left, wisps of fog curled along the surface of a large lake.

"Is that Lake Erie?" I asked, trying to remember my geography.

"Not quite," Chase said. "We're at the southwest end of Sandusky Bay. Humans didn't want to give the fae direct access to the lake proper. Too hard to monitor."

If I squinted, I could just make out a row of bright-red buoys in the water. There looked to be iron chains connecting them. To my right, beyond scattered snow-dusted trees and the dry husks of reeds, I found a row of twelve-foot iron poles topped with razor wire. The poles were close enough together to interrupt the scene beyond, and looped with thick wire, but they cordoned off the little space without providing any real privacy.

Following the path of the fence with my eyes, I found the thicker structures of the main gate. I moved behind a tree trunk to obscure it from view.

"We're awfully close to the boundary," I said.

He nodded. "This reservation is about a quarter of the size of the one in Colorado. It's mostly the domain of the freshwater fae who need access to the lake for their—"

Water surged up the bank, flooding the nearby grass and racing over the frozen ground. But it didn't rise evenly. The water twisted and rolled to the side before it hit us, splitting and rising to a waist-high wall that enveloped our little group.

"Intruder," hissed a voice.

Chase grabbed James's shoulder and shoved him to the center of the dry patch so the rest of us stood between him and the vortex encircling us.

"Trespasser. Abomination." The voice came from all around us, carried on the wind and water. "Die."

Ribbons of water rose above the swirling mass, tapering into translucent spears—each pointed directly at James.

I stepped closer to him, blocking the path of one of the spears, and waved my arms. "He's not an enemy."

"Lies."

The water spears reared back, as though lifted by unseen hands.

I grabbed Morgan. "Get him out of here!"

She rolled her eyes, but shook me off and took James's hand, pulling him into the shadow of a leafless old oak.

He met my gaze as he stumbled backward.

Chase tackled me, grinding my side into solid earth.

Eight shimmering spikes pierced the space where James had been standing.

"He's gone," Haru shouted at the circling waves. "Go back to your patrol."

I stared at the place where James might have died, had Morgan been a second slower. The spears softened, losing their shape. They dropped to a puddle and ran back toward the larger body of water swirling around us.

A new shape emerged from the water wall. A female torso, arms, the impression of a face. "What is your business here, travelers?"

"We're only passing through," Haru said.

"Why did you bring the abomination?"

I shivered at the word, feeling it could just as easily be directed at me as at James. Anger blazed through me. "He meant you no harm!"

"His kind is a pestilence," the figure said. "They bring death, no matter their intent."

"The threat is gone," Haru said. "Let us pass."

I wanted to argue his admission that James was a threat, but I bit my tongue. My pride would serve no purpose here, except maybe to get us killed.

The shimmering woman continued to observe us, unblinking. Then she gave one small nod and sank back into the surrounding whirlpool. "Be on your way."

The water receded as quickly as it had risen, settling back to lap against the icy banks of the bay. I was suddenly very glad I didn't live near any large bodies of water.

Chase rose, smacking dirt off his knees. He looked visibly shaken. "I hadn't expected an elemental guard here. Hardly anyone bothers with this reservation."

"Why did Morgan bring us directly into the reservation anyway? I assumed she'd take us to the way station."

"Maybe she didn't know about the guardian either," Chase said.

Haru snorted. "More likely she was hoping for a little violence to liven up her trip."

Anger bubbled inside me at the suggestion. Would Morgan risk James's life to sate her boredom? Yes. Most fae wouldn't hesitate to sacrifice a vampire . . . for any reason.

I reached out along the silvery thread that connected me to James. *Are you all right?*

A long moment passed with no response. Then feelings of reassurance mixed with frustration filtered back to me.

I'm fine. Morgan and I are just outside a nearby town where I should be able to secure a safe house for your return.

I should have thought to specify where she brought us out. I never—

I'm fine, he reiterated. *Though I would have liked to kiss you goodbye.*

I wish you were coming with me. The thought slipped past my guard before I realized.

You forget, I am always with you.

I bit my lower lip. I knew from experience that our bond thinned with distance. Even now he was harder to hear than when we were together. With two realms of separation between us . . .

I tried to quash my doubts, to focus on saying my goodbyes with as much optimism as I could, but facing my imminent return to Enchantment, my worries bubbled up and leaked through our link. *What if I'm not strong enough, even with a name? What if Shedraziel takes control of me? I couldn't bear to be her puppet.*

You are no one's puppet, Alex. You are the strongest person I know. Then he whispered the name I'd shared with him.

Fire raced through my veins, and my bones thrummed. Every nerve in my body tingled, as if coming back to life after too long in the cold.

So long as I hold your name, Shedraziel cannot command you. Now do what you must, and come back to me.

"You okay?" Chase set his hand against my back, making me jump.

James's presence faded on a last note of encouragement, leaving me with the silence of my own head.

"Yeah, I just . . ." I shook my head. I wished I shared James's confidence. "Which way to the portal?"

We both looked at Haru, who pursed his lips, turned, and strode away from the water's edge.

Chase and I fell in step behind him. We walked for a few minutes in silence. As we moved farther from the shore, patches of snow blanketed the ground under the trees and bushes. Pines were interspersed with the naked branches of oak, ash, elm, and a dozen other species. I kept glancing toward the distant PTF guard towers. Was someone watching me through a pair of binoculars right now?

I shuddered and rubbed the back of my neck. I could only hope the misdirect I'd gambled on at the gas station wouldn't be undone so easily.

Haru stopped in front of a pair of trees—an oak and an ash. They looked just like the trees around them.

"Here we are," he said, indicating the space between the frost-coated trunks.

Yeah, I would never have found the portal on my own.

I glanced at Chase. He didn't look surprised, but he hadn't known which trees led to Enchantment, either. Even as limited as this reservation was, we could have wandered it for days without a guide.

"I'll go first," Haru said, "since I'm the only one of us who won't be arrested on sight if the other side is guarded."

He didn't wait for a response, just strode confidently toward the space between the trees. He winked out of sight between one breath and the next.

"Go," Chase said to me. "I'll be right on your heels."

Taking a deep breath, I stepped into the portal.

There was a moment of disorientation, when up was down, down was up, and I was turned inside out. Then my boots sank into calf-deep snow.

The trees were much closer than I expected, looming right in front of me compared to the vast clearing I usually arrived in. Some were bare of leaves, but most wore shaggy coats of green, burgundy, purple, or blue.

The forest also wasn't as quiet as I expected.

I turned. Behind me, ice creaked and tumbled in a sluggish current. The river was at least twenty feet wide, but it was hard to tell precisely where the banks began, because drifted snow camouflaged its edges. Bright afternoon sunlight glinted off the sculpted ice of a nearby waterfall.

"Alex!"

I turned toward Emma's call.

Haru was moving toward Mica, who stood beside a purple-needled tree a little ways away.

Emma ran awkwardly across the snow, her feet sinking deep with each hopping step. She reached me in six bounds and scooped up my hands, squeezing my fingers tight. "Did you do it? Were you able to get a true name?"

I nodded.

Relief washed over her face. "Then you'll be safe from Shedraziel." Her expression hardened. "We're going to get May back."

I returned the pressure in her grip. "We are."

Chase appeared beside me. He glanced at us, then turned his attention farther afield. He froze. A crease furrowed his brow. The corners of his mouth turned down.

I followed his stare to Haru, whose hands were tightly twined with Mica's. Both men had a soft, dreamy expression that seemed to indicate all the world had disappeared except for the person standing in front of them. Mica said something, too quiet for me to hear. Haru smiled. Not the sarcastic smile he usually wore, but the genuine smile I'd only seen a few times. The smile that lit up his whole face.

Then Haru blinked and stiffened, as though suddenly remembering where he was. He glanced back at us. His gaze settled on Chase for a moment, then slid away. He pulled his hands out of Mica's and took a step away from him. Both their smiles were gone.

I cleared my throat and refocused on Emma. "How'd things go on this end?"

"Fine. That scary guard lady didn't seem to suspect anything when you left. Mica and I have just been hiding here since. One person came and looked around, but Mica hid us. He said it was just a normal patrol, and we'd see them a few more times before you were back. We thought you'd take longer."

I tried to smile, but it came out as more of a grimace. "We took a shortcut."

"Whatever the case," Mica said. "Now that we're all here, we should move out. The forest patrols will be back this way soon."

We all looked to Chase, the only one of us who'd actually seen the entrance to the prison.

"There's a rocky outcropping to the south of the guard station," he said, "where we can check the lay of the land and make sure nothing has changed. From there, it's only a short walk to the gate, assuming we make it past the guards."

"How long will it take to get there?" I asked.

"It took *me* about twenty minutes." He looked pointedly at my feet, buried in the snow.

"Can we take gaala?" Emma asked.

Chase and Haru shook their heads at the same time I said, "That would be too conspicuous."

"Besides," Mica said. "I have something else in mind."

Chapter 24

MICA GESTURED FOR us to follow him into the trees, but stopped as soon as we all stood in the shallower drifts of the sheltering forest. Then he turned to face the area we'd just vacated. Clumsy mortal tracks covered the snow.

He closed his eyes for a moment and muttered something so quiet it came out as more of a hum. Then he opened his eyes, raised one hand perpendicular to his chest, and made a sweeping motion beneath it with the other.

I blinked and stared at the space I'd just left. The snow was pristine, sparkling in an unbroken sheet in the afternoon light.

"Nifty," I said.

"No point raising suspicion before we have to." He led the way farther into the forest, stopping twice more to clear our tracks.

We stopped at the edge of a second clearing, this one even smaller than the first. The rumble of the river was distant and muffled. The light was speckled across the snow, blocked by towering trees.

Mica pressed a finger to his lips. Then he reached into a pocket and tossed a scattering of deep-red seeds across the ground.

Chase raised an eyebrow. Haru crossed his arms and leaned against the nearest tree trunk.

I stared at the little seeds. They looked like drops of blood against the snow. *Guess we're just supposed to wait for something to—*

Branches rustled to my right.

A small, black nose attached to a short, furry muzzle poked out from beneath the waxy leaves of a bush covered with yellow berries.

Mica raised a hand in restraint, as though concerned one of us might suddenly rush the beast.

A moment later, a face emerged from the obscuring shadows, followed by foot after foot of rust-colored fur. The creature darted across the open space and started gobbling up the scattered seeds.

The creature was long, but not very tall—the fur on its belly brushed the ground. It had a raccoon-like face, short legs, and a bushy tail with faint rings in the fur. Other than its legs, which were dark, it was covered in shaggy, orange-red fur. It reminded me of pictures I'd seen of red pandas, if a red panda could grow six feet long and weigh two hundred pounds.

Another, slightly smaller creature shot into the clearing. Then another, and another, until the previously empty space was filled with tumbling, furry bodies.

Emma was practically vibrating beside me, her eyes wide and bright. "They're beautiful."

The mass of scurrying bodies rolled together for another moment. Then every wide, striped face turned in our direction, pinning us in the cross hairs of eight sets of shiny black eyes. The twitch of a whisker here or an ear there was the only movement.

I scanned the ground. Every last seed was gone.

Mica grinned and patted me on the back hard enough to make me take a stumbling step forward. "Let me introduce you to your new mount."

Mica took my hand and strode forward.

I leaned back, dragging my feet. "What are they?"

"Pyaku," he said. "Not as versatile as a gaala, but they're fast and sly. They'll get us where we need to go without drawing attention." He stopped two feet in front of the nearest pyaku and tugged until I stood even with him. "Open your hand."

I did, and he dumped a handful of the blood-red seeds onto my palm.

"Now kneel down and hold out the seeds," he said. "Don't drop them."

"They'll swarm me," I hissed through clenched teeth. I couldn't look away from the beady black eyes locked on my hand.

"No, they won't."

I remained standing.

None of the creatures moved.

Mica sighed. "Do you want to get to the prison today or not?"

I clenched the fist not holding the seeds and sank to one knee in the snow. I stretched my arm as far as I could, sure I was about to lose at least a finger or two.

One of the creatures scuttled forward, clawed toes scrabbling against the crisp crust of ice on the snow. None of the others moved.

The brave pyaku paused just shy of my outstretched hand. It sniffed the air. Then a quick, pink tongue darted out of its mouth and scooped the seeds out of my hand.

I blinked.

The pink tongue flicked out again, this time sliding around its furred lips as if searching for stray seeds that hadn't made it into its mouth. Then it plopped down on its haunches and stared at me, waiting.

"Congratulations," Mica said. "You've made a friend." He reached out and scratched the pyaku behind the ears.

"We're really going to ride these?" I asked.

"We are."

Emma stepped forward. "Can I try?"

"Of course." Mica pulled a small leather pouch out of his pocket, took a handful of seeds for himself, and tossed the bag to Chase. "Get her sorted, shifter."

While Chase helped Emma coax another of the pyaku over to her, Mica stepped away and called his own.

I buried a hand in my pyaku's fur. It was coarse and warm. Its wet nose snuffled my side, searching for hidden seeds. The seeds had left a slightly sticky residue against my palm. I sniffed it. The smell was sweet. My mouth began to water.

"What kind of seeds are those?" I asked, stroking down the pyaku's back to distract myself from the tantalizing smell.

Mica caught my gaze. "Goblin fruit."

My hand froze mid-stroke. I glanced at Emma. She was snuggling with the pyaku who'd come to her. Chase was holding the little leather bag.

I glared at Mica and scrubbed my sticky palm along my thigh. "Are you insane? What if one of us had eaten them?"

"Are you in the habit of eating animal bait?"

I compressed my mouth. For the fae, and apparently the pyaku, goblin fruit was a sweet treat that provided a mildly euphoric effect. For mortals, it was insanely addictive. "Where did you even get them? Do you just carry that bag around like you do your box of pixie dust, for when you need a hit?"

He frowned. "I borrowed them from Marron before I left. Why are you so upset?"

"Because you didn't warn us."

His frown deepened. "I hadn't realized mortals had so little self-restraint."

"That's not—" I groaned. "Never mind. Just let me know the next time you're going to put something toxic and potentially habit-forming in my hand, okay?"

He shrugged. "As you wish."

"So how do we ride them?" Emma asked, oblivious to the danger she'd held.

Mica demonstrated by scratching his pyaku behind one ear while he circled around behind it and straddled its back. Then he gripped the fur along the sides of its neck, just above the protruding shoulder joints.

"Hup," he said.

His pyaku stood, lifting Mica with him.

"Unlike the gaala, you'll need to sit low against the pyaku's back." He leaned forward until he was practically lying down and tucked his feet up against the pyaku's hips.

Emma was snuggled on her pyaku's back before Mica finished talking. I took a little longer. I buried my fingers deep in its coarse fur and leaned forward until the pyaku's spine was a hard line against my stomach. Then I gripped with my knees and tucked my feet up behind me to keep them from tangling with the pyaku's when she ran.

Chase tossed the leather pouch of seeds back to Mica, then stripped off his clothes. "Stay close," he said, and shifted to his cat form.

I nodded to the pile of abandoned fabric. "Want me to take your clothes?"

"We're better off without them," Haru said, shucking his own garments. "Mortal modesty will only get in the way if we need to shift quickly."

He nodded to Mica, who nodded back and whispered something into the ear of his mount. Then Haru shifted into the form of a large white fox with seven red-tipped tails. He turned his nose to the sky and gave a *yip*.

Chase took off, a gray streak over the snow.

The pyaku began to run. They didn't move with the forward-back motion I'd grown used to from the gaala. Instead, their legs blurred beneath them while their bodies zipped forward with an almost serpentine slither. Pressed as I was to the pyaku's back, there was hardly any jarring at all.

Despite the smoothness of the ride, I sank lower until the pyaku's coarse red fur tickled my chin. If the gaala ride had been a Ferris wheel, offering unobstructed views of the land below, the pyaku was a roller coaster. We streamed between trees and over boulders at breakneck speed. The ground was a blur. Thin branches whipped my sides, there and gone before I ever saw them coming. My hair streamed behind me, flying back from my face, and cold wind made my eyes water. I was hanging on for dear life, rushing headlong into danger, unsure where I was going—just like every other experience I'd had with the fae.

In front of me, Mica's pyaku ran neck-and-neck with Haru, as though the two were having a race. I couldn't see Chase. Around me, the other pyaku from the field wove around obstacles like streaks of liquid fur. I could barely see their legs moving. Together, the herd swept through the forest like a rolling red wave.

Emma's pyaku ricocheted off a tree and tipped sideways to scramble along the steep incline of a rock face, its claws scoring the surface. I didn't have more than a second to marvel before my own pyaku catapulted off the top of a rocky outcrop. I went weightless for a moment, then the pyaku twisted and streamed down the side of an enormous tree, its claws easily finding purchase in the bark as we raced headfirst toward the ground.

The mad dash through the forest lasted only a few minutes, but the experience left me wide-eyed and breathless.

"That was . . . amazing," Emma said as she slid off the back of her mount, holding its side to steady herself.

I could only nod. My legs shook slightly when I dismounted. The pyaku had taken us across a great distance, over terrain that would have otherwise slowed us to a crawl, in the blink of an eye.

Chase shifted back to human. "The overlook is this way," he said, and started walking.

Mica emptied the last of his bag of seeds onto the ground, and the pyaku once more became a roiling mass of scrambling bodies as they gobbled them up. I walked wide around the chaos and followed Chase up a steep incline.

He crouched at the base of some crumbling gray rocks. When he saw me, he pressed a finger to his lips and crawled to the edge of the outcrop.

I dropped to my belly and inched forward until I could see over the edge of the precipice.

Below, an area of the forest had been cleared away. A dozen tents were pitched at one end of the clearing. Beside them were several tables made from thick slabs of rock circled by various-sized tree stumps. Three of the stumps were occupied—one by a pale sidhe who sipped from a wooden bowl, and two by eloko who seemed to be playing some kind of card game. All the fae were wearing the green and leather livery of Bael's court.

Beyond the tables was a fire pit where a short, shaggy-haired gnome stood on a rock stool so he could stir a pot of bubbling stew.

Three fae sparred near the edge of the camp. Two held silvery swords, probably made from a nickel alloy, and attacked a lithe, pale-haired woman wielding a bronze spear.

A large wooden platform dominated the center of the clearing, with a guard posted at each corner. The platform itself seemed to be empty.

On the opposite side of the camp from the tables and guard tents stood a single, larger tent.

The flap of that tent pushed open and a face with an elephant trunk and tusks and a lion's mane peeked out. The long, leathery nose lifted into the air, sniffing. A large, gray-furred shoulder appeared, and a wide paw settled on the muddy ground. The baku lifted its head higher, stretching its trunk. It turned slightly in my direction.

I ducked behind the rocks. I knew that baku. I'd met him at the Winter Festival.

Baku ate bad dreams, and I'd been having plenty of those lately. Could he smell them from this distance?

Chase and I slid down from our perch, trading places with Haru, Mica, and Emma so they could take in the scene below.

"That baku is the captain in charge of guarding Shedraziel's prison."

I nodded. "Zhang."

The others joined us.

"Zhang is going to be a problem," Mica said. "We'll need to deal with him first."

"I'd like to do this without killing anyone," I said. Bad enough I was going against Bael's wishes—he'd probably never trust me again—but I didn't want to hurt his guards.

Haru chuckled. "As if the old bastard would go down that easy."

"Still, I agree." Mica smiled at me. "We should avoid shedding the guards' blood."

"And what about our blood?" Haru grumbled.

Chase smirked. "Guess you've gotten rusty in your exile."

Haru lifted his lip in a snarl.

I held up my hands, a palm toward each of them. "This isn't helping."

"I might be able to put the guards to sleep," Emma said.

The rest of us turned to her.

"Might?" I asked.

"Well, the spell isn't designed for fae." She shrugged. "But it's what Luke uses to anesthetize the werewolves when they're too worked up to hold still. It doesn't put them to sleep exactly, but it makes them numb and they aren't able to move."

Chase pursed his lips. "A spell that can sedate a raging werewolf should have a similar effect on most fae."

Haru nodded, looking impressed. "Can you cast it over the whole camp?"

She shook her head. "I have to touch the individual."

"So you'll need to get up close and personal with each guard to put them under." I frowned. "That's gonna be tough."

"We can hit the tents first," Chase said. "Take out the reinforcements."

"And the rest of us can deal with the active guards," I added.

"One of the guards posted on the platform will be holding a signal horn," Mica said. "We need to incapacitate them before they can blow it."

"And we still need to deal with Zhang," Haru said. "There's a good chance the knockout spell won't work on him."

I pursed my lips and turned to Mica. "When I met Zhang at the festival, and again when I was up on the rocks just now, I got the feeling he was attracted to me. Not sexually, but like—"

"A predator scenting prey," Mica finished.

I nodded. "Could we use that to lure him away from camp?"

He tapped his chin. "Baku are drawn to dreams and other emotionally-charged thoughts." He looked between Emma and me. "If one of you tempt him into feeding from you, I can ensnare him while he's distracted."

"How close would we have to be for him to notice us?"

Chase crossed his arms. "Baku can scent dreams over quite a distance, but negative emotions work best. If you had a nightmare just beyond the patrol perimeter, he might be enticed to investigate. But the dream would have to be tempting."

I frowned. "Humans don't have control over what we dream."

Mica waved my comment away. "I can put you in an enchanted sleep that guarantees nightmares."

"Lovely." I hugged myself. "What happens if he eats the dream?"

The three fae shared a look.

Chase cleared his throat. "We won't let that happen."

Emma turned to me. "Rock, paper, scissors for who's bait?"

I shook my head, remembering the way Zhang had sniffed the air when he came out of the tent. "I'll do it. I've got plenty of nightmares these days."

Chapter 25

CHASE DROPPED another broken branch on the ground, finishing the "bed" under the wide branches of an enormous tree that looked a lot like a weeping willow—except that it had needles instead of leaves and was bright pink. The tips of the lowest branches reached nearly to the ground, but they attached to the trunk well above head height, creating a drooping shelter around the open space at its base.

Rubbing my hands nervously, I settled onto the gathered branches that would insulate me from the frozen ground and tried to relax. The smell of pine needles and fresh sap filled the air. I looked at Mica.

He knelt beside my head. "Are you ready?"

I tried to still my shaking hands, wishing unreasonably that Emma was still there. Haru had taken her to the far side of the camp in preparation for the next phase of our attack.

Chase crouched and set a hand on my shoulder. "I won't let him steal your dreams."

I nodded.

Mica tugged the collar of my borrowed coat up to obscure my face. Then he placed chilly fingers lightly against my forehead. "I'd wish you pleasant dreams, but . . ." He smiled sadly.

I closed my eyes.

I'm standing in a valley. Warm wind blows the scent of decay into my face, whipping my loose hair into tangled knots. I shake my head, hoping the scene will change. I've been here before.

Corpses litter the ground around me, and every face is familiar. My mother, Oz, Aiden, O'Connell, Johnson. They all stare at me with wide, blank eyes.

Rows of humans in shining armor stand under the banner of the Church's sorcerer troops on the hill to my right. The patchwork specter of my father sits on a white stallion at the front. To my left, the faerie hoards scream their battle cry, Bael central among them.

But they aren't the only armies in this valley anymore.

Behind me, dozens of horse-size wolves stand shoulder to shoulder, a wall of snarling teeth and hungry eyes. I recognize Marc, the alpha, at the head of the column, Sophie beside him. At the opposite end of the valley, golden charms hanging around every neck, are figures with shining, metallic eyes and elongated teeth. James stands between Victoria and Bryce.

A horn sounds. Hazy red sunlight glints off armor, blades, teeth, and claws as the four forces descend into the valley. They will converge where I stand.

I try to move, but my legs are sunk in bloody mud up to my thighs. The ground shakes, as it did during my naming trial.

I twist and strain, but there's nothing I can do. I'll be crushed in the impending conflict. I'm helpless.

"No." I say the word out loud even though there is no one near enough to hear it. "The moment I give up is the moment I fail."

I continue to struggle as the armies advance, and one of my legs begins to pull free. But something is wrong. Great swaths of the sky have turned shimmering black. Holes appear in the oncoming ranks like faces burned out of a photograph, empty and charred around the edges.

Something slammed into my gut with the force of a dropped bowling ball.

I jolted awake, gasping.

Claws dug into my side as the weight lifted. I cried out. But mine wasn't the only voice.

"—hold him forever!" Chase was at the edge of the tree, kicking at the angry baku filling most of the space beneath the branches.

"I'm trying." Mica shouted. His voice came from somewhere beyond the obscuring needles. "You need to keep him there."

"She's going to get trampled." Chase failed to dodge a swipe from Zhang's front paw that sheared through several dangling branches, opening a hole in the living curtain. Four crimson lines appeared across Chase's chest and he tumbled into the snow with a howl of pain.

Bracing one hand against the rough bark of the tree, I sat up and pulled my feet under me. My body responded sluggishly, as though I were still swamped in the thick mud from my dream.

That gave me a nasty thought. Was this really happening? Or was I still dreaming?

I shook my head. Dream or no, my choice was the same. My friend was in trouble.

Zhang hunched, preparing to spring on the injured shifter.

I jumped first.

I landed squarely in the middle of Zhang's back and grabbed fistfuls of mane to keep from being thrown off when his body jerked. He bucked like a wild bronco. My back slammed into the drooping branches above, and a shower of needles rained down around us.

Zhang growled and shook.

My leg slipped and I flopped to one side, dangling off his back, but I still had a grip on his mane.

He swung his head. One ivory tusk skimmed my leg, snagging on the loose fabric over my dirty bandage. His trunk whipped back to lash at my head.

I buried my face against the spotted gray fur on his heaving side, but a sharp pull on my hair lifted my face.

There was a bright flash of crimson light. White sparks danced in my vision.

My feet hit the ground. Then my knees.

An arm snaked around my ribcage from behind, tearing me away from the falling baku. When I looked down, clumps of yellow mane were still trapped between my fingers. I glanced at Zhang, who'd collapsed onto his side, then up at Chase, who held me pressed to his injured chest.

"Thanks."

He cringed and released me. "Don't."

I frowned as he pushed through the curtain of battered branches and walked away. Fae didn't like thank-yous—not the way mortals used the term. For fae, debts and favors were a sort of complex currency, not to be treated lightly.

I crawled out after Chase, brushing dirt and needles from my clothes.

Mica was kneeling in the snow, breathing hard. That seemed ridiculous since he hadn't been the one fighting, but magic took a lot of energy.

I looked back at the fallen baku, realizing why my dream had changed at the end. Zhang had been draining it out of me, feeding on my feelings. I frowned. "Wasn't the point to hit him with your enchantment *before* he had time to react?"

Mica glared at me.

"He recognized you," Chase said. He was panting, each breath stretching the gashes in his chest so fresh blood welled out. "He pulled back before the princeling had a chance to spring his trap."

"Good job keeping him under the tree." Mica rose, bracing against his knees.

I shook my head. "I was just trying to keep him off Chase."

"Whatever the case," Mica said. "It worked out. Zhang will sleep under that tree for the next six hours."

"But we made a racket." Chase looked in the direction of the camp. "The patrol might have heard."

"Then we'd better get moving." I took a few unsteady steps before my legs started moving normally—the lethargy from my dream finally dissipating.

Chase and Mica hurried to join me.

HARU AND EMMA were crouched in a thick patch of bushes just beyond the perimeter of the camp, near where the guard tents were staked.

"Any sign of alert?" I asked as I dropped next to Emma, breathing hard from my jog. We'd skirted wide around the camp, and the terrain wasn't exactly level.

Emma shook her head.

Haru glanced at the scabbed-over gashes on Chase's chest. "How'd it go with Zhang?"

"He's down for the count," I said. I set a hand on Emma's shoulder. "Are you ready?"

She gave a stiff nod, lips pressed tight. We were counting on Emma's magic, which had never been intended for offensive use. I glanced at the three fae, meeting the eyes of each. If Emma's spell didn't work, we'd have to fight every guard in the camp. Even if she did manage to take some of them out, that still left plenty for the rest of us to subdue.

I swallowed to clear the lump in my throat. "Let's go."

We waited until the perimeter patrol passed before moving closer. Chase led the way, since the small, gray tabby was best suited for stealth and scouting. Emma inched along behind him, staying as low as she could. When Chase darted to the back of the nearest tent, Emma followed. The rest of us kept to the tree line.

Chase slipped under the lip of the tent. A second later, his little pink nose poked back out, then disappeared again. Emma wriggled under the fabric.

I held my breath.

Seconds ticked by.

Finally, when my lungs felt like they would burst, the edge of the tent lifted. Emma's sideways face appeared in the gap and she waved her hand in a "come" motion.

Haru, Mica, and I scanned the trees to make sure the patrol hadn't made it around yet. Then we scampered across the stretch of open space at the edge of the camp and darted under the side of the tent.

Inside, dim light filtered through the white fabric. There were two cots, one on either side of the tent. One was empty, the other held a sidhe woman with purplish skin and long, dark hair pulled into a braid. Her breath was deep and even. A woven gray blanket was pulled up to her chin.

I caught Emma's gaze and tipped my head toward the sleeping woman.

She gave me a smile and a thumbs up.

Mica knelt beside the occupied cot and set a hand against the woman's neck as though measuring her pulse. "So far so good," he whispered. "The test will be to see if it works when the target is not already unconscious."

Chase poked his head through the tent's front flap. His tail lashed back and forth. Then he looked back at the rest of us and gave a quiet "meow."

Time to move.

We made our way from tent to tent. Some were empty. Some held sleeping fae. Occasionally, Chase would peek into a tent, then immediately move on to another. Haru, Mica, and I stayed in the fourth tent. It was empty, and close to the tables where the active guards were eating, drinking, or playing. Haru kept lookout at the entrance. I peered under the side of the tent to keep an eye on Chase and Emma as they continued their work.

Emma managed to clear over half the tents before our luck ran out.

One of the fae I'd seen sparring near the edge of the camp walked toward a tent Emma was slipping into from the back.

I tightened my fists, resisting the urge to shout a warning.

The fae, a man with greenish skin, long ears, and a braid of rust-colored hair, pulled back the flap of the tent. He was wiping sweat off the back of his neck with a towel. Otherwise, he might have reacted sooner to the naked arm that shot out and dragged him through the opening. Unfortunately, his surprise didn't stop him from shouting.

It was only one short cry, but it rang through the camp.

"The guards are moving." Haru shifted to the form of a huge white fox. Mica stepped up to the tent flap and pulled a long blade from his boot.

"No killing," I hissed.

"No dying." He flung the knife into the dirt near my knee. Then he pulled back the flap, and Haru launched through the opening. Mica followed him out.

I grabbed Mica's knife, scrambled to my feet, and charged after them.

Haru was up on the stone table, his fangs deep in the shoulder of an eloko who'd been too slow drawing his weapon. The pale sidhe who'd been sipping soup lay on the ground holding a gash in his neck.

So much for avoiding bloodshed.

Mica had commandeered the downed fae's sword and was using it to devastating effect on the remaining guards. His attacks were fast and precise, and I was reminded that fae nobles were raised with a sword in their hand from a very young age.

I turned away, heading for Emma.

A goblin stepped out of a tent to my right. He was shorter than a human, with dark-green skin, a wide mouth, and bright-yellow eyes that widened when he saw me.

Our mutual surprise lasted only an instant. Then he grabbed for the sword at his belt.

Dropping my weight, I planted my boot in his gut, right over the dark-bronze blade clearing his scabbard. My kick pressed the sword flat against his stomach and sent him reeling back through the tent flap with a grunt. He grabbed the fabric as he fell, tearing it, which gave me an idea.

Gripping Mica's knife, I sliced through the guy lines holding the tent in place. The structure wobbled. I kicked the nearest pole, and the whole tent collapsed on top of the thrashing goblin.

But cloth wouldn't slow him for long.

Kneeling, I reached out with my free hand and touched the fabric. I felt the threads, tough but flexible. I called up my magic—not the untamed magic of the demons, but the warm, roiling mass at my center. Then I told the fabric to stiffen. The heavy canvas was already prone to stiffness, so it responded quickly to my coaxing.

The fabric snapped into place, folds and ripples frozen like cast metal. Half the goblin's snarling face was covered by a fall of fabric, holding his jaw closed while his lips pulled back from jagged razor teeth. He'd managed to pull his sword free as he fell, but the blade swung uselessly from a hand trapped in the air by a loop of the tent flap that had encircled his elbow. One enormous green foot flopped at the end of a trapped leg.

I stifled a laugh, picturing the ridiculous tableau displayed in James's gallery beside my other sculptures.

I call this one "Swaddled Goblin."

A panotti charged between two nearby tents, his elephantine ears tied back into a fleshy ponytail. His sword was out, but he stopped short, mumbled something, and drew a quick circle in the air with two fingers. Silvery needles flashed in the sunlight.

I dove away from the struggling goblin, rolling when I hit the ground, but I wasn't fast enough. Slivers of pain pierced my leg. Not debilitating, but a burning distraction that flared when I regained my feet.

I darted forward, closing the distance between us as the panotti sketched another shape in the air.

My knife arced toward the his chest, making him skip back, interrupting his spell.

Suddenly, pale arms wrapped my opponent, pulling him off-balance.

"Now," Chase shouted. His silvery hair was just visible over the pinned panotti's shoulder.

Emma stepped around the panotti and slapped her palm against his cheek. His eyes rolled back. His jaw sagged open, and a string of saliva leaked from the corner to dribble down his chin.

Chase dropped the limp fae, letting him crash to the ground. Then he pointed to the wooden platform at the center of camp. Somehow, in the few seconds I'd been fighting, Haru had made it to the platform and engaged the four guards stationed there. It looked as if he'd seriously injured one, and was keeping the other three from reaching their companion. Beside the downed fae, a white horn rolled across the wood and dropped into the mud.

"Get that horn," Chase said. Then he grabbed Emma's wrist and dragged her toward the stone table where Mica was keeping the remaining guards in check.

I raced across the open ground, but the woman I'd seen practicing with the bronze spear was headed for the horn as well. I was closer, but she was faster.

We reached the horn at the same time, but before she could grab it, I swung my knife at the woman's head. My blade slammed into the shaft of her spear, ringing out with the distinctive sound of clashing metal.

Face to face, the woman's skin, which had seemed only pale from a distance, was actually the nearly translucent blue of an aquamarine gem, and her eyes were milky white from edge to edge.

My mind stuttered for a moment as it tried to place her species. In that moment, she twisted sideways, and the lower end of her spear swept into my ankle.

My back hit the ground, knocking the air from my lungs and the knife from my hand. The tip of her spear dropped toward my face as I struggled to inhale. I rolled, and the bronze point buried itself in the ground, shearing off a lock of my auburn hair.

She stabbed again, this time landing a thin slice along my upper arm above the one James had wrapped earlier. The spear stuck in the ground, and I used the opportunity to roll up to my knees.

She grunted as she yanked her weapon free. Was she slowing down? Bronze was dense, heavy, and the spear she was swinging around was cast solid, rather than wood with a metal tip.

Surging to my feet, I grabbed the metal shaft, matching my grip to hers.

She pulled back. Her eyes widened with surprise, then narrowed as she settled back into her stance.

I concentrated on the metal beneath my hands.

The woman tried to shake me loose. When that didn't work, she twisted the spear so our arms crossed and swung it to the side. My shoulder slammed into hers, the spear pinned between us. She untwisted, stepping around me, and tried again to swing me loose. We moved together, both still gripping the weapon.

It was hard to focus on my magic while trying to keep my footing. When the warmth flooded me, I pushed it toward the spear.

Bronze is heavy, solid. That's the core of its existence. I only had to give it the slightest nudge to encourage those traits.

I released my grip the second I felt the spear start to sag.

The woman, still holding tight to the disputed spear, was pulled down by the unexpected weight. I brought my knee up to meet her descending chin.

Her head snapped back with a terrible *crack* as her teeth slammed together.

The spear hit the ground at my feet, sinking an inch into the frozen earth. The woman landed flat on her back. She didn't get up.

"Alex!"

I spun toward Emma, but she was pointing behind me as she ran toward the platform.

Two guards assaulted Haru on the far side of the platform while the third dropped from the near edge and scooped up the muddied horn.

I took two steps and launched myself at the goat-legged guard who was lifting the horn's golden mouthpiece to his lips. I tackled him mid-chest and we both toppled over, but not before a single, clear note rang out.

Chapter 26

I KNOCKED THE horn from the satyr's hand and pressed my forearm across his throat. Emma dropped beside us a moment later and set slim fingers against his forehead, carefully avoiding his curved horns as he lashed his head from side to side. As soon as the satyr fell limp beneath me, Emma moved on, climbing onto the platform where Haru had locked his jaw on the leg of the last conscious guard. The dark sidhe he'd been fighting lay gasping, one hand holding closed a gash across his abdomen while he dragged himself away from Haru with the other. A bright-red smear streaked the wood behind him.

Emma grabbed the outstretched wrist of the gutted fae. His head drooped to his shoulder. His body went limp. She hesitated before the final fae, probably mostly because Haru stood snarling over him with blood dripping from his fangs.

Chase and Mica came jogging toward us. Behind them, bodies lay scattered between tents and near the tables where the guards had been relaxing. The cookpot had been overturned, the fire doused. Chunks of meat and root vegetables littered the ground.

"You need to hurry," Mica said as he approached. He didn't even seem winded. "Now that the alarm has sounded, Bael will be on his way."

I groaned as I pushed to my feet. "How long?"

Mica shook his head. "Mere moments, but you'll have more time once you're through the portal."

I nodded. For once, the time distortion would work in our favor.

Mica vaulted onto the platform. "Stand back."

Emma moved to the very edge of the platform. Haru hopped off the side, once more in human form. The blood around his mouth was still there.

Mica dropped to one knee. He pressed his fingertips to the wood, closed his eyes, and let his chin sink to his chest. Then he started chanting.

"Is he casting a spell?" I whispered to Chase, who'd come up beside me.

He shook his head. "Breaking one."

I frowned.

A moment later, the air in front of Mica flashed. My ears popped. An oval of shimmering space floated in the middle of the platform. Mica stood, wobbled, and gestured to the portal. "The door to Shedraziel's prison."

Emma strode toward the shimmering distortion in the air, but Mica grabbed her wrist. He shook his head. "This is as far as you and I go."

She yanked her arm, trying to break free, but Mica had the strength of a fae, and Emma was so terribly mortal.

"May is *my sister*. I have to go."

"Not if you truly hope to see her survive this."

She blanched.

"He's right," I said. I'd been dreading this, dreading the look on Emma's face when I told her she had to stay behind. "Without a name, you'd have no protection against Shedraziel's magic." I hardened my heart. "You'd only be a burden."

"Besides," Chase added, "you've got plenty to do right here." He pointed toward the fallen guards near the stone table. The eloko who'd been playing cards was starting to stir.

Emma pressed her lips to a thin, white line. She tugged her arm again, and this time Mica let her go. She turned to me.

"Promise me," she said. "Swear you'll bring May back."

Retrieving Mica's knife, I climbed onto the platform and hugged her tight. "I promise. I won't come back without her."

The eloko was on his feet now, and some of the other guards were starting to move.

Emma hugged me back. Then she pushed me toward the portal.

"Go," she said. "And come back safe."

"We'll hold them as long as we can," Mica said. He looked from Chase to me, and finally to Haru. "Hurry."

I stepped up to the shimmering air, Chase on one side of me, Haru on the other.

"Not going to run away?" Chase said. He didn't look at Haru.

Haru lifted his chin.

Sighing, I rolled my eyes and stepped through the portal.

There was a disorienting jolt, then my boots crunched in hard gravel. From side to side, in front and behind, lay a field of tiny, smooth, black stones. Half a mile away in any direction was the dark line of a forest, except the trees seemed oddly tilted.

I frowned, tipping my head to one side.

Then I looked up. The cloudless sky was the color of rust and shone with uniform light. There was no sun. No moon. Not even the hint of a hidden light source on the horizon. The entire landscape seemed disturbingly flat, lacking highlights or shadows.

Chase landed beside me a split second before Haru.

Chase turned his bright-green gaze on the kitsune, as though surprised the latter had actually followed him through. "The odds are against us."

Haru looked away. "I know."

"Do you care so much what the princeling thinks of you that you would go against your own nature?"

"You knew my nature best." Haru's words were strained. "I am not a coward."

Chase scoffed. "A traitor then."

Haru spun on Chase, his eyes bright. His fists shook at his sides. "It was Anika who betrayed us by withholding information."

"Such is the right of a lord."

"And it was your blind loyalty that doomed us. If you'd run too, Nia might still be alive."

Chase stumbled back as though he'd received a physical blow, but he didn't deny Haru's words. The fae couldn't lie.

Haru took a noisy breath and blew it out. He seemed to deflate. "But I should not have abandoned you. During the mission . . . or after."

The three of us stood frozen on that desolate plain for a quiet moment. There was no wind, no sound of animals or running water, just the beat of my own heart and the rasp of my breath.

I cleared my throat. "As great as it is that you two are finally hashing out your issues, this isn't the time."

I set out across the disturbingly uniform landscape without looking back to see if the others would follow. Bael was on his way. I had to find and free May before he caught up.

It didn't take long to reach the edge of the forest, and when I did I found the trees weren't as slanty as they'd looked. I glanced back across the rocky field. The trees on the far side had nearly vanished beneath the horizon.

I rubbed my eyes. "There's something wonky with the angles in this place."

"It's the size," Haru said.

I looked at him blankly. "The size of what?"

Chase spread his arms. "This place," he said. "You could walk the circumference of this world in less than an hour."

"Is that why time moves so much faster here?"

He shook his head. "That is the whim of the lord. Some fae crave stability, others invite change. Bael slows his land so that the mortal world moves quickly by comparison, providing new delights to ease the passing of years. Shedraziel is also one who craves new experiences, so—" He gestured to the trees around us, which I noticed for the first time were not made of wood and leaves.

I rapped my knuckles against what should have been bark and found the solid resonance of stone.

"He built her a prison where nothing ever changes," I said with a shudder.

We continued through the stone forest until a sound caught my attention. Chase and Haru had already stopped, but I tromped a few more steps before my mortal ears caught on. Coming from somewhere ahead was the sound of running water.

"Wait here."

Before I could respond, Chase had shifted to the small gray cat I knew so well and darted ahead.

I looked at Haru. He shrugged one shoulder and settled into a crouch.

I was too anxious to sit, so I settled for wringing my hands while I waited.

I lost track of the number of times I glanced over my shoulder— wondering if I'd see Bael or Rhoana there—before Chase returned. He shifted back to human.

"Shedraziel's dwelling is up ahead," he said. "The children are being kept in a separate building"—he pointed to his left—"that way. I didn't see any guards, but there are at least two servants."

I frowned. "Servants? She's supposed to be in prison."

Chase raised his hands, palms up. "A hob and a brownie. They were carrying trays of food."

I wasn't expecting anyone besides Shedraziel, but the news that the kids were kept in a separate location was good. Maybe we could get through this without a direct confrontation after all.

I nodded to Chase. "Take me to the kids."

THE STONE TREES pressed right up to the sides of the building

Chase led us to, and I blessed their cover as we approached, since the land had no hills or valleys to hide us. The building looked more like a stable for animals than the kind of dwelling a person might live in. It had open sides, gaping slat walls, and only a thin lattice for a roof. Then again. . . . I looked up at the empty orange sky. . . . Without wind or rain, there wasn't much point to a sturdy structure in this place.

Along with the shabbiness of its walls, the building was also strangely shaped—a collection of long, narrow spaces that curved and wound between the encroaching trees. A curl of smoke rose from a stone chimney in the section farthest from my hiding spot. A moment later, the brownie Chase had mentioned exited the structure with a silver platter of steaming meat. He had spindly limbs draped in gray rags, and long, sharply tapered ears that were flattened by the tray balanced on his head. He walked barefoot over the smooth black pebbles that seemed to cover this whole world.

Once the brownie passed out of sight, we crept closer, Haru and I on human feet, Chase back in cat form. When only the haphazard slats separated me from the interior, I placed my hands on either side of a medium-sized gap between two boards. The surface was rough. I frowned at the feel of splinters seeking purchase in my skin. This structure wasn't part of Shedraziel's unchanging prison. Where had she gotten the wood?

Pushing the thought away, I pressed my eye to the gap.

Beyond the wall was a narrow aisle, on the far side of which were small, fenced-off areas. A pair of dirty, calloused feet stuck out at the edge of one. A grimy, tear-streaked face stared blankly from another.

My cheeks and limbs tingled as my blood raced with anger. Somewhere in that squalor, May was being held prisoner.

There was a scuffing sound to my left, and a short, fat hob with straw-colored hair stepped into the room from the far end. She wore gray rags similar to the brownie, but over them hung a thick canvas apron stained by rusty-red smears. In her plump arms, she carried a basket.

"Feeding time," she said as she strode into the room.

The penned children, so still before the woman entered, grew suddenly alert. Some reached through the planks of their stalls, others rattled the walls. The room filled with a multi-voiced, inarticulate moan.

The hob reached into her basket and pulled out a round, golden fruit that seemed to glow in her hand—goblin fruit.

The clatter in the cages grew more intense.

"Let's see who eats today." She tossed the fruit into one of the pens.

Beyond the rickety fence, a stick-thin boy with yellow eyes elbowed a purple-skinned girl in the face. Blood surged from the girl's broken nose as the two of them tumbled in the gravel, groping for the fruit. The girl kicked out, but the boy's backhand caught her across the cheek. She slammed into the wall.

The boy devoured his prize in three gluttonous bites. Red juice ran over his chin as the girl's blood had run over hers. The boy's yellow eyes rolled up. He shivered, then went still.

A shudder ran through me as the sweet smell of honey and citrus assailed me, making my mouth water, my stomach roar with wanting.

"Who's next?" the hob called.

I pulled my face away from the peephole, horrified. Horrified . . . and hungry.

Chase and Haru had found their own places from which to spy, but they both pulled back when I did.

"Can I kill this one?" whispered Haru.

I didn't know if Bael had assigned the hob here, or if she'd come into Shedraziel's service some other way, but she clearly enjoyed her role as warden. I handed him Mica's knife.

"Good." He slipped along the side of the building, toward where the hob had entered at the far end.

I pressed my face to the boards once more. There was a scuffle in the second pen, another fight for another fruit. The hob watched on, glee at her own importance written plainly across her face. Her smile was still in place when the knife slid across her throat, opening it wide like a second mouth. There was a gurgling sound. The basket fell. Golden fruits rolled across the floor.

The frenzy in the stalls increased as fruits tumbled tantalizingly close. Hands reached through gaps, fingers straining.

I frowned. The wood containing the children was not all that thick, nor were the gaps too narrow to squeeze through, given enough motivation. The fences were four feet high at most and open on top. Why not just climb out?

Chase and I circled around the near end of the building, coming in through the open side. The smell hit me like a hammer. Not just the tantalizing odor of the goblin fruit, but the rancid stench of waste and unwashed bodies—sweet, and sour, and sharp.

The hob lay face down in the gravel, her wound hidden.

Taking a careful breath, I kicked a nearby goblin fruit back toward Haru. "Can you get rid of these?" Chances were every kid in there was already addicted, but I didn't want to give them any more. I turned toward the cages and raised my hands in what I hoped was a soothing gesture. "You don't need to fight anymore. We'll make sure you all get fed."

I reached for the fence blocking the first pen. It was tied in place with a simple leather strap. No locks. No traps. The knot came undone easily, and I pushed the wooden gate aside.

The children in the pen cowered away from me, piling into the far corner. There was a goblin boy with olive-green skin and a bulbous nose, a pixie whose tattered blue wings were wrapped around his body like a blanket, and a human girl who couldn't have been more than four years old. All three had wide, frightened eyes.

I stepped inside the stall and held out a hand. "It's okay. We're going to get you out of here."

The goblin shook his head. The little girl burst into tears.

"We can't," shouted the pixie. "We'll die."

I jerked back. Could Shedraziel have placed some kind of curse on the kids so they couldn't leave? That would explain why they didn't try to escape, despite the poor quality of their cells, or rush the servant with the fruit, despite how hungry they clearly were.

I glanced back at Chase, who sat in the aisle, his tail flicking. Then I looked at Haru. He was down on one knee, sweeping the last of the goblin fruit back into the basket. Mica's knife was tip down in the gravel beside him. A long, thin blade was poised above his back.

I gave a strangled cry of warning, but I was too far, too slow, to be of any use.

Haru started to turn.

The blade dropped.

The tip of the sword slid into Haru's shoulder, and he let out a startled, angry yell.

Then my ears rang with a lower, louder sound, and a streak of white blurred across my vision. Paws the size of my face slammed into Haru's attacker, throwing them back. There was a snarl, a scream, and the sound of bone crunching.

In the time it took my heart to beat twice, the sword was on the ground, along with the attacker. An eight-foot-long white tiger stood over them.

Haru was sitting on the ground, one hand over his shoulder trying to stop the blood seeping between his fingers. His eyes were wide and unblinking, his jaw slack. But he wasn't staring at his attacker. He was staring at his savior.

I looked in the direction the tiger had come from, at the empty space where Chase had been sitting a moment before, then back at the tiger. Chase was larger as a tiger than he was as a man. Unlike the gray of his smaller cat form, he was covered with thick white fur with black stripes. He looked just like the tiger in the paintings in his room. The ones of Nia.

The figure pinned beneath his front paws twitched, and Chase's upper lip curled to reveal three-inch fangs. A low rumble shook my bones.

"Chase?" I stepped up beside Haru and gasped. I'd expected the person trapped beneath Chase to be the other servant, the brownie, back from his duties, but I was wrong.

Pinned with one clawed paw resting squarely on her chest, and the other covering her sword arm, lay a sidhe woman I recognized. A woman I'd hoped never to see again. Though I had to admit, I wasn't hating the view.

I didn't bother hiding my smile as I knelt down beside her. "You're a long way from court, Lady Pimm."

Chapter 27

THE WOMAN WHO'D orchestrated my humiliation at my court debut, who'd called for Kai's imprisonment, smiled up at me. Even flat on her back, with four hundred pounds of snarling tiger in her face, Lady Pimm managed to seem as though she was looking down at me with her diamond-white gaze swirled with silver. "As are you, half-breed."

I narrowed my eyes, but didn't rise to the bait. "What are you doing here?"

She sneered. "It seems you've found new fools to take the place of your lost knight. If you want an answer, call off your pet."

The rumble in Chase's throat grew louder.

I rested my hand against his furry shoulder. "Perhaps I should tell him to rip out your throat and be done with you."

"Would our lord look kindly upon you murdering a member of his court?"

"*Your* lord. And the threat of his displeasure didn't stop you trying to sheath your sword in Haru's back." I glanced at the kitsune, but he hadn't moved. He sat in the black gravel beside the basket of goblin fruit, his wide eyes fixed on Chase.

Pimm sniffed. "A mere consort, not sworn to the court."

I shook my head. "I don't have time for you."

Something like fear flickered through her gaze, there and gone in an instant. "You can't kill me."

"I can, actually." I wrapped my fingers around the hilt of her dropped sword and stood. "But I'm not going to."

I moved toward her slippered feet and grabbed the thick, green fabric at the hem of her dress. I pulled the fabric taut, then slipped the tip of the sword into it, severing the threads. I cut three strips off the bottom of the dress, exposing Pimm's pale ankles and calves.

Her feet kicked out. "What are you doing, you insolent mongrel?"

Circling back to her head with my three freshly cut strips of fabric, I planted the sword tip-first in the ground and knelt once more.

Pimm's head lashed from side to side as I pressed the fabric between her lips and cinched it tight with a knot that tangled into her pale-blond hair.

I patted the side of her face. "If you don't want me to turn that gag to iron, I suggest you stop struggling."

Pimm froze. Her eyes went wide, then narrowed. Hatred simmered in her diamond gaze.

I looked at Chase. "Let her sit up, but only sit up. If she makes any other move, kill her."

The white tiger backed slowly down the length of Pimm's body. He stopped with one paw resting on her knees.

Retrieving the sword, I rested the tip against the side of her neck. "Sit up."

She did, struggling slightly when her right arm wouldn't respond. Probably at least one of her bones was broken. When she was upright, her nose was less than an inch from Chase's exposed teeth. To her credit, she didn't look afraid.

Setting the sword aside again, I tied Pimm's arms together behind her back, careful to keep the cloth away from any exposed skin. I used the final strand of fabric to loop her waist and lock her bound arms in place, then I tied the trailing end to one of the more sturdy looking posts supporting the fenced pens. Once the knots were tight, I reached for my magic.

It had been easy to stiffen the tent canvas, or add weight to the bronze spear. I'd simply compounded a trait that was already there. When I'd forged a knife of pure magic to fight O'Connell, I'd created something from nothing. That had required me to call forth every drop of magic in the surrounding area, and drew all the demons there with it. I didn't have time to fight for control of my body. What I needed was something in the middle.

I probed the fabric, finding the truth of it, the bonds that held it together and made it what it was. I found the label "silk." Turning that truth in my mind, I found all the ways it fit together with other labels like "strong," "flexible," "smooth." I sorted those labels, discarding ones I didn't need, strengthening ones I did. Then I twisted the "silk," and replaced it with "iron."

Pimm gasped.

I opened my eyes, unsure when I'd closed them.

The circles of fabric around Pimm's waist and arms were now cast of solid iron, as was the drape of cloth holding her to the fence.

Chase backed up, settling onto his haunches just out of kicking distance.

Pimm squirmed and struggled, grunting into her gag.

I grabbed the collar of her dress, forcing her to focus on me. "This is for Kai." I balled my fist and slammed it into her beautiful face.

Pain lanced through my knuckles, and I shook them with a hiss. But the blood pouring from Pimm's narrow nose and the way her cheek was changing color was totally worth it. Maybe I was just an emotional mortal after all, but knocking the smug smile off her face felt good.

"Haru, keep watch for the other servant," I said. "He could return at any time."

Haru didn't respond. He hadn't taken his eyes off Chase, who for his part, stared at the gravel between his huge, white paws.

"Haru," I said again, with more force.

He blinked. "I never thought to see her likeness again."

Chase shimmered and shifted so he was once more in the shape of a man. "And I never meant to show it," he whispered. He looked at the open palm of his hand. "What you said before was true. If I'd run with you, Nia would have lived. She stayed to protect me, so I could get out. She saved me then . . . and again . . . after you left."

Haru looked away. "I heard you were lost to wilds for a time."

Chase nodded. "And when I came back, I carried her form."

"You were right to hate me," Haru said.

Chase frowned at the kitsune. "I never hated you."

Haru gave a small laugh. "Then you're the only one. I've been running since the day she died."

I set a gentle hand on Haru's shoulder. "A person can't outrun their past."

His voice dropped to a whisper. "Or their cowardice."

Chase sighed and tipped his face toward the lattice ceiling and the burnt-orange sky. "You're not the only one who's been running."

Both men lapsed into a silence made unnaturally thick by the lack of ambient sounds.

I cleared my throat, making them both jump. "Congratulations. That only took, what, six centuries?"

It was nice to know I wasn't the only one struggling to climb free of the emotional baggage from my past, but we had more pressing concerns.

Haru finally climbed to his feet. Color stained his cheeks. "I'll go keep lookout."

He scooped up the basket of goblin fruit and left without a backward glance.

I turned to Chase. "You okay?"

A small smile played on his lips. He nodded.

"Then let's get these kids out of here."

Returning to the cage I'd opened, I crouched in front of the three children still huddled in the corner. At least they seemed calmer.

"What did you mean when you said you'd die if you left?"

The pixie boy straightened up. He seemed to be the spokesman for the group. "The lord told us, 'Should you pass beyond your cells without escort, your heart shall stop and you shall fall down dead.'"

"I've seen it happen," the goblin added in a whisper.

I looked over my shoulder at Chase.

"We told you she was a powerful enchantress," he said. "Once she has a person enthralled, if she commands them to stop their heart, they will."

"Is there a way around it? Can we"—I waved my hands, groping for words—"un-enthrall them?"

He shrugged. "Someone like Mica could maybe break the enchantment, given time, but not you or I."

I turned back to the pixie boy. "You said 'without escort.' Does that mean you can leave if you have someone leading you?"

He nodded. "We're led to the lord when it's our turn to entertain her at court."

"So you could leave with us," I prompted. "If we were to escort you."

The boy frowned, his lips drawing down in a thin arc. "We serve Lord Shedraziel. I do not think she would want us to leave."

Bad enough these kids had been brainwashed into killing themselves if they disobeyed, had Shedraziel made them willing accomplices to their own imprisonment? Anxiety gnawed at my gut. I remembered the way the vampire Merak had used his magic to make me want to serve him, to please him, even as he hurt me. Would these kids fight us if we tried to make them leave?

I plastered on my best customer service smile. "Lord Shedraziel has asked me to fetch you and take you to a new court."

"Will the lord be there?"

"She will join you there. She commands that you go on ahead."

The pixie boy frowned. "You'll escort us?"

I gestured to Chase. "My friends and I will take you." I held out my hand. "Come with me."

Hesitantly, the pixie boy slipped his grimy fingers into my hand. I led him to the edge of the enclosure, held my breath, and pulled him across.

When he didn't collapse instantly of heart failure, I let out a noisy sigh.

He looked up at me.

"Wait here while we collect the others."

Chase and I set to work opening cages and coaxing out the children, my heart sinking a little further each time I failed to recognize any of the frightened faces. Finally, the pens were empty. A total of three humans and nine fae, ranging in apparent years from four to eight, stood in a wary cluster in the middle of the aisle. May was not among them.

Squashing the wobbly feeling twisting in my guts, I looked over the gathered children. "I was expecting to find a human girl, a little older than any of you. She has dark-brown eyes and black hair." I lifted my hand to chest height. "She's about this tall."

The pixie boy I'd first spoken to raised one quivering, stick-thin arm. He pointed behind me, in the direction the hob had come in from. "Older kids are kept separate. That way."

I smiled my thanks, but held back the words.

"Chase, you take this group back to the portal. I'll find the others."

He shook his head. "I don't like the idea of splitting up."

I gestured to the children. "They can't go alone, and we don't have time to argue." I turned away. Something tugged my pant leg, and I looked down to find a tiny hand gripping the fabric.

"You're not coming?" The tiny girl I'd found in the first cage looked up at me with wide wet eyes, fear plain on her human face.

I patted her tangled, brown tresses. "My friend will be your escort. He's going to take you where you need to go, and I'll be right behind you. But I have to bring the rest of the kids."

Her lower lip shook. Then a low grumble came from her belly and she dropped both hands to cover it.

I fought to keep my smile in place. "Then we'll have a big meal, and you can all eat as much as you want."

She stared down at her hands, clenched over her stomach.

I ruffled her hair one more time, then looked at Chase. "Get them out."

Past the open end of the building where the hob had entered was a cluster of trees that separated the prison stalls from the next structure.

This second building was wider than the first, more a room than a hall, but it was almost circular, due to the slats of its outer wall being secured trunk to trunk between the surrounding trees. There was also a single tree rising from the middle of the space, baskets hanging from its branches.

The chimney I'd seen before rose from a stone fireplace on one side of the room. A large black pot hung above the flame. I peeked inside and gave a sniff. Chunks of meat simmered in a thick red sauce.

I frowned. I hadn't seen any indication of animals in this world—not even the call of a bird.

Aside from the opening through which I'd entered the kitchen, there were two others. Movement caught my eye through the gap directly across from where I'd entered. I hurried in that direction, trusting Haru would not have let the brownie past him.

Jutting off the far side of the kitchen was another holding pen fenced by loose boards. Like the first pens, a wide range of fae and a few humans were contained within the flimsy barrier, but these people weren't spaced a few to a cell, and they weren't children.

Limbs tangled together, the corral's occupants lay in a heap. Their chests expanded and contracted, but their eyes were blank and staring. The two humans present had to be at least in their twenties, though the lines around their eyes made them look older. It was harder to tell the ages of the fae, but they all struck me as mature.

I rattled the fence. "Hey."

They didn't respond. Not a twitch, not a blink.

"Hey," I said louder. "I'm here to rescue you."

No one moved.

I glanced side to side. Not far from the pen was a large, flat stone with a slightly depressed middle. The top and sides of the stone were dark. Lying beside it was a pile of rust-stained fabric scraps. A piece of dull-white bone stuck out from the heap.

I looked back at the simmering pot. Bile rose to the back of my throat.

Yanking open the pen, I grabbed the shoulders of the first person in reach, a sunken-cheeked sidhe man, and shook him.

His head flopped back and forth. When I released him, he slumped back onto the pile.

I stumbled away, horrified. I'd felt the give in his flesh, the warmth of him. He was definitely still alive. But looking into his eyes was like staring into the eyes of a corpse. *Or a thrall*, I thought, remembering the blank stares of Merak's mindless minions.

Shaking my head, I retreated to the kitchen. May wasn't here, but I wasn't ready to accept defeat. I had to believe she was through the kitchen's final exit.

The next building was farther, tucked behind a thick cluster of stone trees.

Like the first, the long room was a collection of fenced animal pens. And like the first, children sat behind the flimsy wood gates. Some jerked away when I yanked open the doors to their cells. Others barely twitched. I searched each grimy, tear-streaked face. These kids were older than the first lot, but not yet adults. My heart sank as I opened cage after cage.

May was not among these children either.

Did you learn nothing from your last mistake? Bael's scornful words filled my head. *What proof do you have that your friend is there? Vague hints from an enemy lord? This is likely a plot to sow discontent between us.*

Discontent would be an understatement when Bael caught up with me. I'd blatantly defied him. And I'd dragged Mica, Haru, and Chase into it as well. Had that been Anika's goal from the start?

But there *were* missing kids here. Anika hadn't lied about that. Even if May wasn't among them, coming here had been the right thing to do. But if May wasn't here . . . where was she?

I forced my thoughts away from the boiling pot in the kitchen with a shudder, and tried to focus on the task at hand. I didn't have time to wallow in worry and self-doubt. There were plenty of children who needed saving right in front of me.

"I'm here to escort you," I said to a young woman in the open pen before me. Then I raised my voice so it carried to all the cells. "All of you. But first, have any of you met a human girl named May?"

"May?" A dull, grayish lump I'd mistaken for a large rock filling the back half of the pen began to move. Muscles rippled under translucent skin. The long, thin tip of a tail lashed the gravel, spraying stones. Then one golden eye focused on me from beneath a bony ridge, its vertical pupil narrowing to a slit. The tips of fangs peeked out along the edge of a long muzzle like that of lizard. Wide nostrils flared.

Dragon. The word popped unbidden into my head, but looking at the sinuous body I knew it to be true.

The girl in the cell shied back, pressing herself hard against the wall to give the great beast space.

"I know May," the creature said. Except its mouth didn't move. It was as though the words were spoken directly into my mind with no need for clumsy sounds.

I choked down a stiff swallow. "Where is she?"

The dragon tilted its head, and a tinkling sound drew my attention to the delicate silver chain around its neck. "You are not one of Shedraziel's creatures."

I indicated the chain. "Nor, it would seem, are you."

"The enchantress cannot take my soul, so she binds my body."

"You have a true name."

The dragon dipped its head. "But you may call me Zeraldi."

I jolted. "Lord Anika sent me to find you."

It was the dragon's turn to look surprised, though the expression was barely recognizable on the reptilian features.

I frowned. "I thought Shedraziel was only stealing children. How can you have a name?"

She straightened up, and for the first time I noticed the folds of leathery skin near her shoulders that suggested wings. "My kind do not have the same limitations as the younger fae. We are born with names."

I shook my head. "Then why did she take you? Surely she must have known you'd be hard to control?"

"But worth the effort." Zeraldi sighed. "Shedraziel craves unique experiences . . . and unique beings. I am the only opal dragon alive since the destruction of our home."

I opened my mouth, wanting to ask more about what an "opal" dragon was and why it was special, but now wasn't the time. "I'm going to get you home. But I need to know what happened to May."

Zeraldi nodded. "She came here a few days after me. Though she was frightened, she was brave and kind. But"—she turned her gaze away—"she was mortal. And no mortal can resist the enchantress's call."

I clenched my hands over the worms in my gut and thought of bloody meat being delivered on silver platters. "Is she dead?"

"No, but she is Shedraziel's plaything. She is in the pavilion, entertaining the lord. She is quite beyond your reach." She pinned me with her golden stare. "Now go. Take what children you can and flee this place."

I set my jaw, trying to stop my hands from shaking. May was with Shedraziel. I could save some of the kids. Most, even. But not her. Not without facing Shedraziel directly.

Would Bael listen now that I had proof of Shedraziel's crimes? Would he free the remaining kids? But then, he might leave May to rot just to spite me for acting against his wishes. I couldn't take that chance.

"Let's get that chain off you." I stepped into the pen and reached for the silver links.

"You cannot," Zeraldi said with a shake of her long snout. "The chain is enchanted. Only the hand that bound me may lead me."

"Shedraziel leads you back and forth herself?"

Again the huge face swung in the negative. "Her handmaiden fetches me when I am called to court."

I thought for a moment of the hob throwing fruit to the children. Then I shook my head. "Pimm."

Chapter 28

"ANY SIGN OF THE brownie?" I asked as I approached Haru.

"He'd be dead at my feet if there were."

"I've got the second batch of kids ready to go, except for one. Come on." I waved and headed back into the first structure.

Inside, I knelt beside Pimm, who I was gratified to see was sporting the first signs of two beautiful black eyes. Blood stained the gag in her mouth, but no longer flowed from her nose. She glared through puffy slits when I came close.

"We're going for a little walk." I reached for the iron fabric pinning her to the post and called up my magic.

"What are you doing?" Haru demanded.

"I need her." The cloth softened beneath my hand and I slipped the knot loose. The bands around her wrists were still solid.

"Stand up," I said.

She continued to glare at me.

"I'm pretty sure I only need your hand, and it doesn't have to be attached to your body. So stand up now, or I'll turn your whole dress to iron and watch you burn."

Pimm stiffened. Her gaze slid to the side. Then she struggled onto her knees and finally her feet.

I wrapped the end of her bindings around my hand like a leash and tugged her toward the second set of stalls.

The kids were waiting where I'd left them, frightened but docile. All except Zeraldi, who was still chained in her pen.

I led Pimm into the smaller space, dragging her forward when she shied back from the dragon. I couldn't blame her. I wouldn't want to face a person I'd imprisoned and tortured when they were set free.

"Remove the chain," I commanded.

Pimm whimpered. She shook her head.

I jerked the iron bindings and leaned forward to hiss in her ear. "Now, if you want to save your flesh."

She mumbled something, but the words were garbled by the gag.

"She says she's impressed," Zeraldi translated. "Mongrel or no, you're every bit as ruthless as your grandfather."

Zeraldi's words sent a shard of ice into my heart. I didn't want to be anything like my grandfather—a man who'd decimated a world, pushed a species to the brink of extinction.

I'd once asked Bael how he could be so cold.

Practice.

Bael's expression when he answered had been stern . . . but also tired. Had he started out cold? Or had things like compassion and sympathy drained out of him as the result of a million tiny compromises to his conscience over the centuries? If I lived long enough, would I be just like him?

Pimm turned sideways and stretched her fingers toward the danging silver chain.

"No tricks," I said, tightening my grip on her leash.

The silver links fell away from Zeraldi's neck. The dragon stood, forcing Pimm and me to shuffle backward lest we be knocked down. Zeraldi shook herself, wings spreading slightly before settling along her back. Her head reached the lattice ceiling.

"Um . . . you're going to be a bit conspicuous running for the gate," I said. Then I looked around at the small entrance to the pen and narrow aisle. "How did you even get in there?"

Pimm mumbled something else. It didn't sound like a compliment.

Zeraldi shimmered and shrank.

In the dragon's place stood a human-looking girl of about eight years old. Human-looking, that is, except for the vertical pupils in her bright, golden eyes and the sharply tapered ears peeking out of her pale purple hair. Her skin was chalky white.

The girl Zeraldi knelt and scooped up the silver chain from the gravel. She stepped lightly out of the stable and stopped before Pimm, but her eyes went to me. This time when she spoke, her lips moved.

"Would you hand over your prisoner, so that justice might be served?"

I recalled Kai telling me, what felt like forever ago, that fae justice rested in the hands of the wronged party. Zeraldi had every right to serve as judge, jury, and executioner of the woman who'd imprisoned her. Even if Shedraziel had been the mastermind, it had been Pimm's hand on the chain.

Pimm was mumbling again, shaking her head.

"As long as you take her away from here to dole out your justice. I still need to find May, and I can't have her making a ruckus."

"Your friend isn't among these?" Haru swept a hand over the waiting children who stood in the middle of the room with vacant expressions.

I shook my head. "She's with Shedraziel."

"Then she is lost."

"I can't leave without her."

"To face Shedraziel directly is a fool's errand."

"I have my name to protect me."

"And did a name protect her?" He gestured to Zeraldi. "The power to enthrall is not her only weapon."

I gripped his shoulder. "Take the kids to the portal. I'll give you as much of a head start as I can."

"Chase will not forgive me if I abandon you here."

"You're not abandoning me. You're helping me. I can't face Shedraziel while these kids are still in danger. If I fail, I need to know that they, at least, are safe."

He pursed his lips. "We'll come back for you as soon as the children are beyond Shedraziel's reach."

Nodding, I turned back to Zeraldi. She waited patiently, the silver chain clutched in her fingers. "You suffered at Pimm's hands, so she's yours."

She smiled a very inhuman smile and slipped the silver chain around Pimm's neck. The links sealed into a smooth circle with a dangling tail, which Zeraldi held tight.

"Please remove your toxic metal," she said. "She will cause no more trouble. Her magics are bound."

I wasn't thrilled to use more magic, and therefore energy, when I was about to face Shedraziel, but I could understand Zeraldi's request. The bindings were a hindrance to more than just Pimm. With the iron in place, no fae could touch her.

I coaxed the fabric back to its natural state.

Pimm started to slump as though the metal had been her only support, but a slight tug on her chain had her standing ramrod straight again.

"Good luck," Zeraldi said. "I hope you're able to save May. And . . . thank you." She flinched as the words left her lips. "I am in your debt."

An awkward silence fell as I nodded to acknowledge the importance of those words. Then I helped Haru herd the children toward the exit.

Zeraldi brought up the rear, with Pimm in tow. When the group was far enough away that I couldn't hear the mortals' footsteps, I set off in the direction of Shedraziel's court. I still had a promise to keep.

I SLUNK ON MY belly through smooth, black gravel until I was level with the last stone tree before a bare stretch of land like the one surrounding the portal. But at the center of this clearing stood a white marble floor. The trickle of water in a fountain and lilting music drifted to me on the still air. Ionic pillars stood at each corner of the marble square and halfway along each side, all overgrown with creeping vines and thick, heart-shaped leaves. Goblin fruit hung heavy from the plants. A small dais with a carved divan sat at one end of the wall-less "room," backed by a lattice overgrown with more of the golden fruits.

Upon the divan lounged a woman with cerulean skin and long falls of curled hair that faded from indigo to teal. Unlike most court fae I'd seen, Shedraziel left her hair loose; it fell over her shoulders and draped her curves. She wore a translucent cream-colored gown that slithered and slipped over her skin when she shifted positions.

The brownie I'd seen earlier knelt on one knee beside the divan. He held the silver tray steady before him—a table for his mistress. She plucked one red morsel off the pile and popped it into her mouth.

Bile rose to the back of my throat as I recalled the blank expressions and unresponsive forms of the people in the corral and the simmering pot on the fire.

On the far side of the mock court a man leaned against one of the pillars. I couldn't make out his face, but I recognized the green sash he wore. He'd been Pimm's companion at the Winter Festival, and he'd taken particular pleasure in my humiliation.

Beside him, a malnourished teen painted a monochrome sunset upon a large canvas. He smeared a streak of bright red with his fingers. He didn't seem to have any brushes. I blinked and frowned. He didn't seem to have paint or palette either. Then I saw him reach for his wrist. He lifted a dark glob on his fingers and splattered it across the foreground with a flick of his hand.

Two children spun through my line of sight, breaking my fixation on the thick, red paint that wasn't paint dripping down the canvas. The dancers—a boy with pale-green skin and hair that resembled gnarled bark, and a girl who looked to be a mortal teenager—moved together, but never touched. They danced for the entertainment of their lord and captor, and where they passed, bloody footprints decorated the white marble.

At the farthest end of the mock court stood the musicians.

Nearest me was a short, round fae with a body like a brown balloon and a mop of coal-black curls. Fur covered his legs, and his cloven hooves clicked against the marble when he moved. Trilling notes drifted from the pan flute pressed to his lips, and his chest swelled and heaved like a bellows to keep the flute from falling silent even for a moment.

Beside him sat a woman with skin the color of sea foam and greasy gray hair that matched the faded rags hanging from her shoulders. A pair of delicate horns grew from her forehead and curled above her ears. Across her lap lay a stringed instrument from which she coaxed a wide range of notes in rapid succession, alternately pounding the strings with a felted hammer and strumming them with her wickedly long nails.

The final musician was tall and willowy, with straight black hair that trailed to her waist. Her right arm blurred as she slid a black-haired bow over a battered violin. Her fingers flew over the strings. Blood dribbled down her hand and arm from split fingertips, dripping from her elbow. She wore a pair of faded jeans that ended mid-calf in a tattered hem. Her pale-pink shirt fell short of covering her abdomen and was worn so thin the fabric was nearly transparent.

The girl turned, tracking the motion of the dancers who swirled past her.

A wave of nausea swept over me. The violinist was far older than the eleven-year-old I'd come to save . . . but her face was a younger version of Emma's.

I took a deep breath and forced my muscles to relax as I studied the girl. May had grown taller, but it looked as though she'd been stretched without adding any new material. Her cheeks were sunken, her limbs thin, and her eyes bore the same hopeless, glazed quality as the children in the animal pens. But she was not beyond recovery. Not yet.

I glanced over my shoulder. Had Haru gotten the remaining kids to safety? Were he and Chase headed back, or were they captured by Bael when they crossed the portal? Even if Bael hadn't arrived yet on the other side, I had no idea how long the handful of moments it would take to pass the kids off to Emma and Mica and get back through the portal might take here in Shedraziel's nightmare realm. I was not mentally, emotionally, or educationally prepared to do that math. Somehow, I'd missed calculating time differentials between realms as a college course.

I sighed and turned back to Shedraziel's grotesque court.

Gaining a name had been a safety precaution—a measure of protection should Shedraziel get hold of me. It was by no means a guarantee that I could stand against her if I was foolish enough to challenge her flat out.

I tried to swallow, but my mouth was a desert. My throat constricted over nothing.

Looking at Shedraziel and her puppet prisoners, fear gripped me. The thought of being a slave to another's will, a helpless passenger in my own body as I had been while enthralled to Merak, made my blood freeze. What good would a fae name be in the hands of a mortal mongrel like me?

I imagined the mirror me from my naming trial gesturing back the way I'd come, offering me the exit. But this time my quarry was not a phantom from my past, but a promise to the family I'd built. To the future I wanted. This time, turning back wouldn't just be letting go. It would be giving up everything I'd been fighting for.

This was my choice. Kai's voice echoed in my head as it had off the walls of his prison cell in Bael's dungeon. *What kind of knight would I prove myself to be if I ran away?*

I was no knight, but I was starting to understand where Kai was coming from when he chose to face his sentence. We all made choices to either protect or abandon what was important to us, and those choices changed us, defined us. My father went to war to fight for his beliefs, misguided though they might have been. He tried to build the future he wanted. My mother ran from her past and her memories and spent her life adrift. The past and the future were two roads stretching out from every person, in every moment, and we each had to choose what mattered most to us.

I'd come to save the children. I promised I wouldn't return without May. For better or worse, I'd made my choices. The only question that remained was whether I was strong enough to see them through.

I closed my eyes, took a deep breath, and pushed to my feet. Shoulders back and head high, I strode across the empty space surrounding Shedraziel's court.

Though the odds were against me, I wouldn't give up. I would fight for the future I wished to protect, and the people I wanted in it.

Chapter 29

"WELL, WELL." Shedraziel sat up on her divan and swung her long blue legs around so her feet rested on the floor. "I was wondering if you would come out on your own." She closed her eyes and lifted her face to the rusty sky. "From the flutter of your heart, I thought you might flee."

I forced myself to keep walking, to keep my expression blank, though the realization that she'd known I was there the whole time was like a bucket of ice water dumped on my head. If I'd chosen to run, would she have hunted me down? Or simply let me go to wallow in my own cowardice and shortcomings?

A cruel smile curved her lips. "I'm pleasantly surprised."

I stopped just before my feet crossed the line where black gravel pressed against white marble.

"I've come for the children," I said. My voice was strong and steady. It sounded nothing like how I felt.

"Then you shall have them," she said. "For as long as they last."

She plucked another juicy morsel from the silver tray and popped it into her mouth.

I glanced away and tried not to gag as the meat passed her lips.

Elliot was no longer leaning against the pillar, but neither did he seem concerned by my arrival. He watched me with slitted yellow eyes, a sneer on his lips. The painter continued to paint, the dancers to dance, and the musicians to play. May had not missed a single note, nor did her expression change. Her blank stare drifted over me without recognition.

I looked back at Shedraziel, who swallowed, then licked the tips of each dainty finger.

"Come here, child," she said. Her voice held a musical quality that put the nearby minstrels to shame, and I found my boot on the marble before I realized what was happening.

I pulled my foot back from the white line and set it solidly on the gravel.

I have a name, I reminded myself. *I am my own person. I don't have to do what she says.*

Her eyes narrowed, her deep green gaze focused on me. One arched, indigo eyebrow rose.

"I said, come . . . here . . ." Her fingers coiled shut one at a time— a trap sliding closed over her palm—and as each joint curled, her pull grew stronger. Her fist closed, and it felt as though her fingers gripped my heart rather than empty air. I struggled to breathe. Then she leaned forward and I felt myself falling into the green abyss of her eyes. "Alyssandra Blackwood."

Her power slammed into me.

I swayed, feeling my control slipping away. I clung to the name I'd fought for and found, praying it was enough to keep me afloat in the storm, but even as I chanted it in my mind, I lost sight of it . . . of me. I was drowning in the tsunami of Shedraziel's will.

My foot moved again. I strained against the motion, tensing my muscles till they screamed. Sweat beaded on my forehead. I bit my lower lip hard enough to break the skin.

My boot came down on the line, bridging the gravel and marble. Not exactly a loss. My weight shifted. My other foot rose.

Again I strained. My body shook. My foot came down.

A sob escaped me as my boot touched down entirely on the white floor. I wasn't strong enough. Even with the added protection of a true name, my will was no match for Shedraziel's magic.

If I give up . . . I die . . . and every choice that led me here will have been for nothing.

My teeth ached under the strain of my clenched jaw. My eyes watered. Cold sweat drenched my back. My whole body vibrated as Shedraziel and I played tug-of-war with my muscles.

She shifted in her seat and the corners of her mouth turned down slightly.

At least I'm making her work for it. But the thought was cold comfort as my heel lifted away from the gravel and I moved one step closer to my doom.

I might fail. But I wouldn't give up. I wouldn't do her work for her.

Three steps and I was ready to collapse. My muscles twitched and cramped as though I'd run a marathon. I was lightheaded with exhaust-tion. When the call came for the next step, I used the last of my energy to stop it dead.

I wavered on one foot, the other frozen precariously in the air. Shedraziel's power bombarded me like waves against a rocky shore, eroding my will.

My control cracked. My leg started to move again. I wasn't strong enough. But just as Shedraziel's will surged to victory, the memory of James's voice flared in my mind.

So long as I hold your name, Shedraziel cannot command you.

My every cell seemed to come to attention, singing with his words. Where Shedraziel and I struggled, James dominated. For the first time, I fully realized the terrifying power I'd given him. The power to control me. His word was law, etched in my very soul.

Now do what you must, and come back to me.

James's remembered command shattered Shedraziel's hold, and I found myself in control of my own panting, shaking body once more.

Now that I wasn't struggling for every breath, I was able to think. Pushing aside thoughts of what James's new authority might mean for our relationship, I focused on Shedraziel. Her pull was still there, but like the call of an impulse buy at the grocery store. I could resist. But then what?

The power to enthrall is not her only weapon.

Controlling me was only the beginning of what she could do. When she realized I wasn't in her power, the battle would begin in earnest. Even carrying Pimm's pilfered weapon, I didn't relish my chances against one of the best swordsmen in Enchantment. And that was assuming she didn't set Elliot, the brownie, or the brainwashed children on me. What if Shedraziel fought through May, using her like a puppet?

Her call hadn't eased any, so she still thought she could win our struggle for dominance.

When the next impulse to step hit me, I let it pull me forward. Now that I had the choice, being dragged forward wasn't nearly so scary. I wanted to go to Shedraziel, to get as close as I could. Close enough to strike before she knew what was happening.

As my feet shuffled forward, I unfocused my eyes and forced my jaw to relax, mimicking the glazed expressions of the children still dancing around the court.

"That's it," Shedraziel crooned when I'd crossed three quarters of the distance between us. "Stop there."

The pull to move eased, so I let my weight settle evenly in place.

She turned to Elliot. "You said she was weak."

"You disagree?"

"She put up more of a fight than I expected."

"Mortals burn bright," he said. "But they can't sustain it."

Shedraziel's laugh was like chimes in a tornado, high and wild. She stood and walked closer to me, stopping just out of striking distance.

"You won't be needing that." She pointed to Pimm's sword. "Drop it."

The blade rang against the stone floor.

"Good girl. Do you have any other weapons?"

I shook my head.

"Let's be sure," she said. "Clothes off."

I hesitated for a second, then slipped off Mica's borrowed coat and let it fall to the ground. The oversized orange sweater joined it. I stepped on the back of each boot and pulled them off. Keeping my expression carefully neutral, I unzipped my pants and slid them down my legs. The air was neither warm nor cold against my skin, but I shivered.

Shedraziel walked a slow circle around me as I stripped, and I struggled to keep the humiliation off my face.

Let her believe she's won. Wait for her to drop her guard.

My sword was on the ground. The only other weapon I saw was hanging on Elliot's hip. Shedraziel seemed to be unarmed.

Turning my focus inward, I tugged at my magic. The amount of power inside me wasn't enough to create a sword, or even a dagger. Not on its own. And I couldn't risk a struggle with the demons who seemed twined with the other energies I could call. I'd have to stick with something small. Something subtle.

Slowly, carefully, I funneled magic into my index finger.

"That's enough," Shedraziel said from behind me.

I froze, hands on the hem of my shirt. Had she sensed my magic?

She stepped closer, her breasts pressing against my back. Then she reached around so her arm lay across my throat. She dragged one tapered nail over my cheek.

I held my breath, clamping down on the urge to react.

She rested her chin on my shoulder and smiled at Elliot. "Were you enjoying the show?"

He cleared his throat and looked away, scowling. "Even for a mortal, this child is far from beautiful."

"Then why were you blushing?"

"Due respect, but this is hardly the time for—"

"Perhaps you weren't," she cut him off. "It's so hard to tell with that complexion of yours."

Now the greenish tinge of Elliot's skin really did take on a blush of red, though I doubted the shift had anything to do with me.

Shedraziel turned so her lips touched my ear. "You mustn't judge Elliot too harshly," she whispered. "He takes what comfort he can from tormenting the likes of you to ease the sting of his own shameful origins."

Elliot's scowl shifted to something resembling fear. "My lady—"

"Lord." The single word was spoken with a voice like iron.

Elliot's chin dropped to his chest. "Apologies, my *lord*, but I don't see why the girl need know any more about me."

She pressed her cheek to mine and looked directly at Elliot. "He doesn't want you to know he's part goblin."

Shame and anger warred on Elliot's face. If not for the fact that I hated his guts, I might actually have felt sorry for him. Why was Shedraziel teasing him like this? Weren't they allies?

I flexed my finger, testing the shape of the magic I'd gathered, but I didn't dare glance down. I was forging by feel, like shaping clay with my eyes closed.

Just a little more.

Shedraziel stepped away so abruptly I nearly fell into the space she left. "Mongrel though he is, he's fae through and through. Which is more than I can say for you." She sauntered back to her divan and sat down.

I silently cursed the distance she'd put between us. I needed to be close for any hope of success.

She leaned back, crossing her long, blue legs. "Mongrel is too plain a term for you."

From inside her gown she pulled a length of chain. A small, silver locket swung at the end. A stylized letter "A" was engraved on one side.

My breath hitched. I barely stopped myself from darting forward to snatch back the necklace I'd lost in Enchantment—stolen from my room during the Winter Festival.

"Imagine my surprise when Elliot brought me this," she said, gaze fixed on the locket as it spun slowly at the end of its chain. She flipped it open.

I couldn't make out the details of the picture inside, but I knew it well enough. Six-year-old-me smiling at the camera, wrapped in my father's arms. Etched into the opposite side was the last promise he made before he walked out of my life forever: *I'll give you the world.*

"I knew about your connection to Bael, of course. But Darius?" Her wild laughter broke out again. When it subsided, she licked her lips.

"How delicious. Do you suppose Bael knows yet?"

It was a struggle to keep the confusion off my face. My father's name had been Darren Carter. He didn't have any siblings, or even cousins, that I was aware of. So who was Darius? Had she made a mistake?

Shedraziel frowned and her gaze lost focus, as though she was looking at something far away. "That was such a long time ago," she whispered. "Tell me, child. Does your father yet live?"

I opened my mouth, unsure what to say. How would I react if I were properly enthralled?

"My father died," I said at last. "During the war."

One arched eyebrow rose. "He was alive at the signing of the treaty."

The words were a kick to the gut. This time, I couldn't keep my expression slack as her statement warred with the truth I knew.

"You really believed that." Shedraziel was studying me. "But then, you would have been little more than a child, and mortal memories are so unreliable."

I schooled my expression as quickly as I could. Would she realize the truth?

But she just tipped her head back and sighed, a wide smile spreading her lips. "Darius was a wonderful adversary—the strongest practitioner I ever faced."

So I'd guessed right about my magic's strange properties, assuming Darius and Darren were one and the same. The confirmation should have been gratifying, but it wasn't. The truth just opened up more questions—about my magic, about my father, about the demons who welcomed me when I called on their power.

She shifted her gaze back to me. "Come." She patted the space beside her. "I shall tell you of the glorious battles we had before the politicians got in the way."

I shuffled forward as I had before—slowly, taking care with each step—but every inch of distance that shrank away sped my heart until my pulse was a steady flutter of indistinguishable beats. I turned when I reached her, and lowered myself to the divan. I was once again within striking distance.

"I wonder how your father would have felt about having an abomination for a daughter?" She spoke the question offhandedly, like she was asking my opinion on the weather, but the words echoed those of the patchwork man in my naming trial.

Abomination.

"Darius seemed a practical man," Shedraziel continued. "Like Bael. Hardly one to throw away a useful tool, no matter its origin."

She turned slightly away from me to retrieve a bloody morsel from the brownie's tray. Her back was exposed.

Moving as fast as I could, I pressed her flat to the divan, pinned her arms, and plunged my index finger, now wrapped in a sheath of sharpened magic, toward her neck. I slowed only once the tip of my magical needle pierced the surface of her skin.

Shock rippled across Shedraziel's face. Then her laughter filled the court.

Elliot stepped toward us, his sword out.

"Ah-ah," I said, pressing the needle deeper into Shedraziel's neck.

Her laughter cut off and Elliot froze.

I frowned down at Shedraziel. I'd gotten the upper hand. A little more pressure and I'd slice her carotid artery. She couldn't move without inflicting more damage. . . . So why was she smiling?

"Well done," she said. When she spoke, blood seeped out around the wound in her neck. "Tell me, how did you break my enchantment?"

"I'm under no obligation to answer your questions," I said. Then I looked at Elliot. "Drop your sword."

A muscle worked in his jaw. His eyes were narrow slits—apertures to focus his hatred. He glanced at Shedraziel.

"Do as she says." Again, the words released a trickle of blood over her throat.

Elliot's sword clattered to the floor.

I shifted my weight over Shedraziel. Everything was going to plan. So why was I the only one who seemed to be off balance in this situation? The brownie hadn't moved, the chunk of meat Shedraziel dropped when I shoved her down lay on the floor at his feet, a bloody splat pattern streaked the white stone around it. The children continued their endless entertainment, oblivious to their captor's plight or their would-be rescuer.

"Release your hold on the kids," I said.

She pouted her lip. "But life here is just so *boring* without them."

I leaned in harder, pressing my weight into her shoulder. "Your spell will break if you're dead."

Her gaze slid up to me. Her smile was back in place. "Are you sure about that?"

I licked my lips. I wasn't sure. But even if the enchantment didn't end on its own, I'd find a way. Maybe Mica could fix them. I twisted the needle. "Do it."

Still smiling, she snapped her fingers. The six children dropped like discarded puppets. Blood continued to seep from the dancers' raw feet, and a pool formed under the painter's left wrist. May's violin cracked against the ground.

I stared at her limp form, longer and thinner than the girl I remembered. I shook my head. "You're sick. Taking kids to be your own personal playthings?"

"Oh, child. Did you think I took that girl for her musical merits?" Her grin grew. "She's talented, no doubt. But a prodigy to warrant my attention? Hardly. She was an invitation, a means to an end. Her fate rested entirely with *you*."

The accusation chilled me. Emma had been beating herself up because she believed she was to blame for May's abduction. Would she be able to forgive me when she learned her sister's predicament was not her fault, but mine?

Unsettling as Shedraziel's statement was, I wasn't entirely surprised. It was too much of a coincidence that May was targeted by Bael's ex-general. Bael had even speculated I was being set up, though he'd gotten the details wrong. Much as I tried to protect the people around me, Loni was right. I *was* a bad influence. My friends would always be targeted because of their relationship to me. And I'd continue to be targeted because of my relationship to Bael.

"Bael's newest toy," she teased. "How could I resist? But what really decided me"—she twitched the locket in her hand—"was this."

I once again resisted the urge to snatch my necklace back. If I let her goad me, I'd play right into her hands. Just as I had with Pimm and Elliot at the festival.

"Part practitioner, part fae. You, my dear, are unique, and a fitting addition to my collection."

I smiled. "You mean your collection that used to be locked up in those animal pens?"

Her smile faltered, her expression shifting to annoyance before smoothing out once more. "They cannot live without me."

"They seem to be managing just fine."

"But for how long?" she asked.

I glanced again at May, crumpled at the far end of the court. None of the children had moved since collapsing.

Haru and Chase would be on their way. I just had to keep Shedraziel contained until they showed up. . . . Unless Bael held them on the far side of the portal.

I sighed. I couldn't wait. Not with the kids bleeding out on the floor. I had to get them out now.

I looked between Elliot and the brownie. The former would do his best to undermine any order I gave him, but maybe Shedraziel's servant would be more cooperative.

"You," I said. "Brownie. What are you called?"

He held perfectly still, the tray steady in his arms, but his gaze rolled toward Shedraziel.

I glowered. I was the one in control here. Why did people keep looking to Shedraziel for permission when she was my prisoner?

"Answer," Shedraziel said. A fresh bead of blood oozed from her neck.

"Never mind," I snapped. "Swear to me you'll carry these children through the portal, alive and unharmed, or say goodbye to your bitch of a lord."

Again the brownie looked at Shedraziel.

I gritted my teeth.

Shedraziel continued to smile, her expression relaxed, as though she was reclining on the divan by choice and not because I'd pinned her there. "Do as the girl says."

The brownie finally set down his tray. He stared at me with dark, unwavering eyes. "I swear I shall take these children through the portal, alive and unharmed."

"The portal to the guard station in Enchantment," I added. Pimm and Elliot surely had another way to come and go as they pleased.

"I will take them to the main portal," he said.

I nodded toward May. "Start with that musician and the painter."

He gave a slight bow, then scurried over to where the painter lay. I worried about the size of the puddle under him—coupled with the "paint" on his canvas, he had to be close to bleeding out.

The brownie slung the unconscious boy over one shoulder, then moved to May and draped her over the other. Both children were taller than the brownie, but brownies were strong. He straightened without visible strain. Then he walked across the gravel and into the stone forest without a backward glance.

Once they were gone, I breathed a little easier. May was out of immediate danger.

I frowned down at Shedraziel. "Kidnapping my friend's sister was a pretty convoluted way to get my attention. What if I hadn't come for her? It's not like you left a ransom note."

"Then she would have died after however many years it took for her mortal body to wear out, and I would have sent you another invitation, and another, until you took heed."

My finger twitched, wanting to plunge that last little bit deeper and end this woman. But without my hostage, I'd have to fight Elliot head-on, and there was little hope the month of lessons I'd gotten from Kai would keep me alive against a fae noble, even if I could reach my sword before he cut me down.

I glared at Shedraziel, still tempted.

"You want to kill me," she said. The prospect didn't seem to bother her.

"You want to die?"

"The game is only fun if there's something at stake."

Looking at her expression, I was reminded of Marron as she spun through her tower and burned her menagerie of paper creations. I hadn't noticed at first, because Shedraziel seemed to be functioning normally, but madness danced in her eyes.

I shivered. Once the kids were out, I'd finish her and take my chances with Elliot. She was too dangerous to leave alive.

Her eyes slid shut and a small pout puckered her lips. "It seems our time together has come to an end."

Gravel crunched at the far end of the court.

When I looked up, Bael and his entourage stood at the edge of the white marble floor, framed by the overgrown columns.

Chapter 30

BAEL WORE GOLDEN plates of armor over a deep-maroon tunic. His dark braids seemed more purple than black in the flat orange light, and across his forehead sat an intricately woven, thin metal circlet. Rhoana was on his right. Her long, green cape hung loose, pushed back over her shoulders to keep her sword arm free. Her right hand rested on the hilt of her sheathed blade.

A dozen guards in green and leather livery spread behind them. One, a dark sidhe, gripped Haru's hair in his fist and held a sword to his throat. A satyr held Shedraziel's brownie servant in a similar fashion.

I scanned the remaining troop. May wasn't among them. Nor were any of the other children.

"What happened to the kids?" I called.

"They're safe." Bael strode forward alone, passing the fallen musicians and dancers without seeming to notice them. "My guards are looking after them."

Elliot shrank back behind his pillar, maybe hoping he'd be overlooked. Bael shot a glance in his direction and Elliot froze in place. The blood drained from his face, making his green complexion stand out even more.

"And my friends?" I cut my gaze to Haru. "Are your guards looking after them, too?"

"I thought I'd be coming to your rescue after you so foolishly ignored my warnings." Bael spread his arms wide to encompass the scene as he approached. "You continue to surprise me."

"And you continue to disappoint me," I shot back. "All this could have been avoided if you'd helped me when I asked."

He lowered his arms, a condescending smile on his lips. "I couldn't act without evidence."

I shifted my grip on Shedraziel. "Is this enough evidence for you?"

He nodded. "You've done me a favor, rooting out the traitors in my midst." He indicated Elliot.

I snorted. He'd already known Elliot and Pimm were out to get him—their antics at the festival had made that clear. I'd just given him the excuse he needed to strike without reprisal from their supporters at court.

"In light of that," he continued, "I might be inclined to overlook your minor rebellion."

I glanced at Haru, blade at his throat, and felt the notable absence of Chase, Mica, and Emma—invisible hostages to this negotiation. "If?"

He chuckled. "It really is a pity you weren't fae enough to be my heir."

"May I get up now?" Shedraziel said in a bored voice.

I increased the pressure on her neck. "You're not going anywhere."

"Actually," Bael said, raising one hand to forestall me. "That's what I'd like to discuss."

I looked from Bael to Shedraziel and back again, trying to wrap my brain around his last sentence. Finally, I asked, incredulous, "You want me to spare her?"

He nodded.

"She's a traitor."

"As a prisoner here, she was not technically bound to my court."

"She found a way out of your prison."

"*Actually*," Shedraziel chimed, "I haven't left this place since Lord Bael put me here. I have others for such tasks." Her gaze flicked to Elliot.

"It seems she has not breached the terms of her imprisonment," Bael said.

Realization dawned. "You intended to free her all along. You expected to find me here in her thrall, and you would have offered her freedom in exchange for sparing my life."

"I came here to save you," he said.

"But that's not the only reason. And if the situation had played out the way you expected, I would have been in your debt."

He sighed. "I invited you to stay with me by choice after the festival. I tried to keep you by force when you came yesterday. Neither swayed you." He pressed his fingertips to his forehead—a gesture that reminded me of my mother when we fought. "What must I do to convince you that you are safer by my side?"

I scoffed. "You pretended to be a knight in shining armor to gain my allegiance."

"Not a knight," he said. "A lord."

"And now that the tables have turned, you'll bargain for *her* life instead." I nodded at Shedraziel. "How could I ever feel safe around someone like that?"

"Believe it or not, I am only trying to protect you."

The words passed his lips, so they had to be true, but to what degree? Did he actually care about me, or was he simply protecting the possibility of an heir he still hoped I would produce some day? If I let him, Bael would keep me on a shelf like the magic-eating artifact he'd used to destroy the dragon home world, or shuffle me into a corner of his keep, like Mica, on the off chance I could prove useful.

Hardly one to throw away a useful tool, no matter its origin.

I stifled the urge to ask if he knew about my father, my unique meld of magics. If he learned the truth, would that change the way he saw me? Interacted with me? Would he still want me at his court?

I looked down at Shedraziel. If Bael didn't know about my mixed magics already, he'd learn the truth soon enough.

"If you want me to feel safe, let me kill this bitch."

"I understand you wanting to finish what you started, but you must consider the bigger picture. You've already bested her. There's no need for further violence."

"She kidnapped and tortured *children.*"

"Her proclivities are . . . distasteful, but not pertinent to this discussion. Release her into my custody. You have my word the abductions will stop."

"You couldn't control her before. Isn't that why you had to lock her away?"

"I couldn't curb her appetite after the war. But it seems the treaty is breaking down. If tensions in the mortal realm continue to rise, we'll be at war again soon enough, and I'll need my best general." He gestured to Shedraziel.

The bottom dropped out of my stomach.

"You intend to go to war against the humans?"

"I intend to be ready for war when it comes."

My gaze slid to Shedraziel, who appeared to have dozed off during the conversation. She wasn't afraid of the needle in her neck. Had she known Bael would come? That he would release her from this prison? Reinstate her as his general? Had they planned this together?

"Did you know about her stealing the kids?" I kept my gaze on Shedraziel, afraid of what I might see in Bael's face. "Were you a part of it?"

"I would never condone the needless suffering of children," he said.

Needless. But who's to say what he considered necessary?

"Did you know what she was doing?" This time I did look up.

He stared straight at me with unblinking eyes, black and gold embers swirling in the red depths. "No."

A small thread of doubt that had been strangling my heart loosened at his denial. Bael was an immortal jerk, but he was also my only living relative. Alien though his motivations were to me, he was family. I wanted to believe there was common ground between us.

"Will you release her?" he asked.

I stared at the glowing tip of my finger where it pierced Shedraziel's skin, and the trail of blood that traced the curve of her neck and stained her collar red. If I let her go, she would lead an army. She was crazy and bloodthirsty, she'd slaughter the mortals. Someone like her shouldn't have that kind of power. I could stop her here, now.

"Not only will I forgive you and your friends for this trespass, I'll even release Kai from his imprisonment."

I closed my eyes, weighing the lives in my hands. The life of the woman beneath me; the lives she would surely take if I let this opportunity go; the lives of my friends and the children we'd come to save. I pictured Chase with a sword to his throat and Kai in his cell. I imagined Shedraziel at the head of a fae army marching across the mortal realm. I couldn't see a clear path. No matter what I chose, people would suffer.

But there were lives that I could save today. As for the threat Shedraziel posed to the mortal realm, I'd fight for those lives when the time came. Perhaps I would regret my decision when I saw her at the head of an army, but if war came, it would come with or without Shedraziel.

"All the stolen children will receive treatment and safe passage home. None of my friends will be held accountable for any wrongdoing. Kai will be pardoned and reinstated as a knight. Elliot will be executed for treason, and Pimm will be given to the dragon Zeraldi to do with as she pleases." I looked up at Bael. "Agreed?"

He smiled. "Agreed."

"Also," I added, "promise you'll never again try to keep me in Enchantment against my will."

Bael pursed his lips. "For all the good it did."

"Promise."

He sighed, but set a hand over his heart. "I shall never again attempt to detain you in Enchantment against your will. You have my word."

I grabbed the silver locket out of Shedraziel's hand, then lifted my magic needle away from her neck. A fresh stream of blood trickled out and dribbled down her collar. Holding my breath, I backed away.

When I was clear of the divan, Shedraziel sat up. She rolled her head from side to side as though easing stiff muscles. Then she pushed to her feet and sauntered toward Bael.

"Your new pet is fun," she purred, pressing up to his side.

Faster than I could follow, she wrapped her fingers around the hilt of Bael's sword and pulled it free of its sheath.

A cry of alarm lodged in my throat. I took a step, one hand raised uselessly.

Shedraziel spun. The blade flashed.

Elliot dropped to his knees, taking a handful of goblin fruit vines with him as he clutched at the pillar. Bael's sword was buried in his chest nearly to its guard.

Bael crossed his arms and regarded Shedraziel with a stiff frown.

She shrugged. "His death *was* part of the deal, was it not?"

"And what didn't you want him telling me?"

She clasped her hands behind her back and strolled across the blood-streaked floor toward Bael's waiting troops.

"You can't control her," I said.

He shrugged. "I only need to aim her. It's my enemies who must deal with her."

I shuddered, thinking of Shedraziel let loose on the mortal realm. And I'd have no one to blame but myself.

My choice. My consequences.

But at least I didn't have any blood on my hands today.

I nodded toward Haru. "Keep your word."

"Always." Bael gestured to the guard holding Haru. "Release him."

Once the blade was off his throat, Haru stepped away from his captor, but he didn't go far.

"Now," Bael said, "let's take care of your other demands."

THE KIDS I'D SENT with Haru sat in a huddled, wide-eyed group at the edge of the prison's gravel field around the portal. A handful of guards stood watch over them. Zeraldi was at the edge of the group. Pimm knelt beside her, the silver chain still around her neck, her arms still tied by the strips of fabric I'd cut from her dress, but her gag had been removed. Two guards stood behind her, hands on their weapons.

I turned to Shedraziel, who walked on Bael's other side. "Release your hold on the kids and erase any lingering commands."

She crossed her arms and lifted her chin. "That wasn't one of your requests."

"It falls under treatment," I countered. "They can't get well with you still in their heads."

"Do it," Bael commanded.

She pouted her lower lip, but addressed the group of quivering children. It was disgusting to see the worship in their eyes when they looked at her.

"Once you leave this place, you will have no memory of your time here and you will no longer be subject to my commands." She glared at me over her shoulder. "Happy?"

Not by a long shot. I nodded.

Bael gestured to Zeraldi and Pimm. The two guards behind them brought them forward. He focused on Pimm. "You'll be going with the dragon child."

"My lord, I beg of you—"

Bael lifted a hand, and Pimm fell silent. "I am not your lord. You forsook your oaths when you swore allegiance to Shedraziel."

Pimm's gaze darted to her new master for help, but Shedraziel merely smiled.

Bael placed his fingertips against Pimm's forehead. There was a brief, red glow against her skin. Then he said, "Tell me the name of my granddaughter."

Pimm glanced at me, frowning.

"Well?" Bael crossed his arms.

"Her name is A—" The first syllable of my name turned into an anguished scream and Pimm collapsed to her knees.

I took a step back, shocked and unsettled by her wails.

"Should you attempt to share information about the Realm of Enchantment or any of its people, this will be the result."

Pimm's cries turned to whimpers and finally quiet panting.

Bael shifted his focus to Zeraldi. "She is yours to do with as you please. Enchantment holds no claim on her."

Zeraldi's expression was unreadable as she stood face to face with Bael—the man responsible for the destruction of her world, the fall of her people. Was she old enough to have witnessed that devastation firsthand, or had she been born in the aftermath?

There was a tense moment of silence, then she gave the silver chain a tug.

Pimm climbed unsteadily to her feet.

Zeraldi turned to me and offered the bow she'd withheld from Bael. "Until we meet again."

"Until then," I replied.

Pimm swayed slightly as she followed Zeraldi back toward the waiting children.

I wasn't sure if I'd done the right thing in giving Pimm to Zeraldi. Deciding another person's fate was a heavy burden, and Zeraldi was still a child. Perhaps I should have sentenced Pimm with Elliot and been done with them both.

"Let's finish this up," Bael said, and he stepped through the shimmer of air that would lead us back to Enchantment.

Shedraziel made a little bow. "After you, *princess*."

I hated the idea of exposing my back to that wicked smile and had the sudden thought that I should have worked some kind of "no harm to me and mine" clause into her release. Who knows if Bael would have agreed, but the oversight rankled. Still, I couldn't keep my back to a wall forever. I was impatient to see my friends and verify for myself that they were all right. It seemed watching my back would have to be my new normal.

May was with the other children, one hand pressed to her temple like she had a headache. At least she was awake.

Shuffling sideways to keep Shedraziel in sight, I moved to May's side before going through the portal. I touched her shoulder. "Can you walk?"

She jerked as though startled and looked up at me, her dark eyes scared. "Alex? Is that really you?" She stretched out one tentative hand as though she expected it to pass through me.

I squeezed her fingers. "Yes, I'm here. And your sister is waiting. Are you ready to go?"

Tears welled in her eyes. She nodded.

I pulled her to her feet and led her to the exit.

Shedraziel was still smiling at me, but at least Rhoana was beside her. Surely Bael's captain wouldn't let the crazy bitch attack me while my back was turned?

Towing May, I stepped through the portal at an angle, never taking my eyes off Shedraziel.

Chapter 31

BAEL WAS BARELY two steps ahead of me, but he was already issuing commands by the time we came through. Chase, Mica, and Emma knelt in the dirt near one side of the platform, along with the group of younger kids I'd sent with Chase. I led May in that direction. As I approached, a guard sliced the ropes holding my friends' hands behind their backs.

Mica and Chase rubbed their wrists. Emma just let her arms drop to her sides. She was staring at May with a mixture of relief and horror.

When May noticed Emma, she pulled out of my grip and raced toward her sister, tackling her around the middle so they both toppled over. May was sobbing, her face buried against Emma's stomach.

Emma touched May's hair, her heaving back. Then she looked up at me with tears in her eyes. "She's like, fifteen years old."

I nodded.

"Was she suffering?"

I wouldn't insult her by lying, but I wasn't about to tell her about May's bloody fingers as she played the violin endlessly for Shedraziel's amusement, the horror of having her will overridden by another, or the addictive, intoxicating fruit she'd had to fight for to survive.

"Once she's home, she shouldn't remember her time here."

Emma's gaze shifted to something over my left shoulder.

I turned. Shedraziel stood on the platform. She spread her arms wide and tipped her head to the sky. Her mouth split in a wide grin as a breeze fluttered her long, loose hair. She shivered, and her wild laughter filled the air.

Everyone in camp looked in her direction, even Bael.

"Is that her?" Emma hissed.

I nodded.

Her grip tightened around May. "You should have killed her."

"It was her . . . or all of you." I pulled my gaze away from the sight of Shedraziel reveling in her first taste of freedom in centuries. May was safe. My friends were safe. I'd done what I came to do. But seeing

Shedraziel basking in the afternoon sunlight, the day didn't feel like a win.

Haru materialized on the platform behind Shedraziel and gave her a shove that could totally have been an accident, but the look in his eyes said otherwise. He walked past her without apology. When he reached us, Mica and Chase were standing. Haru took Mica's hand. Small though the gesture was, the pull between them was palpable, like two magnets held at a distance and finally allowed to snap together.

I strummed the cord in my heart, feeling James at the other end, my magnetic north guiding me home.

When Haru finally pulled his gaze away from Mica's, he looked at Chase. The two shifters stared at each other. The silence between them made my skin itch. Then Chase nodded. Haru smiled. Not the wide, teasing smile I'd grown used to, but a small smile. A quiet smile that spoke volumes without saying a word.

Bael strode up to us, sunlight glinting off his armor. He looked over the gathered children and called over his shoulder to Shedraziel, "Release these ones as well." Then he turned to me. "My men are preparing clothes and food for the young ones. They are welcome in my keep until they are fully recovered."

I glanced at Shedraziel as she approached the kids. The thought of making them spend even one night under the same roof as the monster who'd abducted them made my blood boil.

"No," I said. "I want to get them out of here as quickly as possible."

He shrugged, the plight of the children seemingly already forgotten. "The mortal realm is no longer safe for you. My offer stands. Stay. Learn more about your magic." He extended his hand, inviting. "More about me. And help me learn more about you so we can avoid this kind of . . . predicament in the future."

I looked at his outstretched hand, and for a moment I pictured myself taking it. I could learn more about my family and my magic. I'd be safe from the PTF manhunt awaiting me at home. But if I accepted Bael's protection now, I'd be giving him control over me. Besides—I shifted my gaze to the huddle of dirty, frightened children—my work wasn't done yet.

I shook my head.

"Conflict with the mortal realm is inevitable."

"Maybe," I said. "But I'm not giving up just yet."

"And when that conflict comes?" he asked. "Will your allegiance lie with the fae or the humans?"

I glanced at my friends, human and fae, and smiled. "Yes."

Bael blinked. Then he burst into laughter. Grinning from ear to ear, he clapped me on the shoulder with the hand he'd offered earlier. "I hope someday you'll come around to my way of thinking, preferably before the mortals you so love turn against you. But I respect your resolve to handle things your own way. You truly are my kin, if not my heir. Never back down."

He gave me one last thump on the back, then went to rejoin his troops.

"What about Kai?" I called.

He waved a hand without looking back. "He'll be reinstated, as promised."

I bit my lip. "Reinstated" didn't mean he'd get to join me in the mortal realm anytime soon. Another oversight. For all I knew, Bael might assign Kai to guard a rock at the farthest edge of the kingdom.

I sighed. At least he'd be free.

"Rhoana," he shouted. "Assist Lady Alex with whatever she needs. I will take Shedraziel and the court guard back to the keep."

Rhoana bowed low, fist to her chest, as Bael swung onto the back of a huge gaala with glossy, jet-black fur.

Shedraziel hopped up behind him without invitation and slipped one arm tight around his waist in a way that suggested more intimacy than a simple shared ride. She looked down on me with eyes like the ocean—beautiful, powerful, and merciless. Then she smiled and blew me a kiss. "Until next time."

Bael flicked the reins, and his gaala leapt into the air. The remainder of Bael's entourage scrambled to follow their lord as he streaked across the sky, golden armor shining like a second sun.

"Your orders, my lady?"

I turned to find Rhoana watching me, her stern frown etched deeper than ever. Behind her, the remaining guards watched me. The children watched me. My friends watched me.

I swallowed, and the sound was loud in my ears. Three months ago I'd spent my afternoons curled up in my favorite chair with a blanket and a cup of tea, enjoying the solitude of my mountain retreat after a hard day of metal work. But that life was gone. That *person* was gone. I hadn't picked up a hammer in weeks, and what I was shaping these days wasn't metal. With every choice I made, I was shaping lives. I was shaping the future.

A heavy weight settled around my heart as I took in the sea of expectant stares. My shoulders sagged. My legs shook.

Then my stomach let out a long, loud grumble.

Everyone's gaze shifted down, drawn by the noise.

I covered my abdomen with my hands and forced a smile. "Let's start by getting everybody clean and fed."

IT TOOK MOST OF the remaining daylight to get the kids to the nearest portal, the one leading to the reservation in Ohio. Once everyone had eaten and dressed in clean clothes from those available in the camp, we'd packed them onto gaala, each behind a guard, and flown them to the small clearing by the ice-rimmed river. The fae children had taken the ride in stride. The mortals had responded with a wide range of emotions, from elation to terror. Most enjoyed the experience of skimming over treetops on their six-legged steeds. I found myself hoping those memories would persist even after the kids returned to the mortal realm.

Memories of their time in Shedraziel's prison were already fading. May could no longer recall specifics of what had happened, but her sunken eyes still looked haunted. I suspected she'd have plenty of nightmares from this experience, even if she couldn't remember their source.

"You ready?" Chase stepped up beside me. He'd borrowed a pair of tight tan pants from one of the guards.

"Are you? There are a lot more fae than mortals."

"But less explaining," he said. "Besides, I've got help."

Chase had volunteered to escort the fae children back to their respective realms. And much to my astonishment, Haru had offered to join him. We both watched the kitsune as he helped herd the fae children into a line in preparation for departure.

I cast a sidelong glance at Chase. "You two gonna be okay?"

He frowned. "I don't know. But we're better than we were."

Beside the line of fae, Emma stood at the head of a much shorter line—the mortals I'd be taking back with me. I just hoped James had found somewhere safe to stash them until we could return them directly to their families.

"Everyone's ready," Mica said, as he, Haru, and Rhoana came to join us in front of the portal. "I've double-checked all the kids. Shedraziel's enchantment is gone."

"That's good." I studied his frown. "What's the bad news?"

"The children were sustained on a diet of goblin fruit."

I nodded.

"The fae kids will have little lingering effects. The mortals, however . . ."

"They're addicted." I'd assumed as much, but a cold dread twisted inside me as I said the words out loud.

"They're going to go into withdrawal," Haru finished.

I nodded. My gaze flickered to May. "Will they survive it?"

"Not without help," Mica said.

"As per your demands of treatment," Rhoana said, "I'll request an order of distilled goblin juice and have it delivered to you in the mortal realm. If you wean them slowly, they should survive."

"I'm not sure where I'll be."

She held out the glass orb she'd used to communicate with Mica when we were at Marron's. "Keep this with you."

I tucked the ball in my coat pocket, my mind racing. I might have to keep the kids hidden longer than I originally thought. I couldn't very well return them to their families just to have them die a gruesome death. No, we'd have to get them clean first.

"All right," I said. "Let's get this party started." I turned to Mica and extended my hand. "I couldn't have done this without you. If I can ever return the favor . . ."

He gripped my hand, but instead of shaking it he lifted it and placed a soft kiss on the back. "I'm sure I'll come up with something."

The words rang in my ears like a promise.

He released my hand and pulled Haru aside. They spoke in low tones. I looked away when they kissed.

I nodded to Rhoana. "Give me a couple minutes' head start before you send them through." Then I turned to the shimmering patch of air, nearly invisible in the dusky light of the sunset, and stepped through.

My boots sank into slush. Above me, familiar stars twinkled in the night sky and the pale crescent of Earth's single moon hung low on the horizon, partly obscured by the skeletal branches of the forest around me. I took a deep breath of frigid air that carried with it subtle wisps of industrial pollution, absent in the fae realm, and let out a relieved billow of steam.

Focusing inward, I strummed the cord in my heart that was tethered to James. I felt the resonance, and turned like the needle on a compass. *James?*

I'm here. Relief and worry swirled together in his response.

I smiled and pushed reassurance through the line. *I'm safe.*

I'll believe that when you're back in my arms.

For a moment, the pressure of a phantom hug wrapped around me, and I could almost believe we were together. I took a deep breath, and the feeling passed.

Is Morgan with you?

Yes.

Good. Tell her we need a ride.

I SNUGGLED DEEPER into the space between the armrest of the overstuffed chair with its nauseating floral upholstery and James's side. The two of us had crammed into the seat together, unwilling to separate for even a moment since being reunited on the front steps of the tiny cabin James had rented using a mixture of barter and illusion.

On the far side of the room, Morgan sprawled on the cabin's only couch, pressed to the wall to make space for the children. She'd been grumpy and exhausted after a dozen back-and-forth skips to ferry the frightened kids, since we couldn't trust them not to let go of one another in the shadowy space between. She'd passed out nearly as soon as the last trip—mine—was done. I still owed her the full story of what transpired between me and Shedraziel.

Beyond the rough wood walls and sheer curtains of the main living area, the first blush of dawn painted the eastern horizon. I yawned and scanned the ashes behind the fireplace grate for any lingering embers of the blaze we'd lit to keep the kids warm as they settled in among the mattresses, blankets, and pillows spread on the living room floor.

You should get some rest. James's voice thrummed through my mind, rich and clear at this distance. *You've kept your vigil long enough. Your charges are asleep. The fire has burned down.* He stroked the back of his finger down my cheek. *You're exhausted.*

"Just a few more minutes," I whispered, staring at the sea of bodies filling the space between my chair and Morgan's couch.

It seemed that after the endless procession of trips to the bathroom, requests for water, and aborted attempts at sleep, the children had finally passed out. Emma snored softly in the middle of the group, May tucked against one side. A small boy with dirty blond hair snuggled under her other arm. The remaining children pressed in around the edges like puppies in a pile, huddled together for comfort and warmth.

I smiled. Emma put the children at ease in a way I couldn't, addressing their needs and concerns before I even considered them. Maybe it was a side effect of being an only child, or my general lack of social experience, but Emma's ability to effortlessly connect with people was a constant mystery to me. I got the feeling these kids would be okay so long as Emma was around.

Or as okay as any of us could be with war on the horizon.

Conflict with the mortal realm is inevitable.

The sleepy threads of my thoughts drifted away from the comfortable scene.

It seemed, despite all my efforts, another war was brewing between the humans and fae.

The current treaty wouldn't hold, that much was clear. Neither side was respecting their part of the bargain. And now, with the werewolves and *me* thrown in the mix. . . . I sighed and nuzzled closer to James, which caused him to hold me tighter. At least the humans didn't know about vampires yet. That revelation would cause a shit storm for the ages.

But I was in a unique position. I might not be able to find a path to peace on my own, but I could see the conflict from multiple sides—human, fae, and those caught in-between. If I could help them under stand each other better, even a little bit . . .

I worried my lower lip between my teeth.

I needed to talk to Agent Harris again, open a line of communication. Now that my mission to save the kids was over, I had to focus on doing what I could to clean up the mess my video confession had made in the mortal realm. If nothing else, I had to warn her what was coming if the humans and fae went to war. I'd chosen to let Shedraziel live. Any blood she spilled would be on my hands.

My gaze drifted back to May, followed by a familiar twist of guilt. Too many people had already been caught in this game being played between mortals and fae, but it was naive to think there wouldn't be more. Every choice had the potential for collateral damage. All I could do was make the best decisions I could with the information I had.

You're spiraling. James's reprimand pierced my thoughts.

"Sorry," I whispered, turning my face toward his. "I've got a lot on my mind."

He placed his index finger against my forehead, right between my eyes. "There will be time enough for thinking tomorrow." He traced down the bridge of my nose and poked the tip. "Just savor the moment."

A small shudder passed through me. His words weren't exactly a command, and he hadn't said, or even thought, my true name. Still, the echo of his authority swept over me and I found myself relaxing, letting my worries drift away. All but one.

"Promise me something." I traced my fingers along the arm draped around me. I trusted James. That's why I'd given him my name in the first place. And that trust had saved my life. Without his preexisting order, I would have been no match for Shedraziel. Still. . . . "Promise you'll never use my name against me."

James kissed the top of my head. "I promise."

The last remaining embers of the fire glowed deep red, casting long shadows across the sleeping kids. Kids I'd helped save. James was right—for tonight at least, I deserved to savor my victory. I snuggled closer and let my brain shut off. As James had said, there'd be time enough for thinking tomorrow.

Want more?
Continue the adventure with
Of Mettle & Magic
Book 5 of The Magicsmith series.

Acknowledgements

This book wouldn't have been possible without the help of Debra Dixon, who helped refine my story, and my beta readers, David and Connie, who generously donated their time to make sure the book still made sense after I ripped it apart and stitched it back together. I'd also like to thank Alexandra Christle for her copy editing services, and the many people at BelleBooks who worked to make this product the best it could be. Thanks to my friends and family for their unending support. And finally, I want to thank you, the reader, who makes all the work worthwhile.

About the Author

L. R. Braden is a bestselling, multi-award-winning author of dark-yet-hopeful urban fantasy stories. Her published works include the *Magicsmith* series, the *Rifter* series, and several works of shorter fiction. A bit of a recluse, she enjoys collecting skills that may (or may not) prove useful in the event that she is suddenly transported to an inhospitable alternate reality. Since that hasn't happened yet, she mostly spends her days weaving fantastic tales, playing with her family, and getting lost on purpose. Her writing has won many awards, including the Eric Hoffer Book Award for Sci-fi/Fantasy, the Next Generation Indie Book Award for Paranormal Fiction, and the Imadjinn Award for Best Urban Fantasy.

Connect with her online at lrbraden.com

www.ingramcontent.com/pod-product-compliance
Lightning Source LLC
Chambersburg PA
CBHW022031240626
47154CB00007B/2358